AF267396

Arrested LOVE

Based On A True Story

Arrested LOVE

Based On A True Story

KAREN KRUEGER

QUANTUM SHIFT
PUBLISHING

Port St. Lucie, Florida

Copyright © 2026 Karen Krueger

All rights reserved. No portion of this book may be reproduced in any form whatsoever without permission from the publisher. For permissions and information about special discounts for bulk purchases, please contact: Karen@KarenKruegerWriter.com

Editing, Cover and Interior Design by Quantum Shift Media
Author photos by MarilynGarrisonPhotography.com

ISBN: 978-1-955533-49-2 (paperback)
ISBN: 978-1-955533-50-8 (eBook)
ISBN: 978-1-955533-51-5 (audiobook)

Library of Congress Control Number: 2026906647

Content Advisory: This book addresses sensitive and potentially distressing subject matter, including mental illness, betrayal, infidelity, and criminal behavior involving minors. There is no graphic content, and these themes are explored within the context of a fictional narrative inspired by real-life experiences. Reader discretion is advised. Some scenes and topics may be triggering for individuals who have experienced similar situations. The author's intent is not to sensationalize, but to shed light on complex emotional, psychological, and relational dynamics with honesty and care.

Donations for each book sale will be given to the National Alliance on Mental Illness (NAMI)

Printed in United States of America

QUANTUM SHIFT
P U B L I S H I N G

Port St. Lucie, Florida

DEDICATION

To my younger self: you were stronger, more courageous,
and resilient than you ever realized.

ACKNOWLEDGMENTS

I always dreamed of being a novelist. Yet this was never the book I expected to write.

During the pandemic, I joined a women's connection group called Polka Dot Powerhouse. It was during a virtual meeting with another member that the idea for this book was born. We had an immediate connection and shared some deeply personal things about ourselves, and I shared my story with her. And when she heard it, she said, "You need to write a book. You need to share your story with others."

Thank you, Lisa Harris Gore, for sharing your story with me, giving me a safe space to share mine, and encouraging me to write this book. My book would not exist without you.

I also want to thank Keren Kilgore of Quantum Shift Media. Keren, whom I first met through Polka Dot Powerhouse, is my author coach, editor, publishing guide, and a dear friend. I could not have published my book without her help. I have learned so much from her and am deeply grateful for her guidance throughout this process.

Thank you to my beta readers and launch team. Your help in getting this book to the finish line is greatly appreciated.

Thank you to my family—the one I was born into, the one I married into, and the many friends who have become family along the way. Your support and encouragement sustained me throughout the writing of this book. My parents may not have fully understood why I felt called to write it, yet their love and belief in me never wavered. Though they both passed before its publication, I carry the quiet knowing that they would have been proud—not only of the finished book, but of my perseverance in bringing a lifelong dream to life.

Thank you to my husband, Dean. You have been my rock through hard times and my joy through all times. Thank you for always being there for me. I love sharing life with you! There isn't anyone else I could have trusted as much to be the first to read my book. I love you with all my heart!

CONTENTS

PROLOGUE

Friday, October 2, 1998

Damn, it's hot! I thought as I waited for my dark blue Honda Civic's air conditioner to kick in. My long brown hair stuck to the beads of sweat dripping down my neck. I couldn't wait to get home, see Finn, put my feet up, and sip a cold Shiner Bock after a tedious day of software testing.

It was unusually hot, even for early October in Texas, so I was careful not to touch the scalding steering wheel more than was necessary as I turned the key and started the engine. I opened the windows to let some of the hot air out of the car, cranked the air conditioning to the coldest setting, pointed all the vents toward me, and let it blow full on.

Despite the heat, I was happy. I waited for the air conditioner to cool the steering wheel, letting my mind drift to the weekend ahead. Finn and I were planning to see the newly released *Waking Ned Devine*, a small luxury we'd been anticipating all week. He was a Ph.D. student at the University of Texas at Austin, often up late working on his dissertation about the geochemistry of rocks he had collected in Antarctica. With money tight and his research demanding most of his time, weekends were sacred—set aside for being together. A movie was a rare treat, and we were both looking forward to it.

And after ten years of marriage, I still got excited when I heard his voice on the phone. He was the only one I wanted to share any adventure with.

One of my favorite adventures early in our marriage was our spontaneous trip to Italy. Finn had been invited to present research at a conference and, despite our budget, he insisted I come along. "We've got a chance to explore another country together—how can we pass that up?" he asked. "Besides, it won't be half as fun without you, Kass!" That was all it took—I was in.

After the conference, we took the train to the Dolomites to hike and relax before heading home. In the passenger section, we sat across from an older gentleman who smelled of garlic and wine and continually talked to us joyfully in Italian, which we didn't understand. Finn pretended to understand the man by studying him intently, mimicking his facial expressions, nodding in agreement, and laughing along. Later, we made up stories about what the man was saying and laughed about that for years.

Finn was the one I trusted to do new things with. We met in college, where we both studied geology and attended a geology field camp together in Utah. On our way home from field camp, we stayed longer to do some additional hiking and camping, and to explore areas we had not yet seen.

While hiking in a slot canyon, we reached a narrow, 30-foot section where water blocked our path. We had no way of knowing how deep the water was. It was too steep to climb out the way we came. The only way to go was forward.

"How are we going to get through this, Finn?" I asked nervously.

"We'll have to put our backs against one wall of the canyon and our feet on the other and shimmy our way above the water to where we can climb out on rocks on the other side," Finn explained confidently.

Terrified, I exclaimed, "I don't think I can do it! It's too far!"

"Take a breath, Kass. It's okay. I'll help you." Finn replied calmly.

He tied a rope to one of the rocks near where we stood and carefully shimmied his way across to the other side, tying the rope off when he arrived.

He had made the traverse look easier than it was, being six feet tall and having no trouble putting his back against one wall of the slot canyon and his feet on the other. But I was half a foot shorter and knew it would be a much bigger stretch for me.

"Okay, now it's your turn!" he encouraged me. "Just hold onto the rope as you shimmy your way across."

I was still scared, but I trusted him. I grabbed the rope with an underhand grip, as if I were going to do a pull-up. The rope was rough, and I wish I had thought to pack gloves. I moved slowly, first moving my hands along the rope, then my feet along the wall. I stopped to take deep breaths every few feet of progress across the gap. As soon as I got within arm's reach, Finn grabbed me and pulled me to the other side, embracing me reassuringly.

"I've got you, babe! I would never let anything happen to you," he whispered as he held me tightly.

I knew then that I could trust him with my life. "I love you, Finn!" I said, looking up into his beautiful blue eyes.

He pulled me closer and said, "I love you, too, Kass!"

A few months later, we finished college and got married. We knew each other inside and out, having grown up together as we navigated life, shimmying our way over the obstacles in our path. With Finn, I truly felt loved and safe.

Finn was almost done with his dissertation and graduate school. Soon, we would move on to our next adventure together. We hadn't yet determined where life would take us, but it was fun to speculate and dream about what was to come. Finn was intelligent and dedicated to his research; I knew he had a bright future ahead of him. He wanted to get a teaching position at a college or university where he could continue his research and share his passion for geochemistry with students.

"I can picture us in a small college town, where you will become a tenured professor," I shared as we lay awake at night speculating about our future.

"And you can return to working in environmental geology. I know you hated to give that up for your current job," he replied.

"Yes, that would be nice! But technology jobs in oil and gas pay significantly better, and I don't have to travel as much as I did working in environmental geology. So I don't mind working in tech until you graduate. We need the money," I told him. "And when both of us are working, we can finally start a family!"

"And we can take the kids with us when I travel to give lectures around the world!" Finn exclaimed happily.

I liked the idea of traveling as a family so our kids could experience different cultures and also develop a love for adventure.

"Yes, that will be wonderful! I can picture them all lined up by age to get on the plane - Christopher, Lauren, Matthew, and Emily!" I teased.

During our pre-marriage counseling, as encouraged by the Catholic church, we discovered that we both wanted to have four children. Finn had surprised me with that revelation because, as the youngest of five, he had always said his family was too big.

"Don't you mean Finn Junior, Jack after my dad, Myra after my mother, and Emily?" Finn countered playfully.

"We're not naming our kids after family members! Especially not your mother!" I protested, although the thought of having a little Finn was not unpleasant. "And we will need a house with a big yard for the kids and dogs to play!"

"When we're not traveling," Finn laughed. And then he pulled me close, and we fell asleep, each of us dreaming about our future.

It was nice reliving those memories as I continued to wait for the steering wheel to cool enough to drive without blistering my fingers.

I mused that it was almost like we were dating again, even though we had celebrated our tenth wedding anniversary just a few months earlier. The anticipation of Finn finally graduating brought a fresh spark to our relationship. It felt like we were standing on the edge of a new chapter—dreaming together, planning together, and cheering each other on with renewed hope and closeness.

Thinking of Finn made me anxious to see him. I put the car in gear and rushed home.

As I arrived home, I pulled into the parking spot behind our townhouse beside my husband's white Acura Integra. Finn was usually home early on Fridays. As I exited the car, I felt crushed by the humidity and heat. I rushed to unlock the door and escape into the cool air conditioning.

I braced for the usual chaos—our dogs barking and pressing their noses to the dining room window in eager welcome.

But the house was silent. Unsettlingly silent. Maybe Finn had taken them for a walk without me, though he almost always waited so we could go together. I shrugged it off, thinking maybe he was restless about our evening plans—eager to get to Alamo Drafthouse early enough to snag our favorite seats and order dinner before the movie. Still, something about the quiet made me pause.

As I stepped into the dining room, the stillness deepened. The dogs—normally bounding toward me—were locked in their crates, watching quietly.

Why are they crated? I wondered, my pulse quickening. *We never crate them except to keep them safe, like when we had that cracked pane of glass in the front window replaced*, I thought.

Lizzie was lying down, whimpering quietly, while Sam was sitting up, wagging her tail nervously, anxious to be released. They were not barking as usual when I walked through the door.

Something was wrong.

"Finn! Are you here?" I called out.

Silence.

It was too quiet in the house. And too dark. The blinds had all been drawn shut. Finn never shut them. He'd walk around naked and not care if they were open.

My heart pounded in my chest, and the hairs on my arms stood on end. The air was filled with the unfamiliar, warm scent of spiced aftershave or deodorant.

Someone else had been here.

I suddenly felt unsafe in my own home, although I could not pinpoint why. All kinds of thoughts were suddenly running through my head. Perhaps Finn had injured himself, and a neighbor took him to the emergency room. But that wouldn't explain why the dogs were in their crates.

Had we been robbed?

I went to the phone and called Finn's office at the university, hoping he would answer. Just hearing his voice would reassure me. His tenderness could calm me in any situation. He wouldn't make me feel silly for worrying; he would understand that my concern was out of love for him.

But there was no answer.

Where was Finn? Had he put the dogs in their crates to keep them away from danger? Or had a spice-scented stranger put them in their crates?

I leaned over to unlock the crates when something caught my eye.

A yellow piece of paper lay on the dining room table. I let out a big sigh of relief. I was being ridiculous. Finn must have left me a note, letting me know he had gone to grab a beer with his friend, Kevin, and he'd be back in time to catch the movie for our date night.

But why would he have put the dogs in their crates if he was just going out for a beer?

I picked up the paper. It was not a note from Finn.

It looked very official and had the word RECEIPT in large letters at the top. It offered a lot of information and very little at the same time.

I stared at it briefly as my brain registered what it was. It was from the Austin police department and indicated that they had taken our computer, along with a few other items. The date and time were two hours prior.

I was very confused. *Why would the police take our computer? I thought. Where is Finn? Why is his car here if he is not?*

I left the now silent dogs in their crates and hurried upstairs to the guest bedroom we used as an office. I pictured Finn sitting at the desk just as he always did, his long legs stretched out under the desk, deep in thought, intently typing away at the computer as he worked on his dissertation. I loved watching him while he worked - his brow furrowing when deep in thought, his face lighting up when he solved a problem or made an exciting discovery, his hands tousling his sandy blond hair when he was thinking.

But what I saw jolted me.

The room had been ransacked. The drawers of the desk had all been pulled open, and someone had rummaged roughly through them. Papers were strewn haphazardly on the floor. The drawers of the filing cabinet were also opened, and several folders had been pulled out and scattered on the bed. The closet door was left ajar. A pair of blue rubber gloves, turned inside out as they had been pulled off, lay in the trash bin. In the mess, it was hard to tell what, if anything, had been taken except for the empty space on top of the desk.

The computer monitor and CPU tower were gone.

The receipt on the dining room table had said as much. The missing computer still didn't explain the strange energy I felt in my home. Something dark and ominous was hanging in the air. It was almost palpable, yet I couldn't quite grasp it. The quiet dogs felt it, too.

I crossed the hallway to our bedroom. It appeared to be untouched. I opened the closet, and all of Finn's clothes were still hanging there. I opened a few of his dresser drawers; nothing appeared to be missing.

Confused, I tried to piece together what little I knew. Finn was gone, but his car and other belongings were here. And the police took the computer. *At least Finn wasn't injured, and we had not been robbed,* I thought as I slowly walked down the stairs. *Did the police take Finn with them? And why wouldn't they just let him drive his own car?*

As I headed down the stairs, Lizzie heard me and, no longer able to contain herself, let out a high-pitched bark, asking to be let out of her crate. I rushed over to the crates to free the anxious pups. I let Sam, our black lab mix, out first because she hated being in the crate. I patted Sam's head and then quickly unlatched Lizzie's crate. Although the crate was her safe spot, Lizzie darted out of it, pushing the gate aside before I could open it. Although she was a terrier and smaller than Sam, she ran into me with a force that nearly knocked me over.

Sam and Lizzie circled me in greeting, wagging their tails and licking my face as I bent down to pet them, but they still seemed afraid to make much noise. They paced around me, agitated, then back and forth to the window.

"Are you looking for Finn, Sam?" I asked.

I grabbed the black cordless phone from its base on the counter and checked for messages. There weren't any.

I called Finn's office again. Still no answer.

I had no other way of contacting Finn. I would have to wait until I heard from him or until he came home.

I finally let the dogs out into the front yard after they had been patiently waiting while I tried to call Finn. I sat on the stoop of our townhouse and watched them explore the small, unfenced yard that we shared with our neighbors. Sam attempted to entice Lizzie to play by nipping at her playfully. Lizzie ignored her and continued sniffing the area for scents from the other dogs that visited the yard.

The sun was low in the sky, but it was still hot. I realized I was still wearing the green silk blouse and dark-washed jeans I'd worn to work. I would have been much more comfortable in shorts and a t-shirt, but I couldn't make myself move. Instead, I sat there sweating, gripping the phone, and biting a few of my fingernails, a bad habit I had when I was nervous. I was waiting for something, but I didn't know what.

Sam and Lizzie tended to wander a bit, but were not wandering far tonight. They lacked their usual enthusiasm. I was so lost in thought, I barely noticed the sun slipping away—until the first few mosquitoes found me. As I swatted them off, I looked up to see the darkness closing in around us, quietly urging the dogs inside.

There was still no word from Finn, and my anxiety grew with each passing minute.

The house was dark, but I didn't stop to turn on a light until I got to the kitchen. Sam and Lizzie stood by their food bowls, waiting for their dinner. Lizzie pawed at her empty water dish to get my attention.

"Oh!" I exclaimed as the noise roused me from my thoughts. "You need water!"

Both dogs quickly lapped the cool water, thirsty from being locked in their kennels and then outside for so long. I grabbed a couple of cans of dog food from the pantry and opened them. The dogs whined excitedly when they heard the can opener, as they usually got dry food in the evenings. After being locked up for a couple of hours, I felt they deserved a treat.

I probably should have made myself something to eat after feeding Sam and Lizzie, but I was too anxious to eat anything. I ignored my growling stomach and headed into the living room with a glass of water, switching on the lamp next to the couch.

"What could the police possibly want with our computer?" I muttered to myself, pacing the living room floor.

Only one thing came to mind, but it felt like a stretch. A graduate student from California came to use the lab where Finn was conducting his research. They had a state-of-the-art mass spectrometer and special software to analyze data. I remembered Finn telling me that the student had not finished analyzing his data before he had to return to California.

Maybe Finn had shared the software with him so he didn't have to make another trip to Texas to finish his work, I speculated. The thought seemed ludicrous, but it was the only thing I could think of that might involve the police.

It would have been a violation of the licensing agreement, and authorities were cracking down on illegal software sharing because software companies were losing money and complaining. Even so, it was hard to believe that two graduate students would have gotten caught doing something like that or that the authorities would even care about it. They mainly were going after the mass sharing of licenses, not individuals.

It was now almost 9:30. I had been clutching the phone's handset with the antenna up since I had arrived home four hours ago, carrying it with me as I paced. When it finally rang, the sound made me jump. My heart raced as I gripped the phone.

"Hello?" I stammered, my voice shaking.

"Hey, it's me," Finn said, his voice sounding strained.

"Where are you? What's going on?" I blurted out, panic rising.

"I've been arrested," Finn uttered, "I need you to find a lawyer for me."

His words shot through me, and I hung onto a dining room chair to avoid collapsing.

"Arrested!? You need a lawyer!? Why would you need a lawyer? What happened? Why did you get arrested?" I asked, desperate to understand what was happening. Surely, they had the wrong guy, I thought.

"I can't tell you now. This is the only call I'm allowed to make, and I only have a few minutes. I just need you to find a lawyer and have him call this number," he instructed. "They will give him the information he needs about the charges against me and the bail I need to be released."

As Finn read off the number, I frantically scribbled it down on an envelope from the stack of mail on the counter.

"What charges? What kind of lawyer do you need?" I asked, my brain trying to understand everything but failing to make sense of it.

"A criminal lawyer!" Finn spat out angrily.

"Please," I stammered, "please tell me what's going on?"

"I can't!" he yelled. And before I could say another word, he hung up.

I felt adrenaline coursing through me. Finn needed an attorney, and I was the only one who could help him find one.

I have no idea how to choose a criminal attorney! I thought as I got out the phone book and frantically began searching, going down the list, calling lawyers with addresses near us. At 9:30 on a Friday night, most didn't answer, and the process was, to put it mildly, inelegant. Had I been looking for an attorney at any other time, I would have done more research. But there was no time for that now.

After leaving seven voicemails, one finally answered.

"Jordan Jensen here," he said.

"Uh, hi!" I stammered. "My name is Kassidy Haggerty. I need to hire a lawyer for my husband, Finn. He was arrested, and he needs a lawyer."

"Okay, what was he arrested for?" the lawyer asked.

"I don't know. He wouldn't tell me. He just asked me to hire a lawyer for him. He is in the Austin jail."

I gave the lawyer the limited information I had.

"Okay, I'll take care of it," he said after I had rattled off the information. "I charge an hourly fee of $150. I'll get back to you once I find out what is happening. Do you agree to pay my fee?"

"Yes!" I replied. What choice did I have? My husband was in jail, and I didn't know why.

"I'll give you a call as soon as I have more information for you," he said and hung up the phone.

"Thank you," I uttered softly, although he had already disconnected.

Two hours later, well after midnight, he finally called back.

"Kassidy," he said, very business-like, considering the late hour.

"Yes," was all I could manage to squeak out.

"I'm going to post bail for Finn in the morning," he told me.

My brain was crashing against the sides of my skull, and I couldn't think straight. I stupidly asked, "Does that mean Finn's spending the night in jail?"

"I'll call you with a time and place to pick him up," he said.

"But why is Finn in jail? What do they think he did?" I asked the lawyer. I could feel the tears welling in my eyes. I felt confused and out of control.

"I can't tell you that due to attorney-client privilege. I suggest you get some sleep and wait for my call in the morning," was all he said.

The receiver cradled against my face was now wet with tears. And then he hung up.

I slid down to the floor, my breathing coming in ragged breaths as I gasped for air. My chest ached, and my limbs went numb. My head and chest felt like they would both explode. *Am I having a heart attack?*

No, it wasn't a heart attack. I was having a full-blown panic attack, and Finn was not here to help me.

I closed my eyes and tried to slow my breathing with deeper breaths. I felt a cold, wet nose nudge my left hand and instinctively knew it was Lizzie. Without opening my eyes, I stroked her soft fur, and soon, I was breathing almost normally again, and the pain in my chest subsided. My head was still pounding, and I was still filled with fear, but Lizzie infused me with a little courage.

As I sat on the floor, the same question kept rolling around in my head: *why had Finn been arrested?* I was worried about him spending the night in jail with criminals. Thinking of my husband as a criminal and picturing him in jail made my heart hurt.

I opened my eyes and found Lizzie's nose inches from my face. "Lizzie, how in the world are we going to pay back the bail money and the lawyer's fees?" I asked her. Cost had not figured into my frantic phone book search for an attorney.

I felt lost, and there was nothing I could do about it.

Sam heard the question, too, and got her favorite toy and set it in my lap next to Lizzie's head. Each seemed to be doing their best to comfort me. Or maybe they were hoping I would comfort them.

Finally, I dragged myself off the floor and climbed the stairs. When I saw the ransacked room at the top of the stairs, I froze. I quickly shut the door; the sight was too much to bear.

I crossed the hall to the bedroom, set the alarm, and crawled into bed. I hadn't even bothered to change out of my work clothes or wash my face. I wanted to be ready to go when the next call came. I patted the bedspread, and Lizzie jumped up on one side and circled Finn's empty pillow to make her nest. But Sam whined on the floor, looking up at me. They both knew something was wrong, and as I looked at them, I realized they knew as much as I did.

Finn was gone.

I jumped out of bed, pulled Sam into my arms, and carried her back into bed with me. The three of us comforted each other that long night, but none of us got much sleep.

I spent the night tossing and turning while wondering what the police thought Finn had done to land in a jail cell. None of this made any sense.

A slow, creeping dread unfurled in my belly, rising into my chest and radiating through my limbs like cold lead. With each tick of the clock, the heaviness grew, as if the weight of not knowing had anchored me in place, pressing against my skin from the inside out. I knew that whatever put him in jail was bad. It was the only way I could account for Finn rudely hanging up on me. Why wouldn't he just tell me what had happened? We told each other everything! My pulse pounded, and my blood felt hot within my veins. Each time I shifted positions to try to sleep, Sam whimpered nervously.

It wasn't just fear that tightened my throat and wet my eyes. I felt something unformed hovering above me. It was cold and out of reach, but if I concentrated hard enough, I began to recognize the edges of loss. My breathing fell into rhythm with the alarm clock's ticking as exhaustion mercifully brought me to sleep.

The dogs snuggled close to me that night as we tossed and fussed until the alarm clock finally ended our struggles. At the shrill sound, I thought, for an instant, that I had been having a nightmare. But when

I looked over and only saw Lizzie on Finn's pillow, the reality hit me that my husband of ten years was not there, lying beside me. We always slept with our bodies touching in some way - one leg entwined around the other, his arm draped over my waist, or my head resting on his shoulder. Instead of his arm wrapped around me protectively in our bed, he had spent the night in jail.

The nightmare was real.

CHAPTER 1

THE CONFESSION

I stumbled into the bathroom and caught my reflection in the mirror. My green blouse was wrinkled and sweaty in places. My green eyes were red and swollen, and my face was streaked with tears and yesterday's mascara. How different my life had been when I had applied it yesterday morning! My long brown hair was a knotted mess from my restless night. I decided to wash my face and change my clothes, but I would not get in the shower for fear of missing the call from the criminal lawyer.

It was still dark outside, and I knew it was unlikely that the attorney would call that early. But, still, I was not going to take the chance. I had never been in this situation and had no idea how it all worked. I wanted to be prepared when he called. I wanted to be ready to pick up Finn when he was released from jail.

Jail! I still could not believe this was happening.

As I searched the closet for something to wear, my gaze settled on the one bright exception on Finn's side—a boldly striped polo shirt tucked among his otherwise practical clothes. It had always made me smile; it felt like a glimpse of the playful man beneath the serious scholar. I slipped it from the hanger and pressed the fabric to my face, breathing in the faint trace of his scent. It was barely there, but it was enough. Somehow, that small closeness steadied me.

I suddenly wondered what he had worn the day before. *Was he still wearing it in jail, or had they given him prisoner's clothing?* It was too much to bear, and I shut my eyes tightly to make the image disappear. I brushed my hand across the row of his shirts, hoping to feel him there with me.

I headed downstairs to the kitchen. As I scooped the coffee into the coffee maker, the aroma of the grounds made me think of Finn. He usually made the coffee on the weekends. He would take the time to grind whole beans, and the smell filled the kitchen. I loved that smell, and it made me miss him even more. I glanced at the phone, willing it to ring. It sat silently in its cradle.

My stomach was churning. I realized I hadn't eaten since lunch the day before. I should have been hungry, but I felt nauseated. I forced myself to eat a few bites of a slice of toast with butter just to have something in my stomach to absorb the coffee.

"Do you want some toast?" I asked Sam and Lizzie as I handed them the rest.

The dogs sniffed tentatively at the toast, disappointed that it wasn't the usual weekend breakfast of eggs or pancakes. But they ate it anyway when they realized that was all there was. Then they hovered by the door, reminding me to let them out.

I took them outside, but I left the door open to hear the phone, which I had left to charge in its base on the kitchen counter.

The dogs would have liked a walk, but I did not dare leave the house for fear of missing the lawyer's call.

I tried to busy myself with mundane tasks, like cleaning the kitchen and doing laundry. But the tasks did nothing to take my mind off Finn. I was restless, and Lizzie and Sam anxiously watched as I paced from the kitchen to the living room and back again. I still felt queasy and tense, my neck and shoulders knotted from the stress.

Around ten o'clock, the phone finally rang, and I snatched the handset from its cradle. "Yes! This is Kassidy!" I answered, breathlessly.

"Hello, Kassidy. This is Jordan Jensen, Finn's attorney," he said calmly. "How are you this morning?"

I exhaled heavily in relief that it was the call I'd been expecting, not realizing until then that I had been holding my breath. "Not very well," I sighed, choking back the urge to cry. "I hope you can tell me what's going on."

"Finn and I went before the judge this morning," the attorney declared.

"I didn't know judges heard cases on Saturday!" I exclaimed.

"They can only hold someone in jail for 48 hours, and they don't work on Sunday," he explained.

"Oh," I replied, dully.

"He told us the charges and then set bail at $7,500," the attorney revealed.

I audibly gasped when I heard the bail amount. My mind was reeling. *How are we going to pay for this?*

The attorney continued, "Do you understand how bail works?"

"Not really."

"Bail is the fee the court sets for a defendant to be released from custody until their trial. I made arrangements with a bail bondsman at Finn's request. The bail bondsman puts up that money on the defendant's behalf. You'll need to pay ten percent to the bail bondsman and put up some collateral for the rest."

I cringed at the word "defendant." Finn was now a defendant, and I still had no idea why.

"Collateral?" I asked, my voice a dry whisper.

"Yes, it's standard procedure in these cases," he replied.

"These cases?" I queried, although the answer hit my brain before I got the question out.

"Criminal cases, Kassidy," he confirmed. "I know this is all a lot to absorb. I can explain everything when you and Finn meet me at my office on Monday at 9:00 AM. You can then give me the money and information on what you'll be using as collateral for the bail bondsman."

"Collateral," I echoed, dazed.

"We will also settle up on my fees for representing Finn last night and this morning. And we will discuss my fees for additional representation, should Finn decide that he'd like me to represent him going forward," Jordan continued.

I felt dizzy, and my body began to shake. *Going forward means that this is not over*, I realized.

"Going forward," I repeated numbly.

"I'm sorry, Kassidy. I know this must all be overwhelming for you," the attorney comforted. "Let me give you the address where you need to go to pick up Finn."

I grabbed a pen and scribbled down the address as he read it. My eyes welled with tears, and I shook my head so that I could see clearly enough to write.

Then Jordan told me, "Finn should be released between eleven and eleven-thirty this morning. You won't be able to go inside, so just try to find a place along the curb to park and wait. Good luck, Kassidy! I will see you and Finn in my office on Monday."

"Thank you. I'll see you then," I muttered, leaning against the counter, my forehead on my hand, and then hung up the phone, laying it heavily back in its cradle.

My mind was racing. *$7,500! Plus, lawyer's fees! How are we going to pay for this? Where are we going to find the money? we're already heavily in debt!*

What is Finn charged with? And what are we going to use as collateral? The only thing we own that would cover that amount is the townhouse! Or both cars together, and that is a stretch!

I put those thoughts aside and concentrated on picking up Finn. I had to go to the downtown jail. Visiting the jail had never been part of our lazy Saturday adventures.

As I drove downtown, I focused on the directions and tried not to think about why I was going there. But not thinking about it was impossible. I didn't know what to expect. But no matter what, I felt sure that Finn and I would get through this together, just like we always did.

A few blocks from the jail, the intersection was closed due to an accident. As I waited for the first responders to clear the scene or direct us around it, I twirled the ring Finn gave me for our anniversary. As my mind wandered back to our recent and unforgettable weekend on Padre Island National Seashore, a soft smile formed on my face.

We decided to celebrate our 10th anniversary with a weekend trip and wanted to make it special. To stretch our budget, we decided to camp on the beach for the first night and spend the last night in a hotel.

The first night was unbearably hot in the tent, and neither of us could sleep, so we decided to take a walk along the moonlit beach. The stars twinkled above us, and we could see the bright lights of oil rig platforms at a distance offshore. Despite the heat, we held hands and kept each other close, gently bumping shoulders as we walked. The sensual feel of hot and sweaty skin on skin was exhilarating.

As we walked, Finn leaned in and brushed his lips against my ear as he whispered, "You're so beautiful." He drew out each word slowly in the deep, sexy voice he used when he wanted to seduce me. A warm tingle spread through my torso.

"Mmmm…" I replied, practically purring with delight. "Are you sure you're not looking at the moon?" I teased.

"Why would I look at the moon when I have you?" he murmured as he took my hand and twirled me like we were on a dance floor.

The breeze was thick with summer heat, brushing against our skin like a lover's breath. It carried the sweet scent of coconut oil mingled with the tangy, salty kiss of the sea—a perfume that clung to our bodies and filled our lungs. The waves murmured a soft, rhythmic lullaby as they lapped the shore, each one a soft heartbeat against the white sand. We felt the movement of the breeze and water, but everything was calm and peaceful.

Barefoot, we wandered into the warm shallows, water swirling around our ankles, toes sinking into the cool sand, until a rogue wave rose without warning and crashed over us, drenching our sweaty skin in a rush of saltwater and laughter.

I gasped, breathless, as the water splashed over my body, making every nerve come alive. Finn was already watching me with that look—the one that made my stomach flutter and heat pool low in my belly. He stepped closer, his voice low and teasing.

"When was the last time we went skinny dipping?" he asked, his fingers lacing through mine, tugging me gently but firmly toward the deep. His touch said more than words, a promise carried on the wind and the waves.

"Our honeymoon in St. Maarten," I replied, fondly remembering that romantic evening on the beach.

A moment later, we were stripping off our clothes, laughing, and running naked into the ocean for a swim.

When we reached the deeper water, Finn dove beneath the surface and slid his hands along my body as he emerged, water droplets tracing his path. I wrapped my arms around his neck as he pulled me in for a long, passionate kiss.

Our bodies, buoyed by the salty water, danced together as we playfully teased one another, each familiar with the other's secret spots that would elicit the most intense responses. Cooled by the water, our bodies soon radiated a different kind of heat – a longing that can only be ignited by a lover's touch. Finn took my hand as the heat grew all-consuming, leading me out of the water and onto the beach.

Finn spread his t-shirt on the sand, sat down, pulled me into his lap, and started kissing me again.

"Finn! We should get dressed! What if someone decides to walk the beach?" I whispered, glancing around nervously.

We had passed several other tents at campsites along our walk. As hot as it was, we were probably not the only people to think about a moonlit stroll or swim. The bright moon cast an ethereal glow on the beach, exposing us.

"Who cares if someone sees us?" Finn replied, his blue eyes sparkling with mischief. "I want to make love to you right here on the beach under the stars!"

He kissed me again, and we rolled off the t-shirt onto the soft, white sand, his hands caressing my body. The pleasure I felt heightened the excitement and outweighed the risk of getting caught. I would never take such a risk on my own, but with Finn, I felt safe and loved in a way I never had. Trusting him completely, I let go of my fears and inhibitions and surrendered to the passion that engulfed us both.

Finn was wildly passionate that night. I gave myself completely to the urgent demands of our bodies, and the sand clung to us as we moved together as one. It was beautiful and fierce, loving and lascivious, tender and unrestrained.

When we were both satiated, Finn found the t-shirt again, laid me on it, and pulled me close. We held each other there, our limbs entangled, staring at the stars. "Look there, low in the sky to the south!" Finn said, pointing in the direction he wanted me to look. "See that bright red star? That is Antares. It's part of Scorpius, the hooked-shaped constellation there."

"Yes, I see it!" I exclaimed.

"And do you see those three bright stars that form a triangle? Those are Vega, Altair, and Deneb. They make up the Summer Triangle," he explained while pointing toward the eastern sky. "Vega is also part of Lyra the Harp, Altair is part of Aquila the Eagle, and Deneb is part of Cygnus the Swan."

Finn continued pointing out other features in the night sky as he held me close. Astronomy was one of Finn's hobbies, a nice complement to studying geology. The depth of his knowledge of the earth and sky never ceased to amaze me.

After a few minutes of stargazing, I suggested, "We should probably start heading back to the tent and try to get some sleep."

"Yeah, you're probably right," Finn replied.

As we stood up, the sand clung stubbornly to our bodies. It had dried, allowing us to brush most of it off. But there were spots that we couldn't reach, so we relied on each other for assistance. Finn stood behind me, gently brushing the sand off my back. His touch sent shivers down my spine. He wrapped his arms around me, his hands tenderly cupping my breasts. He gently kissed the back of my neck, knowing it was my most vulnerable spot. It didn't take long before we found ourselves back in the sand, making love again.

When we were finally exhausted, we brushed ourselves off, put our clothes back on, and walked hand in hand back to our tent. We whispered, careful not to disturb the other campers as we passed. We crawled into our tent and lay together on our sleeping bags, holding each other close despite the heat.

"I'll be graduating soon, you know," Finn said in a hushed voice.

"Yes, you've been working so hard on your dissertation–all the late nights," I responded, smiling.

"Yeah, I did a lot of writing while you were traveling for work," Finn agreed. "I'll be able to start applying for research or teaching positions at other colleges and universities soon. Where do you think we should go next?"

"Some small to medium college town where we can put down roots and raise a family. Somewhere that doesn't have extreme heat or cold," I said dreamily.

"Maybe I'll find something on the East Coast," Finn suggested.

I was surprised that Finn had mentioned graduating. He never seemed to want to talk about it when I brought it up. Perhaps his dissertation was progressing better than I thought. That made me happy. We fell asleep in each other's arms that night, dreaming about our future together.

Suddenly, I was roused from my daydreaming by the honking of the car behind me. A policeman was waving me through the intersection past the accident. I waved to the driver behind me in acknowledgment, my feelings of happiness and contentment dissolving as I was pulled back into the reality of driving to the jail to pick up my husband.

As I continued to drive, I thought about the ring. After our passionate night of sandy lovemaking on the beach, we moved to the resort hotel for the final night of our getaway. We checked in and hurried up to our room, anxious for air conditioning, a much-needed shower, and a meal that didn't require cooking on a single propane burner. I hopped into the shower first, letting the water wash away the salty residue of our beach adventure. As I stepped out of the shower and toweled off, I wrapped the towel around me. Then, I called Finn to say it was his turn, but he didn't answer. I poked my head out of the bathroom door to call him again, only to find him kneeling by the door and holding a small red jewelry box.

"Happy anniversary, Kassidy!" Finn said, smiling broadly.

"Oh my! What is this?" I replied, my heart racing with surprise and excitement.

"You'll just have to open it to find out!" he said, rising to his feet.

I opened the box and found a beautiful, simple silver ring shaped like a love knot.

"It's beautiful, Finn! Thank you!" I beamed as I put my arms around his neck and kissed him, careful not to let the towel slip as I did so.

At that moment, I could not have been happier. Many women would have preferred something more extravagant, like a diamond necklace or a tennis bracelet. But that simple ring was perfect for me. I recognized the jewelry store where he had bought it and knew he had given me a gift we could genuinely afford for the first time in our ten-year marriage. Money had often been a source of tension between us, but with this heartfelt gesture, I felt like my husband finally understood that the true value of a gift was not measured by its cost but by its thoughtfulness. And that was everything!

I slowly drove my car forward, merging with the other cars in the lane as the police officer directed. As I passed the wreckage, I noticed two damaged cars. The paramedics were examining the drivers of the vehicles. Fortunately, it looked like no one had been seriously hurt.

I had been wearing the ring every day for the last three months; it reminded me that Finn and I loved each other and were a team. I couldn't imagine anything he could have done to change that. We were always there for each other, and I would be there for him now.

The voice in my head kept telling me that this was all just some terrible mistake. Finn was a good man, and I couldn't imagine him doing anything that would land him in jail. Yes, this had to be a mistake, and whatever was happening now, we would get through it together.

But if this was all a mistake, why hadn't Finn told me why he had been arrested? Why hadn't he tried to reassure me that everything would be alright?

When I got near the jail, I looked for a place to pull over and park on the street, but nothing was available. I drove around the block and tried again. I saw people coming out of the jail who looked like they might have spent the night there. Some were young men who looked hungover, blinking in the bright sunlight as they scanned the waiting cars for their rides.

There were scantily dressed women of all ages. One young woman was barefoot and carried her stilettos as she made her way down the street. It was a dark reality that I had never seen before.

It wasn't until my third trip around the block that I saw my husband. I almost didn't recognize him. His shoulders were stooped, and his head was bowed. He showed none of his usual confidence. He positioned himself away from the others on the sidewalk as much as possible, trying not to interact with anyone. He was usually outgoing and friendly, happy to talk to anyone. It was a shock to see him this way.

I pulled over and stopped as close as I could get to the curb. Finn saw me and approached the car. The look on his face revealed shame. *He must feel really bad for having spent the night in jail,* I thought as he walked around to the other side of the car.

He climbed into the passenger seat and fastened his seatbelt without saying a word.

I stepped on the gas and navigated the one-way streets of downtown Austin toward home.

The tall, gray office buildings we passed seemed to close in on us. The jail would have looked like any other office building if it hadn't been for the disheveled people filtering out from inside. It was remarkably plain, meant to blend in with its surroundings. But to me, it was an ugly monster that had just spit out my husband after holding him hostage overnight.

Once we were out of downtown, I looked over at my husband. He looked terrible. His eyes were red, his hair was uncombed, and his face bore a scruffy stubble. There was a feral energy about him. He smelled of body odor, and the underarms of his blue-striped, short-sleeved, button-down shirt were stained with sweat.

There was also another smell that I couldn't quite identify. Something musty or earthy, like the smell of a basement. He remained silent and stared straight ahead. He wouldn't look at me. We always shared everything, and now he felt so distant. The man I loved felt like a stranger to me. *His night in prison must have been even more traumatic for him than I had imagined, if he can't even speak to me*, I thought.

But it had been traumatic for me, too! I still didn't know why Finn had been arrested or why they had pressed criminal charges against him. I needed answers, and I needed them now! And Finn was the only one who could give them to me.

It was going to be up to me to break the ice. I proceeded as gently as I could, while inside I was screaming to find out what had happened.

"Finn! Are you okay? I was so worried! Can you help me understand what happened?" I began.

I grew more concerned when he didn't respond, and my need for answers took over.

"What is going on? Why were you arrested?" I demanded anxiously.

Finn didn't look at me, and his voice was barely above a whisper when he responded, "I don't want to talk. Just take me home."

His response did nothing to calm my rising anxiety. I was gripping the steering wheel so tightly that my fingers hurt. My entire body was one big knot, and I felt the bile rising from my stomach into my throat.

"Look, Finn, I understand you had a very difficult night. But so have I! I have been worried sick about you, and you can't even explain why this whole nightmare is happening! Why did you ask me to call a criminal attorney? What happened, Finn? What did you do, or what do they think you did that they arrested you for it?" My voice was high and tight, but I couldn't control it.

We were at a stoplight, and I looked over at him. His eyes welled with tears. He swallowed hard.

"I was arrested for soliciting a minor for sex," he told me in a shaky voice.

My breath caught in my throat, and the world spun around me. *Soliciting a minor? My husband? My Finn?* I couldn't believe what I was hearing! But the way he kept his eyes fixed anywhere but on me—on the floor, the dashboard, his hands—was all the confirmation I needed. The unthinkable was true.

Silence filled the car as we drove home. I felt lightheaded and shaky as his words sank in. It didn't make sense. I struggled to breathe as tears dripped down my cheeks. Finn sat there looking straight ahead, silent, as I processed what felt like an earthquake inside me. The small car seemed to constrict around us, and I felt like all the oxygen had been sucked out. I could barely breathe, my throat and chest feeling tight.

I wanted to be as far away from Finn as I could get, and yet he was right there, less than an arm's length away. I couldn't escape what Finn had just told me, or the stream of thoughts that raced through my head as the telephone poles blurred past me.

My husband solicited a minor? This is not my Finn! There must be some mistake! Why isn't Finn telling me he didn't do this, and they have the wrong guy? Why isn't he telling me this is all just a horrible mistake?

I don't know how I managed to drive. I was sobbing so hard I was nearly blinded by my tears. I gulped for air with every breath. I was sweating and nauseous. I didn't notice traffic lights or any of the sights we passed. It was all just a blur of indistinct shapes and colors that I couldn't make any sense of. But somehow, we made it home. Finn just sat in his seat, not saying a word, not trying to comfort me, staring blankly out the window, tears dripping off his face.

I parked the car behind our townhouse, and we just sat there; neither of us could move. Finn broke the silence by opening the glove box and rooting for napkins. He often joked that I needed napkins handy because I always spilled the ketchup for my fries on road trips. He found a napkin from a happier time and used it to wipe his tears.

But he didn't offer me one.

I sat there motionless, not wanting to bring this awful thing with us into our home. The first home we purchased together no longer felt like a home. It was just a place where our lives happened before Finn's arrest. Suddenly, a crevasse had opened between the before and the after, and, peering into the dark abyss, I couldn't see what the after would bring.

How do you go on after your life has been shattered? I wondered. I felt Finn looking at me for the first time since he got into the car. He was waiting for me to say something. But now I was the one who could not look at him. What was there to say?

There were many things I wanted to know. I wanted to scream at him, *How could you?* I wanted to ask: *Have you done this before? How old was she? Or was it a he? How did you know them? Was it one of your students?*

I wanted to tell him I was appalled and sickened. After ten years of marriage, who are you?

I hadn't asked any of the questions out loud, so Finn didn't answer me. But my brain frantically searched for the answers it needed. *He's still my Finn! Of course he is! Right? But my Finn would never have betrayed me! He promised to love me forever. My Finn would never do something this terrible!*

But this is no longer my Finn! When did he stop being my Finn to become this person I barely recognize? When did he become a person who would betray me, lie to me, and be so selfish as to not even hand me a napkin to wipe away my tears, tears that he caused?

But surely my Finn is still there. Any minute now, he'll tell me it was all a mistake, that the cops made a mistake, that I misheard him. He will once again be my protector. My Finn!

I wanted him to take it all back and make everything okay again, to go back to how things were and to prevent this from happening. But I couldn't utter a word and knew I couldn't make him say what I wanted to hear.

I was in shock, and my tired brain was wildly trying to understand everything. My mind desperately tried to find a way to make his words take on a different meaning, but couldn't.

He was my husband, the person I knew most intimately.

But now, he was also a stranger—a dangerous one.

He was a man who had done something unimaginable! I did not know the man who had been accused of soliciting sex with a minor. The moment he told me, everything shifted. Feelings of love and safety turned to feelings of betrayal and uncertainty. Trust and faith in my husband became clouded by fear and doubt. I thought I knew my husband, but now I wondered if I had ever really known him.

In a single, shattering heartbeat, my world cracked open like fault lines tearing through solid ground. Everything I once trusted splintered into Before and After—no gentle in-between, only a yawning chasm where my hopes and certainties tumbled into darkness.

I don't remember how long we sat in the car. Our silence was interrupted by the dogs' sharp, incessant barking at the dining room window. Afraid that the neighbors might complain, I knew we had to quiet them. I wanted to get out of that car and away from Finn. I didn't want him near me. But where else could he go?

"We should go inside," I finally said.

I didn't recognize my own voice; it was hoarse and ragged, stripped of its usual warmth and kindness. It belonged to a cynical woman who had been robbed of her faith in the world and the man she loved.

And so, because I didn't have time to process the seismic shift that happened to me in the fifteen-minute car ride, I followed Finn into our home, which suddenly no longer felt like a home.

Lizzie and Sam greeted me with unshakable love but sensed a change in Finn. They sniffed the jail scents on him distrustfully. They knew that something was wrong. When Finn tried to pet them, they pulled away, eyeing him cautiously. When he ran upstairs to shower, I was left alone with Sam, Lizzie, and my thoughts.

Finn normally used the shower in the spare bedroom. For a split second, I wondered if he would be shocked when he saw the ransacked office. But then I remembered. He already knew.

I sat on the sofa, Sam and Lizzie on either side of me. Instead of fighting for my attention as usual, they sat quietly, occasionally wagging a tail or moving a paw or head onto my lap. They wanted to console me, but I was lost in my head, barely aware of their presence. Part of me was listening for the shower to stop so I could prepare myself for Finn coming back downstairs. I had so many questions. *Why did he do this? What exactly had he done? Where do we go from here? How could this be happening?*

I needed details to help me sort this all out. My mind could not reconcile the husband I knew—or thought I knew—with the person who had just confessed to me that he had committed this horrendous offense.

The anger burning in my stomach felt like I'd swallowed a whole habanero. *How in the hell had this happened? How could Finn have been accused of having sex with a minor?*

And then the self-doubt crept in. *Maybe I did something? Maybe I didn't give him the love he needed. Maybe I didn't satisfy his sexual needs. How could I not know what was going on?*

Underlying my anger and fear was the thought that I had missed something and could have prevented this. My world had been capsized instantly, and I had to make sense of it.

What exactly did soliciting a minor mean, anyway? What exactly had he done?

He had confessed in the car, but it was like a stone skipped across a pond. I knew I must prepare for deep diving now. And I feared that the implications of the coming conversation may last the rest of my life.

CHAPTER 2

DEEP DIVING

Finn came downstairs, freshly showered and clean-shaven. On the outside, he looked identical to the man I married. He was wearing one of my favorite shirts in a shade of blue that perfectly complemented his eyes. He smelled like my Finn again, too - sandalwood with a hint of citrus - the odors of his night in jail washed away. For a split second, I felt he was the man I fell in love with, and I couldn't believe he could have done this. Surely, the police had this all wrong.

But his demeanor was completely different. I was used to Finn's free and easy spirit; this cautious darkness was utterly unknown to me. A sinister moodiness replaced his usual vivaciousness. His face was fixed in a scowl. His bloodshot eyes were moist as if he were on the verge of tears. A part of me wanted to hug him and tell him everything would be alright. But that thought repulsed me.

He sat there as though he were the victim, not the man who had just confessed to something unspeakable. My feelings fought each other—grief, fury, disbelief—while I watched for even a trace of the Finn I once knew. If that Finn still existed, he was buried beneath the scowl of this sullen, angry stranger.

Hope faded as the minutes dragged on. Finn sat there brooding silently. He offered me no explanation, no apology—nothing to soothe the raw ache tearing through me. My tears slid uninvited down my cheeks as the ugly truth emerged: a child was somehow entangled in his crime, and I'd been blind to it all. Guilt clawed at me for not seeing the signs, for failing to stop any of this before it began.

Finn did not explain that it was a misunderstanding. He didn't insist that the police had made a mistake. His heavy silence said everything: he did it, and life, as we knew it, no longer existed.

Finn sat on the opposite end of the couch. Sam went over to greet him and then quickly came back to me. Lizzie never left my side and positioned herself in a defensive position with her back against me, facing Finn and not taking her eyes off him. She seemed to sense that I needed protection and that he was responsible for whatever was happening.

I wanted to shower, but the weight of my questions anchored me to the sofa. My body felt as if it were made of granite blocks, and I sank deeper into the couch. I needed answers before anything else. I knew—of course, I knew—that I wouldn't like hearing those answers. They would tear me apart.

It was mid-afternoon. I'd cracked the blinds just enough to let in a sliver of light—enough to see, not enough to feel exposed. The rest of the world remained shut out. Still, the room felt dim, thick with a heaviness that no sunlight could lift.

My eyes drifted to the mantel above the stone fireplace, where framed moments from other lives stood in quiet formation—beaches, holidays, laughing faces from both our families. But it was our wedding photo that caught and held me. I looked closer.

The couple smiling back at me looked untouched by doubt, radiant with certainty. I didn't recognize them. Their joy felt almost cruel now—an accusation, a taunt. They didn't know what was coming. And I no longer knew who we were.

The antique clock on the mantel was the only sound in the room, and I could hear it ticking away the time. Its staccato quickened as I grew impatient. Although I dreaded hearing what Finn would reveal, I had to know.

The clock suddenly chimed the hour, startling us both, but goading me to speak since Finn wouldn't.

"Tell me what happened," I pleaded, tears threatening to flood my eyes again. "Tell me everything. And tell me the truth because you know I'll find out anyway. But I need to hear it from you."

Finn took a deep breath and started to cry. "I don't even know where to begin," he whispered. "I'm so sorry. I never meant to hurt you. I did not want to do this. It just happened," he stammered.

It just happened, I thought, *as if he had nothing to do with it!*

"Tell me exactly what happened!" I shouted, my voice edgier than I intended. I was clenching my fists in anger, and I felt my face getting hot.

I could tell he was stalling.

"It all started when you were away on business a lot. I was lonely and bored," he said.

Was he seriously going to blame this on me? I thought.

"That's when I got online and found a chat room," he continued. "Just to talk to people. I never intended to meet anyone in person. It just happened," he repeated.

I grabbed a pillow and clenched it to my chest, my fingernails nearly ripping the fabric. Finn crossed his arms defensively across his chest. I could feel the wall between us building as we assumed protective positions.

"Things like this don't just happen! You made a choice." I was shouting at him, and my body felt like it would spontaneously combust. "You know right from wrong! You do know right from wrong, don't you?"

When he didn't respond, I slammed the pillow against the wall, nearly knocking down the picture above the sofa. Finn made a move toward me to try to calm me down. But Lizzie growled menacingly, baring her teeth and snapping at Finn as he attempted to approach me, her protective instincts in full force. Finn recoiled, stunned.

"She almost bit me!" he cried.

"Consider that a warning," I said coldly. "Now tell me what happened!"

"I started by chatting with different people in the chat room, mostly women. And then one of them was a girl I thought was eighteen," he stated.

"How old was she?" I asked, holding my breath as I waited for his answer.

Finn paused before answering, looking at his hands. Then he took a deep breath before he quietly muttered, "Eleven. She was eleven. But I didn't know that when I went to meet her."

I gasped in horror as this just kept getting worse. My thoughts were spiraling. *She was just a little girl! What in the hell was he doing chatting online with a little girl?* I tried to keep my emotions in check as I continued my interrogation. If I went off now, Finn might shut down completely.

"What made you think she was eighteen?" I asked, waiting for more details.

Finn's voice was tinged with frustration as he explained, "She told me she was eighteen, okay! I didn't know she was lying. I just wanted someone to talk to and make me feel less alone."

He looked and sounded pitiful, but I felt little sympathy for him. He should not have been online chatting in the first place.

"How many children were you having online chats with? Have you ever met with any of them?" I queried.

"I wasn't talking to other children! I've never done anything like this before! How could you even ask that?" he countered.

I didn't respond to his question but continued with my own.

"How did the girl get into the chat room?" I asked.

"It was just a public chat room on AOL. Anyone with an AOL account could get in," Finn explained.

"What did you talk about?" I thought a conversation with an eleven-year-old would be much different than one with an eighteen-year-old. A young girl would talk about school, her friends, and her pets. A young woman might discuss more mature subjects and be flirtatious. Their choice of words and perspectives would be different.

"How could you not tell the difference between an eleven-year-old and an eighteen-year-old based on your chats?" I queried, as doubt about his not knowing her actual age crept in.

"Our chats at first were just fun and playful. I don't remember what we talked about, exactly. We were just having fun," Finn replied without answering my question.

"But what do you mean by fun and playful? Again, I think those would be very different for a young girl and a young woman," I countered.

Finn was getting annoyed at my questioning. He was fidgeting in his seat and picking at his fingernails. He avoided looking my way.

"I didn't know she was only eleven!" he shouted.

I still wasn't convinced, but decided to focus on something else Finn had said.

"You said 'at first' the chats were fun and playful. Did something change?" I asked, becoming more uneasy with what I was hearing.

Finn hesitated and looked at his hands before continuing.

"Yeah," he said, frowning, "things changed."

I noticed his hands shaking as he said it. It was clear that I would have to drag the details out of him. It was hard enough to listen to the details, but his persistent hesitation made it necessary for me to keep digging. It was infuriating, and rage was boiling up inside me.

I clenched the pillow protectively to my chest, bracing for what might come next. My heart raced, and I felt the blood throbbing heavily at my temples. My chest ached, whether from the stress or the breaking of my heart, I wasn't sure. But I had to continue.

"How did things change?" I challenged.

With a heavy sigh, Finn rubbed his tired eyes before finally responding.

"Things started to take a more…sexual turn," he said.

My fingers dug deeper into the pillow as I fought to hold back my tears.

"Who took it in that direction?" I asked, suspecting that I already knew the answer.

Finn cleared his throat and avoided my gaze while I waited for him to respond.

"I did," he finally replied in a meek voice, looking at me tearfully.

"And what made you do that? Even if she were eighteen, why would you do that? Did she give you any indication that she was interested in that sort of thing?" I demanded.

"No," Finn admitted, "I just - I mean - I enjoyed our conversations and wanted to take it to another level."

"Even though you were married? Even though you knew it was wrong?" My voice was a screech in my ears, but I could not control it, no matter how hard I tried. The dogs shifted nervously, fearful of the sound.

"You weren't here! I was lonely!" Finn offered as a defense.

"Stop blaming me for your actions!" I shouted as I jumped up from the couch and began pacing. "So, is that when you went to meet her?"

"No," he said, no longer looking at me. "At some point, without my knowing, she got scared and told her mother. Then her mother started chatting with me, posing as her daughter."

"Did you say something that scared her?" I asked, my apprehension rising.

"Not that I know of," Finn replied, not looking my way.

"Then how do you know she got scared?" I probed.

"The prosecutor said it at the bail hearing," Finn explained.

"And the prosecutor didn't say what scared her?" I queried.

"No," Finn said, turning away from me.

I suspected he knew more, but I let it go. He was already forcing me to extract every detail. If I pushed him too far in any area, I was worried he would shut down entirely, and I still had a lot of ground to cover.

"Did you know it was the mother chatting with you?" I asked.

"No," Finn replied.

"I'm still a little confused how you couldn't tell the difference between chatting with a child and an adult. What kinds of things did the mother chat with you about?" I pressed further.

"I don't remember - just stuff!" Finn replied, getting agitated again.

"How can you not remember? Tell me what happened next!" I retorted, getting more impatient with his unsatisfying responses.

"Things continued to escalate, I guess." Finn fidgeted in his seat as he said it.

I stopped my pacing and looked straight at him. He wouldn't meet my gaze.

"Who escalated it? And how?" I wasn't letting up.

"I did," he said, gritting his teeth. "I did."

"So, is that when you asked to meet her?" I drilled.

"No," Finn replied, shaking his head as tears rolled down his cheeks.

Frustrated at having to drag out every detail, I threw the pillow at him, barely missing his head.

"Hey!" he shouted with surprise, finally looking up at me.

"Tell me what happened!" I shouted back.

"At some point, the girl's mother had enough evidence that our chats were not…innocent," he said, pausing to clear his throat. "And that was when she called the police."

"But how did it come about that you went to meet the girl?" I asked, still not getting the whole picture.

Finn sighed heavily before responding.

"A policewoman posed as the girl and continued our chat. When it escalated again, she suggested that we meet," Finn said softly.

"And you agreed? That didn't sound like a bad idea to you?" I asked incredulously.

"I don't know. Maybe a little," was all Finn could manage in response.

"Where did you go to meet her? Did you suggest the spot, or did she?" I pressed on.

"At the shopping center on William Cannon. She said it was near her house," he replied sheepishly.

I knew that shopping center. I passed it on my route to work.

"None of this raised any concerns for you? If she were eighteen, why would she want to meet at a shopping center near her house and not at a restaurant, coffee shop, or some other place that would have been safer for her to meet some unknown man?" I asked, still not believing he was telling me the whole story.

"I don't know. I've never done anything like this before!" Finn shouted as his frustration level rose at my interrogation.

"So you went to meet her at the shopping center. What happened when you got there?" I kept probing, needing to hear the whole story.

"I went to the shopping center and saw who I thought was the girl. She told me what she would be wearing: jeans, a pink t-shirt, and purple sneakers. I pulled my car into a parking spot, rolled down the window, and called out to her," Finn said, still avoiding my gaze. "She asked if I was Finn, and I said yes. But when she came to the car, I saw that she wasn't a girl but a petite woman dressed like a girl."

"Wait, if you thought she was a young woman, an eighteen-year-old, why would you think she would be dressed like a girl and not a woman?" I asked, suddenly realizing that he was lying about knowing the girl's age.

"No, I mean, sh-she looked a lot older," Finn stammered.

"You knew all along that you were talking to a young girl!" I paced the room as this thought sank in.

"That is why it didn't seem odd that she would ask to meet at a shopping center in her neighborhood. A child wouldn't understand how dangerous that would be! You knew all along that she was a child!" I sat down hard on the chair opposite the couch as this new information came to light.

Finn remained silent, still looking down at his hands.

I was nauseated, but I had to know the truth, so I continued my interrogation. "And if it had been the girl and she had gotten in the car, what were you planning on doing?" I asked, my heart racing and my stomach churning.

"I don't know. I guess we would have driven somewhere," Finn said, squirming in his seat.

"Where would you have gone?" I probed, barely able to get the words out.

"I don't know," Finn replied, shrugging. "I didn't have a plan. As I said, I have never done anything like this before."

I paused for a moment and studied Finn as he pulled at a thread on the hem of his shirt, still avoiding eye contact with me. I didn't believe he had no plan, and the thought sickened me.

"What happened next?" I continued, forcing down the bile I felt rising in my throat.

"She pulled out her badge, and as I tried to roll up the window and drive away, a bunch of police cars pulled in behind me, blocking my path," Finn said. "The police got out, pulled their guns, and ordered me out of the car. They arrested me right there. They had warrants to search my car and my house. One of the cops drove my car here, but I had to ride in the back of the police car. It was humiliating!"

"Oh my God, Finn! It was a sting operation! They were waiting for you, and you played right into it! What were you thinking?"

"I don't know. I guess I just wanted it to be over," he mumbled.

Confused, I asked, "What do you mean you wanted it to be over? Going to meet someone doesn't sound like the end of something. It sounds like the beginning of something more!"

"I was so relieved that the police were there and it wasn't the girl. I just wanted it to be over," he repeated.

Again, this didn't make sense to me. Was he really that naïve? Or was he trying to elicit my sympathy?

I pressed on.

"And who were you expecting to show up? An eighteen-year-old or an eleven-year-old?" I asked, even though I had already figured it out; I needed to hear him say it.

"I was expecting the girl," he answered in a small voice, his eyes fixed on the floor. The weight of it all hung in the air.

I felt hot rage boiling inside me and couldn't sit still. I jumped up and paced around the room, my hands on my hips, trying to find a more appropriate way to dissipate it than wrapping my hands around his throat.

"What the hell were you thinking? What were you expecting to get out of this? How could you do this?" I implored.

My husband was a pedophile. My whole world had just been cut to shreds, and he was holding the knife.

"I don't know. It just happened. I was under a lot of pressure with school. Everyone was pushing me to finish my dissertation and graduate – you, my family, my professors. And you were gone so much with work. It's not my fault!" he shouted.

He turned my way and saw my open-jaw reaction. I stopped my pacing and silently glared at him. We froze for a moment, staring each other down, each waiting for the other to make the next move.

Then, I strode over to where he was sitting and leaned over him, my jaw set hard, and my eyes narrowed. Through gritted teeth, I said, "Don't put this on me! Yes, I was gone for work a lot, but that's what I had to do to support us! You don't even bring in enough to pay for your tuition! And now, you're blaming me for the crime you committed - a harmful act against a child?"

He was still sitting, and I towered over him. He looked small and afraid, yet I could feel his defiance.

"I cracked under all the pressure I was under! You have no idea what it's like!" he retorted.

My head was pounding, and my sight blurred. An electrical charge ran from my skull to my fingertips, making them tingle. I was outraged that he refused to accept responsibility for his actions. My body shook in rage as I clenched my fists, trying to control myself.

"You had other options! You could have talked to me about being lonely. You could have hung out with Kevin more often. But you chose to go online and chat with a child with the intention of having sex with her. That is sick! And what would have happened if it had been the little girl who showed up and not the cops? Would you have acted on your intentions?" The thought of what could have happened terrified me, but I had to know if he was capable of hurting a child.

"I don't know," Finn said, shaking his head, "I really don't know."

"That is not the same as saying no," I replied hoarsely, a sick feeling washing over me. My heart was beating out of my chest, my palms were sweating, and I felt dizzy. I grabbed a tissue from the kitchen and wiped away the tears so I could see.

"I thought I knew you, Finn," I said softly as I returned to the living room. "I thought you loved me. After ten years, this is not something I ever saw coming. What other secrets have you been hiding?" I asked with raw emotion.

"I do love you, Kass! I didn't do this to hurt you. I was the one who was hurt because you weren't here. I was the one hurting because of all the pressure I was under. And now you think I'm some kind of monster who would hurt a child? How could you think that of me if you truly love me?" Finn's face was red with anger. Like a snared animal, I could see him twisting and manipulating this to make me the bad guy.

I took a step back, feeling like someone had punched me in the stomach.

"Considering your actions, what am I supposed to think? Yes, I love you - loved you! I don't know anymore! I don't even know who you are!"

I couldn't look at him for another second. Finn remained silent, looking down at the floor. The air in the room felt heavy and suffocating, and I struggled to catch my breath. The man I thought I knew was gone, replaced by a stranger who had committed an abhorrent crime and denied he was responsible.

I needed to get out of that room. I needed time to think about what to do next. I left and ran upstairs to shower, the dogs faithfully following me. Lizzie lay by the bathroom door, keeping watch.

Although her head rested on her front paws, she was tense and alert. She would not let Finn come in if he tried – that was obvious. Sam paced in the small space, not knowing what to do.

As the hot water washed over me in the shower, I tried to focus on what to do next. It was Saturday afternoon, and our meeting with the lawyer was not until Monday. I began considering what I could control.

I need to take some time off work while we sort things out. We can't afford that, but I have no choice! I've got to go with him to see the lawyer to know what's coming legally and financially. Whether I like it or not, he has dragged me into this because we're married, and all our assets are joint. He's reckless with money. If I kick him out, he'll max out the charge cards, and if he's in jail, I'll be the one paying them off. I can't kick him out until I figure out how to financially disentangle myself from him.

I dropped the soap, and when Lizzie heard the noise, she poked her head into the shower to check on me.

"I'm okay, Lizzie!" I reassured her. Satisfied, she lay back down on the bathroom rug.

I'm in no shape to do much today, but I can go to work tomorrow and put in some time while Finn assists on that field trip with the undergraduates. He has to leave early and will be gone all day.

I rinsed my hair, lingering under the stream of hot water.

That takes care of tomorrow, but what about after that? And what about tonight?

My mind was spinning. I wanted the water to wash away my tension and fears, but even a waterfall couldn't have managed that.

I wanted to call my parents. I was very close to them and knew they would be there for me, no matter what. But each time I thought about grabbing the receiver to dial their number, I chickened out. What would I say to them? How could I tell them what the man I married - the man I had brought into our family - had done? They would be so disappointed. I was embarrassed and didn't think I could handle their disappointment. My own shame was hard enough to bear.

And then there was Finn. I couldn't rely on him to help me. The fact that he took no responsibility and was actually blaming me made me want to scream.

Still, I felt some sympathy for him. No matter who he blamed, he would have to face the consequences of his actions, and one of those consequences would likely be prison.

And what about our marriage? I had loved him and made a lifelong commitment to him. But could I ever trust him again? No! How could I?

Then there was the guilt about not knowing what my husband was up to. And more importantly, not being able to stop it. A little girl could have gotten hurt! Thankfully, the child's mother intervened. Things could have been much worse. A shiver ran down my spine as I thought about that.

As I stepped out of the shower, I toweled off and wrapped my hair in the towel. I reached blindly for the closest robe hanging on the door. Realizing it was Finn's blue robe, not my white one, I dropped it as if it burned my hand. I slowly reached down to pick it up, then brought it up close to my face. It smelled like Finn, the way I remembered him smelling before this all happened. I carefully placed it back on its hook, then grabbed my robe and wrapped myself in it.

I walked into the bedroom and over to the closet. I took the towel off my wet hair, folded it in half like a pair of trousers, and hung it neatly on a hanger. It felt like my brain and body were no longer connected, and my actions no longer made sense.

I opened my dresser drawer, grabbed a bra and a pair of panties, and put them on. I jammed a turtleneck over my head, then, grunting, pulled on my favorite pair of well-worn jeans. Lizzie looked at me questioningly. I glanced in the mirror and sighed, realizing the turtleneck was inappropriate for the hot weather we'd been having. I pulled it back over my head, tossed it on the floor, and grabbed a favorite t-shirt instead.

"I'm going to have to be the strong one, Lizzie. He's not going to be there for me. I will have to figure our way out of this mess if that's even possible! I have no idea where this is leading or what it will cost us! Money, his career, our marriage?" I bent over and gently stroked Lizzie. She gazed up at me, cocking her head as if she were trying to understand.

Sam walked over and licked my hand, wanting to be petted. Both dogs watched me with a mix of love and concern. They stayed close to me, ready to offer me comfort. I felt so disconnected from Finn now, but with Lizzie and Sam beside me, I felt much less alone. I gave each of them a quick pat on the head before opening the bedroom door.

I could hear sounds from downstairs - cupboards and drawers opening and closing, a plate placed heavily on the counter, and a knife scraping on a cutting board. Lizzie and Sam led the way, and we found Finn in the kitchen making a sandwich.

"Hey," he said, smiling slightly, "Can I make you a sandwich?"

"No, thanks," I said, still feeling nauseated. "I'm not hungry." It seemed so normal and so absurd at the same time.

How could he eat at a time like this? I judged him, but then my compassion for him stepped in. *I guess a night in jail can leave a person hungry.*

Mentally, I vowed never to find out for myself if jail causes hunger. But I would never end up in prison. The thought of it was laughable. I was always the good girl, doing what everyone expected of me. The hard worker. The loyal friend. The devoted wife. I had given up a job I loved in Virginia to move to Texas with Finn so that he could pursue his academic career. No, it wasn't likely that I'd ever end up in jail.

But then, I never thought I'd be married to a pedophile, either. But here I was, married to a criminal. Someone had rearranged the puzzle pieces of my life, and they no longer fit together.

CHAPTER 3

NAVIGATING A NEW REALITY

We barely spoke the rest of the day. I avoided Finn by busying myself with mindless tasks - cleaning the bathrooms, cleaning out the refrigerator, organizing the junk drawer. Finn parked himself on the couch in the living room to read Rocket Boys: A Memoir, which his oldest brother, Jack, had recommended.

As the sun set, I realized Sam and Lizzie had not yet gotten their evening walk. I put their leashes on them and opened the door.

"Hey, where are you going?" Finn asked.

"For a walk. The girls need their walk," I replied.

"I'll come with you!" Finn said, "I just need to put on my shoes."

"No!" I replied a little too forcefully.

Finn looked a little stunned.

"Why not?" he asked.

"I just want to go alone. I have a lot to think about," I replied.

"But we always walk the dogs together!" Finn protested.

"We did," I answered in the past tense.

"We *did?* What does that mean?" Finn asked angrily.

"It means I need to be alone to think!" I shouted as I walked out and slammed the door behind me.

Sam and Lizzie were happy to be outside as they led me through the neighborhood. They knew the routes we usually took, so I followed them, lost in my thoughts.

As the sky darkened, I started thinking about going to bed. That brought up new questions. *Where am I going to sleep tonight? In the same bed with Finn? God no!*

I pulled back gently on Sam's leash as she lunged at the neighbor's cat as we passed.

But I can't kick him out! We have too much debt, and I know Finn. He'd find a nice hotel, order room service, and run up more debt on my credit card! But I don't want him in my bed either. Last night, all I wanted was for him to come home!

I stopped before crossing the street, making the dogs sit as we waited for a car to pass.

But that was before I knew what he did. Could he really be a pedophile? He never showed any signs of being interested in children in that way. Did I miss something?

I stooped and used a bag to pick up the pile of poop Lizzie had deposited.

How can I lie next to him, knowing he might be a pedophile? He will have to sleep in the guest bedroom.

I paused to wave absently to a neighbor across the street.

But how do I tell him? He got angry when I said I wanted to walk alone. He is not usually one to get angry like that!

I waited as the dogs sniffed a spot in the grass beside the sidewalk.

This new Finn is not the man I married. Has it all been an act, and this is who he really is? Or did he crack under the pressure, as he claims?

I stopped and made the dogs sit so a woman with a stroller could pass.

But the way he blames me and everyone else for his actions feels like he knows he did something horrible, but doesn't want to admit it. He's deflecting - I think that's what they call it. Or he's in denial. Because what he did is horrible! There's no way he's sleeping in my bed!

I was still trying to figure out how to tell Finn I needed some space when I realized the dogs had led me back home. I took a deep breath before opening the front door, uncertain which version of Finn I would find inside.

Sam and Lizzie led the way into the living room. Finn was sitting on the couch watching television, a bottle of beer and a bag of chips on the coffee table in front of him. I realized then that I hadn't eaten and was starting to feel a little hungry.

"How was your walk?" Finn asked as I entered, not looking away from the television. His voice was tinged with resentment.

"Fine," I replied curtly.

I went into the kitchen, drank a glass of water, and filled the dogs' water dish, as well. Then, I made myself a sandwich. I grabbed a beer from the refrigerator and carried my sandwich into the living room. Finn didn't look away from the television when I sat on the couch. I had picked my spot out of habit and was already sitting when I realized I didn't intend to sit so close to him. Getting up now to move would likely set him off again, and I didn't want to do that before I told him he needed to sleep in the guest room. So, I stayed put.

I took a bite of my sandwich and washed it down with a swig of beer. Then I steeled myself for the conversation I knew I had to have with Finn.

"What are you watching?" I asked, breaking the silence between us.

"I was just flipping through channels. It's *Lethal Weapon*," he responded, still not looking my way.

I found it ironic that he was watching a cop movie, considering he'd just been arrested the night before. Arrested! My brain was still getting used to that word in the context of our life together.

"We need to talk," I said, then took another sip of my beer.

Finn sighed heavily and then finally looked my way.

"I have already told you everything!" he shouted in frustration.

No, you haven't.

"I know," I replied gently, although I was skeptical that he had told me everything. "But it's almost bedtime."

"Yeah, so what?" Finn said, staring at me questioningly and not anticipating what was coming next.

"I think you should sleep in the spare bedroom tonight," I said, still trying to be gentle and not elicit a reaction.

"You want me to sleep in the spare bedroom? Are you serious?" he asked angrily, his face turning red.

Lizzie jumped up on the couch and put herself between us protectively.

"I don't feel comfortable sharing a bed with you right now," I replied.

"That's insane." Finn shot to his feet so fast the sofa cushions recoiled beneath him. "I'm still your husband. I still live here." His voice rose, sharp and incredulous. "Or are you planning to throw me out now?"

He was looming over me before I realized he'd moved. Lizzie sprang up at my side, a low, warning growl rumbling from her chest.

"Lizzie! Stop that!" I said reflexively and petted her to calm her down. "Sit down, Finn! I'm not kicking you out!"

"Then why do you want me to sleep in the spare room?" he asked, still standing, his hands on his hips.

"Finn, please sit down so we can talk this through!" I pleaded.

Finn sighed and sat down heavily on the couch. Next to him, Lizzie was still on high alert.

Finn's voice broke the silence. "I'm sorry, Kass! I never meant to hurt you." His fingers pulled at the frayed edge of his t-shirt, his blue eyes filling with tears. "Lizzie's wrong—I'm not going to hurt you. But making me sleep in the spare room? Is that really where we are now?"

I kept my arms crossed, holding together the pieces of my resolve. I was torn. I still felt love for the man I had married, and I was looking at those blue eyes for some sign that he was still there. Finn sensed my hesitation and moved closer.

"I love you, Kass." His words slipped out in a whisper, as though speaking any louder might shatter what was left between us. Tears spilled over and trailed along the curve of his jaw. "Please… don't push me out of our bed. I need you now more than ever."

I could feel his pain, and it stirred something deep in my chest. I felt it first in the tightening of my throat, then in the way my grip slackened around myself. Logic reminded me of his heartbreaking confession, but guilt weighed heavier: for better or worse. The room smelled faintly of his aftershave, comforting and cruel all at once. His shoulders sagged, the weight of what he'd done pulling him inward. Suddenly, the question was no longer whether he deserved forgiveness—it was whether I could stand to watch him fold in on himself without offering my hand.

My heart wavered, loud in my ears, drowning out the sensible arguments still fighting for space in my mind. No one could do that to me better than Finn.

I was still uncomfortable with letting him sleep next to me. He felt like a stranger now, although I still hoped the Finn I knew was in there somewhere. But he had done things I had not thought he was capable of doing. He had shown anger toward me earlier in a way he never had. Still, I didn't think he would hurt me physically. He never had before. But I never thought he could harm a child, either, and clearly, he'd had intentions of doing that. I no longer trusted him the way I had. Neither did Lizzie, and I knew she would protect me if he tried to hurt me. She had already put some fear into him. So, against my better judgment, I relented.

"Okay," I replied, although my voice held no conviction. "But you stay on your side of the bed. I'm still hurt and angry, and the thought of you touching me right now is repulsive. I'm sorry, but I'm just being honest."

"Repulsive? Are you repulsed by me now? Because I made one mistake?" Finn was angry again.

It was more than one mistake, I thought bitterly. But I wasn't going to point that out. Finn was already angry.

"I'm just having a hard time reconciling what you did with the man I thought you were! It's like you're a different person, Finn!" Now, I was the one crying.

"It's still me, Kass! I just made a mistake. But it's still me! I'm still the man who loves you! And still the man you love, right? Don't throw away everything we have, Kass! Please!" he pleaded.

He reached out to hug me, but Lizzie intervened with another growl. And although I did not move to hug him or stop Lizzie, he had struck a nerve with me. I was not ready to throw away our marriage, not while I was still in shock and trying to sort it all out. My guilt at the thought of turning my back on Finn, or at least the old Finn, and our ten years of marriage, won out.

"Yeah, okay, you can sleep in my bed tonight. But I'm serious about not being touched. Stay on your side of the bed or sleep in the guest room!" I declared firmly.

"Fine," Finn said. "I guess I'll just have to prove to you that I'm the same man."

My thoughts were racing. *If I keep Finn close and observe his new behaviors, maybe I can figure out who he really is. I need time to sort this out and decide what I want.*

A part of my brain realized I was talking myself into it, while the other part was in complete denial that I was actually doing so.

I delayed going to bed as long as possible. When I could barely stay awake, I finally headed up the stairs without saying a word, the dogs on my heels. Finn followed a few minutes later. In the bathroom, I changed into my nightshirt. I did not feel comfortable undressing in front of Finn. He felt like a stranger now. But I didn't want to sleep in my clothes another night. When I came out of the bathroom, Finn was already lying on his side of the bed, with his back to me. I slipped quietly under the covers on my side. The dogs quickly jumped up and settled in the middle of the bed, creating a barrier between us. This was not entirely unusual for Lizzie, but Sam usually slept at my feet.

I fell asleep, but it was not a deep sleep, and I reacted to every noise and movement from Finn's side of the bed. Lizzie moved closer until she was lying against my back, always my protector. As exhausted as I was, I forced myself to stay awake until I heard the familiar pattern of Finn's snoring. Then, eventually, I fell into a fitful sleep, unable to fully relax with Finn in the same room.

At six o'clock, the alarm went off, and as I reached to turn it off, I noticed the room was still dark. It took me a moment to realize that it was Sunday and we had to get up early. Finn was co-leading a geology field trip with another teaching assistant named Dennis, and he needed to be on time. They were heading to Enchanted Rock, where pink granite was exposed in a dome. I was groggy, but I snapped awake as soon as I thought of Finn. He was still lying on his side of the bed, with Lizzie creating a barrier between us.

Suddenly, yesterday came flooding back. *Finn was arrested! I should have made him sleep in the guest room. But he is still my husband. And what about the field trip? Can he even go on the field trip today? Do I even ask him that?* My thoughts were running wild, and I hadn't even sat up yet.

Finn hadn't stirred yet, so I sat up and nudged him. "Finn! You need to get up! You're supposed to lead the Enchanted Rock field trip with Dennis today!" I shouted, knowing Finn was typically a heavy sleeper.

"Uh-huh," he mumbled, "field trip."

I got up, grabbed my favorite sweatpants and a t-shirt from the dresser, and went into the bathroom to change and wash my face. When I stepped back into the bedroom, the dogs were lying in front of the bathroom door, waiting for me. Finn hadn't moved.

"Finn! Get up!" I yelled.

Then I headed down the stairs, the dogs following close behind. As we passed the front door, the dogs stopped and whined. They were ready to go outside.

I opened the door and let them into the courtyard. The Sunday newspaper was lying on the stoop, so I picked it up as I waited for the girls to finish up and come inside. The dogs didn't linger, anticipating Sunday breakfast. I shut the front door and dropped the newspaper on the coffee table as I passed through the living room on the way to the kitchen. I started the coffee and soon heard Finn in the shower upstairs.

"It's about time he got up!" I said to the dogs, who eagerly wagged their tails, hoping for handouts.

I was still wondering whether his arrest would prevent him from going on the field trip. I hadn't thought to ask him yesterday whether the judge or lawyer had given him any instructions about what he could and couldn't do. I had been in shock and not thinking clearly. I was going to have to ask him when he came down.

The coffee maker beeped, indicating that the coffee was ready, and out of habit, I grabbed two cups and filled them. Finn rounded the corner into the kitchen, carrying his backpack, just as I finished pouring the coffee.

"Good morning! Thanks for making the coffee! I don't want to be late!" Finn said cheerily as he picked up his cup and added cream and sugar.

"Yeah, about the field trip," I began.

"What about it?" Finn asked, not letting me finish.

"Did the judge or lawyer tell you anything about what you can and can't do? I mean, did they give you any restrictions?" I asked hesitantly.

"No! Why would they do that?" Finn replied, irritated.

"Well, you were arrested! And I don't know the protocol in a situation like this. I've never been through anything like this before. I just thought they might have said something." I shrugged and tried to act casually as I sipped my coffee.

"Oh, and you think I have?" Finn shouted. "No! They didn't tell me there were any restrictions! It's not like I'm a criminal!"

I nearly spat my coffee out.

Actually, you are. You committed a crime! I thought to myself, but didn't dare say it out loud. He was already angry.

"Besides, it's not like anyone knows," he added, pulling out bread and lunch meat from the refrigerator to make himself a couple of sandwiches to take with him.

I stood there watching him as I sipped my coffee. Finn was packing his lunch as if nothing horrible had happened in the last two days.

He shoved his sandwiches into his backpack and flung the pack on his shoulder. And then he leaned in to kiss me. I pulled away from him, but he caught me by the arm.

"What the hell, Kass? I can't even kiss you goodbye?" he said, sounding hurt.

"I'm not ready, Finn!" I declared, twisting out of his grip.

He stared at me in disgust for a second and stormed out the door.

I stood there, feeling shaky, waiting for his car to pull away. Then I slid to the kitchen floor and cried. The dogs tried to console me by licking away the tears that slid down my cheeks. I wrapped an arm around Lizzie's thick neck and hugged her. Sam whined, feeling left out, so I wrapped my other arm around her and hugged her, too. Then I picked myself up off the floor and blew my nose.

I grabbed the leashes to take the dogs for a short run. Excited at seeing the leashes, Lizzie circled me, whining happily, while Sam nearly knocked me over, trying to lick my face as I bent down to put on her leash. For them, the run was a reason for joy. But I needed to run to clear my head before heading to work.

How could he do this? I thought angrily as I ran through the neighborhood with the dogs. I had picked a route we didn't usually take, hoping to avoid neighbors I knew. I didn't want to have to explain why I was crying. *And how are we going to pay a lawyer? We're already so far into debt. The lawyer said something about collateral. The only things we have of value are the house and cars. Oh my God! Could we lose our home?*

I suddenly felt my stomach retch, and I rushed to some nearby bushes to throw up. As I wiped my mouth, I looked around to see if anyone had seen me. I felt mortified. I walked the dogs the rest of the way to our townhouse. Since it was still early, I managed the trip without anyone seeing us.

I quickly showered and pulled on jeans and a short-sleeved t-shirt. Then I headed downstairs to the kitchen to make myself a sandwich to take to work, and I treated the dogs to a few pieces of lunch meat. They were hungry after our run and waited patiently for the handouts.

I didn't normally work on Sundays. That was usually our day to have a leisurely breakfast and drink coffee while reading the newspaper. Then, we would take the dogs to the park, have a late lunch, and lounge on the couch, reading or watching a movie. But today was not a typical Sunday.

I was the main income earner, and I knew I might be unable to work while we sorted everything out. I had limited vacation time; once I used it up, I would have to take time off without pay. We couldn't afford that under normal circumstances. But this new reality Finn had thrown us into was anything but normal. We needed the money now more than ever. Finn would have to pay legal fees for his defense, and we still had no idea what other expenses might be on the way. We didn't have separate accounts. For now, I had no choice but to figure out how to keep us from going under financially.

Finn's defense! I was having difficulty comprehending those words.

Sam and Lizzie looked up at me anxiously as I grabbed my purse and lunch and prepared to leave. They were hoping we were going to the park.

"I'm sorry, girls!" I said as I petted them and gave each of them a treat before walking out the door. "I'll be back as soon as I can."

CHAPTER 4

THE SHIT HITS THE FAN

As I drove to the office, I stopped at a light and realized I was in front of the shopping center where Finn was arrested. I sat there staring at the parking lot, picturing Finn in his car waiting for the girl. I imagined the petite police woman walking toward him. I pictured the shocked expression on Finn's face as he realized the policewoman was not the girl he wanted to meet. I visualized him panicking and putting the car in reverse as the police cars surrounded him.

Suddenly, I heard honking behind me. I hit the gas and roared through the intersection, happy to escape that awful scene. But the pictures still flooded my imagination, and I realized I was sobbing again as I drove toward my office.

Although the parking lot was empty, I chose an isolated spot. I pulled myself together and surveyed the lot to ensure no one would see me as I walked quickly toward the building. I walked like a robot to my shared office space, relieved it was windowless and dark. I sighed in relief as I sat at my desk and turned on my computer.

My work as a software tester required a lot of focus, and that was exactly what I needed after the previous 48 hours. I was usually very detail-oriented, but my thoughts kept drifting, and I couldn't get the scene from the convenience store out of my mind.

I ran a test on the software, but I got an "error" message. I scoured the code and found my mistake easily. I fixed the problem, but it errored again several minutes later. I was obviously not fit for work. My brain refused to refocus on anything but my situation. I couldn't be here. I shouldn't be here.

I finally completed the task, but it took me twice as long as it should have. I wanted to go home, but I had more to do. More importantly, we needed the money. So, I forced myself to keep going and focused as best I could. After several hours, I had completed only three-quarters of what I had planned, and I was exhausted.

I shut down my workstation and left a note for my boss explaining that I needed some time off to deal with a family situation. I told him I would call him as soon as I knew when I could return to work. Since I wasn't sure when that would be, I left my timesheet with the hours I had just worked. It was a small portion of the usual time I worked during a week, but I knew we would need every penny.

There might be other expenses I hadn't thought about yet. If we were going to repair our marriage, we would probably need counseling. But would that even help? Considering what Finn had done, I wasn't sure rebuilding the trust was possible. But I wasn't sure I could give up on our marriage without trying.

In my family, divorce was not an option. Marriages went through difficult times, but you worked through them. Although no one I knew had ever been through anything like *this*. Finn's parents had just celebrated their 50th wedding anniversary. And no one in Finn's family, except for his brother, Hayden, had been divorced. Hayden and his wife were under a lot of pressure from the family to work things out. Especially from Finn's mother, Myra, who thought divorce was somehow a reflection on her. I wasn't ready to face that kind of pressure. I was in survival mode now; that was all I had the energy for. It was going to be hard enough to tell our families about Finn's arrest and what led up to it.

My hands shook as I walked to my car, and I struggled to find my keys in my bag. I chose a different route home to avoid passing by the scene of the crime again. It's funny how people use that as an expression; it actually applied to my life now.

When I got home, I stopped at the community mailbox to retrieve yesterday's mail.

I'll hop out quickly and avoid talking to anyone, I thought.

But just as I opened my mailbox, I spotted Julie and Ben, a lovely couple we had recently gotten to know, coming around the corner. Their Great Dane, Moose, trotted up to me.

"Hey, Moose!" I said, patting him on the head and scratching him behind the ears as Julie and Ben walked over.

"Hi, Kassidy! How are you doing?" Julie asked, concern evident on her face and in her voice. She reached out and put a gentle hand on my arm.

That was not how she usually greeted me. A sudden panic flooded over me. *Had they seen the police at our townhouse?* I thought. We lived in a small complex, and I suddenly realized that many of my neighbors had likely seen what happened on Friday afternoon.

"Hi! I'm doing great," I said with a weak smile. I was falling apart, but I felt the need to maintain appearances.

Julie and Ben exchanged a look, which told me they knew something. Thoughts raced through my mind. *What had they seen?* So much for keeping things quiet. They were probably not the only neighbors who knew.

Ben cleared his throat and shifted nervously from one foot to another.

"Um, how's Finn? We saw you walking the dogs alone this morning," Ben asked.

"Oh, Finn's on a field trip today," I replied quietly. It was the truth, but it sounded like a lie. I wondered if they thought "field trip" meant jail.

"So everything's okay then?" Ben asked, still looking worried.

"Yeah, thank you. I'm okay. Really," I said as convincingly as possible.

"Okay, but please let us know if you need anything," Julie countered with a strained smile.

"I will. Thank you!" I said, fighting back tears. "I appreciate your concern, but really, I'm alright."

I was not alright, and I knew they saw right through my lie. But they smiled and waved as I quickly climbed back into my car, drove around the corner, and parked behind our townhouse.

As I got out of the car, another neighbor from a few doors down started heading my way. I waved and quickly ran into the house. I was not ready for this! I was not ready to discuss what had happened with my neighbors or anyone else, for that matter. I wanted to keep it private for as long as possible.

As I shut the door behind me, the dogs greeted me with wagging tails and kisses. Lizzie whined happily as I petted her. Sam brought me Piggy, her favorite stuffed toy, and offered it to me. I was so grateful that they were there. They provided a sense of normalcy that I needed. It calmed me as I tried to put the awkward conversation with Julie and Ben out of my thoughts.

I let the dogs outside and then went to the kitchen. It was nearly six o'clock by then. Even though I had taken a sandwich to work, I hadn't eaten all day and was finally hungry.

Then I noticed that the light on the answering machine was blinking. It was probably a message from my parents. I usually talked to them every other Sunday.

Did I forget it was our week to talk? I wondered. *I need to call them back, but I'm not ready to tell them what happened!*

As I walked over to the phone, the message light indicated not one but eight messages! *Eight messages! Mom wouldn't call that many times unless there was something wrong.*

I nervously pushed the play button. And that was when the next bomb dropped. When I heard the first message, my knees went weak, and my eyes welled with tears.

"Hey, Kassidy, this is Max. It's about 9 AM on Sunday. I'm just calling to check on you. I saw something in the newspaper today about Finn getting arrested," my boss said. I could picture him pacing as he talked, a habit he had when on the phone. "I'm sorry, Kassidy. I was shocked when I saw it! I imagine you don't want something like this getting out, so I won't say anything. Please let me know if you need to take some time off to deal with this."

It was in the newspaper! I felt queasy, grabbed the counter's edge to steady myself, and pressed play again. The next message was left just a few minutes after Max's.

"Hello, Finn and Kassidy! This is Professor Huntington," Finn's thesis advisor began in his smooth New Zealander accent. I had always liked his accent, and for a split second, I felt soothed. But the feeling did not last.

"I just read this morning's newspaper, and I must say I'm quite shocked! Kassidy - I can't imagine how you're feeling! Such devastating news!" he continued. "Finn, you must know that these are severe charges that you are facing! I don't know how the department or the university will handle this situation. However, considering the nature of the charges and that you are accused of committing a felony, I doubt you will be allowed to continue with your degree until the matter is resolved."

Professor Huntington paused for a few seconds before continuing. "And, of course, you would need to be found innocent of the charges," he added before pausing again. I felt the gravity of that statement as he let it hang in the air before he continued. "I will contact the geology department's head to determine how to proceed. Please call me back as soon as possible, Finn. I hope you and Kassidy are both holding up despite the circumstances. I still cannot believe this is happening! Okay, please call me Finn!"

Finn very likely destroyed his career, as well as our marriage. The situation was going from bad to worse.

The next message was from my best friend, specifically directed at me, not Finn. "Hi, Kassidy! This is Steph. Macy called me to tell me about the article she saw in the morning paper about Finn getting arrested. I can't believe it! I hope it's not true! I hope you're okay! You're welcome to stay with me if you need a place to stay. You can bring the dogs, too. I can't believe Finn did this! I'm so shocked! I can't imagine what you are going through! If it's true, you need to get away from him immediately! Macy said the geology department at the university is already buzzing about it. Wasn't Finn supposed to go on that field trip? I'm meeting Macy for lunch in about an hour, and you're welcome to join us. Please call me! I'm so worried about you!"

I wanted to call her right back, but I needed to listen to all the messages, even though it was painful. I wanted to know who knew.

The next message was from our friend, Ed. He and his wife, Laura, were our close friends. Finn had been doing office work for Ed to earn some extra income. "Hi, Kassidy and Finn! This is Ed. Laura and I just read the newspaper. Frankly, we're shocked! We just wanted to check to see if you're alright and if you need anything. Give us a call when you can."

I felt relieved that Ed hadn't mentioned whether Finn could continue working for him. I wouldn't have blamed Ed for firing Finn over this.

I pushed play again.

"Hi, Kassidy! This is your neighbor, Martha. Joe and I saw the newspaper article this morning. I nearly spit out my coffee when I read it! I guess this explains why the cops were at your house on Friday! I hope you kicked him out, Kassidy! What Finn did is despicable!"

I felt sick to my stomach. If Martha knew, then the whole complex must have known. She was the complex gossip. I took a deep breath before listening to the next message.

"Hi! This is Eric. Susan just read the article in the newspaper. Kassidy, you're welcome to stay with us if you need a place to stay. Finn—I don't know what to say! I can't believe what you did! I hope it's not true, but if it is, we've got kids! We can't have you around them. How could you do something like that? Kassidy, please call Susan when you can."

My heart broke as I heard Eric's voice crack when he mentioned his children. Eric and Susan were a couple we met when we lived in our first apartment in Austin. We hung out with them a lot back then, but hadn't seen them as much since they had the kids. Of course, they wouldn't want Finn around now. But I was glad to hear I was still welcome in their home.

The next message was another from Professor Huntington. "Finn, it's been three hours, and I haven't heard back from you. Did you go on that field trip this morning? Not the best choice, considering everything. Call me as soon as you get this message!" His voice was now much sterner and lacked the compassion it had earlier. Again, I felt the weight of the consequences of Finn's actions. Would he also feel it? Or would he continue to deny responsibility?

I pushed the play button once more.

"Hi! It's Cindy! Kassidy, what's going on? Did Finn really do what we read in the newspaper? Luke is so angry! He doesn't understand how a friend of ours could do something like that! Neither do I! But mostly, I'm just worried about you, Kass! Did you kick him out? Let us know if you need a place to stay. We don't have a room, but my sister has a guest room, and she said you can stay there."

Cindy and I had worked together at a previous job and became good friends. When we got together with our husbands, they hit it off too. Luke and Finn sometimes played frisbee golf when Cindy and I went shopping or caught a movie that the guys didn't want to see. I felt another one of our close relationships contracting. The losses were compounding.

As I listened to message after message, my knees gave out, and I dropped to the floor, head in my hands, and sobbed. Nothing in my life could have prepared me for this.

After listening to our friends' messages, I realized people were judging Finn, and that how they looked at us would never be the same.

I could hardly blame them. Many suggested that I kick Finn out or leave him. Although I agreed with them, I still wanted to believe this was all a mistake and that this wasn't my life now. I was waiting to wake up from the nightmare.

Lizzie and Sam circled me nervously, and then Sam settled next to me with her head in my lap. Lizzie licked my face and hands, anxiously moving from one to the other until she finally settled beside me, opposite Sam, and put her head in my lap, too. Gently stroking their soft fur helped to calm me. I wanted to call Steph back, but couldn't pull myself up from the floor yet.

Just then, Finn walked in the back door and saw me on the floor.

"What's wrong?" he asked.

"Listen to the messages," was all I could muster in response.

Still sitting on the floor, I watched him as he listened. He turned pale and sweaty, looking like he was about to get sick. I jumped up and grabbed the wastebasket, just in case.

Hearing the messages again was like another gut punch. I felt a mixture of anger, sadness, and fear. Now that it was out in the open, I didn't know how to face people. I was certain that the neighbors I had talked to at the mailboxes had read the article, too. I felt extremely exposed.

I sat on the floor with Lizzie, Sam, and a wad of wet tissues next to me and watched the tears streaming down Finn's face. *Was he crying in remorse for what he had done or because his actions had been exposed?* I wondered. Since he hadn't taken responsibility, I assumed it was the exposure. *Does he even realize that all this is a result of his choices and actions?* I wondered.

Blowing my nose on another tissue, I asked, "Did Dennis or anyone on the field trip or at the university say anything to you?"

"No. I'm sure it was too early for anyone on the field trip to see it. And I dropped everyone off at the geology building and then took the van back to the parking area, so I never went inside the building when we got back," Finn replied.

"We should probably read the newspaper article so we know what everyone else read," I said, dreading seeing Finn's mess in print.

Finn nodded slightly in agreement but didn't speak.

I retrieved the paper from the coffee table and set it on the dining room table. As I scanned the headlines, I saw that the Cleveland Indians, my hometown team in Ohio, had won their playoff series. Thankfully, there was nothing on the front page about Finn.

With Finn looking over my shoulder, I opened the newspaper and searched through the pages until I found the article in the Metro section. My pulse raced, and my chest constricted. I was afraid that the article might reveal new details, but I was intent on finding out the truth.

Finn was standing close enough that I could hear his breathing quicken.

The article took up nearly a quarter of the page and was very detailed. The headline announced, "Grad student used Internet to seek child sex, police say."

Fear and anger filled me, but I pressed on.

```
A 34-year-old University of Texas graduate
student was arrested Friday and charged
with sexual performance by a child, Austin
police said Saturday.
```

Sexual performance by a child? But Finn said nothing happened! I thought. I continued reading, my distress rising.

The article then gave Finn's full name and listed our address. There was no mistaking that it was him, and it was clear why we had so many calls. And why our neighbors had shown concern.

I kept reading.

```
Police said Haggerty had gone there to meet
an 11-year-old girl he had contacted over
```

the Internet. According to a police affidavit for his arrest, the following events
occurred: Haggerty initiated a chat session with an 11-year-old girl on a computer Internet service in early August.
Haggerty asked the girl for her picture
and asked several personal questions. The
girl's mother later accessed her daughter's account and had a second conversation
with Haggerty, who again asked what she
looked like. The mother replied that she
was a "normal 11-year-old girl." Haggerty
described himself and said he was a graduate student at UT.

This confirms that he lied to me about knowing her age before he met her! And this has been going on for two months! I was nauseous, but I kept reading, wondering what else he had lied about in his version of the story.

After the mother had contacted authorities
in late August, a police officer accessed
the girl's Internet account and received a
private message from the on-screen account
'Dex32tx,' according to the affidavit. The
court document said Haggerty again asked
several personal questions and sent two
pornographic images.

I had to grab the edge of the table to steady myself. Two things stood out to me in that statement. That Finn had neglected to tell me about sending pornographic material, and that his online name contained the number 32.

It's common for people to use their age in an online name. But Finn is thirty-four! Had he been chatting online for two years? My skull felt like it would shatter from the questions rattling inside my brain, but I continued reading.

> Authorities obtained a subpoena directing American Online Computer Service to release subscriber information for the screen name 'Dex32tx.' A driver's license search provided a description of Haggerty, which matched the one he gave over the Internet.
>
> Authorities had more online conversations with Haggerty, who tried each time to set up a meeting with a person he thought to be an 11-year-old girl, the affidavit said.
>
> The document said Haggerty talked about sexual experiences and offered to expose his genitals. He also offered to allow the girl to touch his genitals and asked to touch hers, the affidavit said.
>
> On Thursday, authorities engaged in one last computer conversation with Haggerty, and a meeting was arranged for 3:30 pm Friday at the shopping center.
>
> Haggerty arrived and approached an undercover female officer, called her by the girl's name, and told her to get in his vehicle, the affidavit said."

I knew now that most of Finn's story had been fabricated. He was the one who asked to meet the girl; it was not the policewoman who asked to meet him. And he had done so much more than he led me to believe. His story about how the arrest went down was also a lie. Had he made it sound more dramatic to garner my sympathy? It was all there in black and white, everything Finn had done and everything he had lied about.

I ran for the bathroom to get away from Finn. I was sobbing so hard that I could hardly breathe.

Everyone knew not only *that* Finn had been arrested but exactly why.

I wanted to call my best friend, Stephanie, but did not want Finn there when I did. It would have been comforting to talk to her, but I was in survival mode now and knew she would have tried to convince me to leave him. Calling Stephanie would have to wait for now. I had to figure out what I needed to do to escape this situation.

There was also the question of what more devastation leaving Finn to his own devices would bring. *Has he ever done something like this in the past? Was this just the first time he got caught?* I no longer knew what he was capable of, and I was frightened. I was already feeling guilty about not knowing what was happening and being unable to prevent it.

I composed myself as best I could and returned to the living room. Finn was sitting on the couch, staring straight ahead, motionless, and not making a sound.

I needed a plan, but my mind was reeling.

But the next move was Finn's. He had to call Professor Huntington.

CHAPTER 5

ANOTHER BLOW

"Hello, Professor Huntington? This is Finn," I could hear Finn saying uneasily. "I got your message. I guess we need to talk."

I was in the living room but within earshot. I could sense Finn's pause as he listened to what Professor Huntington had to say.

"Is that necessary? Can't I even get the stuff from my office?" Finn pleaded.

Finn paused again to listen before shouting, "But I haven't even been convicted! Don't I get to have my day in court before you make these decisions about me and my future?"

Professor Huntington must have been speaking again. Finn's breathing was ragged as he listened.

"Yeah, I understand," Finn said sullenly, hanging up the phone without saying goodbye.

Finn walked slowly into the living room and plopped down on the opposite side of the couch.

I was hugging one of the blue pillows to my chest. Lizzy and Sam were at my feet, looking up at me. When Finn sat on the couch, Lizzy stiffened, eyeing him closely. My fingers tensed, and I realized I was clutching the pillow in a death grip.

Finn stared straight ahead, speechless.

I was enraged that he was making me dig for what he should have willingly offered. "Are you okay?" I asked.

"Not really," he replied, choking back tears.

"What did Professor Huntington say?" I asked, eager to know what we were dealing with next.

"I'm suspended from classes immediately, both the ones I'm taking and the ones where I'm a teaching assistant. I'm not allowed on campus unless I get permission from Professor Huntington. And I must have a good reason – like cleaning out my office! The department heads will meet on Monday to decide on the next steps. Professor Huntington made it clear that this is the end of my career at the university. He also said that having something like this on my record would probably keep me from getting accepted anywhere else. And it doesn't even matter what the outcome of the case against me is! It's so unfair!" Finn said.

What did he think was fair for the eleven-year-old? I thought.

I suddenly realized that he hadn't asked me how I was doing or expressed any concern for the young girl whom he had victimized. Finn was used to charming his way through life. He had a way of making people feel special. But had it just been an act all along to get what he wanted? Why hadn't I seen that before? Again, my brain was struggling to decipher who the real Finn was. The picture I was seeing now was aligning less and less with the man I thought I knew. But now was not the time to bring that up. I needed to focus on how to get out of this.

"Now, what do we do?" I asked, needing to find a way to take action and gain some control.

He must have felt my empathy because Finn reached out to me for a hug, and when Lizzie saw me pull back and raise the blue pillow to keep him away, she made a guttural growl.

"I'm not ready to be touched," I stated firmly, wishing I had sat in one of the chairs on the other side of the room instead of my usual spot on the couch.

"Will you ever be?" he asked dismally.

"I don't know. I really don't know. I feel like nothing will ever be the same. I don't know if I can ever trust you again! I don't know how we're going to get past this!" I replied angrily.

I got up from the couch and went to the kitchen, steadying myself on the counter and fighting to compose myself. I thought about going for a run or taking the dogs for a walk, but the thought of running into any neighbors stopped me in my tracks. I wasn't ready for another encounter like the one I had earlier with Julie and Ben.

I grabbed a beer from the fridge and twisted off the cap. I chugged half the bottle before setting it on the counter. I paced the length of the small kitchen a few times before picking up the bottle again and heading back to the living room. I needed action. I needed to feel like I was doing something besides wallowing in my grief and watching my life fall apart. I needed a plan, or I was going to lose my mind completely.

"I think we need to deal with the immediate issues first," I declared as I walked back into the living room and continued pacing there.

"Did you bring me one?" Finn asked, nodding toward the bottle of beer I was still clutching.

He can get his own damn beer! I thought to myself, ignoring him. As if he heard me, Finn got up and went to grab one for himself. I waited for him to return and settle back on the couch before continuing.

"We need to figure out how we're going to pay for the bail bondsman and the lawyer tomorrow. We have no money, and our credit cards are already pretty much maxed out. Do you think your parents would lend you the money?" I asked. I sipped my beer while I waited for his reply.

Finn looked at me and yelled, "No! We are not telling my parents!" When I didn't respond, he continued, "I have a credit card that I can use to pay the bail bondsman and hopefully the lawyer for tomorrow. After that, I don't know."

"Wait, what credit card? You have a credit card I don't know about?" I responded in shock. I didn't wait for him to answer before continuing. "And you have to tell your parents!"

He took a beat before he spoke again. "Yes, they were offering credit cards on campus, so I signed up for one. I didn't tell you because I knew you would be mad. And I needed it for…things."

I was stunned. It was bad enough that he had gotten us into more debt without telling me. *Do I want to know what those "things" were, I thought, especially considering he had just been arrested for soliciting an eleven-year-old girl for sex?* My thoughts were churning, and so was my stomach. I ran for the bathroom and heaved up the beer. And that's when I realized I hadn't eaten anything today. When I came out of the bathroom, the dogs were waiting for me and followed me back into the living room. I took a seat in the chair by the window. Sam was now also avoiding Finn and stuck close to my side. I slumped down in my seat heavily, feeling weak.

"What did you use the credit card for?" I asked, dreading his response. But I had to know.

"Stuff for school, mostly," Finn replied, not meeting my piercing gaze.

"What else?" I asked. When he didn't respond, I repeated the question more forcefully. "What else? Answer me! I need to know!"

"Some dinners while you were away working," he said, still not looking at me.

I had been on a project at my previous job where I would go on location in Louisiana during the week and come home on weekends. But I had quit that job over a year ago, and he had been hiding this card all this time.

It wasn't adding up for me. "Why didn't you use our regular credit cards like you normally did?" I queried.

"Because they were almost maxed out. I knew you'd be mad if I kept running them up," Finn replied.

Something still felt off. I knew he was hiding something, but he wasn't going to give me a straight answer.

"Have you been paying on this credit card?" I asked. I had not seen a bill.

"Yes. Just the minimums," Finn said, looking down at his hands.

"And how have you been doing that?" I asked.

"When I cash my stipend check, I've been keeping enough cash for me to pay it, and also just to have some cash. That way, I wouldn't have to take it from the ATM, and you wouldn't get mad at me," he said.

I felt like I was just scratching the surface of unraveling his deception. However, further probing now would likely result in more lies. There was another way I might find out what he had been using the credit card for.

"Bring me the statements so I can start paying the card and include it in our budget," I told him. He might not give me all the statements, but once I had the account information, I could look them up online.

"I can pay the bill!" he protested.

"But if you're going to use it to pay the lawyer, the minimum is going to go up by a lot! It's going to affect how we pay our other bills. Just give me the statements, and let me handle it!" I retorted.

Finn sighed, knowing I was not going to let this go. I don't know whether he suspected I had another motive for wanting the statements, but he couldn't dispute my logic about the bills.

"Okay," he relented, "I'll let you pay it."

"Go get the statements," I instructed.

"Right now?" Finn asked.

"Yes!" I shouted. I was not going to let him get out of giving them to me by stalling later or claiming he forgot.

He sighed heavily, got up slowly, and trudged up the stairs. I followed him. I wanted to see where he hid the statements and if there was anything else he was keeping from me.

I waited at the door of the spare room while Finn waded through the mess left by the police search. He grabbed his backpack from the closet, pulled out the statements, and handed them to me. From where I was standing, I couldn't see what else was in the backpack. I'd have to search the backpack and the closet later.

Having settled that for now, we headed back down the stairs. I grabbed a glass of water in the kitchen before returning to the living room. I sat in one of the chairs by the window. Sam and Lizzie came and sat near me, Sam wanting to be petted and Lizzie keeping her gaze fixed on Finn, who had taken his usual seat on the couch.

I took a few small sips of water before speaking again.

"You are going to have to tell your parents," I told him, even though I probably should have quit after the first battle.

Again, he yelled, "No! I can't!"

We sat there quietly for a few minutes at an impasse. And then Finn finally spoke again.

"I will tell them," he said softly. "But not yet. Let's wait until we talk to the lawyer and find out what we need to do. Then I will tell them. I promise."

It wasn't exactly what I wanted to hear, but I understood it. I wasn't in a hurry to tell my parents, either. I felt so alone right now, and it really would have been nice to have their support. But for now, we would wait until we talked to the lawyer. At least we could cover the immediate expenses with the credit card Finn had hidden from me. At the moment, I had to settle with taking things one step at a time.

Frankly, it was all I could handle.

My head was spinning from the beer and the barrage of information. But somehow, I had to stop myself from falling apart. One of us had to be strong to get through this, and I knew it would not be Finn.

I also needed to deal with one more thing before going to bed tonight. There was no way that I was going to let Finn sleep in my bed after reading the newspaper article that exposed the depth of his lies and the extent of his actions. I wasn't sure I had the emotional energy for another fight with Finn, but I had to do it.

"There's one more thing, Finn," I began.

"Now what?" Finn responded, exasperated.

"You will be sleeping in the guest room," I declared. "And you'll need to clean it up!"

"But why? I thought we settled that last night!" he asked, seemingly shocked.

"Because you fucked up! Read that article again!" I said coldly.

I headed up the stairs to prepare what I might need for our meeting with the attorney the next morning. The titles for our cars, which might be needed for collateral, were in a fireproof lock box in our bedroom. Finn followed behind me, the dogs on his heels.

"You can't do this, Kass!" he shouted.

"I can and I will! You are the one who brought all of this on yourself and me! After everything you have done, I can barely look at you, let alone share my bed with you!" I shouted back at him.

When we reached the bedroom, something inside me split open.

I didn't pause. I crossed to his side of the closet and dragged out an armful of clothes—shirts tangled on hangers, jeans half-folded—and flung them into the hallway. Plastic cracked against the wall. A hanger skidded across the carpet.

"You can sleep in the guest room," I said, my voice unsteady but rising. "Move the rest later."

Behind me, Finn hadn't moved. He just stood there, staring, as if this were happening to someone else.

Maybe it was.

Because the woman who tolerated, explained, and absorbed—she was gone.

Sam paced nervously up and down the hallway, unsure of what to do. Lizzie stood on high alert, watching Finn.

The dogs followed me into the bedroom. Panting from exertion, I shut and locked the door, sat down on the bed, and breathed heavily, resting my head in my hands. Lizzie jumped up on the bed and licked my face. Sam jumped up on the other side of me and nudged my hand with her soft muzzle, wanting to be petted.

"This is why I have two hands," I told them, scratching them both behind the ears. They instinctively knew that I needed them.

I felt as though all of my energy had left my body.

I felt loss, and I felt lost.

CHAPTER 6

THE LAWYER

I woke the next morning with the same hollow ache in my chest, the same disorienting sense of being untethered. We were still married—at least on paper. What affected one of us was supposed to affect us both. That's how it worked. That's what vows meant.

But I didn't feel partnered. I felt alone.

This wasn't like navigating a job loss or deciding to buy a house—hard seasons that required strategy and teamwork. This was something else entirely. This was the ground beneath us shifting, and I had the terrible sense that I was the only one trying to keep my footing. Finn had made horrible choices and was acting like the victim. He was not taking responsibility for fixing things and was leaving it all up to me!

As I lay there thinking about the situation I found myself in, the alarm clock rang. It activated another alert in my brain. *It's Monday! We're meeting with the attorney this morning!* I suddenly remembered. *He'll guide us through this nightmare!*

Relief washed over me. I had taken the lead on fixing things out of necessity, but I had no idea what I was doing. I couldn't do it alone and hoped I would soon have the attorney on my side. And maybe Jordan would help Finn, so I wouldn't have to. I wanted to concentrate on getting myself out of Finn's mess.

I got out of bed, grabbed my clothes from the chair where I had laid them out the night before in preparation for today, and jumped in the shower. Lizzie insisted on entering the bathroom with me, standing guard while I showered. Both bedroom doors were closed, but I could still hear Finn snoring. I knew it would take more than the sound of the shower to awaken him.

Did he even set an alarm? No, I'll probably have to wake him. He can't even take responsibility for making sure he's on time for his appointment with his lawyer. He disgusted me.

I got dressed and dried my hair. As I walked down the hallway toward the stairs, I banged on the door to the spare bedroom and yelled at Finn. "Get up! We have an appointment with the lawyer, and I don't want to be late!"

Finn mumbled something unintelligible from behind the closed door.

"I mean it, Finn! Get up!" I shouted as I headed down the stairs.

The dogs trailed behind me as I opened the front door and let them out. The cool morning air slipped inside for a moment before I shut it again and headed to the kitchen.

Coffee first. Always coffee.

I reached for the bread to make toast, then hesitated.

No. Not today. This is a critical day, I'm having eggs, I thought.

I pulled the carton of eggs from the refrigerator. The dogs were already scratching at the door, so I let them back in, their paws clicking across the floor as they followed me to the stove. Their tails began to wag the moment they saw the eggs. Scrambled eggs were usually reserved for weekends.

I made a plate for myself and spooned a little extra into their bowls. They devoured theirs happily while I carried mine to the table with a mug of coffee.

I was halfway through when Finn walked into the kitchen. He poured himself a cup without a word, then glanced at the stove, at the dogs' bowls, at my plate.

"Where are my eggs?" Finn asked, looking at the empty frying pan.

"If you want eggs, you can make them, but I'm leaving for the lawyer's office in 15 minutes," I replied.

Finn huffed and popped some bread into the toaster. I finished my eggs, rinsed my plate in the sink, and then headed upstairs to put on some makeup and fix my hair.

As I finished, I heard the shower in the spare room, where Finn usually showered. It had always been easier for us to use separate bathrooms, as we often had to get ready at the same time. I was relieved that we had already been doing that; it wasn't something new I needed to demand now. I headed back downstairs and waited anxiously for Finn. I was just about to leave when he finally came down the stairs.

"Let's go! I don't want to be late!" I said as I handed each dog a treat and headed out the door to the car. Finn followed but stopped when he saw that I had gone to the driver's side of my car.

"What are you doing? I can drive!" Finn said.

"Get in!" I said as I slid into the driver's seat. Finn hesitated for a few seconds, arms crossed, and then relented. Although I was tempted to leave without him, I wanted to ensure he showed up to see the lawyer. I wasn't sure where his head was at and didn't want to risk him skipping the appointment.

We didn't talk on the drive to the lawyer's office. The office was in one of those lovely old houses downtown that had been converted into office space, primarily for law offices. We walked through the grand front door and were greeted by a curved wooden staircase with an intricately carved, painted white banister that contrasted with the dark wood of the stair treads. We found the directory to the left of the stairs. The lawyer's office was on the second floor, and as we climbed the beautiful old staircase, the stairs creaked under our feet.

We found the lawyer's office, and he stood up and welcomed us inside. His office was small, and papers were stacked on the desk. His wrinkled suit jacket hung on the back of his chair. It looked expensive, and I was surprised he didn't have it hung neatly instead. His shirt sleeves were rolled up to the elbows, and he was already hard at work despite the early hour. I guessed his age to be in his late thirties or early forties.

He offered me his hand to shake and said, smiling, "Hello. I'm Jordan Jensen. You must be Kassidy."

His warm smile immediately put me at ease.

Then he turned to Finn and said, "Good to see you again, Finn. How are you doing?"

"Alright, I guess," Finn replied, though he did not sound alright.

Jordan motioned for us to sit in the chairs on the opposite side of his desk, and then he got down to business. As Jordan began to speak, Finn reached for my hand, but I pulled away. Jordan noticed my reaction as he took a sip of coffee from a large mug that read "World's Greatest Uncle." I spotted Jordan's University of Texas Law School diploma hanging on the wall behind him next to a Bachelor of Arts degree from Penn State.

"I know this is a very uncomfortable situation," Jordan began. "But I'm here to help guide you through the legal process. The first thing we need to do is settle the fee for the bail bondsman and for the services I provided Friday night. I also need the information on what you are using as collateral for the bail bondsman."

"Finn's car," I blurted out. "Finn has a 1994 Acura Integra. We bought it used, but it is in good condition."

"No way, Kass! I don't want to lose my car!" Finn retorted.

"You'd rather put my car up for collateral then?"

Jordan cut in, "As long as you don't skip out on bail, Finn, you won't lose the car. Think of it as insurance for the bail bondsman that he will get his money back once you go to trial or a plea deal is made."

"Fine!" Finn said, crossing his arms across his chest, "We can use my car for collateral."

I breathed a sigh of relief, grateful that Jordan had intervened and Finn had backed down. This was another consequence of Finn's actions, but he still didn't want to take any responsibility.

"I'll need the title for the car. Do you have that with you?" Jordan asked.

"No, I don't have it with me! I didn't know you needed that!" Finn said angrily, looking at me.

"I have it right here, Jordan," I said as I calmly pulled it out of my purse.

Finn glared at me but didn't say a word.

"Thank you, Kassidy," Jordan said as I handed him the title. "I also need to collect the money to pay the non-refundable premium for the bail bondsman and my fees for last night. Then, we can discuss what happens next and whether you'd like to retain me as your lawyer. You do not have to retain me just because you hired me Friday night, but I can continue as your lawyer if you want."

Finn handed him his secret credit card, and they settled the fees Finn had incurred. Anger filled me when I saw the secret credit card Finn handed Jordan. As Jordan processed the card, my anger melted into relief. I didn't know how we would have paid him otherwise.

I sat there, watching the men complete the transaction and listening to the traffic on the street outside. Sunshine streamed in through the window, and its warmth on my shoulders felt comforting despite the hot and stuffy office. I noticed a bead of sweat was forming on Finn's brow. Whether it was due to the heat in the small office or the weight of the situation, I didn't know.

The small wooden chair I was sitting on was hard and had no cushion. It was not terribly uncomfortable, but it did not invite guests to stay longer than necessary. *I guess when you're a criminal lawyer, you don't want people to get too comfortable*, I mused.

"The authorities will conduct a thorough investigation into all the allegations and what transpired. As it stands, they have charged Finn with sexual performance by a child. That is a felony, and if convicted, Finn could face from three to ninety-nine years in prison plus a ten thousand dollar fine," Jordan stated, looking from Finn to me and back to Finn.

I gasped, but Finn sat there looking at the floor. I wondered if the information Jordan had just delivered had registered with him. Maybe he already knew?

"What exactly does 'sexual performance of a child' mean? Finn told me he didn't have physical contact with the girl, and there was no mention of physical contact in the newspaper article," I asked, wondering if Finn had lied about that, too.

"For sexual performance of a child, there does not have to be actual physical contact. Intent is enough to make the charge," Jordan replied.

I shot Finn a look. Intent. There was clear evidence of that, although Finn denied it.

"They seized Finn's computer, and they will be doing a thorough search. They will check for anything they could not get from the girl's account. They will check for things like what sites Finn visited, child pornography, and evidence of other victims," he continued.

"Other victims! I have never done anything like this before! You make me sound like I'm some kind of a monster!" Finn shouted indignantly.

I was shocked at his response. He was still in denial about what he had done.

"I'm just telling you what they will look for in their investigation. But, Finn, you've been charged with a felony. And if you retain me to represent you, I will need to know what they will find so that I can best defend you," Jordan said in a calming voice.

Finn didn't respond and looked away from Jordan.

There must be something more on his computer that he doesn't want Jordan or me to know about! I thought.

"Kassidy, you are likely to be questioned at some point during the investigation, as well," Jordan said, looking my way.

"But I knew nothing about this until I picked Finn up from jail!" I protested.

"I understand, Kassidy," Jordan said gently, "But since you are Finn's wife and you share a home, they will want to question you."

I felt hot tears welling up in my eyes again. The thought that I could be pulled into Finn's offense was sickening. What he had done was so far beyond my comprehension of conceivable behavior. Panic crept up my spine. *Will people think I'm somehow involved?*

I was repulsed by the thought of being married to a pedophile. And I was horror-stricken about what people would think of me now that Finn's secrets were exposed.

"There may be some pre-trial hearings, depending on whether or not there are questions about evidence or if the prosecution offers a plea deal. Those would be determined as the case unfolds," Jordan explained.

"So there is a chance for a plea deal? Would that mean I wouldn't have to go to jail?" Finn asked, suddenly taking a greater interest in Jordan's words.

"It's hard to say, and that will depend on the evidence they have. A minor was involved, and it's unlikely that the prosecutor will go easy," Jordan replied.

Finn's shoulders slumped.

"But that is all speculation at this point," Jordan reassured him. "We just need to wait and see."

Jordan paused before continuing. "I also recommend that you seek counseling. The courts may decide more favorably if they know you've taken that action. I suggest that you do that sooner rather than later," Jordan suggested, looking directly at Finn.

"I also know the emotional toll these situations take on individuals and a marriage," he continued, glancing my way.

"And the nature of your deeds indicates that you may have some issues to deal with," Jordan concluded, looking squarely at Finn again.

"I don't have any issues," Finn said. Then, almost as an afterthought, "But if it helps Kassidy trust me again, I'm willing to try counseling." His eyes locked on mine as he spoke, as if this were proof of something.

Jordan and I exchanged a brief look. The concern passed between us without words. Finn didn't believe he had a problem. That much was clear.

Neither of us challenged him. He wasn't ready to hear it. And for now, his willingness to go to counseling would have to be enough

— even if the idea that therapy would simply "help me trust him again" felt like an expectation too heavy, too premature, to name.

Jordan broke my thoughts by clearing his throat before speaking again. "My standard fee for representation in a felony case is $150 per hour for out-of-court work and $200 per hour in court."

His words hung in the air. "How are we going to pay for this?" I asked, overwhelmed by what I had just heard.

Finn remained silent and wouldn't look at me or Jordan.

Seeing my discomfort, Jordan turned to me and asked, "Do you own your townhouse? Perhaps you could take out a home equity loan to cover the costs."

Tears burned behind my eyes as the reality pressed in: we could lose our home because of what Finn had done.

His transgression. Not mine.

Why was I the one bracing for impact? Why was I the one who might lose everything? The walls around me suddenly felt fragile, temporary — as if the life I had built could be stripped away by choices I hadn't made.

There had to be another way. There had to be.

I shifted in my seat, my body unable to settle under the weight of it.

Looking at me, Jordan continued, "In many cases like this, it is not uncommon for couples to divorce."

Was he reading my mind and seeing my doubts?

"If that happens in your case, I can represent you at a discounted rate since I'm already representing Finn," Jordan continued. He glanced at me, then back at Finn, waiting.

The room felt suspended in that pause, but neither of us spoke.

"Finn, would you like me to continue representing you?" Jordan asked, his gaze steady.

"Yeah. I would." Finn turned to me. "What do you think, Kass?"

The question landed heavily. The decision was his alone, yet he was still looking to me—as if I were his partner in this, as if I were meant to steady him while he stood in the consequences of his own choices.

"Yes," I said quietly. "I think that's best." The thought of retelling everything to another attorney felt unbearable. I didn't have the strength to relive it again.

A fresh wave of nausea rolled through me.

How did I get here?

The question pulsed louder than the room around us. Had I missed the signs? Had I mistaken charm for character? I felt a lump in my throat as I fought the tears threatening to surface once more.

I had never doubted Finn before. He was intelligent, driven, and respected. When we met in college, he was the guy everyone liked—the one who could strike up a conversation with anyone and make them feel interesting. I admired that about him. It was part of what drew me in. He had always treated me well. I believed he loved me.

I stared out the window while Jordan had Finn sign the agreement that officially made him his criminal defense attorney. Absentmindedly, I turned the simple silver ring on my finger.

He had given it to me for our anniversary—a quiet departure from the expensive gifts we couldn't afford. I remember thinking we had finally turned a corner. That he understood.

But the ring stirred another memory.

One of our worst fights had started with a gift—an ornate necklace and matching earrings that weren't my style. When I saw the price, my stomach dropped. I suggested we return them.

"Why would you return something I picked out just for you?" Finn had asked, wounded.

"Because they're too expensive. And I don't even like them," I shot back.

I saw the hurt in his face immediately. Guilt followed fast behind. In the end, I kept the jewelry—and paid for it myself—just to smooth things over. I never wore it.

In recent months, I'd felt us growing closer again, almost like we had in the early years of our marriage. But sitting there now, watching him initial legal documents, I realized I didn't know this man at all.

Jordan finished the paperwork and shook our hands. We left his office in stunned silence.

As we walked to the car, a sharp thought surfaced.

I'll sell that jewelry. At least it can help pay down the debt.

For the first time, it might actually serve a purpose.

CHAPTER 7

COUNSELING

We drove home in silence, both lost in our thoughts. The gravity of Finn's actions and their consequences were sinking in for me. I looked over at Finn, and judging by his furrowed brow and frown, perhaps the severity was sinking in for him, too. Since Jordan told us about the potential jail term, Finn stopped conversing unless asked a direct question. His face was ashen and glum. I was more worried about Finn's mental state than my own.

On the way home, I stopped at the grocery store closest to our townhouse. When I got out of the car, Finn didn't move.

"Are you coming?" I asked.

"No. I'll wait here," he mumbled.

Normally, Finn would have jumped at the chance to shop. One of his favorite things to do was to spend money. I shrugged, shut my car door, and headed into the supermarket without him. When I returned half an hour later, he was still sitting there, staring out the window.

When we got home, Finn went straight to the living room, turned on the television, and settled into the couch as if it were any other day. I carried the groceries into the kitchen and began putting them away.

For a moment, I felt sorry for him. The possibility of jail time was unthinkable. No one imagines their life narrowing to a cell.

But the sympathy didn't last. This was his doing. His choices. And while he might be the one facing a sentence, I was living inside the fallout. The anger rose quickly, hot and steady.

I retreated to the laundry room and pulled the clothes from the dryer, folding them with more force than necessary. The ordinary rhythm of it—fold, stack, smooth—did nothing to quiet my thoughts.

My marriage is on the brink. Financially, he's dragging me down with him.

It was hard to think clearly, but I forced myself to slow my breathing. Stay calm. Stay rational.

I had been crying for three days. Drowning in hurt. In humiliation. But at least I had taken action—we had an attorney. Still, I knew that wouldn't be enough. I needed support beyond legal strategy.

I needed counseling. And whether he admitted it or not, so did Finn.

I found the Employee Assistance Hotline number through my company. It took me several minutes to dial. My finger hovered over the last digit before I finally pressed it.

A woman answered. Her voice was calm, practiced. I gave her only the bare facts—we needed a counselor, as soon as possible. She asked a few questions and located someone nearby. I thanked her, wrote down the number, and sat there staring at it, my chest tight.

Then I called.

I expected a voicemail. Instead, a man answered on the second ring.

"How can I help you?"

The question undid me.

"My husband…" My voice wavered. I swallowed and tried again. "My husband was arrested."

The words sounded foreign in the air.

"My husband was arrested for meeting with a young girl he met over the Internet with the intention of having sex," I continued, forcing each syllable past the lump in my throat. "His attorney suggested we seek counseling."

Saying it aloud made it real in a way it hadn't been before. I felt exposed—like I had just opened a door I could never close again.

"I see," he replied calmly. "I had a cancellation this afternoon at two-thirty. Could you come to my office then?"

Of course, we were available since Finn was banned from campus, and I was taking time off from work to deal with this mess.

"Yes, we'll be there," I replied. "Thank you."

As he gave me the address of his office, I felt my shoulders relax with the relief of being able to share this burden.

The counselor's office was in a modern medical office building not far from our home. The practitioners shared a common lobby and receptionist. I felt self-conscious that everyone would know why we were there. It was irrational, but since the arrest, my thoughts had become irrational.

The young woman behind the reception desk greeted us as we approached.

"Hello! How may I help you?" she asked cheerily.

"I'm Kassidy Haggerty. This is Finn. We're here to see Robert Sonders," I replied.

"Please take a seat, and I'll let him know you're here," she replied with a smile.

A few minutes later, the counselor came out and led us to his office. As we stepped inside, I noticed it was much neater than Jordan's had been—no papers strewn about, just an appointment book and a notebook on his desk. The desk had clean lines, a wood top with a light-colored stain that showed the grain, and black metal legs. The walls were light gray and held a few abstract art pieces.

He motioned for us to sit on the dark gray couch opposite a large, comfy-looking chair, where he took his seat. He was graying at the temples, and I guessed him to be in his fifties. He was more casually dressed than the lawyer, wearing gray wool pants and a navy sweater. He seemed relaxed and calm. I was tense, and my arms were crossed protectively across my chest. Still, I felt better just being there.

"I'm Robert," he said in a soothing voice. "You must be Kassidy and Finn."

His smile was warm and kind.

"It's nice to meet you, Robert," I responded, smiling back, although my arms remained crossed.

"Yeah, nice to meet you," Finn added without a smile.

Robert picked up the pitcher of water on the table between us and poured a glass for each of us.

"Have either of you been through counseling in the past?" Robert asked.

"No," we replied in unison, the first time we'd been in sync in days.

"Finn, why don't you explain why you are here?" Robert continued.

"I thought Kassidy already told you that!" Finn replied, shooting me an angry look.

"Kassidy gave me a rough overview, but I would like to hear it from you," Robert responded, calm and controlled.

Finn sighed deeply before speaking again.

"When Kassidy was traveling for work, I got on a chat room online to meet people because I was lonely. It was just to talk," he stated, tapping his foot nervously.

"And how often did you go online to talk?" Robert asked.

"Not a lot. Just a few times," Finn replied.

That didn't ring true with me, but I didn't say anything and let Finn continue.

"And who did you talk to?" Robert asked.

"Women mostly," Finn disclosed, shifting in his seat.

"Was there anyone in particular that you talked with?" Robert probed further. Robert was very patient, but once again, I felt like getting Finn to share anything was like pulling teeth.

"Yeah, I met a young girl, but I thought she was an adult when we started chatting," Finn stated.

"What kinds of chats did you have with this young girl?" Robert asked, still speaking in a calming voice.

"The chats were innocent at first, but then…" Finn paused, rubbing his brow before finishing his sentence, "Then they turned to a more sexual nature. But I thought she was 18!"

I looked at Finn, surprised.

If he is going to lie to his counselor, how can he get to the root of his issues? And since I'm sitting here witnessing his lie, how does he think he'll regain my trust?

Robert continued his questioning. "How did things take a turn toward a more sexual nature? Who initiated that?" he asked.

"I did!" Finn confessed, his face turning red. Whether it was from embarrassment or anger, I wasn't sure. But I suspected it was the latter.

"Kassidy told me that you were arrested, and charges have been filed. What have you been charged with?" Robert asked.

Finn didn't respond immediately. He rubbed the back of his neck and stared at the floor, jaw tightening. When he finally spoke, his voice was raw.

"Sexual performance of a child," he stated.

"Did you have sex with the girl?" Robert asked.

"No, I went to meet the girl, who I thought was older. But the cops were there instead, and that was when I got arrested," Finn said, continuing his lie and not looking at Robert.

"Thank you, Finn. I know it wasn't easy to share that with me," Robert said. "But I also know that was just the summary, and there is much more here that we need to dig into."

At this point, Robert stopped and looked at me, smiled, and said gently, "I know how hard it is for you to hear all this, Kassidy. But beyond that, there is another issue – Finn's legal case."

I picked up the glass of water in front of me and took a sip, bracing for what was coming next.

"Going forward, it is in your best interests for Finn to see me on his own. Anything he says in our sessions that you hear, they could ask you about in an investigation or at trial," Robert continued.

I glanced at Finn, but he looked at the floor and did not want to make eye contact with Robert or me.

"I know this may be too much for you, or for anyone to handle. And so, I recommend seeing another counselor on your own," Robert suggested.

I nodded in agreement, although I wasn't sure how I felt about seeing a counselor separately.

"My wife is a counselor, too, and her office is here. She would be a good fit for you, but you are free to see whomever you'd like. If you want to meet her now, I can see if she is available," Robert offered as if reading my mind.

Everything was happening so fast! But I knew I needed to talk to someone. I was overwhelmed, and without feeling able to talk to my family and friends, I felt alone and in way over my head. I would worry about the cost later. It was something I needed to do.

"Yes," I finally replied, "Yes, that would be great."

He called his wife and asked if she had time to come to his office. A minute later, there was a knock on the door, and a thin, sharply dressed woman in a light blue skirt and matching cashmere sweater stepped inside. Robert introduced her as Dianne. She looked toward me, her elegant blonde bob swaying as she did. Although her colored hair was not showing signs of graying, I guessed she was also in her fifties. She had a kind smile and spoke in a soft voice. Something about her immediately put me at ease.

Dianne sat in a chair next to Robert, who gave her a brief explanation of our situation.

"I see the need for having separate counselors," Dianne agreed. "Kassidy, if you would like, we can talk in my office."

It was clear that Finn's legal issues would be the dominant factor in how we handled everything.

"Yes," I replied. "I would like that."

"We want to do a preliminary session with each of you right away, and then we can discuss how to proceed," Robert told us.

I grabbed my purse and followed Dianne into her office just a few doors down the hall. Her office was less stark than Robert's and had a more feminine atmosphere. She had boxes of tissues on the coffee table in front of the couch, on the side tables, and on the desk. She motioned for me to sit on the couch and sat in a chair across from me. A light lavender scent filled the room. I found it calming.

"So, tell me," she began softly, "how are you doing? You're free to say anything at all here. This is a no-judgment space and completely confidential. I have dealt with situations like yours, where someone finds out their spouse has done something shocking and hurtful. Some of them have also been involved in criminal cases. So you can tell me anything."

I wasn't exactly sure where to begin. So many feelings were running through me: sadness, anger, fear, disbelief that any of this was happening.

"This is the first time I've talked about this with anyone! I guess I'm still in shock!" I began.

"That is understandable," Dianne soothed.

"How is this even possible? It's like I don't even know him! How could he do this?" I cried.

The flood of emotions that I had kept bottled up while dealing with the logistics of our situation now threatened to overwhelm me.

Dianne nodded and handed me a box of tissues. Two minutes into the session, I was already a puddle.

"Please tell me what you know about the situation," Dianne requested.

"Not much. I knew nothing about it until I picked Finn up from jail on Saturday morning. I only know what he told me, and then I found out what really happened in the newspaper yesterday. And frankly, his story didn't match the newspaper account very well," I replied.

"In what way?" Dianne asked.

"He lied about a lot of it. He keeps denying that he knew the girl was underage, but there is evidence that he knew all along that she was only eleven. And he left out that he sent pornographic photos and made suggestions of what sexual things they would do when they met. He also lied to me, saying he thought the person he was meeting was a young woman, but he didn't. He still thought it was the young girl! And he made his arrest sound like he was the victim," I explained.

"Why do you think he is choosing to act like a victim?" she asked.

"I think he was trying to make me feel sympathy for him," I replied.

"And did that work?" she asked.

"I don't know. Maybe a little, just because it was all so shocking, and it was hard to understand how this was happening to my husband. But much of his story didn't ring true to me. I felt like he was hiding things, and he was," I acknowledged.

"It sounds like your intuition was trying to tell you something. I want you to keep that in mind going forward. It may take Finn some time to tell you the truth, or he may never be completely honest. He needs to be honest with himself first; it sounds like he is in denial. But I want you to listen to your instincts, recognize when something feels wrong, and let that guide you," Dianne advised.

"Just now, he lied to Robert about knowing her age, too, which worries me. If he isn't going to be honest with his counselor, I don't think he will take counseling seriously. I believe he's doing it just to make his lawyer, the courts, and me happy. He said he was willing to do it if it helped me trust him again. I'm not sure that is even possible, especially if he continues to lie!" I continued.

"Again, it may take some time for Finn to accept what he has done. But we'll leave that to Robert to work out with Finn. You and I will focus on your well-being. It's normal to have mixed feelings about all of this. You're still processing it all," Dianne replied.

"Everything changed in a split second!" I lamented.

"What has it been like since you picked Finn up from jail?" she asked.

"Surreal. It's like I don't even know him anymore! He looks like my husband, but he has done something horrible, something I never thought he was capable of doing. And now I find myself second-guessing whether I ever knew him at all. And I wonder what else he's hiding, what else I don't know. Then he keeps blaming this on me, his family, and his professors - everyone but himself. He's not taking any responsibility for any of it. He shattered our life together, and I don't know where we go from here!" I sobbed.

I pulled the last tissue from the box, and Dianne handed me another box. After I'd taken what I needed, she grabbed a few for herself. She was crying along with me, and for the first time in days, I didn't feel so alone. Talking to Dianne was like talking to a friend.

It took us a minute to regain our composure. When she had finished dabbing her eyes, Dianne continued.

"How were things between you before Finn's arrest?" she asked.

"Not perfect, but good. We have a lot of debt, and money has always caused contention between us. That was the main thing we fought about," I told her.

"Money issues are very common in couples," Dianne replied. "Did you talk about money before you were married?"

"No, but I wish we had. Before we were married, he lived at home, and his parents took care of all his financial needs. He could spend money whenever he wanted. After we married, he continued spending the same way," I shared.

"Unfortunately, it is common for many couples not to discuss how to handle money before they get married," Dianne said.

"Now, ten years later, we're heavily in debt, and he has added legal fees, counseling fees, and who knows what else we don't know about yet! We could lose our house, our cars, everything! And that terrifies me!" I wailed, blowing my nose again.

"And yesterday I found out he has a credit card I didn't know about!" I said, almost shouting. "It's overwhelming! What he did makes me sick! I'm hurt! I'm angry! I'm confused! And betrayed by the one person I most trusted in this world! I don't know how I'm going to get through this!"

My tissues were saturated, so Dianne passed me the box of tissues again. "I'm so very sorry you're going through this. You've had the rug pulled out from under you in the harshest way. And I recognize that you may not even be through the worst part of it - there may be more coming," Dianne said in a soothing voice.

"What do you mean?" I asked, not thinking clearly at this point.

"More may be revealed either through the police investigation, or Finn may tell you himself," Dianne explained.

I already sensed this, but hearing someone else say it out loud made it more real. "I don't know if I can handle much more!" I moaned.

"I want you to know that I'm here for you, whatever happens. Don't worry about the cost. We can bill your insurance to cover it completely," Dianne continued. "What you need to focus on now is healing and getting through this. And you *will* get through this! It will just take some time. I would love to help you if you are open to that."

I nodded in agreement, still trying to compose myself again. I knew I needed her help. I told her I wanted to continue the sessions.

I was still raw, still unsteady, but saying the words out loud—admitting I needed support—lightened something inside me. For the first time in days, I felt like I was doing something constructive instead of simply reacting.

Then the phone on Dianne's desk rang.

She listened for a moment, then nodded. "We need to go back to Robert's office," she said.

When we returned, we took the same seats as before; the familiarity of it was almost surreal. Robert folded his hands on his lap and began to speak.

"Kassidy, thank you for coming back. I know this isn't easy. I have completed my initial assessment of Finn and his situation. He has given me permission to share that with you, Kassidy. But first, I'd like to ask you both a few more questions leading up to the arrest."

Finn fidgeted in his seat; his leg bounced restlessly.

"Okay," I said, my voice flat. I didn't look at him.

His knee bounced against the leg of the chair until he caught himself and stilled it, then sagged into the cushion as if the effort had exhausted him.

"I think I've told you everything already," Finn grumbled. "I don't even remember most of it."

"You told me that you weren't sleeping," Robert began, but Finn cut him off.

"I wasn't! I couldn't! I was restless, like I was chasing something, but I don't really know what. Noise in my head, thoughts that I couldn't control," Finn explained.

"You were up all night for weeks. You said you were working on your dissertation and that you were 'on fire' with ideas. Then you'd sleep late the next day," I added.

"Is that true, Finn? Were you working on your dissertation during that time?" Robert asked.

Finn's leg began bouncing again, and he tugged at his shirt sleeve.

"No, I was staying up to chat online," he said, looking at the floor. "But the chat room stuff—it wasn't real. None of it felt real."

"Finn, have you ever had stretches where you felt invincible? Like your thoughts were racing faster than you could speak them?" Robert asked.

Finn grunted. "Yeah. All the time. It's like—like my brain's on a bullet train, and I can't get off."

"And then periods where you struggle to get out of bed, lose interest in things, feel worthless?" Robert queried.

Finn looked up at Robert, his eyes glassy.

"Yeah," he said quietly, nodding.

"Finn, I believe you're experiencing bipolar disorder, likely Type I. It's not just moodiness or burnout. It's a brain-based condition. The symptoms you've described—insomnia, hypersexuality, impulsivity, grandiosity, crashing afterward—these aren't isolated. They're part of a pattern."

We sat silently for a moment, each of us taking in what Robert had just revealed.

"So this…it's not just Finn making bad choices?" I asked.

"No. But — and this is critical— bipolar disorder helps explain behavior. It does *not* excuse it all. Especially when it causes harm," Robert explained.

"Shit!" Finn exclaimed, staring straight ahead, looking like he'd been hit by a truck.

"You didn't choose this illness, Finn. But you'll have to choose how you deal with it now. That includes owning what happened— and committing to real treatment," Robert said, focusing directly on Finn.

Finn had dropped his head again, unwilling to make eye contact with Robert.

"That tension—between illness and responsibility—is something we'll walk through together. There is no shortcut. But there is a way forward…for each of you. Whether it's together or apart," Robert said.

I sat there speechless for a moment. Finn's older brother, Hayden, had been diagnosed with bipolar disorder a few years earlier. Robert noticed the shock on my face and the quick look I gave Finn.

"You seem surprised and yet not surprised," Robert declared, tilting his head slightly.

"Did you tell Robert about Hayden?" I asked Finn.

"No, I didn't!" Finn replied, "I was also surprised when Robert told me I might be bipolar!"

Robert and Dianne exchanged looks, and then Robert asked, "Who is Hayden?"

"Hayden is my older brother. He was diagnosed with bipolar disorder a couple of years ago. He went through a very rough time. They had to close the family business shortly after Hayden and my cousin took over from my dad and uncle. He took it pretty hard, having worked there since he was a teenager. And then he and his wife got divorced. He sort of had a breakdown, and that's when he was told he had bipolar disorder," Finn told him.

Robert sat back in his chair. "It's not uncommon to find mental health issues occurring in family members," he told us. "Did his bipolar disorder manifest in behaviors similar to yours?"

It took Finn a beat to realize what Robert was asking.

"No! As I said, he had a bit of a breakdown. He didn't do anything like I did," Finn said, his cheeks flushing red.

For the first time, I thought Finn might feel embarrassed by what he had done. Embarrassment was far from remorse, but perhaps it was a start.

"Can you explain what you mean when you say Hayden had a breakdown?" Robert probed.

"He was very depressed after the business closed, and then the divorce. He got caught trying to shoplift a car battery he didn't need. And that was when he first got some help. But he has changed a lot. He gets agitated easily. He used to be easy-going, adventurous, and fun. And he still is. But just not quite like he used to be. His moods can change quickly," Finn explained.

I hesitated for a moment, unsure how much to share. But Robert was waiting, and if he was going to understand, he needed the full picture.

"There was one visit in particular that stands out," I began, then told the story.

Hayden and his girlfriend, Maxine, had come to visit us shortly after he was diagnosed with bipolar disorder. Hayden was open about telling us what he had experienced. But what Hayden did not share with any of us, including Maxine, was that he had been feeling good and had stopped taking his medication.

One evening, as we prepared to go to dinner, Hayden went outside to get into the car. The car was locked, and Hayden tugged at the door handle anxiously, like a small child, trying to get it open. He looked like he was on the verge of a meltdown. Finn and I saw it from the window, and Finn quickly unlocked the car doors with his key fob. We thought everything was okay, but the meltdown was yet to come.

When we arrived at the restaurant, I was thankful we were seated immediately. We ordered our drinks, and when Hayden got his iced tea, he dumped every packet of sugar from the table into his glass. He stirred it, but there was too much sediment to dissolve. He then interrupted our waitress, who was taking an order at the next table, and asked her for more sugar. The waitress told him she would get some as soon as she placed her current order with the kitchen.

Hayden got impatient waiting for her to return with the sugar and went to the drink station alone. We tried to stop him, but he was like a wild man. He started opening the cupboards, looking for sugar. The waitress came over and tried to stop him, as well. And then the manager came. By this point, Hayden was yelling, and though we tried to console him, he continued ranting.

The manager ordered us out of the restaurant. Finn and Maxine had to drag Hayden to the car while I stayed back to apologize to the restaurant staff and pay for our drinks. The whole restaurant watched me as I hurried out the door.

When I got to the car, Hayden was still ranting and pacing in the parking lot. Finn and Maxine had managed to get him out of the restaurant, but couldn't coax him to get in the car. He was upset, thinking that the restaurant staff had mistreated him, and couldn't understand why Finn and Maxine had dragged him out of the restaurant when he felt he had done nothing wrong. He wanted to go to another restaurant and wouldn't get into the car until we agreed.

Of course, we went home instead, and then there was another meltdown when Hayden realized we weren't taking him to another restaurant. We ended up ordering pizza, and somehow, Maxine convinced Hayden to take his medication, although it would be a while before it kicked in. The whole ordeal had been upsetting, and seeing Hayden in such a disruptive state was frightening.

As unnerving as the scene with Hayden had been, it was nothing compared to what Finn had done.

"Finn, I would like to refer you to a psychiatrist to confirm my assessment, and potentially take over your case. You will need counseling, and you may need medication, as well. I can continue counseling you until the psychiatrist takes over. Is that how you would like to proceed?" Robert asked.

Finn looked at me nervously. I could tell he was worried I'd say "no" due to the cost. But even without insurance, it was clear he needed help more than I did.

"We have insurance," was all I said.

CHAPTER 8

STUMBLING FORWARD

Finn is bipolar! The thought kept reverberating through my brain like a fire alarm. As I buckled my seat belt, I felt like I was going to explode. *Had I missed something along the way? Were there signs I should have seen?* But then, I had no experience with bipolar disorder other than a few encounters with Hayden, so I didn't even know what the signs were.

Finn stared out the passenger window. He hadn't said a word since we left Robert's office. I wanted to know what he was thinking and feeling, but I didn't think I should have to drag it out of him yet again. I was dealing with my own emotional upheaval.

I had no idea what implications a diagnosis of bipolar disorder would have. Would that affect Finn's legal case? Would it affect my decision on whether to leave him or stay?

Because of Finn's legal troubles, Robert and Dianne had suggested separate counseling. I thought a wife couldn't be compelled to testify against her husband, but they were preparing us for an outcome in which we were no longer married.

But now that I know Finn is mentally ill, could I walk away after vowing to be there in sickness and in health? Aunt Emily stayed with her husband even though he was an alcoholic. She endured that for decades. *But his illness doesn't justify his actions, does it? It doesn't change the facts or take away the hurt and anger,* I thought.

It was all so confusing! I no longer recognized my life. I was married to a bipolar pedophile who had an endless supply of secrets. I felt like I had fallen into a deep pool and didn't know how to swim.

Frustrated by my disoriented thoughts, I checked on Finn. I was genuinely concerned for him. It couldn't be easy getting a diagnosis like that.

"How are you doing?" I asked.

He continued to stare out the window and replied, "Not so good."

I took a deep breath before continuing. I wasn't doing so well, myself.

"Did you like Robert?" I asked.

"Yeah, I guess so," Finn replied.

Getting information from Finn was like squeezing blood from a stone. "Do you think he can help you through this?" I continued to query.

"I don't know! I just wish none of this was happening," he said sullenly.

"How do you think I feel?" I shouted, angry that he was still playing the victim.

He didn't answer, and that made me angrier.

"You are not the victim in this, Finn! You caused all this, and now we're both paying the price!"

Finn turned toward me for the first time since we got into the car.

"But it isn't my fault!" Finn insisted. "And how are you paying the price? I'm the one who might go to jail!"

I couldn't believe what I was hearing.

"Yeah, and if you go to jail, who's going to pay the attorney fees? And who is going to pay off your secret credit card? While you're fed and clothed in prison, this could bankrupt me. I'm the one paying the price for your actions!" I retorted.

"All you do is blame me! But it's not my fault! You heard Robert - I'm bipolar! I didn't know what I was doing!" Finn yelled.

"But you still had choices! You could have stopped it long before you decided to meet the girl. You could have come to me and told me what you were feeling before you acted on those feelings. We were supposed to be partners!" I cried.

"We're still partners! Please don't leave me, Kass! Not when I need you more than ever," he said softly.

And then I saw it. He was trying to use his new diagnosis to make me feel guilty. How many times had I fallen for his manipulations in the past?

"I don't know what I'm going to do yet, Finn," I replied, no longer yelling. It was the truth. Things were becoming a bit clearer.

I needed a plan of action. At least for now, we had counselors to help us through the emotional challenges and Finn's psychological issues, and we had secured a lawyer to guide us through the legal issues. I did not feel like things were under control by any means, but at least we had done *something* and were moving forward.

I pulled into the parking spot behind our townhouse. Finn and I sat there for a moment, neither of us speaking.

Finally, I broke the silence. "We need income, Finn. I need to return to work as soon as possible. My vacation time will run out soon, and I won't get paid unless I work," I told him.

"Fine. Whatever you want to do," Finn replied, as if it didn't affect him.

"You can't go back to the university, but I hope Ed will let you continue to work for him part-time," I continued, ignoring his disinterested attitude.

"I'm not sure I'm ready to face Ed or anyone else," Finn said.

"I'm not either! But we need to have income, so we're both going to have to get out there, regardless of how exposed we feel!" I shouted as I got out and slammed the car door.

As I fumbled for my keys to unlock the back door, I could see Finn following me into the house at a more leisurely pace.

I couldn't tell if he was hiding in denial or collapsing into self-pity, but he wasn't taking responsibility. The weight of action settled squarely on my shoulders. If anything was going to get done, I would have to do it.

Finn went into the living room and turned on the television, the sound filling the house almost immediately. I wanted him to call Ed himself, but I knew it wouldn't go well. In his current state, he wasn't going to take responsibility for anything. Pushing him now would only ignite another argument—and I didn't have the energy for that.

So I picked up the phone.

I left a message for my boss, telling him I would be back at work the next day. Then I called Stephanie. I'd hoped she would answer—I needed to hear her voice, to gauge whether the news had already made its way through the office—but her machine picked up instead.

One more call.

I dialed Ed's number. He and his wife, Laura, were among our closest friends. More than that, Ed was Finn's employer. We needed to know whether Finn still had a job. I trusted Ed to be honest with me, even if the truth was hard to hear.

Ed answered on the second ring.

"Hello, this is Ed."

"Hi, Ed. It's Kassidy."

"Kassidy." His voice softened immediately. "How are you?"

There was concern there. I clung to it, hoping it meant something. "I'm… holding up," I said. "All things considered." I swallowed. "Thank you for calling on Sunday. It meant a lot."

"Laura and I are still in shock," he replied gently. "We've been worried about you."

His kindness nearly undid me.

"Thank you. We're doing alright. We've been taking care of the immediate concerns - hiring a lawyer for Finn and seeking counseling," I told him.

"I'm sure it helps to be taking some action," Ed replied.

"Yes, it does," I said, pausing. "Listen, about Finn's job, I was wondering —" Ed cut me off before I could finish.

"Laura and I have been talking about that. Although I have my reservations, as long as we keep his work to filing and not answering phones or dealing with clients, I'm willing to try it. But if anything seems unusual, I reserve the right to let him go."

I breathed a huge sigh of relief, not realizing I had been holding my breath while Ed spoke. "Thank you, Ed! Thank you so much! And yes, you can change your mind, but this will really help us!"

After the call, I walked into the living room, where Finn was still watching television.

"Who were you talking to?" Finn asked, not looking away from the television.

"That was Ed. He said that it's okay for you to keep working for him. He is expecting you on Wednesday," I told him.

"Why wouldn't it be okay for me to keep working for him?" Finn asked, turning my way and frowning.

"You've been charged with a felony. The university has dismissed you. It would not be outside the realm of possibilities that Ed would fire you! Is none of this sinking in for you?" I replied angrily.

Finn opened his mouth to say something, but thought better of it and returned to the program he was watching.

I didn't know whether he was just in denial or actually believed that he didn't deserve the consequences for his actions. But whatever his reasoning, his attitude baffled me. The air in the room was stifling, and I needed to work off the tension I was feeling. As soon as I picked up their leashes, Sam and Lizzie jumped to their feet, eager for a run.

When I returned home, Finn was still sitting on the couch, watching television. An empty plate and a half-empty beer bottle sat on the coffee table in front of him. As I passed him on my way to the kitchen, he didn't bother to look up or say anything. I had no interest in conversing with him, and his silence suited me. I grabbed a glass of water and made myself a sandwich - a task made easier since Finn had left everything on the counter after making his own. I sat at the dining room table and ate my sandwich, a dog on each side waiting for a handout.

Once I had finished, I cleaned up my dishes but left the rest of the mess Finn had made. He could clean it up.

I headed upstairs to set out my clothes for the next day and prepare for bed without saying a word to Finn, who still had not moved from the couch. Although I was apprehensive about returning to work, I was relieved to be leaving the house. My home, once a place of comfort, had become a place of tension and uncertainty.

The next morning, I moved through the house in silence. I dressed for work, made coffee, and ate a few bites of toast I barely tasted. I leashed the dogs and walked them in the cool morning air, their steady pace grounding me.

Finn was still asleep in the guest room. I could hear him shift once as I passed the hallway, but he didn't get up.

By the time I locked the door behind me, the dishes were done, the dogs were fed, and the house was in order. The ordinary responsibilities of the day had been handled—because someone had to.

As I drove to work, the weight of it pressed in. The lawyer. The bills. The uncertainty. The explanations that would have to be made. None of it would move unless I moved it.

And Finn was still in bed.

I felt queasy as I passed the shopping center where Finn had been arrested. That was bad planning; I'd have to find a new route to work.

As I exited my car and headed toward the building, I ran into Patty, the receptionist, in the parking lot. I braced myself for what might be coming next.

"Hi, Kassidy! How was your weekend?" she said, smiling.

Her greeting seemed so normal! Was it possible that she didn't know? It was Tuesday - perhaps she thought I had taken a long weekend for a trip.

"It was fine," I replied, forcing a smile. "How was yours, Patty?"

"Oh, it was great! My husband and I spent the weekend biking. It's our favorite thing to do!" she responded cheerily.

While Patty shared the details of their rides, my mind was focused on the fact that she didn't seem to know. Was it possible that others didn't know? I hoped that would be the case. I did not want to answer questions, nor did I want people to pity me or treat me differently because of what Finn had done. I needed this part of my life away from Finn to be as ordinary as possible.

When I arrived, my boss, Max, was already in his office, and none of my co-workers were there yet. His office door was open, so I paused in the doorway to let him know I was there.

"Hi, Max! I'm back," I told him.

"Hi, Kassidy!" he replied, looking surprised to see me so early. "How are you doing? Come in and have a seat," he said, motioning to the chairs across from his desk.

"As well as can be expected, all things considered," I replied as I sat. I glanced around at the bookshelves, loaded with books on software development and testing, and binders filled with reference materials from various oil and gas companies and professional organizations that we used to validate data.

"Yeah, I'm surprised you were ready to come back so soon. But I'm glad you're here. Is there anything I can do to help?" Max asked.

"Thanks, Max. I appreciate that. But right now, I'm still just trying to figure things out. I'm very nervous about being here and facing people. But I ran into Patty, and she didn't seem to know. That was a relief!" I said.

"I don't think most people know what happened. And the ones who do are concerned about you. Everyone in our group knows. We will keep things quiet as much as possible. And Stephanie has your back. She overheard a couple of the guys in the other group talking about it. She shut them down hard! I think she put a little fear into them. They are not going to say anything," he said with a little laugh.

"I can always count on Steph!" I replied, grateful for having a friend who was so protective and there when I needed her.

I thanked Max and then settled in at my desk before the others arrived. As my co-workers filtered into the office, they greeted me with condolences about what had happened. They were all supportive and asked how I was doing. They didn't ask many questions, which I appreciated.

Stephanie breezed in, wearing a bright scarf around her neck and a smile on her face. She carried two coffees from my favorite coffee shop and placed one on my desk, winking. The smell of the cinnamon coffee– my favorite– warmed me. I could tell that one of the guys was about to ask Steph why she hadn't brought all of them coffee. But then he thought better of it. She took her spot at her desk, facing the opposite wall from the one my desk faced. It took about a minute for her to log into her computer and send me supportive messages via chat. We sat about three feet apart, but since several of us worked in that office, chatting was our standard way of communication when others were present.

Steph: OMG! I'm so glad you're here!

Kass: Thanks! Me too! But I'm worried everyone knows.

Steph: No, only a few of us. Our group. Max talked with us. A couple of guys in the other group heard about it on campus. But that's about it.

Kass: Yeah, Max said you scared those guys into silence. Nice work, my friend!

Steph: LOL! I came down hard on them. Idiots! They deserved it!

Kass: Thanks for the coffee!

Steph: You're welcome! Added bonus is that the guys are all jealous that I didn't bring them coffee!

I let out an involuntary snort, which immediately drew a few glances from our co-workers. Neither Stephanie nor I looked up. We kept our eyes on our screens, doing our best to appear composed.

But we both knew the guys were aware of our ongoing chat thread. And we knew they had one of their own—usually about gaming.

It felt good to laugh, even briefly. I hadn't realized how much I needed it until that moment. Stephanie did.

At lunch, Stephanie and I went for a walk to catch up and talk. She was also a graduate student at the university. We kept the conversation light until we were well away from the office.

"How are you doing?" she asked.

"I'm still in shock. All of this is unreal! And I'm so angry! And hurt. And confused," I replied.

"My offer still stands if you need to get away from him. And I think you should! Or just kick him out if you want to stay in your home. Either way, Kass, I don't understand why you're still there!" Stephanie exclaimed.

"I don't want to leave my home, and I can't kick him out. You know how he spends money! We're already in debt, and now there are all the legal expenses. If I kick him out before I figure out the finances, he'll find a fancy hotel, order room service, and rack up even more debt! No, I need time to figure out what I want to do. In the meantime, he's sleeping in the guest room," I shared.

"Well, at least that's something. So are you eventually going to kick him to the curb?" Stephanie asked.

"I don't know. We went to counseling, and the counselor thinks Finn might be bipolar. If he's mentally ill, can I just leave him? I mean, it doesn't feel right not to try to work things out if he's sick," I confided.

"Yes, he is sick! Did you read the article in the paper? Only a sick person could do that sort of thing!" Stephanie declared.

"Yes. I read the article. It made me ill to think he could do those things. I just need to take things one step at a time right now, Steph!" I replied, my eyes welling with tears.

"I'll support you no matter what you decide, but I will still voice my opinion," Stephanie said.

"Thanks! I appreciate that. And I do value your opinion. But I just need to work through this in my way," I told her.

"I spoke with several other students. The geology department is buzzing with the news of Finn's arrest!" she revealed.

"I'm not surprised," I said grimly.

"The two guys I overheard at work talking about it are the other two graduate students. Only Phil made the connection that Finn is your husband," Stephanie continued.

"Seriously? Tom saw us together at your party! He knows Finn and I are married," I said.

"Yeah, I don't know what Tom was thinking! He got it once Phil and I reminded him. Anyway, I told them both to quit gossiping about it at the office or with our co-workers," Stephanie said.

"Thank you, Steph," I said, my voice breaking as tears spilled over. "It means so much that you did that for me. I don't think I could handle facing everyone right now… not after what Finn did. Just knowing I won't have to explain or answer questions—it helps more than you know."

I paused and took a deep breath. "I'm so grateful for you. You're always there when I need you."

I stopped walking and wrapped my arms around her, holding on longer than I meant to.

"I can't even imagine what this is like for you," Stephanie said, her voice tight with anger. "I'm so mad at Finn. What the hell was he thinking? Sucky bastard."

"Sucky bastard," I echoed, snorting despite myself. It was the first time I'd laughed in days. Leave it to Stephanie to find exactly the crack in the wall where a little light could get in.

Word quietly spread among the few who knew, but no one outside our circle said anything to me. Thanks to Stephanie, the office became the one place I could breathe—a small pocket of normal in the middle of everything unraveling at home.

Finn wasn't home when I returned that evening. He had gone to the university at their request to meet with the administrators. I thought he would be back by now, but I was glad to have some time to myself. I changed my clothes and went to the kitchen to prepare dinner. I didn't feel like cooking, but I was hungry. And with the lawyer's fees now added to our already tight budget, eating out or ordering in was out of the question. So, I made some quick scrambled eggs and toast.

Finn walked in a little while later, carrying a box. The dogs went to greet him, Lizzie still watching him warily. He put the box down on the counter without saying a word.

"How did it go?" I asked tentatively.

His eyes welled with tears, and he took a deep, shaky breath before answering.

"They kicked me out of school and asked me to move out of my office. Most of the other students wouldn't even talk to me and whispered behind my back. Only Kevin and Darcy would talk to me."

A part of me thought, *Well, what do you expect?* The other part of me felt sorry for him. It didn't surprise me that Kevin and Darcy still spoke to him. They were his friends and officemates.

"What did they say to you?" I asked.

"They both said they were shocked at what happened and asked if it was true," Finn said. "I told them it is. And that I have bipolar disorder. It was hard to tell them all of that."

"I'm sure it was," I replied, making a mental note that he had placed the blame on his bipolar disorder. "How did they react?"

"They said they would not end our friendship over this and that they would be there for me."

"I'm glad you have someone else to lean on besides me because I'm struggling to hold myself up," I said as I scraped the eggs from the pan onto a plate. I took my meal and sat down at the dining room table, my back to the kitchen and Finn.

Finn made himself a sandwich and grabbed a beer from the refrigerator before joining me at the table.

We still hadn't figured out how to break the news to our families. Just imagining my mother's voice twisted my stomach—shame crowding out the words I knew I needed to say, even as I longed for her support. Too tired to untangle what came next, I let the subject drift away.

We ate in silence, making the sound of Finn's chewing even more irritating than usual. When we finished, I stood and gathered the dishes. It was his turn to clean up, but the heat of the water over my hands felt preferable to sitting in the thick, unspoken tension between us.

The mayonnaise and mustard he'd taken out still sat open on the counter. I replaced the lids with more force than necessary, sealed the bread and lunch meat, and shoved them back into the refrigerator. I should have left the mess for him. I knew that. But the small, ordinary motions kept me from screaming at him and losing the fragile control I was barely holding onto.

Finn went into the living room and turned on the television to watch the "Everybody Loves Raymond" sitcom. I didn't know if he was watching or was lost in his thoughts and misery. When I had finished cleaning up, I looked outside and noticed the sky had turned dark, mirroring my mood. I couldn't stand to be in the same room with him for another minute, watching him brood about the situation he had created as if he were the victim. His self-absorption consumed the atmosphere.

As I stood there in the archway between the dining room and the living room, scrutinizing Finn, Sam looked up at me and wagged her tail, and I instantly knew what she was suggesting.

I walked over to the door and leashed the dogs for a walk in the cool night air. I would be less likely to run into any neighbors under the cover of darkness. It was October, but the night air was still warm enough that I didn't need a jacket. The stars were out, and for a moment, I just let myself breathe in the night air and soak in the peacefulness of the twinkling stars. Being outside and away from Finn felt good. I felt lighter as the cool breeze swept away some of the tension from my body.

Sam saw the neighbor's cat and tried to give chase, even though her leash kept her from running. Lizzie barked in support. The cat ran under a bush, leaving its tail swaying in sight to tease Sam. The fresh air helped to clear my head. For a few minutes, I almost forgot my troubles.

Almost.

CHAPTER 9

KEEPING SECRETS

As we moved through the next week, not much changed. I went to work every day, and Finn did some office work for Ed to earn extra money. Finn earned a fraction of my income, but every little bit helped. It also got Finn out of the house and doing something constructive instead of wallowing in self-pity. We acted more like roommates than a married couple.

We were both going to counseling; I went once a week, and Finn saw Robert twice a week. Finn also met with the psychiatrist that Robert had recommended, who confirmed through an extensive interview that Finn was bipolar. He also requested that Finn get a physical exam before prescribing medication to treat Finn's disorder, to ensure that there was no other underlying condition causing his behavior, such as a concussion, brain tumor, stroke, or infection.

"How are you doing, Kassidy?" Dianne asked me during our next counseling session. Dianne was a calming presence in my life, always dressed impeccably in soothing colors, much like her office. She put me at ease, and I felt comfortable saying things I'd never say out loud anywhere else.

"Alright, I guess. The psychiatrist confirmed that Finn does have bipolar disorder. Finn had a physical, and he has been prescribed medication to treat the disorder," I replied.

"That's a good step toward Finn getting help. Have you noticed any changes in his behavior since he started taking the medication?" Dianne asked.

"Not really, but it's only been a few days. Should I already be seeing changes?" I queried.

"Medications can have calming effects within a few days, but it can take weeks for them to take effect. Hopefully, he will feel more in control of his emotions soon. But now let's focus on you. I'd like to learn more about your relationship with Finn. How did you meet?" Dianne asked.

"In college," I responded. "We were both in the same core classes in an undergraduate geology program and became close friends. I was shy, and he was outgoing. He could talk to anyone about anything, and I admired that."

"And when did your relationship become more romantic in nature?"

"During field camp. We spent eight weeks in Utah. There were about ten students and four faculty members from the university," I began. "During the week, we did field assignments and learned to understand the area's geology and map geologic features. We usually had free time on the weekends to finish our assignments, do laundry, and hang out."

I took a sip of my water.

"Since Finn and I were already good friends, we spent a lot of our free time together. And we grew closer. One night, we got back later than usual from one of our field camp outings, and the cafeteria was closed. Most of the other students ordered pizza, but we decided to walk the half mile to our favorite restaurant in town. On the way home, Finn took my hand for the first time. When we got to the dorm, he stopped and pulled me close and kissed me. After that, we were a couple and spent all our time together," I explained.

Dianne nodded as she listened and took notes. "And how did you interact with each other?"

"Back then, our relationship seemed so easy," I told her. "I remember one field trip. I was driving the van, and Finn was riding shotgun and talking to me to keep me awake. Most of the other students in the seats behind us were napping. The professors were in another van. Finn and I were discussing politics and disagreed. We weren't fighting; we were just having a lively discussion, listening to each other's points, and countering with our own. After a while, we noticed that the other students were waking up and listening in. A few people commented on how we could disagree but keep our conversation pleasant," I recalled.

"Most of our conversations were like that in the beginning. We truly listened to each other and showed each other respect. I had never had a relationship quite like that before. I don't think he ever had, either. It was nice."

Dianne smiled. "How does it feel to remember that?" she asked.

I took a deep breath before answering, "It feels like that was so long ago, like remembering something that is lost. Like Finn was a completely different person from the man I'm married to now."

A lump formed in my throat, and it was difficult to say those words. For a moment, I was transported back to a happier time, but that time was now long gone. My eyes welled with tears, and Dianne handed me a tissue. We sat quietly for a moment as I dabbed my eyes.

"How on earth did we get here?" I asked in a hoarse whisper, shaking my head as the tears continued to flow.

Dianne handed me the box of tissues and said, "I know this is hard. But it is important to remember the good things as we work through whether you can repair this relationship or even whether you want to."

"I'm not sure I'm ready to give up on our marriage. But after what he has done and all the lies, I'm not sure that is possible," I replied, cleaning up the mascara under my eyes with another tissue.

"Right now, you're feeling angry and hurt, and that is normal. It is my job to help you work through all of it, the bad and the good, to help you determine what is best for you," Dianne soothed.

Everything felt safe in that room. Just sitting there with Dianne, I felt a sense of comfort.

"So how is it going, living with Finn?" Dianne asked.

I let out a sharp breath. "There are days I can't stand the sight of him. The other night I came home late from work, and there was an empty pizza box on the counter. He was on the couch with a plate of pizza and a beer, watching *Home Improvement.* Two empty bottles were already on the table. He'd clearly been there a while."

Dianne tilted her head slightly. "What did you do?"

"I didn't even say hello. I snapped, 'It was your turn to cook!'"

She nodded for me to continue.

"He didn't look away from the TV. Just took a sip of his beer and said, 'I didn't feel like cooking. All I do is work and cook and clean around here.'"

I stared at her. "Dianne, I honestly thought he was joking. Could he really believe that?"

"And then?"

"I lost it. I reminded him we're trying to save money for his legal expenses. I reminded him why we're even in this mess. And he said, 'You just want to keep punishing me for the one mistake I made. It's not fair, Kass.'"

Even repeating it made my chest tighten.

"I told him I wasn't punishing him — that we had agreed no take-out, no eating out. I told him his word meant nothing. Then I went upstairs to change. When I came back down, he was still sitting there, eating pizza, watching TV. Like nothing mattered."

I swallowed.

"I was too angry to eat. I grabbed the dogs and left. He yelled, 'Where are you going?' but I didn't answer. All I could think was, I'm going somewhere where I don't have to look at you. And for the first time, I wondered why I was even trying to save this marriage."

"Why are you trying to save the marriage? Is saving it what you want?" Dianne asked, tilting her head slightly.

I let out a long sigh.

"If I don't try," I said slowly, "I'll always wonder whether I gave up too soon. I need to work through this. I need to know that whatever decision I make is the right one."

Saying it aloud steadied me. That was the truth.

I was grateful for Dianne. She was compassionate, but she didn't rush to take sides. My friends loved me fiercely, but they had opinions—strong ones. Most of them thought I should divorce Finn. Some thought I should have already thrown him out. But I couldn't make a decision based on anger or humiliation. Not yet. I had to be certain. And I had to protect myself financially. Survival had become part of the equation.

"Before this, were there any areas of conflict in your relationship?" Dianne asked.

"Money!" I replied emphatically and without hesitation.

"When we got married, I assumed we were starting on equal footing. I lived alone, paid my bills, and had managed to save about $5,000 while paying down my student loans. Finn lived at home. His parents covered his expenses. I assumed he was saving too.

He wasn't.

A few weeks before our wedding, he had taken out a $7,500 graduate loan—without telling me. I didn't find out until a month into our marriage. I was furious. Not just about the debt, but about being excluded from a decision that would affect our future. Still, when the payments came due four years later, I paid them. We were partners. That's what partners did."

But money never stopped being a problem.

"I'm a saver," I told Dianne. "Finn is a spender."

He bought lunches out when we had agreed to cut back. He charged clothes, CDs, and small things that added up. He withdrew cash from the ATM even after I warned him that checks we'd written hadn't cleared yet. Overdraft fees stacked up. Late fees followed. And when I confronted him, he said I was overwrought—as if I were the problem for caring.

I was the one paying the bills. I knew what we had and what we didn't. But he insisted the ATM balance meant there was money available. It didn't matter how many times I explained it.

As I told Dianne all this, I realized something.

"It's the same pattern," I said slowly. "The overdrafts. The arrest. Denial. No responsibility. He does what he wants and then acts like the consequences are happening to him, not because of him."

Dianne nodded thoughtfully. "That sounds like a pattern."

Finn had never really managed money before we married. His father handled his account and made sure it never ran dry. I had assumed that once we were on our own, he would grow into the responsibility.

He hadn't.

Instead, I became the parent. The monitor. The one holding everything together.

And now I was seeing it clearly: this wasn't just about spending. It was about avoidance. About getting what he wanted and refusing to face the cost.

Dianne shifted gently. "What about your sex life? Was intimacy active between you? And do you know whether he's ever sought out sex elsewhere?"

The question stunned me.

"We had a great sex life," I said quickly. "It was one of the strongest parts of our marriage." I hesitated. "I never had any reason not to trust him. Until the arrest."

The words settled heavily between us.

"He said he was in the chat room because he was lonely when I traveled," I continued. "I used to be gone during the week for work. But we talked every night. And we were together every weekend."

As I said it, something shifted.

"That excuse doesn't make sense," I whispered. "I stopped traveling more than a year before the arrest. So why did this happen now?"

My thoughts began racing. Had he only talked? Had he met others? Had this been going on longer than I knew? The possibility hit like a physical blow. I felt dizzy, nauseated.

Dianne remained still, giving me space.

"I trusted him. When he said he loved me, when he said he was working on his dissertation. I trusted him. And I never questioned any of it."

Anger flared—at him for lying, and at myself for not seeing it.

"I feel so stupid," I said, shredding a tissue in my hands. "How could I not know?"

"You're not stupid," Dianne said calmly. "If he were hiding something, he would have taken steps to keep it hidden. That's what people do when they're protecting a secret."

I nodded numbly.

"Is this something you need to know?" she asked.

I did. Even if I wasn't sure I wanted the answer.

"Then you'll have to ask him," Dianne said gently. "He may not tell you the truth. But you deserve to ask."

My heart sank, and my arms and legs felt weak. I knew Dianne was right. I needed to know the truth. Otherwise, I might only get more lies. This realization revealed just how badly Finn had broken my trust. It would be impossible to get it back.

For the first time, it sank in that my marriage had been irreparably damaged. My chest felt tight, and my head was pounding.

As the room spun around me, my thoughts suddenly shifted from what I could do to save my marriage to what I needed to do to prepare for ending it. This frightened me, and I wasn't sure I was ready for that. I didn't share these thoughts with Dianne at the time. I needed to process this myself first and be certain that was where I was headed before I could say it out loud.

As I left Dianne's office, I began formulating my strategy for asking Finn whether he had met any of the women or children from the chat room. I needed to find out if he had slept with any of them.

What other secrets was Finn keeping? Each new revelation deepened the chasm between us.

CHAPTER 10

THE UNMASKING

When I got home, Finn was not there. I changed into comfortable clothes and took Sam and Lizzie for a walk. I didn't want to be there waiting for him when he got home. I knew my anger would just stew if I waited. As we neared the end of the street, I saw his car come around the corner.

He saw me, pulled to the curb, and rolled down his window. "Hey, I thought it was my turn to walk the dogs," he said out the window as he petted Sam's head.

"I wasn't sure when you'd be home, and the dogs needed to go out," I replied nonchalantly. "I'll be back in a little while." And then I kept walking.

When I walked through the front door half an hour later, he was in the living room watching *Home Improvement* again. I gave Sam and Lizzie their treats, then sat on the other end of the couch, grabbed the remote, and shut off the television.

"Hey, I was watching that!" he yelled.

"We need to talk," I replied, trying to sound calm but unable to hide the shakiness in my voice. "I have questions, and I want honest answers."

Finn suddenly looked worried.

"Questions about what? I told you what happened!" he said in a tight voice.

"No, you told me bits and pieces of what happened mixed with untruths. I didn't find out most of what happened until I read the article in the newspaper," I said coldly.

Finn bristled.

"You told me you never intended to meet anyone in the chat room. You just wanted someone to talk to. But did you? Did you meet any of the other women you chatted with?" I asked, diving right into the deep end.

Finn's face turned pale, and he looked like he was going to be sick. I already knew the answer was *yes*, but I wanted to hear what he had to say. I needed to hear what he had to say. I would know he was lying if he told me he had never met anyone from the chat room. And if he admitted to meeting someone, I had more questions.

"Yes. I met other women," he whispered hoarsely.

I sucked in a shallow breath, realizing as I did that I had been holding my breath while I waited for his answer.

"How many?" My voice was raw.

"A few," he said, turning his eyes away from me and looking at the ground.

And then I had to ask him the hardest question of all. "And did you sleep with them?" I was openly crying now.

He didn't look at me, and he didn't respond. He didn't need to – I knew his silence meant that he had.

"Were any of them children?" My stomach churned as I asked.

"No! They were all adults! I told you before that going to meet that girl was the first time I had ever done anything like that!" Finn shouted.

"You told me a lot of things, Finn! Most of which were lies!"

I got up and walked upstairs to my bedroom. When I kicked him out of my bed, I didn't make him move his stuff out of my room. That had been a mistake. I emptied his drawers from the dresser and dumped his stuff on the hallway floor in front of the spare room. I went back to my room, grabbed an armful of his clothes from the closet, and added them to the pile. He came up to see what I was doing.

"Are you kicking me out?" he yelled.

"No," I replied sternly, "But you will not enter my room or touch me ever again. I will not be cooking for you or cleaning up after you. Until I figure out what I'm going to do about this hideous mess you've dragged me into, consider this a roommate situation. And you will not order take-out, eat out, or spend a single dime without my approval."

"You're treating me like a child!" he protested.

"No," I replied calmly, "I'm treating you like someone who can't be trusted."

I turned, walked downstairs, and began making myself a sandwich in the kitchen. A thousand thoughts were rushing through my head.

I'm not going to kick him out until I have a plan, I thought to myself as I spread mayonnaise on a slice of bread.

I tore a slice of ham in half and handed a piece to each of the dogs, who happily devoured them.

"Do you even taste it when you eat it so fast?" I asked them, shaking my head. Sam cocked her head as if trying to understand my question, while Lizzie just wagged her tail eagerly, hoping for another slice.

I have a lot to figure out—our finances, how to tell our families, and what to do about the upcoming holidays. As I thought about it all, my neck knotted.

I also made a mental note to see my doctor and get tested for any sexually transmitted diseases. Women who were looking for sex in a chat room may not have been very discriminating or have taken any precautions. And I doubted that Finn had, either.

Thanks, Finn, you selfish jerk! What other issues am I going to have to deal with because of your recklessness?

I could hear Finn stomping back and forth upstairs, opening and closing drawers. When he finally came downstairs, he asked, "Can we talk?"

I wasn't sure I was ready to hear more, but I grudgingly agreed.

I was leaning against the kitchen counter, eating my sandwich, while Lizzie and Sam sat in front of me, waiting for handouts. I set the sandwich on my plate and took a swig of my diet soda.

Finn grabbed a beer from the refrigerator, opened it, and took a swig. Then he stood leaning on the opposite counter. The kitchen was small, so he was only a couple of feet away.

"This is hard for me, too!" he began.

I clenched my fists, fighting the urge to lash out at him physically and verbally. But I said nothing, waiting to hear what else he had to say.

"I have known for a long time that something was wrong with me, but I didn't know what it was. And with so much pressure on me to finish my degree, it became too much to handle. I guess I was looking for some kind of escape from it all." He was looking down at his hands, and I was unsure whether what he was saying was the truth or another fabrication.

"How long have you felt like something was wrong with you?" I asked, trying to keep my hurt, anger, and distrust at bay.

"Since I was in high school or college, I guess," he said sullenly.

"That's a long time," I replied, feeling some empathy for him.

"Yeah, like half of my life," Finn agreed.

"But if you knew something was wrong, why didn't you talk to someone? Why didn't you talk to me?" I asked.

"I didn't know how to talk about it. I was afraid to tell anyone. Especially you, Kass," he said, taking a step toward me.

I put up my hand in front of me to stop him from coming closer.

"I feel bad for you, Finn, I really do. But you also made choices. Terrible choices. If you had only talked to me sooner, maybe we could have gotten you help before all this happened. But you didn't. And now we're stuck dealing with the aftermath."

"I'm sorry, Kass! But I didn't mean to hurt you. Those other women didn't mean anything to me. It was just an escape from what I was feeling," Finn replied.

"But you did hurt me, Finn," I said, fighting back tears.

"But it wasn't me. I was sick!" Finn insisted.

And there it was. More denial that he had any responsibility! Did he actually believe I'd keep falling for this routine?

"But you were the one who made the choices, Finn."

I set my plate in the sink, grabbed my soda, and walked away, Lizzie and Sam on my heels.

"Where do we go from here, Kass?" he called after me.

"I don't know, Finn. I really don't."

CHAPTER 11

RED FLAGS

After confronting Finn, I felt hollowed out. There was too much to process alone, so I called Dianne.

"So, did you talk with Finn?" she asked once we were seated.

"Yes," I said. The word felt heavy. "He admitted he'd slept with other women."

Even saying it aloud made my stomach turn.

I told her I had asked whether any of them were underage. He had grown defensive but insisted they were all adults. I wanted to believe him. But after so many lies, belief felt naïve.

"I don't know how I could ever trust him again," I admitted.

Dianne nodded approvingly. For the first time in days, I felt something other than shame. I felt strength. A fragile sense of control.

I explained that Finn had been upset, but then oddly calm. He said he'd known something was wrong with him for years. "He apologizes," I told Dianne, "and then immediately explains it away."

She studied me. "Did you ever see warning signs before this?"

A memory surfaced.

Shortly before our wedding, Finn had shown up drunk at my apartment after a night out with friends. I drove him home, and in the car, he'd kept asking why I loved him. At the time, I chalked it up to alcohol. Now, replaying it, I wondered if it had been something else—an insecurity, a crack in the confidence I thought defined him.

"Was that a red flag?" I asked quietly. "Were there others I just didn't see?"

Dianne didn't answer right away. She simply let the question hang between us.

"You are seeing things from a much different perspective now, Kassidy, and you shouldn't second-guess yourself," Dianne replied. "Now that you have that perspective, were there any other incidents you remember that were out of the ordinary? Any time that Finn's behavior resembled the manic-depressive episodes that he told us his brother had?"

Hayden's meltdown in the restaurant was indeed a manic episode.

"Once, when we were living in our first apartment in Austin, we argued. I don't recall what we were fighting about; it was probably money, if I had to guess. We were getting in the car to go to dinner. I was going to drive, and he refused to get in the car," I told Dianne.

"What did you do?" she asked.

"I got out of the car to talk to him with my keys in my hand. He grabbed the keys from me and threw them into the bushes on the other side of the parking lot. I stood there thinking how irrational he was acting."

"Throwing the keys in the bushes certainly is irrational," Dianne agreed. "What did you do?"

"Finn didn't have his keys, so we were locked out of our apartment. We had no choice but to look for the keys in the bushes. It was getting dark, and it took us about forty-five minutes to find the keys. He was highly agitated the whole time."

"What was he doing to appear agitated to you?" Dianne asked, tilting her head slightly as she listened to my response.

"He wasn't just mad at me about the fight or at himself for throwing the keys; he had a bit of a meltdown. He was talking loudly and breaking the branches of the bushes, which was unnecessary. I asked him several times to keep his voice down and stop damaging the bushes, but that just seemed to spur him on, so I stopped. Then, a neighbor we didn't know walked by and asked if we needed help. Finn snapped at him and told him to leave us alone. The guy asked me if everything was okay, and I just told him we were looking for our keys. The guy just nodded and left us alone, not wanting to get involved in whatever was happening between us."

"It does sound like a manic episode," Dianne suggested.

"Thinking back on that now, it was similar to the scene with Hayden in the restaurant. Finn's actions were completely unreasonable! At the time, I just thought it was his anger that made him respond so out of character," I replied.

I didn't have another frame of reference for Finn's behavior until now. Suddenly, the pieces were starting to fit.

"Were there any other incidents like the one with the keys?" Dianne asked.

"No, I don't remember him having any other meltdowns. There were a few times when I thought he might have been depressed when he was working on his master's thesis. He would get moody and not want to talk. He would stay up all night and then sleep the next day. He even missed classes a couple of times, which was out of character. I just thought it was the stress of working on his thesis. It never seemed to last long and did not seem very much out of the ordinary since he was working so hard," I recalled.

"Well, yes, I suppose it might seem normal for someone under stress to exhibit some of those behaviors. To some degree, we've probably all experienced that ourselves," Dianne offered. "But Finn may have been experiencing something much deeper. I suspect if he had feelings that something was wrong since high school, he had probably gotten pretty good at hiding much of what was going on inside."

"There is something else that has been bothering me. Finn did a season of fieldwork in Antarctica for his dissertation. All team members, including Finn, had to undergo a psychological evaluation to ensure they could handle the isolation and extreme conditions in Antarctica. But he passed it without raising any red flags. Why didn't they pick up on his bipolar disorder then?" I asked.

"It could depend on how rigorous the evaluation was and how much time they spent talking with him," she replied.

"I know the evaluation for the summer season is not as rigorous as the evaluation they do for people who winter over at a base in Antarctica. We had friends at Ohio State who did that," I recalled.

"But still, if a trained professional didn't pick up on it, how could I know there was a problem?" I queried. I had been feeling guilty about not being aware of or seeing the signs. But maybe it wasn't that simple.

"Perhaps Finn's bipolar disorder made him well-suited for the isolation," Dianne suggested. "Or he just hid it well."

Although he could behave normally when it suited him, Finn, I was realizing, was a very good hider. He used his charm to obscure the truth.

"Is there anything else out of the ordinary that you remember?" Dianne asked. Each time she asked, it seemed to spark a new revelation. The floodgates had suddenly opened.

"When I traveled for work, I was only home on the weekends, and things mostly seemed normal then. But I recalled a few times when I noticed items were missing. Sometimes, it was various pieces of clothing that I couldn't find. I assumed maybe Finn had gotten rid of things of mine he didn't like. It had happened before.

Once, he and his mother redecorated while she was visiting, and I was at work. They hadn't asked me or told me they planned on doing it. They had thrown out a gift that a family friend and neighbor had given me. It was a lace doily that she had crocheted and framed. It was not our style, but it had sentimental value. His mother thought I was crazy when I went to the dumpster to retrieve it. Thankfully, it was there and undamaged. I was angry that they had thrown out something that meant so much to me. But the fact that they thought it was right to redecorate my home without involving me was also infuriating! I was livid, and they didn't seem to care.

Finn had also sold all my albums and some of my books to a used bookstore without consulting me. He said we didn't need the albums because we had CDs, and he didn't think I needed the books, either. But it was my stuff!"

I was beginning to see a pattern. Finn ignored my feelings and did what served his interests. Why hadn't I noticed this before?

But besides the clothes, there were miscellaneous pieces of inexpensive jewelry that I could no longer find. Finn told me I had probably misplaced them, but I knew I hadn't.

Once, it was a kitchen knife. I asked Finn if he knew where the missing knife was, and he said it was probably just in another drawer. I searched the entire kitchen and never found the knife. I thought we had accidentally put it in the kitchen trash with potato or cucumber peels and didn't think about it further at the time.

But now I wondered if he had invited some of the women he met online back to our home at some point. Did he give them the cheap jewelry as a token of affection? Perhaps they needed a clean t-shirt to wear home? Or one of them took the knife, thinking she might require it for protection. I shuddered at that thought. At this point, I had no idea what Finn was capable of.

I didn't know what Finn had been up to while I was gone. And I had never suspected anything before. I had trusted my husband.

But now that trust was broken, shattered by his lies and crimes.

Those incidents may not have been a sign of his bipolar disorder, but they were signs that something had been wrong. Finn would work his charm and make it very easy to believe his excuses. Now, I felt like I should have seen all the red flags.

I was furious at Finn! I trusted him, and he used that trust against me. I felt so stupid.

"How did I miss so many red flags?" I asked Dianne.

Dianne paused and then said, "Let's talk about that. Why do you think you should have seen the red flags? Why do you think that you should have known that he had issues? He took deliberate steps to hide it from you."

Dianne waited for me to respond.

"Yes, I get that, but I feel like there should have been something that I should have noticed. Finn is my husband," I said. "He is the person I should have known almost as well as I know myself. We shared our lives and our home. I trusted that my husband was doing what he should have been. And that he was being honest and faithful to me."

Dianne looked at me with a sympathetic smile and said, "Trust is expected between husband and wife. You've done nothing wrong. You simply put your trust in someone who didn't deserve it."

I still didn't feel good about it. I felt guilty for not being able to stop Finn from hurting the child. By blindly trusting Finn, I believed I had a part in putting her at risk.

"But maybe if I had just recognized what was going on, I could have stopped Finn and gotten him help, and maybe things would have turned out differently. I feel like it's my fault for not knowing and not being able to stop it!" I sobbed.

"Kassidy, you cannot blame yourself for Finn's actions or for being unable to stop them! He intentionally deceived you. And when you did question things, he was always ready with a plausible answer. This is not your fault. You are taking on all the responsibility and shouldering the burden of what Finn did. Finn should be the one owning this responsibility, but he hasn't expressed any remorse for what he's done. Don't take that on for him, Kassidy."

I began sobbing.

Dianne had moved from her usual spot in her chair to sit next to me on the couch. She put her arms around me in a warm embrace and tried to console me.

"It's okay, Kassidy! Let it all out! You're going to be okay," she soothed.

We sat that way for a few minutes while Dianne let me sob until I had nothing left. Then she let go of me and handed me the box of tissues. I noticed her eyes were wet with tears, and her mascara was a bit smudged.

I grabbed a few tissues from the box and said, "You should save a few for yourself!"

We laughed at that as we dabbed our eyes and blew our noses. I was amazed that Dianne was always right there with me, no matter what I threw at her.

I was so used to Finn blaming me that I was overwhelmed to find kindness in this woman I barely knew.

Once we had composed ourselves, Dianne pointed out something I had not realized.

"Kassidy, you are currently responsible for everything. His feelings, your finances, the fallout from his actions...Do you see a pattern?" Dianne asked.

"Wow! I never saw it that way before! I always thought of Finn and me as partners. But he has gone from letting his parents take care of everything to letting me take care of everything for him!" I exclaimed as I started to see it all in a new light.

"I understand wanting to control your financial situation and whatever affects your well-being regarding the situation Finn has created. But you need to let Finn handle his mess. It is his mess, not yours," she told me.

"But I worry that he won't handle it," I replied.

"That is his problem, not yours, Kassidy," Dianne said firmly.

I nodded in response. "But I can do whatever I need to do to protect my interests?" I asked.

"Absolutely!" Dianne replied.

I leaned back on the couch and let that sink in. Leaving Finn to his own devices still worried me. But he needed to take responsibility, and I realized he would not do that if I kept doing it for him.

"Have you told your families yet?" Dianne continued.

"No, we haven't," I admitted reluctantly.

"Thanksgiving is just a few weeks away! Aren't you planning on spending it with your family? And Christmas with Finn's?" Dianne asked.

"Yes! And I have pleaded with Finn that we need to tell them before we visit, but he hasn't agreed yet," I replied.

"If he won't tell them, will you tell them or at least tell your own family?" she asked.

"No! He did this! He needs to be the one to tell them. He has to face what he did!" I replied a bit more angrily than I had intended.

Dianne didn't flinch at my response and posed another question, "You don't trust Finn to do the right thing, and you don't trust him to take responsibility or action in resolving the situation. Why are you trusting him to tell his family and waiting on him before you tell yours?"

I pondered that question for a moment, trying to find the words to explain what I felt to Dianne. Dianne patiently waited for me to respond.

"You're right, Dianne. But if I tell my parents before he tells his, then I will be taking responsibility for that, too. I need him to do this one thing. I need him to take this step. I need him to start taking responsibility so that I know he is capable of taking care of himself despite his illness. I need that to be able to move on without regrets."

"By moving on, do you mean leaving him?" Dianne asked.

I nodded in agreement, unable to speak the words out loud.

"It's okay, Kassidy. You will know when you are ready to make that decision. But please understand that Finn may not take that step. You will have to make that decision based on what is best for you and not how it will affect Finn," she said.

"I know," I responded, my voice barely a whisper.

Dianne got up, poured a glass of water from a pitcher on the credenza, and then handed it to me as she returned to her seat.

She asked, "When you tell your family about Finn's arrest, how do you think they will react?"

I hesitated before answering. "They will be upset. And very disappointed in Finn," I stated.

"But do you think they will be supportive?" she asked.

"Of me? Yes, they will be very supportive, even trying to fix things for me. But I need to show them I have things under control and can handle this on my own. I don't want to pull them into Finn's mess, too. I need to have a plan before I tell them, and I don't have that yet," I replied.

"I can understand that. But don't you think they would want to know before you and Finn visit?" Dianne probed.

"Yes, of course! And I hate not being honest with them about this. But I just don't know how I can tell them this. I'm so..." My voice trailed off as I struggled to finish the sentence.

Dianne waited while I pulled myself together and took another deep breath. "You are so what?" she asked softly.

"Ashamed!" I exclaimed. My stomach was knotted, and my shoulders drooped.

Dianne pulled a few tissues from the box and handed them to me. "It's okay. Let it all out," she whispered.

After letting me sob again for a few minutes, Dianne asked softly, "Why are you ashamed?"

I looked at Dianne, and with tears dripping on my quivering chin, I voiced my deepest fears. "Because my marriage is failing. Because I didn't know what my husband was doing. Because Finn cheated on me and is a pedophile, and I didn't know! Because I brought this pedophile into our family! How do I explain that to my parents?"

I began in a hoarse whisper, but now I was hysterical and yelling. Not at Dianne - at myself. How was it that I did not know? I was angry and disappointed in myself for not being aware. And I expected that everyone else would feel the same way. I was afraid people would judge me, as I was already judging myself. Finn had committed this horrible crime, but I thought that it was also a reflection on me. What if people thought I was involved or thought I knew, but had turned a blind eye? What if they held me responsible for not knowing? I was devastated.

And then Dianne said something I will never forget, "You are not responsible for what Finn did. None of us is responsible for anyone else's actions. We are only responsible for our own actions."

She let me sit with that for a minute. My shoulders relaxed, and I breathed in deeply.

I am not responsible. I repeated the words in my head. The words felt both soothing and false. I understood, but I still couldn't help feeling guilty about not knowing. An innocent girl could have gotten hurt. And my life had been shattered in an instant. I wasn't sure that I would ever be able to let go of the shame I felt, and I shared that with Dianne. And, of course, I was crying; I could barely walk into her office without grabbing tissues.

Dianne smiled warmly, leaned toward me, and said softly, "It may take time, but you will get there. And it will get easier once you tell your family and have their support."

I nodded in agreement, even though I didn't fully believe it. Even though I knew my family would support me, I still had a lot of guilt to work through. I still felt shame for trusting Finn and not seeing who he really was. Dianne was right; it would take time.

Our session was almost over, and I had another topic I needed to discuss with her. "I made an appointment to see my doctor. I want to know if I was exposed to anything through Finn's infidelities. I will probably have to tell her what happened so she can do any necessary tests. I'm dreading this, but I need to know."

Dianne smiled and said, "I know it will be hard talking to yet another person about what you're dealing with. But this is a good thing. You are moving forward and taking steps to take care of yourself. Your doctor is a professional, and she will understand. And remember what I told you. It is not a reflection on you. You are not responsible for Finn's actions."

I left Dianne's office anxious about my doctor's appointment the next day. Fortunately, I did not have to stress about it for very long.

As she always did, my doctor took a few minutes at the beginning of the appointment to discuss how I was doing and whether I had any issues. I told her that I was not having any physical issues.

But I blurted out, "I want you to test me for every sexually transmitted disease possible!"

She looked up from her notes with a look of concern and rolled her chair closer to me.

"Did something happen to make you think that you might have been exposed to something?" she asked solemnly, looking at me very directly and searching for any signs of trauma.

I hesitated before responding, which made her more concerned. "It's okay," she said, "You can tell me. I'm here to help you."

I realized then that she must have been thinking I had been sexually assaulted.

"I'm okay. I wasn't raped or anything like that. I just found out that my husband has been meeting women in online chat rooms and having sex with them! I have no idea who these women are or if they used protection. I just need to know if I have been exposed to anything!" I explained.

I saw her body relax, and she patted my arm comfortingly.

"I'm sorry that this is happening to you. I hear this sort of thing all the time. And you are not the first wife who has told me that her husband was using the internet to cheat. I'm hearing that more often now. And you're right to have concerns. We'll run a full panel of tests, and we can code it so that the insurance company will cover it all since it is not the normal panel of tests we run for a routine exam."

She asked me a few more routine questions about my general health, then conducted the exam.

When she finished, she told me, "It will take several days to get the results. Whatever they are, I'll call you personally to discuss everything. Even if everything is good, you may have additional questions."

I left the exam feeling better but still worried about what the results might reveal. The wait was going to be torturous, but I was taking care of myself for a change, and that felt powerful.

CHAPTER 12

LIVING WITH BIPOLAR

Another week passed, and Finn was still living in my home until I could figure out how to extricate myself from the marriage with the least amount of financial devastation. I had worked too hard to build stability for myself. I would not allow what Finn had done to destroy everything.

If being under stress had triggered his behavior before, then the stress of his legal circumstances, our failing marriage, and losing his career could provoke him even more. As long as he lived under my roof, I wanted to know what to look out for and how to handle it if something triggered him. What were the warning signs? What could set him off? And how was I supposed to respond if it did?

At our previous session, Dianne had handed me several pamphlets and written down the names of a few reputable websites about bipolar disorder. "Educating yourself may help you feel less powerless," she had said.

So I read.

I read while waiting for the results of my sexually transmitted disease tests. I read late at night when sleep wouldn't come. The clinical language—mania, impulsivity, grandiosity, hypersexuality—felt sterile compared to the chaos in my home. Still, knowledge gave my anxious mind something solid to grip while everything else felt uncertain.

By the time I returned to Dianne's office, I had pages of notes and even more questions.

She greeted me with her usual warmth. "How are you doing, Kassidy? Did you get your test results back?" she asked.

"No, not yet. The waiting is excruciating!" I admitted. "I've been trying to distract myself by learning more about bipolar disorder. I want to understand Finn—what's illness and what's choice."

Dianne nodded slowly. "That's an important distinction. Bipolar disorder can influence behavior, but it doesn't remove responsibility. You may never know why Finn did what he did, Kassidy. But I do think it is good that you are learning about bipolar disorder. It may help you to deal with Finn and his situation as you go forward," she said.

"Beyond a definition and some information on addiction, I didn't find much else that was useful. Can you help me understand what behaviors I should look for in Finn to know if he might be heading for another episode?" I asked.

"Bipolar disorder can be different for each person who experiences it," Dianne began. "The best way for me to help you with regard to Finn is to talk through some of the behaviors that Finn has already exhibited. Hopefully, we can identify some patterns or flags you can recognize when they occur."

"But I missed all the signs in the past!" I groaned.

"Perhaps. But Finn hid what he was feeling, and you also didn't have the insight then that Finn is bipolar. We have that perspective now, and together, we may be able to reveal some of those indicative behaviors," Dianne said calmly.

Dianne let the silence stretch for a moment.

"You said you have a working definition of bipolar disorder," she said gently. "Tell me what you understand so far."

I shifted in my seat. "From what I read, there are two main states— manic and depressive. Depressive is low energy, sadness…shutting down. Manic is the opposite—wired, agitated, too much energy."

"That's a solid starting point," she said. "Do you remember any times when Finn may have been depressed?"

I had to think about that. Finn wasn't what I would call a gloomy person. He was usually upbeat, charming, and social.

"As we discussed before, when we were first married," I said slowly, "while he was working on his master's at George Washington University, there were periods when he seemed off. Not himself."

"Let's look into that a bit deeper. What did that look like?"

"He'd get discouraged about his writing. If his research stalled, he'd spiral. He'd stay up most of the night working, then sleep half the next day. He even missed a few classes, which wasn't like him."

"How long would it last?"

"A day or two. Maybe three at most."

Dianne nodded. "Did you ever talk with him about it?"

"Once," I said. "I suggested he try sleeping, going to class, maybe talking to his advisor instead of pushing through exhaustion." I gave a small, humorless laugh. "He didn't take that well. Said he had it under control. That I didn't need to worry."

"And you dropped it."

"I did."

Dianne leaned back slightly. "You also mentioned he was staying up late working on his dissertation before his arrest. That could be part of a pattern."

I felt a chill at that word. Pattern.

"Most people think bipolar disorder is just highs and lows," she continued. "But sometimes those states overlap."

"Overlap?" I frowned. "I didn't see that in what I read."

"It's called a mixed episode," she explained. "Someone can feel agitated and energized while also feeling distressed or pressured. It can be volatile."

I sat very still.

"So he could have been overwhelmed by his dissertation," she went on, "and at the same time riding the stimulation of those online interactions. The high may have temporarily relieved the stress."

Relief.

"That makes sense," I said quietly.

But what I didn't say was this: it might explain the intensity… but it didn't erase the choice.

"What other behaviors have you noticed?" Dianne asked.

"He is definitely more moody since the arrest. I guess he feels less compelled to hide his feelings now. He is also watching a lot more television. I don't know if that is because he's depressed about facing a prison term or if it's because he doesn't have much else to do now. It feels more like he is bored than depressed," I told her.

"Boredom can trigger depression, especially in someone who has lost their purpose," she replied.

"Finn destroyed his career, so that fits," I agreed.

"Do you remember any episodes that fit the manic description?" Dianne inquired.

"Yes!" I exclaimed as another memory surfaced, sharp and sudden. "When Lizzie was just a puppy, we were outside our townhouse playing in the grass. Out of nowhere, Finn dropped to a crouch and roared at her—like some kind of wild animal."

I could still see it.

"It startled her so badly she bolted down the driveway and straight into the street. A car was coming. I remember screaming and running after her. Finn just stood there… laughing."

My throat tightened.

"I caught her before she reached the middle of the road. She was trembling in my arms, her little heart pounding against my chest. I asked him why he would do something like that. He said he didn't know. That it just seemed fun at the time."

Even now, saying it out loud, it sounded unreal.

"That does sound like it could have been another manic episode," Dianne agreed. "As time goes by, other memories may surface for you. I suggest you jot them down in a notebook so that we can discuss them. If you decide to stay with Finn, the more situations we can identify, the better we can prepare you to recognize when he might be headed for an episode."

If I decide to stay with him, my brain echoed. *Was staying with him even possible?* I didn't say it out loud. I wasn't ready.

"You mentioned reading about addiction, but you also said that you didn't think that fit Finn. I'd like to explore that a little more," Dianne continued.

"Yes, what I read was that the most common was to use alcohol or drugs to numb themselves. Finn regularly had a beer or a glass of wine but rarely drank too much."

"You don't recall any other times that he might have abused drugs or alcohol?" Dianne asked.

"Oh! I almost forgot!" I cried. "He had a DUI before we met. That was another thing he neglected to tell me before we were married. I found out when we first got car insurance together. It came up when the insurance company checked our driving records. I was furious and asked Finn why he hadn't told me about it. He claimed he thought it had been expunged from his record since it happened in high school. Of course, it caused our insurance rates to be higher than they should have been," I revealed. "I can't believe I forgot about that!"

"Given everything that's happened, it makes sense that some things didn't register at the time," Dianne said gently. "And remember, addiction isn't limited to drugs or alcohol."

I looked up at her.

"There are behavioral addictions too—gambling, compulsive spending, excessive exercise, food, sex." She paused. "From what you've described, we can probably set a few of those aside."

I felt my stomach tighten before she even said the words.

"But I'd like us to take a closer look at two possibilities," she continued carefully. "Sex… and shopping."

The word sex seemed to hang in the air between us.

"What Finn did—meeting women online and especially the interaction with the young girl—was a complete shock to me!" I said, hearing the strain in my own voice. "It wasn't who I thought he was. It didn't fit."

Dianne held my gaze. "I know, Kassidy. But you said that he had been chatting online and meeting other women for sex for as long as two years."

Two years. The number landed heavily.

"When a pattern continues that long," she continued gently, "we have to consider the possibility of compulsive behavior. Sex addiction is one explanation."

The words made my chest tighten.

I stared at the carpet, trying to steady my breathing. Addiction. It sounded clinical. Almost… distant.

"It doesn't excuse what he did," I said finally. "It doesn't make it hurt less."

"No," she agreed quietly.

"But…" I swallowed. "If it's an addiction… then at least there's a framework. It makes the escalation make more sense."

And somehow, that was both relieving and devastating.

"I'm sorry, Kassidy," Dianne said gently. "I know how painful this is. But the more clearly you see the full picture, the more empowered you'll be to decide what comes next."

I nodded, even though I wasn't sure I felt empowered yet.

"There's another area we should look at," she continued carefully. "You've mentioned that Finn's spending could be excessive at times. Can you think of specific moments that stand out?"

I didn't have to search long.

"There was this one time at Dillard's," I said slowly, the memory sharpening as I spoke, and told her the story.

We were shopping together, and I saw him heading toward the checkout counter with three shirts draped over his arm.

I almost laughed at the absurdity of it.

They weren't similar. They weren't different colors. They were identical. Same brand. Same size. Same color. I stopped him before he could get in line.

I could still hear my own voice echoing in the department store. 'Finn, what are you doing? Are you really going to buy all three of those?'

"Yes! I like this shirt a lot! Don't you like it?" Finn asked in reply.

"Well, yes, I like the shirt. But I don't think you need three of them!" I told him.

"Of course I do! I really like the shirt, and if I have three, I will always have a clean one and can wear it more often."

"You could just wash the one," I said, trying to keep my tone even.

"But one shirt will wear out more quickly than three!"

"You already have shirts like this," I reminded him. "They're holding up just fine. And by the time it wears out, you probably won't even want it anymore.".

"But what if I do?" he pressed. "What if it wears out and I can't find it again?"

His voice was getting louder. I became aware of people nearby pretending not to listen.

"Finn," I said quietly, heat creeping up my neck, "we can't afford three identical shirts. And they're not giving you a bulk discount."

"I'm getting all three shirts!" Finn declared, like a petulant child.

"Please," I said, lowering my voice. "Just get one. If the first shirt wears out, you can get another one."

For a long moment, he stood there, jaw tight. I couldn't tell if he was reconsidering or simply calculating whether the fight was worth it. Finally, he shoved two shirts back onto the rack and marched to the register with the third.

He wore the shirt a few times over the next couple of weeks, and then it hung untouched in the closet. It turned out that he didn't like it as much as he thought.

"I'm starting to see something," I said to Dianne slowly. "It wasn't really about the shirts, was it? It was the rush. The moment of deciding. The thrill of getting them."

Dianne nodded. "That's often how compulsive shopping works. The high comes from the anticipation and the purchase—not from owning the item."

"That makes sense," I said, thinking about the closet full of barely worn clothes. "He'd light up in the store. But once we got home, the excitement drained away." I hesitated before adding, "Finn's family members are also big shoppers, so I thought this was learned behavior."

"And it might have been, but then reinforced with a need to self-medicate with shopping, it was a disaster waiting to happen," Dianne confirmed.

"And that disaster helped to contribute to our dismal financial situation," I said glumly.

The more I sat with it, the more other moments began to surface—purchases that had felt excessive at the time but that I had brushed aside.

There was another time, too, when Finn's mania frothed around a fancy new blender that was supposed to be the best. We had a perfectly good blender that we had gotten as a wedding gift. It was nearly new because we only used it twice a year. But Finn insisted we needed this new blender.

"But why would we get a new fancier blender when we don't even use the one we have?" I asked.

"Because it has so many new features! Maybe we would use a blender if it had more features!" Finn suggested brightly.

"What do you think we would use it for? Is it going to solve an issue we have now because we don't have the fancy new blender?" I asked.

Finn had to think about that one. His counterpoint was weak. "I don't know how I would use it because I don't have it yet!" he proclaimed.

That made me laugh! Ultimately, he realized he didn't need the fancy new blender. But we had these types of nonsensical arguments regularly. It was exhausting.

Although I could usually talk him out of something when he included me in the decision, it did not stop him from making purchases I didn't know about. He would go shopping without me frequently while I was at work and sneak the items into the house so I would not see what he bought. Then, he'd wear the new shirt or pull out the gadget in the kitchen at some later date. When I asked him about the items, he would casually tell me that he had just happened to be out shopping the other day and had picked them up. Or worse, since I paid the bills (at least the ones I knew about), I'd see it on the monthly credit card statement before he pulled the item out to use. Either way, we would end up fighting about money. It was a never-ending cycle.

It angered me that he would act behind my back and against my wishes. He was acting alone and not treating me like a partner in those decisions. He forced me to be the gatekeeper. Our finances were tight from the beginning, and we needed to work together to keep our heads above water, but he continually undermined that.

But now it made more sense why he wouldn't stop spending, even when I begged him to. He was acting on compulsion. I was fighting an unseen force.

After sharing all of this with Dianne, there was still a question that we hadn't addressed. "It's still hard for me to comprehend how Finn could have gone to meet a child whom he knew was underage to have sex with her. I still find that part so disturbing and incomprehensible. It's the one thing that I'm not sure I will ever understand or forgive Finn for," I divulged to Dianne.

I didn't want to dig deeper into the subject of pedophiles, but I knew that I had to.

"That is understandable," Dianne replied. "This is difficult to unravel, but we should discuss it. Most adults who molest or sexually abuse children were victims of sexual abuse themselves. Most are abused by someone they know and trust rather than a stranger. Most will also abuse a child who knows and trusts them."

Those words hit me hard. We did not have many children in our lives then, and none were physically near us. For that, I was grateful. I had so much guilt as it was, knowing he had attempted but mercifully had not succeeded in harming the girl he had met on the internet. But had he ever hurt another child? That I did not know.

Finn had never mentioned anything about having been sexually abused as a child. If most abusers came from abuse, was Finn hiding something else from me? Finn told me about his friend Gene. They grew up together. He had been arrested for sexually abusing his girlfriend's two young daughters, and it had really upset Finn. What if Gene and Finn had been abused by an adult in their lives? Their childhood overlapped at school and church. It wasn't unrealistic to think that an abuser could have harmed them both.

A few days after my discussion with Dianne, I decided to talk to Finn about it when we were both in the kitchen making our separate dinners.

"I've been doing some reading on bipolar disorder," I began.

"Why? I don't have a problem anymore! I'm going to counseling!" Finn reacted.

I was surprised at his immediate defensiveness, but continued. "One of the things that I read about is that people who sexually abuse children were often victims themselves. Did anything like that happen to you as a child?"

"No! Why would you even ask that? And I didn't sexually abuse a child!" he yelled angrily.

"You got caught before you could physically harm her. But don't you think that your interactions with her online were harmful? Talking to a child about sex? Sending her sexually explicit photos? Your intent was clear."

"But I didn't sexually abuse a child. And nothing like that ever happened to me." Finn insisted.

"I was just thinking that maybe something had happened. Remember what Gene did? It just occurred to me that you both might have been victims," I replied.

"How could you think that I was anything like Gene? No! Nothing like that ever happened to me!" Finn shouted defiantly.

"But if it did, you should talk to Robert about it," I replied, hoping that if he had been sexually abused as a child, he would at least discuss it in counseling.

"There is nothing like that I need to talk to Robert or anyone else about! Just drop it, Kassidy!" Finn shouted as he stormed out of the room.

If Finn had been molested as a child, he was clearly not ready to deal with it. I'd leave that to his counselor to unravel. But that didn't stop my thoughts from spinning as I finished preparing my meal.

I was starting to understand why he felt relieved at getting caught. It prevented him from carrying out his intentions, and he must not have been certain he could stop himself. That thought made me shudder.

CHAPTER 13

MY SECRETS

The next day, my doctor finally called with my lab results, apologizing for the delay before telling me everything had come back clear—no signs of any sexually transmitted diseases. Relief flooded through me so suddenly that I could feel the knots in my neck and stomach loosen. She offered information for a support group for women with unfaithful husbands, which I accepted just in case, though I told her I was already in counseling. After I hung up, I sat quietly for a moment. I was physically healthy. But there were still enormous emotional hurdles ahead.

My next session with Dianne was scheduled for less than two weeks before Thanksgiving, when I was visiting my family in Ohio. I felt apprehensive—not just about the trip, but about what I knew she would ask.

After we settled in, I told her the good news about my test results. She shared my relief, and for a brief moment, that weight lifted.

Then she gently shifted the conversation. "Have you told your families about Finn's arrest?"

I exhaled slowly. "No. Finn hasn't spoken to his parents, and I haven't told mine. It's only been a month. Nothing new has happened with his case. I'm just trying to regain my footing before the next wave hits."

"I understand," she said. "But what's really holding you back?"

I hesitated. "They'll want to rescue me. And before I tell them, I need a plan. I need to show them I can handle this. I brought Finn into our family. I brought this mess. I feel like I should be the one to fix it."

Even as I said it, I wasn't sure whether I sounded strong... or stubborn.

"Thanksgiving is only a couple of weeks away. Are you still planning on visiting your family?" Dianne queried.

"Yes, we are," I replied.

"We? You're still planning on taking Finn with you?" Dianne asked in a surprised tone.

"Yes, I thought about each of us visiting our own families alone, but that would raise many questions that neither of us is ready to answer," I told her. "And there is also the question of what Finn might do if left alone. We no longer have a computer, so he can't go online. But I'm afraid that he might be more motivated to act on his impulses without the ability to interact through the computer. I need to keep an eye on him."

"It's not your responsibility to keep an eye on him, Kassidy. But I do understand your concerns," Dianne replied.

"I know it's not my responsibility. But if he gets into more trouble, it will make things worse for me, too," I confided.

"With money and vacation time being tight, how can you afford two trips?" Dianne asked.

It was a valid question.

"I had airline miles built up from traveling for work, so the flight for Thanksgiving was covered. But that used up all my miles, so we will be driving at Christmas and sharing part of the trip with Finn's oldest brother, Jack, and his wife, Simone. I have been saving vacation time, but these trips will exhaust that. I won't accrue more until my work anniversary next year. We will be staying with family, so we won't have any hotel costs, either. So our costs for the trips will be minimal," I explained.

"Is Finn even allowed to travel to another state since he's been convicted of a felony?" Dianne asked.

"Yes, but he had to get special permission from the court. Thankfully, Jordan was able to handle that. If he hadn't been able to travel, that would have raised questions with our families," I told her.

"That might not have been a bad thing. It would have forced the issue of telling your families," Dianne pointed out.

"I know. And I hate keeping this secret from my family. But I'm just not ready to tell them," I moaned.

"Didn't you tell me that your sister has young children? Are you concerned about Finn being around them?" Dianne asked.

"Yes, my niece is 6, and my nephew is 4. But we only see them once a year since we live far away. They don't know us very well, so my sister or her husband or my parents are usually with us, so that the kids are more comfortable spending time with us. My sister even shows them pictures of us before we get together, to spark their memories. And I would never let my niece and nephew be in any danger or leave them alone with Finn!" I declared.

"Would you consider talking to your family if an opportunity arises while you're there? You may feel differently once you see your family," Dianne suggested.

"Maybe," I replied, although my voice lacked any confidence. I just couldn't picture how I could tell them. It was enough for me to deal with Finn's transgressions. Telling them and dealing with their shock, hurt, and anger felt like more than I could handle.

"And you are sure you want to go with Finn to visit his family at Christmas?" Dianne continued.

"Yes. I don't think I can convince Finn to tell his family before then. But his oldest brother, Jack, is a psychologist. I'm hoping Finn will feel comfortable talking to Jack about what happened. And maybe Jack could help Finn tell the rest of the family."

"That would be good for Finn and for you. But what if you can't convince Finn to tell Jack? Will you tell Jack?" Dianne pressed.

"As much as I want Finn to start taking responsibility for his actions, keeping his secret is eating me up. If he won't tell Jack, I will,"

I declared. And although I dreaded it, I knew I would have to do it if Finn didn't.

"I'm glad to hear that, Kassidy!" Dianne said, smiling warmly. "Even though it will be hard, it will feel good to unload that burden."

What I wasn't quite ready to share with Dianne was that I also sensed this would be the last time I would see Finn's family, or at least spend a holiday with them. Finn and I were no longer a couple, and I knew there was no going back. I wasn't ready to pull the trigger for financial reasons, but I knew that divorce was inevitable. It made me sad to think it would be my last Christmas with his family. I had always enjoyed their big family gatherings.

Finn was the youngest of five, and when they all got together - his parents, siblings, spouses, and grandkids- there were fourteen of us. My family was much smaller, and there always seemed to be more energy around Finn's family holidays. And his mother, Myra, always made a big deal of having everyone together.

Myra's mother had died suddenly when she was a child, scattering her and her two younger siblings among relatives. Because of that loss, family meant everything to her. She wanted her children close—physically and emotionally—and it pained her that Finn, his older brother Jack, and his sister Joy had all settled in different states. She worked tirelessly to gather everyone for Thanksgiving, Christmas, and a summer vacation each year, though competing in-law schedules made that increasingly difficult. This Christmas would be the first time in several years that we would all be together.

My emotions were a tangled knot about spending Christmas with Finn's family. I was glad to be spending time with everyone. They were my family, too. But I was guilt-ridden, because I knew their world was going to be turned upside once Finn's secret was out. I knew what it felt like, and I wished they didn't have to experience that pain. But there was nothing I could do to prevent it, and I knew that Dianne was right that prolonging it was not going to help anyone. But I didn't want to be the one to tell them about what Finn had done. It had to come from Finn. I hoped Finn would confess to Jack, so I wouldn't have to be the one to break the awful news.

Either way, Jack was going to be told by the end of our Christmas trip. And once Finn's secret was out, there would be no turning back.

But first, I had to get through Thanksgiving with my family without falling apart.

CHAPTER 14

KEEPING UP APPEARANCES

As I prepared for the holidays with our families, Finn's secret hung over me like a black cloud.

By Thanksgiving, my relationship with Finn was very strained. I had expected that the medication he was taking would have kicked in by now, but he still seemed sullen and defensive. I was hoping his demeanor would improve over the holidays. I was tired of dealing with his moodiness. I wanted him to be on his best behavior and not raise any concerns with our families until he spoke to Jack.

We took a direct flight to Ohio to see my parents the day before Thanksgiving. Finn slept most of the way there, and I immersed myself in a book. By the time we arrived, he seemed to be in a better mood. Whether the meds were starting to work or he was happy to have the distraction of traveling, I didn't know.

My older sister, Sela, and her husband, Grant, had driven the day before from New Jersey to my parents' house in Ohio with their two young children, Katie, 6, and Tommy, 4. Sela came to the airport with my dad to pick us up.

"Kassidy!" my dad called out, pulling me into one of his bear hugs. "I'm so glad you're here!"

I felt my body relax into his hug. My dad always made me feel safe, even when he didn't know how much I needed it. I had to fight back tears. I didn't want them to think anything was wrong.

Sela must have noticed I was near tears.

"Geez, you're so sappy, Kass!" she teased, as she embraced me.

"Happy to see you too, Sis!" I retorted, jokingly. "And I'm not sappy! It's just good to be home!"

Finn shook my dad's hand, as he normally did, and then gave Sela a hug. We made small talk about our flight and their drive to the airport, as we headed to baggage claim. Once the suitcases were loaded into the trunk, my dad slid behind the wheel, Sela claimed the passenger seat, and Finn and I settled into the back.

Sela would have preferred to drive, but riding shotgun meant she could twist around and chat with us.. The forty-minute drive home stretched ahead, plenty of time for conversation.

Plenty of time to pretend everything was normal.

"What's new?" Sela asked, not knowing what a loaded question that was.

"Not much," I quickly answered. "What's new with you?"

I knew that asking my sister that question meant I wouldn't have to answer questions for a while. She enjoyed sharing stories about her kids, and I knew my dad loved hearing them as much as I did.

"I can't wait to show you the pictures of the kids in their Halloween costumes!" Sela exclaimed, "Katie insisted on being a sheep! You know how she loves sheep!"

"Oh yes!" my dad replied, laughing. "She wants us to go to the Howell Farm to see the sheep every time we visit you in New Jersey!"

"Her costume was so cute! I got her some white flannel pajamas and a white fleece hooded jacket. I made ears and attached them to the hood. I made a little fuzzy tail and attached it to the back of the pajama bottoms. And she wore black mittens, and an old pair of Grant's black socks over her white tennis shoes for hooves. Then, I made up her face like a sheep's with makeup! Grant teased her that she was a puppy, but she really did look like a sheep!" Sela explained.

"That's a pretty clever costume! And reminds me of how mom used to make ours. She always used flannel pajamas as the base, and then after Halloween, she'd take off any adornments, and we'd have new pajamas!" I mused.

"Yes, it works pretty well that way!" Sela agreed.

"And what about Tommy?" I asked.

"Well, you know how he loves Star Wars. He wanted to be a Stormtrooper!" Sela replied.

"A what?" my dad asked. Much to Tommy's dismay, his grandpa was not into Star Wars and had fallen asleep while watching the movie with Tommy.

Sela looked at me and rolled her eyes, laughing.

"You know, Dad! The white armored soldiers in the Star Wars movie that Tommy made you watch!" Sela explained.

"Weren't they the bad guys?" my dad asked.

"Do not say that to Tommy!" Sela gasped.

"How on Earth did you make a Stormtrooper costume?" I asked.

"Oh, I didn't! We bought that one! Although Grant thought we could make a helmet out of a bucket!" Sela replied.

"A bucket? Thank goodness, you bought a costume! I can't imagine poor Tommy trick-or-treating with a bucket on his head!" I laughed.

"Grant was razzing Tommy about it, and Tommy got upset. But he cheered up when I told him we'd buy him a costume," Sela responded.

"I can't wait to see the pictures!" I said cheerfully.

It felt good to be laughing with my dad and my sister. Finn laughed along, too, but kept quiet and didn't really engage much in the conversation. But he seemed to be enjoying being there with my dad and sister. It was the first time he had laughed in a while, too.

He needs this as much as I do, I thought.

We arrived home, and Finn and I grabbed our bags and carried them into the house. A wave of nausea washed over me as I realized Finn and I would have to sleep in the small room that had been mine as a child. Sela, Grant, and the kids would be in Sela's old room, which was large enough for the kids to sleep on the floor with sleeping bags. Finn and I had not shared a room since I kicked him out of my bedroom. Nausea was quickly replaced by anger, as I thought about what Finn had done and how we had gotten to this point.

My dark thoughts were interrupted by the happy squeals of Katie and Tommy as they ran to hug us.

"Aunt Kassidy! You have to come see the sheep Grandma gave me! His name is Woolly!" Katie yelled gleefully as she pulled me into the living room toward a large stuffed animal sheep that was perched on the couch.

I dropped my bag in the hall, and Finn picked it up and took it up the stairs to our room.

He's on his best behavior so far, I thought.

Not to be outdone by his sister, Tommy grabbed a stuffed dog off the other end of the couch and brought it to me.

"See what Grandma gave me?" he asked, "His name is Buddy!"

My mom came into the living room with a plate of pumpkin bread, followed by Grant with a tray of mugs of tea. My mom gave me a big hug as soon as she set the bread down.

"Oh, honey, it's so good to see you!" she said. "Where's Finn?"

"It's good to see you, too, Mom! Finn took our bags upstairs," I replied.

Grant set down the tea and also gave me a hug.

"Bags? You're only here for a long weekend! We brought one suitcase for the four of us!" he teased.

"One suitcase, but the kids each have a backpack, and I have a small travel bag, too," Sela corrected.

"I have my small bag, and Finn has his. It's just easier if we pack our own stuff. We don't have kids to pack for," I replied.

"You don't have kids *yet*," my mom added.

My mom was anxious for us to have kids. But Sela shot me a look and rolled her eyes. She knew that Finn and I wanted to wait until he finished his PhD before having kids. Of course, none of that would happen now.

After pumpkin bread and tea, Sela, Grant, and I pulled out an old game of *Chutes and Ladders* to play with the kids. The board had belonged to Sela and me when we were little and was now softened at the folds and worn along the edges. Katie and Tommy didn't seem to mind. They squealed over every ladder and groaned at every chute—especially when Grant threw his head back in dramatic despair after sliding down the longest one, sending us all into laughter.

My dad and Finn watched a college football game in the den, an activity that required neither to speak and suited them both. My mom busied herself in the kitchen, heating up dinner. She had made everything ahead of time and insisted she did not need help until she called Sela and me to carry things into the dining room for her.

Dinner was easy and unhurried, the conversation circling the table in bright, overlapping bursts. Tommy and Katie kept us entertained with animated retellings of their school adventures, each story growing more dramatic as they told it. Without fail, my dad would lean back in his chair and begin one of his familiar, "When I was a little boy…" speeches, determined to show them how different life had been in his day. Sela and I exchanged knowing glances, rolling our eyes and laughing—we could have recited those stories ourselves.

For a few hours, I felt something close to peace. I was home, surrounded by the people who had known me longest. Finn appeared relaxed, even cheerful. If anyone had walked in, they would have seen an ordinary family gathered around a table.

And for that moment, it almost felt that way.

After everyone's long travel day, we all decided to go to bed early. I waited until Sela, Grant, and the kids had finished in the bathroom, and then I washed my face and changed into my pajamas. My parents were still awake in their room when I went to my room to put my things away.

Finn was already in bed and appeared asleep. I wasn't going to sleep in the same bed, so I waited until I saw my parents' light go out, then quietly made my way to the den to sleep on the couch. I planned to sneak back upstairs, grab my stuff, and take my shower before anyone woke up. That was not unusual for me, since I was an early riser.

The next day was Thanksgiving, and when I woke up, it was still dark. But I heard my mom in the kitchen, already making coffee and getting ready to stuff the turkey and put it in the oven. She turned when she heard me enter the kitchen.

"Kassidy! You didn't sleep on the couch last night, did you? Is everything okay?" she asked, her tone revealing her motherly concern.

"Yes, I did," I admitted, "Finn was snoring so much I couldn't sleep!" I felt bad about lying. But Finn's snoring often kept me awake, so that made it feel a little less like lying.

"Oh, I know how that goes! Your dad's snoring keeps me awake, too!" she said as she measured the ground coffee.

My excuse seemed to satisfy her, and she didn't ask any other questions. I helped her get the turkey ready, and then we sat at the table sipping coffee and chatting about Katie and Tommy's antics until the others came downstairs for breakfast.

After breakfast, Sela and I cleaned up the kitchen, while my mom entertained the kids - or rather, they entertained her - and the guys watched football.

"Finn seems kind of quiet," Sela said when we were alone in the kitchen. "Is everything okay?"

"Finn's just stressed about his dissertation," I lied. "Things have been a little tense between us because of it."

I felt guilty continuing to lie to my family. The lies were piling up, and we were only two days into a four-day weekend. I wasn't sure that I could keep up the charade. But I could not bring myself to tell my family what was going on since I didn't have a plan to get out of my marriage without destroying my finances yet.

My mom wanted to serve Thanksgiving dinner between football games, so Sela and I took alternating turns helping her in the kitchen and playing with the kids. When dinner was ready, we all gathered at the dining room table. My dad carved the turkey, and my mom fished out the wishbone for Katie and Tommy. She cleaned it off and then handed it to them.

"Each of you take an end, and then make a wish! When you are both done making your wishes, pull the wishbone apart. The wish will come true for the one who gets the biggest piece!" my mom instructed.

The kids each grabbed one end of the wishbone and pulled with all their might.

It didn't budge.

"Grandma, the wishbone isn't breaking! What about our wishes?" Katie cried.

"Oh, that's the best of all! That means you both get your wish!" she replied, avoiding what might have otherwise ended in tears.

"I wished for a real dog!" Tommy exclaimed.

"Me too!" Katie replied excitedly. "That means we're getting a dog!"

The kids had been asking for a dog for a while, and now their pleas would become even more relentless. Fortunately, Grant and Sela had been planning on getting the kids a dog for Christmas. But now they would be in for a long month of pleading until they could surprise the kids on Christmas morning.

"Thanks, Grandma!" Grant said, sarcastically.

"Thanks, Grandma!" the kids joyfully replied in unison.

We all laughed.

My dad served everyone turkey, and then we passed the side dishes around. Since there was a lot of food, the mashed potatoes were passed around twice as we all tried to find an empty place to set the bowl. My dad was not paying attention and served himself another pile of potatoes right next to the pile he already had. I was sitting next to him, and he and I both noticed what he had done at the same time. We both broke out in laughter.

"What's so funny, you two?" my mom asked. My dad and I often had inside jokes, so this wasn't unusual.

We were both laughing so hard, we couldn't respond, so I pointed to my dad's plate. Sela realized what I was pointing at and started laughing, too.

"Dad has two piles of mashed potatoes!" Sela exclaimed.

"Grandpa! Why do you have two piles of mashed potatoes?" Katie asked.

"Well, it was an accident. But I love mashed potatoes, and I was going to have seconds, anyway!" my dad said, shrugging it off with a smile.

"I want more potatoes, too!" Tommy cried. He always wanted to do what his grandpa did.

Sela told him to finish what he already had, and then maybe he could have more. But Tommy was insistent, and she relented.

"At least it's distracting him from begging for a d-o-g!" Grant said.

After dinner, my dad and Finn retreated to the den to watch football. Grant and the kids followed, though Grant's attention shifted back and forth between the television and whatever game he was playing on the floor with them.

Sela and I cleared the table and washed dishes while my mom carefully packed away the leftovers. She preferred to do that herself so she'd know exactly where everything was. Some things, in her house, remained firmly under her control.

By the time the game ended, the day had caught up with all of us, and we drifted off to bed one by one.

When the house finally went quiet, I slipped downstairs to the den again. This time, I wasn't as anxious about being discovered in the morning—my earlier excuse had laid the groundwork. Still, the secrecy made my chest tight.

I would have preferred Finn to take the couch. But my mother still saw him as a guest, and I couldn't bring myself to disrupt her sense of hospitality. So I let her preserve the illusion... and carried my pillow downstairs.

The next day, we all headed to the shopping mall for the Black Friday sales. My dad did not want to go, but my mom insisted, and he relented once she agreed we could eat lunch out. That made him happy, because he wasn't a fan of turkey leftovers, and it would give him a reprieve before dinner.

The mall was crowded, and Finn became very moody and agitated.

"Are you okay?" I asked him after pulling him aside.

"I'm fine!" he said, angrily.

"You don't sound fine," I replied. "Have you been taking your meds?"

"I don't need meds," he retorted.

"Finn, you have to take your meds! When was the last time you took them?" I asked, worried that he was about to have a meltdown.

Finn looked away, shaking his head, but didn't answer.

"Finn, have you been taking your meds?" I asked again, more urgently.

"No, I don't need meds," he reiterated.

"Have you ever taken them?" My voice was high and tight as I felt panic rising.

"Why would I take something I don't need!" he shouted.

"Finn, please calm down! You do need your meds. It feels like you're about to have a meltdown!" I cried.

Then, Finn stormed off and headed into a store. I didn't know whether to go after him or catch up with my family. I decided to let him go, hoping he'd calm himself down before he caught up with us. It was risky, but I didn't know what else to do.

I caught up to Sela, who explained that my parents had gone into the toy store with the kids, and Grant was looking at running shoes.

"Is everything okay with you and Finn?" she asked again.

"Yeah, it's fine," I replied, shrugging it off. "We're just going through a rough patch. Normal couple stuff."

"I get that!" Sela declared. "Why is it that they do one load of laundry and they think they've cleaned the whole damn house?"

That made me laugh, which helped lighten my dark mood. I was tempted to tell her what was happening, but I didn't want to burden her with keeping the secret from my parents, so I kept it to myself.

The rest of the family met back up, and then I saw Finn heading toward us, carrying a shopping bag. I felt my body tense, and I began to sweat. I had no idea what Finn's demeanor would be, so I walked toward him to intercept him before he reached the rest of the group.

"Finn, are you okay?" I asked, nervously.

"Yeah, I'm okay. I'm sorry about before," he replied.

"What's in the bag?" I asked.

"I found two shirts and a sweater!" he replied, smiling broadly.

I started to open my mouth to tell him we couldn't afford that, but then thought better of it. I didn't want to set him off again, and buying something might have been what he needed to relieve his anxiety and avert a meltdown.

"That's great!" I said instead.

Somehow, we managed to get through the rest of the weekend without further incidents.

Sela, Grant, and the kids left after breakfast on Sunday morning because they had about an 8-hour drive home. Then, my parents drove us to the airport. My mom always got teary when it was time to say goodbye, and I got choked up this time, too.

"Are you okay, honey? I'm always a mess when you kids leave, but you usually hold it together better than I do!" she said.

"Yeah, I'm fine. It was just so much fun being with all of you. The kids are growing up so fast! I'm just sad that I won't be spending Christmas with you!" I replied.

"We will miss you, too! But next year is your year to spend Christmas with us!" she responded, trying to sound cheerful.

I hugged both my parents tightly before we prepared to board. Finn hugged my mom and shook my dad's hand, as he always did. Then it was time to go.

I knew my mom would linger at the gate until the plane pushed back, even if my dad was already checking his watch. When I settled into my window seat, I scanned the glass wall—and there they were, exactly where I expected them to be.

I lifted my hand, and they waved back, small but steady figures beyond the window. As the plane eased away from the terminal and turned toward the runway, I kept watching until they blurred into the distance.

And then they were gone.

I was relieved to return to Texas, where we didn't have to keep up the charade. Still, I felt guilty about not telling my family when I could have done it in person. Keeping Finn's secret created an ongoing struggle inside of me. I also realized that I had put my family at risk, especially since Finn wasn't taking his medication.

When we got back into town, we stopped to pick up the dogs from the kennel. They greeted us with frantic tails and happy whines, as if nothing in the world had changed.

At home, we unpacked in silence, each retreating to our own rooms. I changed into more comfortable clothes before heading downstairs. Finn was already there, stretched out in his usual spot on the couch, the television flickering in front of him.

"Finn, we need to talk," I said, picking up the remote and hitting the off button.

"Hey, I was watching that!" Finn cried angrily.

"I'm very concerned that you haven't been taking your medication. Do you remember how Hayden was when he went off his meds? The doctor prescribed them to you for a reason! They will make you feel better," I stated, as calmly as I could muster.

"But I feel fine! I don't need them," Finn insisted.

"Finn, yes, you do need them! If you don't start taking them, I will call your family and tell them what you did and what's been going on!" I threatened. It was a risky move, but I had no other options.

"No! You can't do that! Please don't do that! I will take the meds!" Finn shouted.

"Then get them now and take them in front of me," I said, trying to keep my voice steady.

"Don't you trust me?" Finn asked, annoyed.

"No, Finn, I don't trust you. I haven't since this whole mess began! Now go get your medication!" I shouted.

For a moment, I thought he might refuse. But something in my face must have told him I wasn't backing down. He pushed himself off the couch and stomped upstairs. When he returned, the prescription bottle was clutched in his hand.

I went to the kitchen and got him a glass of water.

"Here. Take them." I demanded, as I handed him the glass.

And then, with tears in his eyes, he took two pills.

"Are you happy now?" he yelled.

"I'm a long way from being happy, Finn!" I replied.

CHAPTER 15

FROZEN IN PLACE

Time crawled between Thanksgiving and Christmas. The tension hung like a thick fog between us. I avoided Finn as much as possible. I kept myself busy with preparations for Christmas - shopping and sending gifts for my family to Sela's house, finding a gift for Finn's family's white elephant gift exchange, and sending out a few Christmas cards to family and friends we wouldn't be seeing over the holidays. The weather was unusually warm for this time of year, and I took every opportunity I could to get out of the house with the dogs to enjoy the weather while it was pleasant. I was sure it wouldn't last.

Finn left his pill bottle on the kitchen counter after the night I made him take his pills. I would check to see how many pills were missing every day. Although the number was declining, I did not witness him taking them, and he was still moody. I suspected he wasn't actually taking them and searched the trash, but found no evidence.

Days before we were scheduled to leave on our trip, I decided to ask him about it. I was in the kitchen making my breakfast when he headed for the coffee pot without saying a word.

"Good morning, Finn," I said, my voice dripping with sarcasm.

"Morning," he grunted back.

"How are you doing? Have you been taking your meds?" I asked.

He grabbed the bottle off the counter and shoved it toward me.

"Look! The bottle is half empty!" he exclaimed.

"Yes, I can see that! But that doesn't mean you've been taking them! Have you been taking them?" I asked again, trying to remain calm.

"Yeah," he said, pouring himself a cup of coffee with his back to me.

"Are they helping you feel better?" I asked.

"That's what they're supposed to do, isn't it?" he turned and shouted at me.

"Yes! That is what they're supposed to do and why I want you to take them." I replied, feeling my neck muscles tightening.

"Yes, I'm taking them. Here is your proof!" he yelled, shoving the bottle back toward me.

"That isn't proof!" I shouted back. "All that proves is that you've been removing the pills from the bottle. You haven't been taking them, have you?" I asked, exasperated.

"I tried. They don't work!" Finn replied angrily.

"Then you need to tell your doctor. Maybe he can prescribe something else,"

"But I don't need medication!" Finn retorted.

And there it was, what I had suspected all along. Was there no end to his lying?

Christmas couldn't come fast enough.

The plan was layered: drive to Memphis on Tuesday to spend the night with Finn's older brother, Jack, and his wife, Simone, then drive north with them the next morning to Michigan, where Finn's sister Joy was hosting the family. We would arrive the day before Christmas Eve, stay through Christmas Day, then retrace our route— Michigan to Memphis, Memphis back to Austin—so I wouldn't miss too much work.

Jack, the oldest by nearly twenty years, hadn't been especially close to Finn growing up, but they'd grown closer as adults. He had stood beside Finn as his best man at our wedding. Jack and Simone had been married twenty-seven years and had one son, now grown and recently launched into a new job in Seattle. He wouldn't be joining us this year, as he was unable to take time off. I felt a quiet pang at that. He was a quiet, thoughtful, and emotionally intelligent young man, who valued meaningful conversation. His steady presence might have been grounding.

I was anxious to see Jack and Simone, but I dreaded the long drive to Memphis alone with Finn. Once Finn told Jack, it would be the gateway to telling his entire family. I felt hope for the first time since I found that receipt from the police officer in my house another lifetime ago.

Although the weather had been nice, a sudden cold front moved through Texas, bringing freezing rain and ice just before Christmas. We probably shouldn't have attempted the trip, but not going - and not telling Jack - was not an option. Finn was planning to talk to Jack after dinner that night, and what Dianne had told me was quickly sinking in for me: you can't help someone unwilling to help themselves. Hopefully, Jack would be able to give Finn the guidance he needed.

Just past Fort Worth, there had been a terrible accident on the other side of the highway, and traffic slowed to a crawl again. As we passed the accident scene, a chill went down my spine.

An SUV's entire front end had been torn away by a semi-truck. Clothing, wrapped packages, and a cooler were strewn around the SUV. It was very sobering, and I wondered if anyone had survived. Finn and I shared our thoughts about what had happened to the family in the SUV. The possibilities made our situation seem less terrible. At least we were alive.

The bad weather put us way behind schedule, so we stopped to find a payphone to call Jack and Simone and let them know we would be late. I also called Peggy, our pet sitter, to check on Sam and Lizzie. We used the restroom, grabbed food, and climbed back into the car to continue. By the time we crossed into Arkansas, darkness had fallen. We were nine hours into what should have been a ten-hour drive—and still had three hours left.

The roads in Arkansas were very bumpy and in poor condition. But things got worse when we ran into another ice storm. This one stopped us between the highway exits, as two tractor-trailers had jackknifed on the road ahead. The accident had just happened, and we had no warning, or we might have been able to get off the highway at an earlier exit. Instead, we were stuck. We hoped we would not be delayed for long.

As we sat there, I reflected on the irony of being physically stuck in the car with Finn. It paralleled where I was in my life at the time: seemingly stuck with Finn in our marriage, unable to move forward until certain obstacles were cleared. I intended to clear a major one when we talked to Jack.

People were getting out of their cars to assess the situation, but doing so was dangerous due to the ice. The poor condition of the underlying road helped a bit, as the ice was rough and not smooth like an ice rink.

Finn decided to get out of the car and see what he could learn. When he returned, his face was tight. A trucker had radioed ahead: no emergency vehicles or tow trucks could reach the wreckage until morning..

We would all be stranded overnight.

We had no way to contact Jack and Simone again. All we could do was hope they were watching the weather and piecing together where we might be.

We did not have any blankets with us, only a few extra layers of clothing, which we pulled on over what we were already wearing. We ran the car briefly when it got bitterly cold hoping we didn't run out of gas. We didn't know how long we would be there, even after the emergency vehicles could get through.

Our two-door Acura hatchback suddenly felt impossibly small. Trying to sleep in the front seat was very uncomfortable, but with gifts in the back seat, there was no room for either of us to crawl back there to sleep.

"I can't believe we're stuck in an ice storm in Arkansas!" I said, shifting in the passenger seat, trying to find a more comfortable position.

"It's not so bad," Finn declared, "At least we're together!"

I didn't respond. I just stared out the window.

"This is just one more challenge that we're getting through together! As long as we're together, we can do anything! Everything is going to be alright, Kass!" Finn continued. His voice had regained the cheeriness it had lost since his arrest. It was unnerving. Was this the beginning of a manic episode?

"Yes, we'll survive the ice storm," I sighed, not fully grasping his meaning.

"No, I mean it, Kassidy! As long as you and I are together, everything will be alright. I love you, Kass!" he said, his voice taking on a more serious tone.

Was he really trying to make up with me right here and now?

"It's not that simple, Finn," I replied.

"I know you're still angry. But what happened wasn't my fault! Because of my bipolar disorder, I just cracked under all the pressure I was under. Why won't you forgive me?" he asked, his voice growing more tense.

"Are you fucking kidding, Finn? You aren't taking responsibility for your actions, you aren't apologizing, and you want me to forgive you? You haven't learned anything in therapy!" I shouted.

"What do you want from me?" he shouted back.

What I wanted in that moment was to be out of that car, away from him, and almost anywhere else. I felt the car constricting around me, and Finn consuming all the oxygen. I felt lightheaded, like I was struggling for air, searching for a pocket to catch my breath. I cracked the window, even though it let in the freezing air. The cold hit my face, and I breathed deeply before quickly shutting the window.

Feeling like I could breathe again, I took a few beats before I responded. Finn was watching me closely now. I faced him and let my words fly.

"What I want from you is to take responsibility for your actions. What I want from you is an apology for what you have done. I want you to realize that it won't be alright. It will never be right again! Your actions broke the bridge of trust with me, with Professor Huntington, with all our friends. Even with Lizzie. You destroyed your career, and you destroyed our marriage!"

I was shouting back at him, and my voice was more shrill than intended. It ricocheted around the car.

"What about you taking responsibility for your actions?" he shouted back. "What about you apologizing to me? This is not all my fault!"

I stared back at him in silence, my fists clenched, and in that moment, I realized that I was done. Done with Finn's lies. Done with keeping Finn's secrets. Done with living in a house filled with anger and resentment. I wanted to be free of the burdens that Finn had saddled me with. I wanted to be free of Finn.

I would do what I needed to get through this trip with his family. And if he did not tell Jack by the time we returned to Memphis after Christmas, then I would.

I didn't say any of it. He was already furious, and I was alone in a stranded car with him. The last thing I wanted was to provoke him further. I could feel the edge in him—his emotions wound tight—and I was afraid of tipping him into something reckless.

He was in the driver's seat. Literally.

When traffic finally started moving again, I would need him to be steady and cautious. The roads were treacherous. Our lives would depend on it.

I couldn't risk pushing him toward mania.

Although I had hit the boiling point, a decisive calm came over me. "What exactly do you think I need to apologize to you for?"

He seemed worried by my sudden calmness. "You were always putting pressure on me to finish school. And you're always mad at me for spending money. And you were gone so much with work – I was lonely!"

Hearing his words further sharpened my resolve. I was done.

I had been married to a master manipulator. A man who could not take responsibility for himself or his actions. I'd been taking care of him for 10 years, while he did what he wanted. I was no longer blind to the real Finn.

I unclenched my fists and my jaw and felt my body relax into my seat. The smell of diesel and exhaust from the vehicles around us permeated the car. And yet, I felt it was much easier to breathe now.

"I have supported your pursuit of more education financially, physically, and emotionally for ten years, through your master's degree and your PhD. I worked to support your career. I quit a job I loved and took one that was not in my chosen field, so I would not have to travel as much. And I had been home for over a year when you went to meet a child. And as for being mad at you for spending money, you have gotten us so deep into debt that I have no idea how I will get out of it. Especially now that you have legal bills on top of everything else. You made choices. They had nothing to do with me." I tried to keep my voice calm, but it had a sharp edge, and I knew he felt it.

He sat there fixated on me for a few minutes.

"It wasn't just you who put pressure on me. It was my family and my professors at school. I was doing my best, and everyone wanted me to do more," he whined, shifting some blame from me but accepting none of it himself.

When he started crying, part of me felt bad for him. He could not grasp that he had been the one to ruin his own life. Perhaps it was too painful for him to accept that he had cut his own throat, and he blamed everyone else as if they held the knife.

"Don't you think it was reasonable to expect you to be close to finishing after ten years? But none of that matters now, you've thrown it all away," I said quietly.

I let my words hang in the air between us, but he didn't respond. From the passenger seat, I could only watch him—his hands fixed on the steering wheel, his jaw set in the glow of the dashboard lights. I couldn't tell whether he was weighing what I'd said or waiting for me to fill the silence.

I didn't.

There was nothing left to add. Mercifully, we didn't speak again until hours later, when the traffic finally began to move.

Nearly ten hours later, traffic finally began to inch forward. We had been trapped in that frozen car all night.

Finn wanted to take the first exit, but the line of cars snaking toward it was already backed up. "Keep going," I urged. The second exit looked no better. We gambled on a third—and rolled into the gas station on fumes.

Stepping out of the car felt like stepping onto solid ground after a storm at sea. I hadn't realized how tightly I'd been holding myself together until that moment.

We found a pay phone and called Jack and Simone. They had already guessed we'd been stranded and were anxiously waiting to hear from us. They had contacted Joy in Michigan to let her know we would arrive a day late.

We still had three more hours to drive before reaching Memphis.

I was overjoyed when we finally reached Jack and Simone's house. Simone had prepared lunch and waited for us to shower and put on fresh clothes before eating. Finn and I shared the room his nephew grew up in, and I was relieved it still had twin beds.

Finn and I were barely speaking to each other, and Jack and Simone could sense that things were rough between us. But it probably didn't seem unusual after the night we had just had.

After we ate, Simone suggested we walk around the lake in their neighborhood. The ice storm had not reached Memphis, and it was still relatively warm. Walking in the fresh air after being trapped in the car for so long felt good. I let Finn walk ahead with Jack while I stayed a few steps back with Simone.

"How's work going?" Simone asked.

We were in similar fields and often discussed our work.

"It's going pretty well. I'm enjoying my new job, even though it's so different from what I was doing. Are you working on any interesting new projects?" I replied.

"Yes! We have a new monitoring program along the Duck River that I'm excited about!" Simone said eagerly.

She told me the details, but admittedly, I was only half listening. I was trying to catch snippets of Finn and Jack's conversation.

"Oh, look! There's a pair of Mallards!" Simone exclaimed, pointing to a pair of ducks paddling lazily about fifteen feet from the edge of the lake as we passed.

"They're so pretty!" I replied, briefly turning my attention away from Finn and Jack.

"And there's a pair of Blue-winged Teals," she added, pointing to another pair of ducks a bit farther out in the water.

On any other day, I would have loved strolling around the lake with Simone, watching the ducks skim across the water. Instead, I found myself listening for the moment Finn might pull Jack aside and finally tell him the truth.

It never came.

We were already two-thirds of the way around the lake—more than enough time. With each passing step, it became clear that he wasn't going to say anything. I should have known. Agreeing to tell Jack had simply bought him time, another quiet maneuver to keep me waiting.

Disappointment settled in, heavy but familiar. Still, I held to my decision. If Finn wouldn't speak, I would—after Christmas.

For now, I would let the illusion stand. I would not be the one to shatter it.

CHAPTER 16

CHRISTMAS SECRETS

The following morning, we all got into Jack's car and headed to Michigan. It was another nine hours of driving, but with Jack and Simone's company, it was much more pleasant than the previous segment of our trip. By the time we pulled into Joy and Matt's driveway, the rest of the family had already arrived from Columbus, Ohio, where Finn had grown up. The house glowed with welcoming warmth, the sounds of familiar voices and shared laughter greeting us as we walked through the door.

Joy was closest to Finn's age. She and her husband, Matt, had been married for about 15 years. They did not have any children, but were considering adoption. They were both working professionals and had a beautiful, large home near Lake Michigan. Joy and Matt had taken on hosting Christmas every year since moving into this house. Joy loved decorating for Christmas. She had special touches in every room and every corner of the house. She truly had a gift for decorating. The beauty of it all immediately lifted my spirits.

Finn's parents and all of his siblings were there with their partners. With so many people in the house, Finn and I could easily avoid each other, and no one would think much of it.

"I'm sorry that there aren't enough bedrooms for everyone," Joy explained. "Mom and Dad are sleeping in the main floor guest room, so that they don't have to navigate the stairs. Jack and Simone are in one of the spare bedrooms upstairs, and Hayden and Maxine are on the futon in the office. Finn and Kassidy, you'll share the family room with Madeline and Patrick."

Madeline was Finn's oldest sister and the second-born after Jack. She and Patrick met at work and had been dating for several years. They had recently bought a house and moved in together. Madeline and Finn had always been close, and Patrick was fun and easy-going, and we all got along well. I wasn't surprised that Joy had put us all together in the family room.

"We brought an air mattress," Madeline stated. "So you can each have one of the couches."

"That works out great!" I replied, perhaps a little too enthusiastically. But I was relieved not to have to share a bed or room alone with Finn.

We stashed our bags in the hall closet and put the Christmas gifts under the tree in the living room. Since Finn's family was so large, they drew names during the annual summer family vacation. Finn and I hadn't attended the vacation this year, so they had drawn for us. I was happy to have gotten Madeline's name. She loved to cook, and I had gotten her one of Paul Prudhomme's cookbooks. We had visited his restaurant in New Orleans when we vacationed there together the previous summer. It was a nice memory we shared.

After we'd gotten all of our things settled, we went to the living room to join the family for a pre-dinner cocktail. Finn's dad, Jack Sr., always traveled with his portable bar, and he set it up in the corner to make martinis for those who wanted them. Myra was sitting in a large upholstered chair, her martini already in hand. Matt was standing near the bar with Jack Sr.

"Oh! You're finally here!" Myra exclaimed as Jack, Simone, Finn, and I filed into the room.

"Finn and Kassidy had quite the trip getting to Memphis," Jack replied. "We're lucky they made it!"

"Well, if they had flown instead of driving all that way, they wouldn't have had that problem!" Myra stated.

I sucked in my breath. It was hard not to respond to Myra's snarky remark.

"They're here now, Myra. Let's just enjoy them while we can." Jack Sr. advised. "Who's ready for a martini?"

After hugging Myra, we headed over to the bar. Jack, Simone, and Finn all grabbed martinis. Knowing I was not a martini drinker, Jack Sr. happily poured me a glass of white wine.

"Cheers!" he said merrily, clinking our wine and martini glasses.

Hayden, Maxine, and Joy had been busy in the kitchen, but they joined us now, bringing trays of appetizers.

"You guys must be starving!" Joy said as she brought her tray over near the bar for Jack Sr.

Hayden and Maxine placed their trays on the coffee table near Myra, then came over near the bar to hug Jack, Simone, Finn, and me. Then, we all sat down so that Myra could be included in the conversation.

"How is school going, Finn?" Matt asked.

I bristled, not sure how he would respond.

"It has been stressful working on my dissertation. I'm glad for the holiday break."

I relaxed a bit.

"Congratulations on your latest promotion, Matt! I'd love to hear more about what you're doing." I interjected, deflecting the attention back to Matt.

Across the room, I caught Myra's expression shift—just a flicker, her lips tightening before she smoothed them into something neutral again. I couldn't tell whether I'd imagined it or not. But I had the uneasy sense she would have preferred the spotlight remain where it was.

"I'm now leading the team of engineers that is responsible for Operations at the power plant. We run the Control Room and the Turbine Room— the areas that are responsible for real-time power generation."

"Wow! That's a big responsibility. How many other engineers do you oversee?" Simone asked.

"I've got a little over 200 engineers on my team now," Matt explained. "It can be a challenge."

"He is on call a lot more now, too," Joy added.

"Yeah, that's definitely a downside. But I enjoy the work, and fortunately, there haven't been too many occasions where I've had to go in when I'm on call. But I need to stay close to home on those weekends, so we're not traveling quite as much as we'd like," Matt replied, rubbing Joy's shoulder tenderly.

"But I'm very proud of Matt," Joy added, smiling up at him.

"And what about you, Kassidy? How is your job going?" Matt asked.

"It's going well. We have a release coming up this Spring, but we're not yet in crunch time. It's sort of the calm before the storm," I replied.

"We're glad you and Finn could take the time off to come for Christmas," Joy said.

"I'm glad, too! It's so nice to be here with everyone," I responded, smiling.

"Not everyone is here. My grandchildren couldn't come," Myra observed.

"Sorry, Mom, but Jacob just started his new job," Jack replied, explaining his son's absence. "He wanted to come, but he didn't have the time off to be able to travel across the country from Seattle."

"And you know Bethany is spending Christmas with her mom this year. Next year will be our turn again, Mom. I miss her, too," Hayden added. Since the divorce, Hayden's daughter spent every other Christmas with him.

"Yes, I know all that. But we should all be together!" Myra responded.

"Cheers to all of us who are here! Merry Christmas!" Jack Sr. cried, lifting his glass in a toast. Jack Sr. was good at steering things to the brighter side and distracting Myra. I loved that about him.

"Cheers!" we all replied in unison as we lifted our glasses.

"I'd better go check on dinner," Joy suggested, getting up from her seat and grabbing one of the empty appetizer trays.

"I'll help you," I offered, picking up the other tray and following her into the kitchen.

"Thank you, Kassidy," Joy replied.

"Your house looks beautiful, Joy! You really have a knack for decorating." I told her when we were in the kitchen.

"Thank you, Christmas is my favorite holiday. I pick up ornaments and other decorations all year. Matt swears it drives him crazy! But he got the boxes out of storage as soon as we got home from Thanksgiving at Mom and Dad's, and I didn't even ask him to do it. I think he secretly enjoys it as much as I do," Joy laughed.

"I think so, too! He was pointing out the new handblown glass Christmas trees on the mantel to Maddie and Simone," I confided.

I helped Joy carry food to the dining room. The table in the dining room was already set.

"Wow," I breathed, taking it all in.

Each place setting held a unique ornament, paired with a handwritten card bearing our names. Joy had thought of everything. The table felt less like a meal and more like a memory in the making.

When I looked up, I caught Joy watching me, a quiet smile spreading across her face.

After we placed the food on the table, we went to the living room and let the family know it was time for dinner. Jack Sr. refilled our drinks, and we all found our places around the table. The conversation was lively as we sat down. Everyone was marveling at Joy's decorations. Matt squeezed Joy's hand and kissed her on the cheek. She glowed under the attention, clearly pleased that her careful planning had been noticed.

It was Christmas Eve, and Joy had prepared a beautiful spread—tender beef roast, creamy mashed potatoes swimming in gravy, roasted vegetables caramelized at the edges, a crisp salad, and warm dinner rolls that filled the house with the smell of yeast and butter.

"This is quite a feast!" Jack Sr. called out merrily. "You must have been working on this for days, Joy!"

" I had a lot of help from Matt, Maddie, and Patrick today," Joy replied.

"And just wait until you see what she's got planned for Christmas dinner tomorrow," Matt added, smiling broadly.

"Oh, I hope it's turkey! With lots of sage stuffing!" Jack Sr. exclaimed.

"Of course it is, Dad! I know that's your favorite," Joy responded.

Before anyone reached for a serving spoon, we bowed our heads as Jack Sr. cleared his throat and began to say grace. His familiar cadence settled over the room, steady and sincere. When he finished, a soft chorus of "Amen" circled the table, and only then did we begin passing the dishes, each platter making its way around until every plate was full.

Conversation during dinner remained light, as the family caught up with each other's news. Hayden and Maxine told us of their recent trip to California, where they drove along the coast and camped. Madeline and Patrick shared about their bike trip to see the fall colors in Vermont, which Jack, Simone, Finn, and I had not yet heard about. Jack and Simone told us all about the trip to Seattle they took to visit Jacob after Thanksgiving.

Finn and I kept quiet and took it all in. I scanned Finn's face, but could not decipher what he was feeling. He seemed in better spirits, but was more subdued than usual. I wondered if anyone else noticed the change in Finn.

After dinner, the evening naturally divided itself. Myra and Jack Sr. drifted into the living room with Matt, Finn, Jack, and Simone, while the rest of us stayed behind to restore the kitchen. Maxine and I cleared plates as Joy and Madeline packed away leftovers, and Hayden and Patrick took over at the sink, water running and laughter rising above the clatter of dishes.

When everything was back in order, we carried dessert into the living room. Madeline and Patrick had baked cherry pies. Maxine and

Hayden brought donuts from their favorite shop in Columbus. Joy unveiled her traditional Yule log—a chocolate cake rolled with cream filling and coated in rich frosting. Finn and I had contributed cookies from a bakery in Austin, and Myra and Madeline added the family's famous Scotch toffee.

The coffee table quickly filled with more sweetness than seemed possible.

"I didn't think I could eat another bite after that wonderful dinner," Jack Sr. declared, piling his plate high, "but these desserts are just too tempting!"

"You always say that, Jack," Myra teased. "And yet you never skip dessert."

"Don't feel like you have to try everything tonight," Joy added with a laugh. "There's plenty for tomorrow."

After an hour of sugar and easy conversation, Jack Sr. pushed himself up from his chair. "All right," he announced with a grin, "you know Santa can't come if we're all still awake!"

Laughter circled the room as we began gathering plates and cups, the house settling into Christmas Eve quiet.

We said goodnight to Myra, Jack Sr., Jack, Simone, Hayden, and Maxine, who were all sleeping upstairs. Joy, Matt, Madeline, Patrick, Finn, and I cleaned up the dessert dishes before heading to our own beds.

I lay awake for quite a while, feeling guilty about the secret Finn and I were keeping from the people we loved. On the other couch, I heard Finn tossing and turning and wondered if keeping secrets was gnawing at him, too. He had talked so easily about school and the stress of his dissertation when questioned. Will his family be able to forgive either of us for keeping up this charade once they learn the truth? The damage is already done, even if they don't know it yet.

Eventually, the exhaustion of the drive from Memphis and my full stomach took over, and I fell asleep. I awoke the next morning to the smell of coffee and cinnamon rolls wafting from the kitchen. Finn and

Patrick were both still sound asleep, but Madeline was already up. I put on my slippers and headed to the kitchen.

"Good morning, Kass!" Matt greeted me while he poured Maddie a cup of coffee. "Can I get you some coffee, too?"

"Good morning, Matt! Good morning, Maddie! Yes, I'd love some coffee." I replied. "Is Joy still sleeping?"

"No, she went upstairs to shower and left me in charge of coffee and cinnamon rolls," he responded, handing me a cup of steaming coffee.

"Thank you! Mmmm…the coffee smells like cinnamon, too." I said, breathing in the aroma deeply. Cinnamon coffee was my favorite.

"It is cinnamon flavored," Maddie confirmed, "Patrick and I bought it on our trip and thought it would be perfect for Christmas morning!"

"It is the perfect Christmas coffee!" I agreed, giving Maddie a hug with my free arm.

The cinnamon rolls were going to take a while to bake, so Matt, Maddie, and I sat down at the kitchen table to talk. We had just taken our seats when Simone walked into the kitchen. Ever the gracious host, Matt was on his feet in a flash, grabbing a mug of coffee for Simone.

"Wow! That's what I call service!" Simone laughed as she took the cup from Matt and slid into one of the chairs at the table. "Good morning!"

"Good morning," we all responded in unison.

"How did you all sleep?" Matt asked.

"I slept well! The guest room bed is very comfortable," Simone replied.

"Patrick and I are used to our inflatable bed. We've used it on a couple of trips, so I had no trouble sleeping," Maddie responded.

"I slept well, too," I replied, although it wasn't entirely true. But it was my guilty conscience, not the accommodations, that disrupted my sleep.

Joy and Jack wandered into the kitchen, followed by Hayden and Maxine. Matt refilled mugs and quickly started another pot of coffee while Hayden retrieved the leftover donuts, arranging them on a plate before setting them on the table. The kitchen hummed with warmth—coffee brewing, chairs scraping softly against the floor, easy laughter rising and falling.

For a moment, I let myself simply be there.

It felt good to be included in the rhythm of this family—to move alongside them as if I truly belonged. A quiet ache pressed against my chest as I realized this might be my last Christmas in this kitchen, at this table, with these people.

I pushed the thought away.

For now, I would stay present. I would gather the warmth while I still could.

The cinnamon rolls were ready to come out of the oven just as the rest of the family made their way to the kitchen. Joy had also made a breakfast casserole, Madeline made a fruit salad, and Hayden made bacon. We gathered up our coffee cups and each carried one of the delightful foods to the dining room table. Once again, the table had been set beautifully. We sat at our previously assigned seats, and each of us found a handmade glass candy cane on our plates, another special touch from Joy.

"Oh, Joy! How did you manage to do all this?" I asked.

"She got up early and did it while you were all still sleeping," Matt answered for her, his voice full of pride.

"It's absolutely beautiful!" Simone added.

"These candy canes are adorable!" Maxine chimed in.

"Did you get these on our summer trip?" Madeline asked. "I remember seeing these in the store next to the restaurant where we had lunch."

"Yes, that is exactly where I found them!" Joy replied cheerfully. "I'm so glad you all like them!"

"My niece and nephew would love the candy canes," I replied.

"I'll take you to the shop next summer!" Joy told me.

My chest tightened as another wave of guilt and sadness gripped my heart.

"That would be nice," I said.

Finn shifted in his chair next to me. His future participation in family trips was also uncertain, and I wondered whether the consequences were weighing on him as well.

Maybe Finn will surprise me and tell his family while we're all together, I thought, although I had strong doubts that he had the courage to do so.

After breakfast, we all headed into the living room to exchange gifts. Matt sat near the tree so that he could distribute the gifts, and Patrick helped play Santa. Once everyone had their gifts, it was family tradition for each person to open one gift at a time, starting with the oldest (Finn's dad) and working their way to the youngest. After everyone had opened a gift, they'd make the rounds again until all the gifts were opened. It took a while, and Finn's dad told of epically long Christmas gift-opening sessions when the kids were young. And although some family members suggested abandoning the tradition, the family hadn't done so.

Finn and I had gotten one gift for his parents, and it was the first one Jack Sr. picked up to open. He cut the tape with his pocket knife and handed the package to his wife to open. She pulled the bow off the package and stuck it in the center of her husband's chest, laughing. It was nice to see that they still shared tender moments after nearly 60 years of marriage.

Myra opened the gift, which was a glass bowl from an art gallery in Austin that Myra liked. She had seen a similar one when she visited, and the blues and greens in the glass were her favorite colors. The one we'd given them was smaller than the one she liked, and more affordable, but she was pleased.

"Oh Finn, this is lovely! You remembered how much I liked this," Myra exclaimed.

Finn jumped up to give his mom a hug. "They didn't have the one you wanted, but I thought this one was pretty close," he said.

You thought? I was the one who remembered Myra liked the bowl and suggested we get it for them!

"Well, it's just perfect! Thank you, Finn!" Myra said, then quickly added, "And you, too, Kassidy."

"Look at this, Jack!" she said, handing the bowl to Jack Sr. "Isn't it perfect?"

"It is beautiful! Just your colors, Myra. Thank you, " Jack Sr. replied, nodding at us.

I was happy that Myra liked the bowl, even if Finn took all the credit.

"Ok, on to the next present. Jack, I think you're up!" Matt suggested.

"But dad hasn't actually opened one yet!" Madeline replied.

Matt shook his head.

"This is why it takes so long to open presents!" he laughed.

Jack Sr. picked out a gift and shook it.

"Oh, stop that! You know what that is! And you kids all have one just like it. You all need to open these together," Myra stated.

Matt groaned. Myra was big on giving matching group gifts. She would designate a day during the family vacation when everyone would wear their matching gifts, and it was mandatory to get a photo with everyone wearing them. We would also take a picture with our gifts before we left Joy and Matt's as our Christmas photo.

"At least that will speed things up, Matt!" Patrick asserted.

We all laughed, including Myra.

We all received t-shirts in different colors. The men's were all bright colors, and the women's were all pastels.

Matt's shirt was bright yellow, and Matt was very tall.

"We'll be able to spot you on the golf course, Matt!" Hayden exclaimed.

"Yeah, he's gonna look like Big Bird!" Patrick added, laughing.

"I like yellow! Thank you, Myra," Matt said, ignoring the teasing and making Myra happy.

Since we had all opened a gift, it was time for the next round of presents. Jack Sr. started with a gift from Myra, which set the tone for everyone else to open a gift from their partners as well. Being the youngest, Finn and I were the last to open gifts in each round. We had not gotten gifts for each other, so Finn selected his gift from Jack, who had gotten Finn's name in the drawing.

"Why don't you open your gift from Kassidy?" Myra asked.

Finn froze. Then looked to me for help.

"Finn and I didn't get each other wrappable presents this year. We decided to put money aside for–" I began, when Finn interrupted.

"The summer trip!" Finn shouted. "So we can come next year. It was going to be a surprise!"

I let out a sigh of relief. It was another lie, but it pleased Myra.

"Oh! That's wonderful!" Myra exclaimed.

"That's why we wanted to drive here. To save money for the trip," Finn added.

Lying comes so easily to Finn! Has it always been this way?

Then, Finn carefully unwrapped his gift from Jack. It was a framed photo of Jack holding Finn as a toddler. Finn's eyes welled with tears. It was a sweet gift, but I was sure that Finn's emotional reaction was due to more than just the gift.

"Thank you, Jack," Finn said softly. "This is really…special."

"You're welcome, Finn!" Jack replied, his voice cracking slightly. "Do you remember when that picture was taken?"

"Yeah, that was the Christmas when I was two, I think. I mean, I don't really remember it, but I've seen the photo before," Finn said, his voice a bit ragged.

"Yeah, I guess you were too young to actually remember it. But I gave you that stuffed dog, and you would not let him go! And then you climbed up in my lap, and Dad took the picture."

Finn got up and hugged Jack. I had renewed hope that Finn would trust Jack enough to tell him about his arrest when we got back to Memphis.

Then it was my turn. The gift I chose to open was wrapped very elegantly in a patterned red foil paper with a shimmery gold bow. It was from Hayden, who had drawn my name. I unwrapped the gift carefully, so as not to tear the pretty paper. I opened the box and found a beautiful amethyst geode. The geode had rich, deep purple crystals that were well-formed and glistened.

"Hayden, this is incredible, I love it!" I cried.

Finn leaned in closer, lifting the geode from the box and brushing his thumb along the jagged edge. He tilted it back and forth so the facets caught the light. "That's a very high-quality specimen," he said with genuine admiration. "Where did you find it?"

"Oh, good! I don't know how to tell the quality of geodes, but I thought it looked like a special one. I got it at the gem and mineral shop on High Street," Hayden told us.

"It is very nice. And very thoughtful of you, thank you, Hayden," I replied.

We passed it around so everyone could take a look.

Before we could begin another round of presents, Jack Sr. rose from his chair and stretched. "Who's ready for a drink?" he called out.

Wrapping paper was pushed aside, and everyone welcomed the pause. I followed Joy and Madeline into the kitchen to set out a few appetizers, grateful for the brief change of pace.

"We're all so happy you're coming on the summer trip next year," Madeline said, lowering her voice slightly as she handed me a plate.

My hands stilled for half a second before I forced them to move again. "We love the summer trips," I replied, choosing words that were technically true. I clung to them like a life raft, even though I knew I was still misleading her.

We headed back to the living room with the appetizers. Jack Sr. had our drinks ready. We all took our seats and continued opening gifts. When we got to Madeline's turn, she selected the gift from me.

"Oh, it's one of Paul Prudhomme's cookbooks! This is perfect, Kassidy. Remember when we went to his restaurant in New Orleans?" Madeline asked.

"Yes, that was such a fun evening, and the food was so good! Remember how we were walking down the street afterwards, and a carriageway gate opened, and there was Paul Prudhomme coming toward us on his motorized scooter?" I asked.

"Oh my goodness, I almost forgot that part! He looked right at you, and you boldly said, 'Hello, Mr. Prudhomme,' and he politely replied, 'Good evening, Madame,' and tipped his hat," Madeline recalled.

"Yup, that was my 10-second brush with fame!" I laughed.

"You met Paul Prudhomme?" Hayden asked. He hadn't been on that trip with us.

"Well, 'met' is a strong word. It was literally an exchange of greetings," I told him. "But I'll never forget it."

After the last gift was opened, we found ourselves in a lull before dinner. The house naturally separated into smaller clusters. Hayden and Maxine joined Joy in the kitchen, the low murmur of their voices blending with the clatter of pans. In the family room, Jack Sr., Matt, Finn, and Patrick settled in front of a basketball game. Jack, Simone, and Myra remained in the living room, deep in conversation.

Madeline and I claimed the dining room table, flipping through her new cookbook and pointing out recipes we wanted to try.

She turned a page slowly, then glanced up at me. "Is everything okay?"

My fingers paused on the glossy paper.

"Yes," I said lightly. "Why do you ask?"

But a quiet ripple of fear moved through me. Had something slipped? Had she seen what I was trying so carefully to hide?

"You and Finn both seem different somehow. I can't quite tell what's different, but there's something," she explained.

"We're both just tired," I offered. "I think we're ready for this year to be over. The New Year always feels like a fresh start."

"I got the impression from Finn that his dissertation isn't going as well as he hoped," Madeline confided.

"Yeah, he's hit a…snag," I told her. It wasn't the whole truth, but it wasn't a lie either.

"That must be hard for both of you," Madeline said. "And we're all hoping he will finish school soon, and that maybe you'd move closer to home."

"That would be nice," I agreed.

"And mom is hoping you'll start a family soon," Madeline added.

I picked at a loose thread on one of Joy's festive napkins.

"Yeah, I know. She has mentioned that to us, too," I acknowledged.

"Well, don't let her pressure you until you and Finn are ready," Madeline said.

"Who knows when that will be," I replied.

We continued looking at the cookbook and bookmarking the recipes she wanted to try first. She marked a half dozen or more.

"Patrick's going to be happy!" I joked.

"Yes, he will be, and luckily for me, he likes to be my sous chef," she laughed.

When we finished flipping through the cookbook, we wandered back into the kitchen to see if we could help. Joy was already moving with quiet efficiency, giving gentle instructions. She sent Madeline to join Hayden and Maxine, then asked me to help set the table.

I found myself curious about what thoughtful detail she might unveil next.

As I laid out the plates and silverware, Joy opened a small box and began placing a hand-carved wooden animal at each setting. Each one was different—a fox mid-step, a bear standing upright, a delicate bird poised as if about to take flight.

"Did you find these on the summer trip, too?" I asked, running my finger lightly along the smooth curve of one.

Joy smiled. "No. Matt made them."

I looked up, surprised. "I didn't know he carved wood."

"He needed something to help him unwind from work," she said. "So he took a class at a local artisan workshop. He really loves it. And he's good at it."

I studied the tiny details—the careful grooves, the polished edges. "They're beautiful," I said softly. "So intricate."

When dinner was ready, and we all sat in our seats, everyone was impressed with Matt's handiwork. As we ate and talked, we passed our animal figures around so that everyone could see each one. The mood was lively, and everyone was in good spirits. It felt good to soak up the family's happy energy after the weight I'd been carrying for the past three months.

After dinner, we returned to the living room for dessert. Jack Sr. had gotten a large box of chocolates from Myra, and he walked around the room offering them to each of us. When someone reached to pick one of the chocolates out of the box, he'd say "No, not that one!" and let out a hearty laugh. It made us all laugh.

I sat next to Hayden and thanked him again for his lovely gift.

"I saw it and immediately thought of you, Kassidy," he said.

"That's really sweet, Hayden! How are you doing?" I asked.

He smiled.

"I'm doing a lot better. I had a couple of rough years there, but things are good now. I'm managing a coffee shop, and I love interacting with all the people. And I'm taking my meds regularly, even when I think I don't need them. Maxine has been a big help with that," he confided.

"I'm glad to hear that, Hayden! And happy that you found something you love to do," I replied.

He got up to get himself another slice of pie, and Maxine came and sat with me.

"Hayden's doing much better," she said, as she watched him cross the room.

"Yes, he is! He told me he really likes his new job at the coffee shop," I told her.

"It's a perfect fit for him. He loves to be around people. I think that was why he had such a hard time after his divorce and the furniture store closed. He was lonely," Maxine said.

"Yes, but now he has you, and he said you've been a big help with keeping him on his meds," I replied. "And how are you doing?"

"I'm happy! Life with Hayden is always an adventure. He always wants to try new things. He wants me to take scuba lessons with him. I'm nervous about it, but I know it will be fun," she said.

After everyone finished dessert and was winding down, Patrick and I volunteered to clean up the kitchen. I was glad to have the opportunity to talk with him while we worked.

"How's the new house, Patrick?" I asked, as I dried a plate and put it away.

"Maddie and I are loving it! Of course, she and Myra have been doing all the decorating. It's too bad the furniture store closed. The family discount would be a big help right now," Patrick joked.

I laughed.

"Myra has big ideas when it comes to decorating. Make sure that you get to have a say in how they decorate. It's your home, too. She redecorated our place when she visited. She and Finn did it while I was at work, and I had no say. It wasn't really my style, and I had to put some of my things back in to make it my own again," I told him.

"Yeah, I feel that way sometimes, too. But Madeline listens to me, even if Myra doesn't," he said.

"That's good! Finn just goes along with whatever she wants," I replied.

"How are you and Finn doing?" Patrick asked.

I paused a few seconds before answering.

"Things have been stressful lately," I confided, which was, at least, truthful.

"Everyone is anxious for Finn to finish his dissertation and get his Ph.D. so you guys can move on to the next step," Patrick said.

"Yes, I'm anxious for the next step, too," I replied. Although the next step now would be very different.

We finished our tasks and headed back to the living room to join the rest of the family.

"We should have some Christmas music, Matt," Myra suggested.

"I'll turn on the music as long as you all promise not to sing!" Matt teased. Finn's family was known for singing out of key.

"You don't like my singing voice, Matt?" Jack Sr. asked, and then started to sing "Jingle Bells" loudly and off-key.

Everyone laughed.

I would miss the fun times like these with Finn's family. But for now, I would just enjoy this last Christmas with them. We'd be leaving in the morning and heading back to Memphis with Jack and Simone.

As I was about to fall asleep, I thought, *Would Finn finally share his secret with Jack? If not, I would.*

CHAPTER 17

THE WEIGHT IS LIFTED

The next morning came too quickly. After a simple breakfast and lingering hugs goodbye, we loaded the car and began the drive back to Memphis with Jack and Simone. The plan was to arrive in time for one more walk around the lake before dinner—a final quiet ritual before returning home.

As the miles passed beneath us, my thoughts narrowed. I replayed the conversation I knew had to happen. Would Finn finally tell Jack the truth? Or would I have to do it myself?

Either way, it would happen that night.

The realization straightened my spine against the seat. The dread I'd been carrying began to shift into something steadier. For the first time since Finn's arrest, I didn't feel cornered.

I felt prepared.

When we pulled into Jack and Simone's driveway, we went inside to change and freshen up, the air thick with the unspoken knowledge that the evening would not unfold like the last.

As we prepared for the walk, I told him, "You know this is your last chance to talk to Jack, right? If you don't do it, I will. But it will be better coming from you."

He didn't answer me immediately but sat on his bed, looking down.

"I don't know if I can do it," he stammered. "This is extremely hard for me."

At that moment, I felt compassion rather than anger for him. He was finally feeling some of the consequences of what he'd done. His actions were about to be exposed to the people he loved. And although they had already been exposed to me, this was different. This time, he had to initiate it himself.

"I know it's hard. But Jack will be able to help you. He might even be able to help you tell your parents and the rest of the family. You know Jack and your family all love you. I saw how they all interacted with you the past few days. The photo Jack gave you was a very loving gift. He will be shocked, I'm sure. But Jack is not just your big brother; he is a professional and has dealt with stuff like this. He will be there for you."

We headed downstairs, and then Jack and Simone led us to the path around the lake. Again, I stayed a few steps behind with Simone so the brothers could talk. While Simone and I chatted about our nice holiday, I watched Finn out of the corner of my eye.

And then the moment came – Jack stopped and turned toward Finn, a look of disbelief on his face. It only took Simone and me a few steps to reach them.

Simone saw the look of shock on Jack's face and asked, "What's wrong?"

Jack didn't answer, but turned to me and embraced me in a tight hug. I held onto him for a moment, not wanting to let go. I felt so relieved that I thought my body might go limp and fall if I let go. I choked back a sob as we released each other.

"I'm so sorry!" he said. "How on earth did you manage to keep this to yourself all this time?"

I was in tears by now, and Simone was still confused.

"What's going on?" she pleaded again.

Jack looked at her and said, "Let's head back to the house where we can all talk."

I noticed then that Finn was also crying. The secret was out, and there was no going back. A deep, aching sorrow washed over me–yet beneath its weight blossomed a profound, liberating relief. At last, this heavy burden was no longer mine to carry alone.

When we returned to the house, Jack grabbed each of us a beer from the refrigerator. We went into the family room and sat down.

When we were all situated, Simone implored, "Will someone please tell me what's going on?"

I waited for Finn to speak up, but he didn't.

Jack looked at Simone and said, "Finn's in trouble. He tried to solicit sex from an underage girl over the internet, and he has been charged with a felony. He has also been diagnosed with bipolar disorder."

Simone was stunned and turned to me, "What? Is this true? Oh, Kass, I'm so sorry!"

"I didn't believe it myself," Jack said. "But when I asked Finn if he was guilty, he didn't look at me or respond. From my years of professional experience, I knew he was telling the truth. I've seen that reaction too many times before."

Then Jack looked at Finn solemnly and said, "Okay, now I need you to tell us everything. Start from the beginning."

I felt mixed emotions as I sat there listening to the story again. I felt sadness and empathy for all involved, even Finn. But as he told the story again, I noticed he omitted some crucial details and spun it to imply he was the victim.

"I guess it started when Kassidy was traveling so much for work," he began. "I was lonely and got online in a chat room."

Jack sensed my annoyance and glanced my way before asking Finn, "What was your intention in getting into a chat room?"

"I just wanted to talk to people, that's all!" Finn replied defensively.

"And what kind of people were you talking to? Men, women, children?" Jack asked.

"Women mostly," Finn admitted.

I felt a surge of heat rising up my neck.

At least he admitted that he mostly talked to women! I thought to myself.

"But you're married, Finn! Did you think it appropriate for you to get online and talk to other women?" Simone queried.

Jack reached out for Simone's hand. Partly to comfort her and partly to quiet her so Finn could continue.

"No! I mean - it wasn't like that! I was just lonely!" Finn replied weakly.

"So, how did you go from just talking to getting arrested?" Jack asked, getting impatient with Finn's apparent stalling.

Finn sighed before responding.

"At some point, I started chatting with a girl I thought was eighteen. I mean - she told me she was eighteen. And I enjoyed talking to her," he said.

"What did you talk about?" Jack asked.

"At first, it was just light and fun," Finn replied.

"And that changed?" Jack asked.

"Yeah, our conversations turned to talking about sex."

"And did she take the conversation that way, or did you?"

"I did," Finn said, unable to meet Jack's gaze.

"You know that regardless of her age, you were betraying Kassie, right?" Jack pressed a little more forcefully.

"Yeah, I know. But I was under so much pressure. Everyone was telling me I needed to finish my dissertation and graduate. It was all so hard, I just cracked!" Finn shouted.

"Okay, so you felt you were under pressure," Jack said gently, trying to calm Finn. "But how did you end up getting arrested?"

"The girl was not eighteen as she told me. She was only eleven, but I didn't know that," Finn continued.

"Eleven!" Simone repeated in shock.

He's still not coming clean about knowing her actual age all along! I thought to myself.

"Yeah, eleven. The mother discovered the chat and started chatting with me, pretending she was her daughter. And things continued to escalate," Finn revealed.

"And who escalated things?" Jack asked.

"I did!" Finn responded angrily, but still did not look up.

Jack paused before asking another question, trying to control his emotions. "Then what happened?"

"When the mother felt she had enough evidence that our chats were not innocent, she got the cops involved. From there, a policewoman started chatting with me, pretending she was the girl," Finn said glumly.

"So the policewoman was pretending to be eighteen or eleven?" Jack asked, clearly doubting Finn's claims that he thought she was eighteen.

"I don't know! She was just pretending to be the girl!" Finn replied, frustrated.

"Okay, keep going. How did you end up getting arrested?" Jack countered, letting the age question drop for now.

"We decided to meet. And when I met her, it was the policewoman and not the girl," Finn said. "When I realized it was not the girl, I tried to leave, but then a bunch of cops surrounded my car, and they arrested me."

I watched Jack and Simone as Finn recounted his story, which was a mix of truths and lies.

"I have been going to counseling," Finn continued. "And I have bipolar disorder, like Hayden. It's not my fault that this happened. I just cracked under the pressure."

"Bipolar disorder," Jack repeated, rubbing his chin. "That makes some sense. But it does not nullify your responsibility in this, Finn."

Tears rolled down Finn's cheeks when he heard Jack's words. He had been hoping that Jack would see him as a victim.

Jack thought for a moment and then had some additional questions.

"What is your plan to tell the rest of the family?" Jack began.

"I don't have a plan," Finn replied, looking at his hands again.

"Do you want to call Mom and Dad together to tell them?" Jack asked.

"No! I'm not ready!" Finn cried. "Telling you and Simone has been hard enough. I need some time to recuperate from this."

"I understand," Jack said. "But don't wait. It will just get harder."

Then Jack turned to me and asked, "How are you doing? How can I help?"

"How can we help?" Simone corrected, patting Jack's arm.

"I'm not sure how to answer that question. But it helps just to have it out in the open and not carry this secret alone," I responded.

"You didn't have to carry this alone," Finn muttered angrily.

I felt the familiar urge to argue rise in my chest, then let it fall. What would be the point? He either couldn't—or wouldn't—see what this had been like for me. And most days, I wasn't sure he even wanted to.

Simone suddenly stood up and said, "We should eat something."

No one was hungry then, but I went with Simone to the kitchen to prepare some snacks. Jack had grabbed a second round of beers, and we needed something in our stomachs to absorb the alcohol.

She hugged me and said, "I can't imagine what you've been going through."

I melted into her loving hug.

"It's been hard," I responded. "And except for my therapist, Dianne, I have felt very alone."

Simone handed me some cheese and a cutting board, and I went to work while we talked.

"You are very strong, Kassidy! I don't know how you managed for the past three months." Simone said, shaking her head.

"Well, Dianne has helped me. Finn has also gone to counseling, but I don't know how seriously he is taking it," I continued.

"What makes you think Finn's not taking it seriously?" Simone asked as she arranged some cold cuts on a plate.

Grateful I could speak openly with Simone, I answered her. "He blames everyone else for his actions." She nodded in agreement and then said something that surprised me.

"I'm not too surprised that Finn and Hayden both have issues. Their mother has had some issues in the past. And I suspect their grandmother did, too."

It was the first time anyone had mentioned their grandmother. I had long had my suspicions about that. She had died suddenly when Myra was a child, but no one ever talked about how she died. There seemed to be some secrecy around the death of their grandmother, and I always thought it was strange that Myra and her siblings were sent to live with different relatives.

But I was curious about something else Simone had revealed. "What did you mean when you said Myra had issues in the past?"

"When Finn was about five or six years old - a little after Jack, and I had gotten married - Myra went through a depression. She didn't want to interact with Finn much during that time. She stopped putting him to bed and tucking him in, and he was left on his own a lot," Simone told me.

"Really? Finn never mentioned it," I said, surprised.

"When Jack and I visited, it was hard to watch because Finn was so young and didn't understand why his mother was suddenly ignoring him. He would act up to get her attention, but she didn't react. Not even to yell at him," Simone told me. "Jack was still in graduate school at the time, so he didn't have the knowledge he has now. When he tried to talk to her about it, Myra just told him she was fine, even though she clearly wasn't."

She handed me some crackers and a plate. Then she washed a few vegetables and cut them into slices.

"When their dad was at work, the older kids cared for Finn, made sure he was fed, played with him, and read to him. Of course, Joy was only a couple of years older than Finn and probably didn't understand what was happening, either. But she was more independent at that point. It lasted about a month, and Myra began to come out of it. No one in the family ever talked about it."

I knew Finn's older siblings, especially Joy and Madeline, always looked out for him, but I thought it was because he was the youngest. This shed new light on their relationships.

"You mentioned something else I've always wondered about. You said you thought their grandmother may have had issues. I've always wondered why Myra and her siblings were sent away to different relatives when their mother died. And no one has ever mentioned how she died. Do you know?" I asked.

"No, I don't know, either. No one has ever said anything about it. But I also thought it was strange that Myra and her siblings were sent away," Simone agreed.

"It seemed like her death was sudden. At least it didn't seem like she had an illness like cancer. And if it had been a car accident or heart attack, I feel like that would have been talked about. And they talked about how their other grandparents died. The grandmother's death always seemed to be a mystery," I replied.

"I know what you mean. I always suspected their grandmother may have taken her own life," Simone said, voicing what I had been thinking.

"Exactly! What other reason would there be to hide it?" I agreed.

We grabbed the snacks and headed back to the family room. Jack and Finn were deep in conversation. They didn't seem to notice us when we set the snacks down and settled in.

"When did you first feel like something wasn't right?" Jack asked Finn.

"I don't know - high school or college," Finn sighed.

"Have you ever acted on your feelings to have sex with a child in the past?" Jack asked boldly.

"No, of course not!" Finn exclaimed.

"What made you act on them now?" Jack probed.

"I don't know. I was just under so much pressure. It was just too much!" Finn shouted.

Finn didn't seem angry, just frustrated.

Jack had experience and backed off when he realized it was too much for Finn. He asked questions similar to the ones I had asked Finn, but Jack asked them without anger or hurt. He kept the emotion out of it as much as possible, something I had not been able to do. I'm sure Jack had a lot of feelings about all of this, but he relied on his experience to keep those feelings separate.

We talked for several hours and had a few beers before finally deciding to call it a night. Finn was exhausted when we returned to our room, while I felt lighter and energized. It was a great relief to have shared this with Jack and Simone.

As I passed the mirror, I noticed that I looked less tense. My shoulders no longer hunched forward tightly, and I was standing straighter. My neck no longer felt knotted and achy. Someone else in the family knew.

"I'm proud of you for telling Jack and Simone," I told him.

And I meant it. It was a big step toward Finn taking action, and I felt I was also moving toward my next step—telling Finn I wanted a divorce. I would wait until we got home so I could discuss it with Dianne. I was unwavering in my decision, but I wanted her advice on how to tell Finn. I wanted to be ready to handle whatever response he threw at me.

The next morning, Jack and Simone made us a delicious breakfast, and then the four of us took another walk around the lake. Finn and Jack talked more, and I noticed that Finn was less irritated this morning than he had been the night before. I hoped that he was starting to feel some of my relief.

After the walk, we packed up the car. It was time to make the drive back to Austin. I had called Peggy, our pet sitter, to let her know that we'd be later than expected, and she agreed to take the dogs for an extra walk before we got home. The dogs adored Peggy, and they wouldn't mind. In fact, I knew that they would be looking for her for the next few days after we returned. They always did.

Once we were on the road, Finn and I had a chance to talk. I asked him how he felt about things now that he had confided in Jack.

"I feel better. You were right to make me tell Jack," he admitted.

I felt the sting of the half-truths he told Jack, but voicing them would spark another exhausting clash. So I swallowed my words, guarding my dwindling strength for the battles that truly mattered.

CHAPTER 18

HELL HATH NO FURY

Finn still hadn't told his family, but he kept talking to Jack that first week home. Jack was helping him figure out how to break the news. They agreed he'd tell his parents over the weekend. Finn wanted me on the line when he told them, but Jack said he needed to do it alone. I was relieved. I felt the same. It would be hard enough telling my own parents.

When I went to counseling that week, Dianne was happy to hear about our trip and that Finn had finally spoken to his brother about his arrest. Then I told her about the plan to tell Finn's parents.

"You must be feeling pretty good about all of that. That is progress." she said with a smile.

"Yes, I am. I'm relieved that I'm no longer the only one in the family carrying Finn's secret," I replied. "But now I also have to tell my parents. It's going to be so hard." My eyes welled with tears just thinking about it.

"And there is something else," I continued, "I know I will never be able to trust Finn again. Our marriage is over. I want to tell him I want a divorce before we both talk to our parents."

Dianne sat back slowly in her chair. "I'm not surprised that you've come to this conclusion. What he did was very hurtful, and he doesn't seem to be taking steps to regain your trust. Are you sure this is what you want?"

193

"Yes," I replied firmly. "How do you stay married to someone once trust is gone? I can't. Not anymore."

"And are you prepared for the consequences?" Dianne asked.

"I've thought about them," I said. "A lot."

"What consequences do you imagine?"

I hesitated. "I'll be a divorced woman in my thirties. A divorcee." The word felt heavy in my mouth.

Dianne tilted her head slightly. "That's an interesting choice of words. What does that label mean to you?"

A memory surfaced before I could stop it. "When I was a teenager, a divorced woman moved into our neighborhood. I remember the way the other women talked about her. They used that word—divorcee—like it was something shameful. They'd wrinkle their noses, like they'd caught a bad smell."

Even now, I could see their expressions.

"That certainly left an impression on you!" Dianne said with a slight laugh. "But there is nothing wrong with being a divorced woman. You are ending a marriage to someone who has betrayed you. You are doing what you need to do to be healthy and happy. People have no reason to judge you."

"I know. But most of our friends are married or getting married. Now, I will be the only single girl in our group. It will change the dynamics, and I worry I might lose some friends," I admitted.

"That may happen, Kassidy," Dianne agreed. "But you will make other friends. What is another consequence you are preparing for?"

I took a deep breath before responding. "I'm going to propose that I take responsibility for all of the debts in both of our names and that Finn has to take responsibility for all the debts in his name only. And I plan on getting it in writing when we talk to the lawyer. I will be taking on the lion's share, but it is the only way to be sure the debts will be paid. I can't trust Finn to pay them."

Dianne paused before responding.

"That is a big responsibility, Kassidy! But I also think that it's smart. You are already the main breadwinner and have been paying those debts. Removing Finn from them and not taking on any additional debt that he has gotten himself into is a good way to protect yourself," Dianne said, smiling.

"Without having Finn's out-of-control spending to deal with, I know I can pay the debt and get myself back to a better financial position."

Dianne nodded.

"I also want to keep the house, the dogs, and my car as part of the divorce settlement. I think I'm in the driver's seat there since I earn more money, and he is the one who committed the felony." I continued. "He may end up in jail."

"I agree that should not be a problem," Dianne replied. "You've got things figured out. I'm very proud of you, Kassidy!"

I felt a wave of strength come over me. Warmth in my core radiated outward to my limbs. Even my fingers felt tingly. I felt lighter than I had in months. I was taking action. I could do this! I was going to be alright.

"Thanks, Dianne. But the hard part will be telling Finn I want a divorce. I have no idea how he will react, but I'm sure he'll be angry and hurt. What should I say to him?" I asked.

"You must be direct and remain calm when you tell him. Are you also going to kick him out?" Dianne queried.

"I have thought about that, too. I'm not planning on kicking him out until our finances are settled and I have everything in writing. I know him and he'll run up more debt on our joint credit cards," I replied.

"Have you considered freezing the accounts or cutting Finn's credit cards?" Dianne asked.

"Yes, I have. But since his name is on the accounts, I'm not sure I can do that legally without having something in writing. He'll probably call the credit card companies and tell them he lost his cards. No, I think it's best to let him stay until things are in writing," I replied.

"Are you worried that he might get violent or hurt you when you tell him you are divorcing him?"

"I don't think so. I know he will be angry, but he has never hurt or threatened me. But he has done other things I didn't think he could do. So, I guess I should be prepared for anything."

"Yes, that's wise. When and where do you plan on telling him?" Dianne asked.

"I'm planning on telling him tonight at home. I want to tell him before we talk to our parents this weekend," I replied.

Dianne nodded, her expression serious but measured. "I'm glad you're telling your parents. And when you talk to Finn, I want you to think about your safety. Keep physical space between you. Make sure you have a clear path to the door—and that it's unlocked. Keep your phone with you. If he becomes aggressive, leave immediately and call 9-1-1. Raise your voice if you need to. I hope none of that will be necessary, but I want you to be prepared."

She paused before adding, "And if it comes to it, you have every right to ask him to leave. Your physical safety matters more than financial concerns."

Her words didn't frighten me. They steadied me.

I was grateful for her experience—for the way she treated this moment with both realism and respect. For the first time in months, I didn't feel trapped.

I felt ready.

I stopped by the ice cream shop on the way home and ordered a double chocolate cone with brightly colored sprinkles to celebrate. It felt lavish and comforting, two things I needed in my life just then. I took a seat by the window, watching passersby as I enjoyed the rich cone.

I wonder how long the divorce will take? I thought. *Jordan Jensen offered to give us a discount. I guess I'll start there. I'll call him as soon as I get home. There's no reason now to wait.*

When I got home, the dogs greeted me at the door. I said hello to them and petted them. Then I walked through the living room toward the stairs, the dogs following close behind.

Finn was sitting on the couch watching television. I passed without saying hello and started to head up the stairs.

"Hi," Finn said, suddenly realizing I was in the room.

"Hi," I replied, stopping on the third step. "Have you walked the dogs yet?"

"No, I was waiting for you. Do you want to walk them together?" he replied.

We hadn't been walking them together lately, but had been taking turns. I wanted to walk them myself.

"I don't feel like cooking tonight. If you haven't eaten yet, maybe we could order Chinese food or pizza. And I can walk the dogs while you go pick it up," I suggested.

I hoped the thought of take-out would distract him from wanting to walk the dogs with me. I wanted that time to clear my head and prepare to tell him I wanted a divorce.

"Yeah," he responded, smiling for the first time since I'd walked in. "Chinese food sounds good."

I wondered if he was curious why I suddenly had a change of heart about getting take-out or if he was simply happy with the suggestion.

I ran upstairs to my room and quickly called Jordan before changing my clothes. He picked up the phone on the second ring.

"Jordan Jensen," he said as a greeting.

"Hi, Jordan. It's Kassidy Haggerty," I replied.

"Hi, Kassidy! What can I do for you?" he said pleasantly.

"I want to make an appointment with you. I want to file for divorce," I responded, firmly.

"I'm sorry, Kassidy. But not surprised. I would be happy to help you and Finn with that," he replied.

"I haven't told Finn yet. I'm telling him tonight," I confided.

"Oh," Jordan responded, sounding surprised. "Do you want to come in by yourself or with Finn? Since this is a no contest state, we could work out the details more quickly if you're both here."

"Yeah, that would be fine. The quicker we can get this done with, the better."

"Are you available on Wednesday at 10 A.M.?"

"Yes, Wednesday at 10 A.M. will be fine," I replied.

"For both of you?" Jordan queried.

"It will have to be," I stated

"Then I'll see you then, Kassidy."

I hung up the phone, smiling. Taking charge of my life felt liberating! Then, I quickly changed and headed downstairs. Finn was already reviewing the menu for our favorite Chinese restaurant. I told him what I wanted and leashed up the dogs. The walk usually took about 30 minutes, so Finn said he'd call in the order about 15 minutes after I left with the dogs and then go pick it up. As I walked out the door, he sat back on the couch to watch television.

I had a pleasant walk around the neighborhood, the dogs leading the way. A new single-story, straw-bale house was being built down the street from where we lived. It was supposed to be more energy efficient, and I enjoyed walking by and checking out the progress. I noticed that the walls were all up now, and they were starting to add windows. The life of the house seemed to parallel my own life. A lot had changed, and more change was coming. But this house was being constructed, while mine was being dismantled.

The closer the dogs and I got to home, the faster my heart raced. My hand shook as I unlocked the door.

Get it together, Kass! You don't want Finn to suspect anything until you're ready to tell him!

When I opened the door, I was relieved that Finn was not back yet. The dogs were happy and tired from their walk. I filled their bowls with fresh water and food, grabbed a beer from the fridge, taking a long swig to settle my nerves.

I got out plates and spoons for serving and set them out on the counter. Then I leaned back against the counter, sipping my beer, taking in the view of the kitchen and dining room from where I stood. The dining set had been a hand-me-down from Finn's aunt: solid oak, with a heavy table and an etagere trimmed in brass. It wasn't my style, but I'd been grateful to have it.

Now I found myself wondering what would happen to it when we divorced. What would happen to all our shared things?

The bed in my room had come from my parents – definitely mine. The futon in the guest room, where Finn was sleeping now, had come from his sister. He could have that. We'd bought the couch together from his family's furniture store. Finn might want it, but if he ended up in a small apartment, maybe the futon would be all he'd take.

I'm mentally splitting up our belongings in my head! I am doing this!

The one thing I was concerned about was whether Finn would want to take Sam with him. He thought of Sam as his dog and Lizzie as mine. But he would likely end up in prison, so keeping Sam wasn't a reasonable expectation, even if the trial took months. He would need his car, but the dogs were staying with me.

The dogs barked, announcing Finn's return. I finished my beer and grabbed a fresh one. I needed a little liquid courage to get through the evening.

As we filled our plates, I noticed Finn had gotten himself an order of egg rolls. He put both on his plate without a thought of offering me one. I felt the heat start to rise up my neck, but then I calmed myself by telling myself that I would not have to deal with his selfishness much longer.

"Did you get me a beer?" Finn asked, noticing mine as we sat at the table.

I responded without looking up from my plate, "They're in the fridge."

Finn exhaled dramatically, got up, and grabbed himself a beer from the fridge. Each act of selfishness only served to bolster my resolve.

I ate slowly, savoring each bite of my Kung Pao Chicken, occasionally washing it down with a sip of cold beer. I was lost in thought, steeling myself for the showdown.

Dianne's words echoed in my head: be calm and direct, make sure you have a clear path to the door, make sure the door is unlocked.

Finn wolfed his meal down and then got up to get seconds.

"Did you walk by the straw-bale house?" Finn asked in an effort to break the silence between us.

"Yeah," I answered, "The walls are all up and they're starting to put the windows in."

"They're making good progress."

"Don't you walk by there when it's your turn to walk the dogs?" I asked.

"No, I haven't been that way in a while. Lizzie always seems to want to take the shortest route," he responded.

She always wants to take the longest route when I walk them, I mused.

We fell back into silence. Finn pushed his food around on his plate, seeming to have suddenly lost his appetite. I sipped my beer, rehearsing in my head what I would say to Finn.

We finished eating, and as we were clearing the dishes and putting the leftovers away, Finn asked, "What's going on? I feel like something's wrong."

His observation was much too little and irreparably too late. Something had been wrong for quite a while! But I knew what he meant, so I simply said, "Let's go into the living room and talk."

He looked pale as he followed me into the living room and sat on the couch in his favorite spot. As Dianne had suggested, I walked over to the chair by the front door, putting distance between us. I had left the front door unlocked and had set the phone on the table next to the chair when we returned from our walk.

Here we go.

Lizzie, always my protector, took her usual position between us, sensing the tension. Sam also felt it and jumped onto the chair by the window, keeping a little distance between her and whatever was going to happen next.

I took a deep breath and let it out slowly. "Since we're telling our families this weekend about what's going on," I began softly, "I've made a difficult decision. I've lost trust in you and don't see any way of getting that back. And I cannot be in a marriage with someone I don't trust."

I paused, bracing myself, gathering what felt like the last of my strength. Then, slowly—steadier than I felt—I said the words.

"I want a divorce."

Even after everything, they were among the hardest words I had ever spoken.

My body locked into stillness, every muscle drawn tight. The air felt thin, as if the room had narrowed around us. I didn't want to end our marriage. But the truth had been forming for months: it ended the moment trust shattered.

Ten years of love, fractured by a secret life unfolding behind a screen.

I didn't realize I was crying until my vision blurred. Across from me, Finn's face crumpled, tears slipping down his cheeks as well.

It took a minute or two before Finn spoke.

"I can't believe this is happening!" he shouted angrily. "Is that why you wanted me to tell my family? So, you could pass me off to them and get rid of me? Is this what you have been planning all along?"

I expected resistance, maybe grief. Instead, he was more upset about the timing than the fact that I was leaving. That said everything.

"No!" I shouted back, "This was not an easy decision, and I tried for a long time, hoping we could work things out."

Lizzy stood up between us, ready to lunge at Finn. I grabbed her collar and pulled her gently toward me, stroking her back to calm her.

"But you did what you did, and you've blamed everyone else along the way and haven't taken responsibility for it. You haven't been taking counseling seriously, I'm sure you're not taking your meds, and you didn't tell Jack the truth about knowing the girl was underage before you went to meet her!" I yelled.

"But," Finn tried to interject, but I cut him off.

"How did you think I was ever going to be able to trust you when you keep lying to everyone?" I asked. I hadn't meant to spew everything I was feeling that way. But his attitude hit a nerve with me. I let my feelings flow.

"I told you the truth and look where that got me!" he shouted.

Something inside me snapped.

"The hell you did," I shot back. "You hid the truth from me. You've been hiding things for years. You were cheating long before this last incident. And you didn't admit you knew her age until I forced you to answer the question."

My voice shook, but I didn't lower it.

"That's not honesty, Finn. That's getting caught."

"I should have known better than to expect your support!" he retorted. "You have been putting so much pressure on me to finish my dissertation and graduate; it's your fault that I cracked under the pressure! What do you expect from me with all this pressure? And you have been pressuring me to tell my family. I told Jack, and that wasn't enough for you!"

"It took you four years to finish your master's," I said, my words tumbling over each other. "And you've been working on your PhD for six years with no end in sight. Six years, Finn."

I shook my head, heat rising in my chest. "I have waited. I have supported you. I have been patient."

My voice broke anyway. "But I'm done waiting."

He said nothing.

The silence only fed the fire. He kept shifting blame, sidestepping responsibility, acting as though this had all simply *happened* to him. Every word made my skin prickle. My muscles tightened, my hands trembled.

I wanted to scream—tear through the air with every ounce of fury I'd swallowed for years.

But I didn't.

I forced myself to breathe, steady and slow, clinging to Dianne's voice in my mind, anchoring me, reminding me how to stay grounded when his words tried to drag me under.

"Your actions broke my trust, and you haven't done anything to regain it," I said as calmly as I could, considering I was shaking. "After what you've done, I'm not sure you even could. I want a divorce."

My words just hung in the air between us. I watched tears stream down his cheeks as I waited for his reaction. Mine had stopped. I was resolute in my decision, and we both knew it. We sat staring at each other, waiting for the other to say or do something.

When he finally spoke again, he said softly, "But I love you. I never meant to hurt you. Please don't do this!"

He was trying to appeal to my empathetic nature. But I didn't trust his words. I knew it was just another attempt to manipulate me. "I need to take care of myself now," I replied.

I got up and started walking out of the room toward the stairs. At that point, he jumped up and ran after me, grabbing my arm in a vice-grip.

Lizzie and Sam ran after him, growling and trying to position themselves between us, but there wasn't room.

"You can't do this!" he yelled directly into my face, ignoring Lizzie's threats.

He had never been violent or hurt me, but I was suddenly afraid. "Let go of me!" I shrieked as I twisted my arm out of his powerful grip. I rubbed my sore arm as I felt the tingle of the blood rushing back into it.

But then, he lunged at me, his hand darting out with a sudden, jarring force, nearly knocking me over, but failing to grab my arm again. Fear and anger erupted inside me, and I shoved him into the chair we were standing in front of, forcing him to sit.

I leaned over so I was inches from his face and said through gritted teeth, "Don't you ever touch me again!"

A look of fear crossed his face. He knew he had crossed a line and that I was serious.

It wasn't until I started walking away that I noticed Sam and Lizzie flanking me, silent sentinels at my side. They were no longer growling—but they were there, ready, reading the energy in the room better than most humans could. I hadn't called for them. I hadn't needed to. They just knew.

But I had stood my ground. I had taken care of myself. And in that quiet, powerful way animals understand, they seemed to sense that too. They stayed close but didn't intervene—like they were honoring what I'd just done.

I started for the stairs up to my room when I turned and said, "Tomorrow, you will call your parents and tell them what is happening. We will decide when you need to move out when we talk to Jordan. Until then, you will be on your best behavior. You will not spend a dime without checking with me – not with the credit cards, not from our bank account. And you will not lay a hand on me or the dogs. Do you understand?"

The edge in my voice surprised me as much as it scared Finn. He was looking at the floor as he listened.

His voice cracked as he said, "Yes, I understand."

He never looked up, but I was sure he had heard my message clearly.

"One more thing," I added. "We have an appointment with Jordan on Wednesday morning."

I went to my bedroom, taking the phone with me, the dogs following close behind. I shut and locked the door behind me. I didn't think he would do anything more, but I wasn't about to take any chances. The dogs were on high alert now, and I knew they would be while Finn was around. But despite our unsettling interaction regarding the divorce, I slept soundly. I had a plan and was acting on it. I was finally taking care of me.

CHAPTER 19

BREAKING THE SILENCE

The next morning, Finn was in the kitchen making coffee when I got up. "Good morning. Would you like some coffee?" he asked pleasantly as I entered the room.

"Yes, thanks," I responded, a bit surprised.

He handed me a steaming cup and said, "I'm really sorry about last night."

"I get that you are upset," I responded, "but you are the one in the wrong here, and you don't get to lash out at me. But I do appreciate the apology. And the coffee."

I managed a weak smile, although I was leery of his sudden behavior change after his angry explosion the night before.

"I know," he replied, "it won't happen again."

We sat down to breakfast, and he asked, "Do you want to take the dogs to the park with me after breakfast?"

"I thought you were going to call Jack this morning for some last-minute advice and encouragement before calling your parents."

I wanted to be there when he called them. I had to see and hear it for myself, or I'm not sure I would have believed him.

I didn't want to start another fight, but I wanted him to follow the original plan, so I took a deep breath before continuing. "We can take the dogs later. I think there are some calls you need to take care of first," I replied in a matter-of-fact tone.

He sighed deeply and said, "Yeah. I know. I was just hoping…" and his voice trailed off. He gripped his mug tightly, like a child gripping a favorite toy.

A part of me still felt sorry for him. I knew that what he had to do would not be easy, but it had to be done. After breakfast, I cleared away the dishes and poured each of us another cup of coffee. The menial tasks had become a welcome distraction in our chaotic new life.

As I handed him his cup, he said, "Thanks. I guess I'd better call Jack."

I stood in the kitchen and watched as he picked up the phone. His voice was thick as Jack answered, and Finn said, "Hi. I guess it's time. Any last words of advice?"

I could not hear what Jack was saying, but Finn nodded and said "yeah" and "okay" repeatedly as he listened. Then they said their goodbyes, and Finn hung up the phone. He sat down heavily on one of the dining room chairs. His face was pale and sweaty. But without saying a word to me, he picked up the phone and dialed again.

"Hey, Dad, it's Finn…yeah, I'm okay. Well, not really. Can you get Mom on the other line? I have something I need to tell you, and it will be easier if I can tell you both together," I heard him say.

He paused as he waited for his mother to get on the line. He nervously tapped his fingers on the dining room table while he waited, shifting in his chair. He tugged anxiously at the hem of his blue t-shirt. Then he slumped over the table, leaning on the elbow of his free hand.

"Hi, Mom," he continued. Then he started to cry.

He took a beat before telling them about being arrested and what had led up to it. He got choked up several times but pushed through and managed to get out enough to give them a pretty good picture of what had happened. He also told them about his bipolar diagnosis and blamed his actions on the disease. He still looked like he was going to throw up, but there was a hint of relief in his voice.

When he finished, he stopped to listen to what his parents had to say. The tears were really flowing then. I grabbed the box of tissues from the powder room and handed them to him. He gave me a little smile at that small act of kindness.

I could hear his father asking questions, and Finn gave them some more details. One of the questions must have been if he knew how old the girl was, because once again, he lied and said that he thought she was 18, or he would not have gone to meet her.

He's trying to convince himself that he didn't know, I thought. I pushed aside my anger. At least he had told them. It was on him if he continued to lie to everyone. His lying was not a reflection on me. Dianne's words that I was not responsible for his actions were sinking in.

After a bit more discussion, I heard Finn say, "Kassidy and I are getting a divorce."

Although it was what I needed, it was hard to hear him say it out loud, and I felt my eyes well with tears. I was firm in my decision, but getting used to saying it and hearing it would take a while. Divorce was something I never thought I'd be doing.

A few minutes later, Finn said, "Yes, she's right here," and he handed me the phone.

I reluctantly took the phone from him. I wasn't ready to speak to my in-laws and had no idea what I would say to them. So, I started with "Hello." It came out like more of a question than a greeting, my voice heavy with trepidation.

My father-in-law, Jack Sr., spoke first.

"How are you holding up?" he asked.

"Not so well," I responded. "As well as can be expected, I guess."

It was a weak answer, but telling them I was hurt and angry at their son's actions would not help matters.

"Yeah," Jack Sr. said, "This is quite a mess he's gotten himself into."

I wasn't sure how to respond to that. I wanted to ask what Finn's parents would do, if anything, to help him. But my mother-in-law cut in before I could ask. I could tell she was crying, and her voice was more like a squeak than a voice.

"I just can't believe this is happening!" she said.

Her voice trailed off, and there was an uncomfortable silence.

Then my father-in-law spoke again and said, "I'm sorry. I think you've really been taken for a ride."

What did he mean by that? I thought. *Had he known that Finn had issues?*

I was about to ask him what he meant, but he abruptly said goodbye and wished me well. I muttered a goodbye and thanked him.

I'll never know what he meant by those words. It was the last conversation I ever had with him.

My mother-in-law was still on the line, and her voice pulled me out of the stupor he left me in. "Why didn't you stop him? You should have stopped him from getting arrested!" Myra shrieked at me.

Her reaction startled me. "I had no idea what he was up to," I stammered.

"Well, you are his wife! You should have known!" she accused.

"He lied to me and hid what he was doing," I countered.

But she continued her tirade. I noticed Finn was biting his lip. He was only a few feet away, but he must have heard her piercing voice, even if he couldn't make out the words.

"And now, when he really needs you, you leave him! You have never been supportive of him! And you were off working when you should have been there for him!" Her voice was shrill.

Anger surged through me, boiling under my skin. She was blaming me—just like Finn had! My fist clenched, my teeth gritted, and the fury bubbling inside me was too much to hold in. When I spoke, my voice cracked with heat, sharp and trembling with the tension I could barely contain. I could feel the rage in every word, as if it was vibrating beneath the surface, ready to explode.

Rather than lashing out at her, I tried to keep my voice from wavering and said, "Finn has lied to me, he has cheated on me, and he has committed a terrible act for which he could go to prison. Those were his choices, not mine! And regarding working and not being here for him, I have supported us financially for the last ten years. I'm hurt and angry. But I'm not to blame for this."

I returned the receiver to Finn without saying goodbye to her and walked out of the dining room.

It took me about twenty minutes to stop trembling. My mother-in-law and I had never had the best relationship. She never thought I was good enough for her son. But I never expected her to lash out at me for what Finn had done. I couldn't sit and kept pacing back and forth across the small living room. The dogs sat close to each other on the couch, watching me and wondering what was next. I heard Finn wrap up the conversation with his mother and hang up. He walked into the living room and started in on me.

"You were very rude to my mom!" he yelled at me. "You didn't even say goodbye to her! She is not happy with you!"

I couldn't help the harsh, angry laugh that burst out. "I was rude?" I responded in disbelief, my voice high and tight with anger. "She acted like this is my fault! I guess I'm not surprised. You're not taking responsibility for your actions, so why should she think any of it was your fault?"

"What do you mean by that?" he retorted. "You wanted me to tell them, and I did! What more do you want from me?"

His face was an angry red. Lizzie jumped off the couch and positioned herself between us.

"You told them, but you also lied to them about the girl's age and not knowing, just like you did with Jack!" I stated, trying to steady my voice but still sounding very angry.

He started to deny it, but he knew he couldn't, so I changed the direction of my questioning.

"What did your parents say to you?" I asked.

"They were shocked. My mom couldn't stop crying. My dad just kept saying that this was a big mess," he said.

"Yeah," I agreed, "He said that to me, too. Are they going to try to help you in any way?"

I was hoping they would give him support, both emotional and financial. He would not have either of those from me for much longer.

"My dad asked if I was looking for a job. I guess I need to do that now. I won't be able to pay rent on what Ed pays me to help him with his filing."

That was encouraging. At least Finn was starting to think about what he would need to do to take care of himself when I was no longer supporting him.

"You'll also need to start looking for an apartment," I added.

At that, he frowned.

"Yeah, I know you want me out. But I think we should talk to the lawyer first and figure out what we need to do," he said.

"You'll need a place to live, regardless of what Jordan tells us to do. We are getting divorced!" I replied sternly.

We had cleared one hurdle today, and although I knew I needed to tell my parents, I felt like that one deed was enough for today. My usual time to call my parents was Sunday, and I decided to call them the next day and tell them what was happening. That would give me some time to steel myself, too. I was about to tell Finn my plan when the phone rang. He went to get it and checked the caller ID before answering.

"It's Madeline!" he announced as he read his oldest sister's name on the caller ID, "Mom must have called her and told her! I don't want to talk to her about it."

"You will have to talk to her sooner or later, so you might as well just do it now." I walked over, picked up the receiver, and handed it to him.

"I can't! I'm not ready," he said in protest.

He took the phone from me gingerly.

"Hi, Maddie," he uttered softly into the phone.

He paused to listen to her reply. Tears started to stream down his cheeks.

"Yeah, it's true," I heard him say.

Naturally, she was shocked and couldn't believe what he had done. I could only hear Finn's side of the conversation, but I could tell from his reactions that she was being compassionate and empathetic.

"Thanks, Maddie! I don't know what help I need right now. But I appreciate you offering," Finn said to her, as the tears continued to roll down his cheeks.

After another pause, he said, "Yeah, she's right here."

"Madeline wants to talk to you," as said as he handed me the phone and grabbed some tissues.

Madeline and I had always had a good relationship. I was worried that would change now that Finn and I were getting a divorce.

"Hi, Maddie!" I said when Finn handed me the phone.

"Oh, Kassidy, I'm so very sorry to hear about what Finn did! I'm so sad you are divorcing, but I completely understand. But I want you to know you are family, and even though you and Finn are getting divorced, that won't change."

"Oh, thank you, Maddie! I really appreciate that!" I said, holding back the tears.

"Thank you for not ruining Christmas by keeping the secret through the holidays. I'm so glad we had such a nice holiday together. Things will be changing now," she continued.

"It was tough for me to bear Finn's secret. But I'm also very grateful that we had a nice holiday together," I told her.

Especially since it was the last holiday I'll be spending with you all, I thought, but I did not say it aloud. It made me sad to think about it.

"Take care of yourself, and please let me know how things are going. And let me know if you need anything!" Madeline said.

"Thank you, Maddie! Take care!" I replied and hung up.

A few seconds later, the phone rang again. This time, it was Finn's other sister, Joy. Finn picked it up less hesitantly after the warm response he had gotten from Maddie.

"Hi, Joy," he replied a little less timidly than he had when he spoke to Madeline.

He paused as he listened to Joy speak.

"Yeah, it's true," I heard him say once again.

I noted that I had not heard him tell either Madeline or Joy any details. They must have gotten those from his parents or Jack. Or maybe they weren't ready to hear all the details yet. Hearing their little brother had been arrested and would have been shocking enough.

"Thanks, Joy! I know you're disappointed in me. But I appreciate your support," I heard Finn reply when it was his turn to speak again.

He handed me the phone and said, "Joy wants to talk to you, too."

"Hi, Joy," I said, "How are you doing?"

"Hi, Kassidy. I'm just so shocked and disappointed in Finn. But how are you doing?" Joy asked.

"I'm doing as well as can be expected, I guess. So not so good," I replied.

"I'm so sorry that you've had to deal with this on your own. But I'm also grateful that you didn't tell us before or during Christmas and we were able to have a nice holiday together. But now that we know, please call me if you need anything. You're still family, and I hope that you won't feel uncomfortable reaching out and staying in touch," she told me.

"Thank you, Joy. I really appreciate that. You're my family, too, and I would like very much to keep in touch." I replied. "And Christmas was wonderful, despite the burden of keeping Finn's secret. I'm so glad we had that time together."

When I got off the phone with Joy, Finn asked if we could take the dogs for a walk together. He needed to get out of the house and away from the phone for a while. Although his sisters had been supportive, it was still draining to talk about what happened and deal with their emotions along with his. I understood how he was feeling and agreed that a walk would be good for us. We decided to go to Town Lake to walk, so we loaded the dogs in the car and drove the two miles to the park.

"There are a lot of people out today," Finn observed, as he pulled Sam closer to the edge of the path to get her out of the way of passing runners.

"It's early January. Everybody has started their New Year's fitness routine," I replied.

"But it's cold out here," Finn retorted. He never did like the cold.

"The sunshine is beautiful, and with a jacket, the cool air is refreshing," I replied, dragging Lizzie away from another friendly dog and out of the path of a couple of bikes.

"I guess," Finn responded without conviction.

"How are you feeling after talking to your parents and sisters?" I asked.

"A little relieved. It was easier with Maddie and Joy. They were shocked, but supportive," Finn said.

"Yeah, it felt good to be able to talk with them openly," I agreed. "But what did your parents say? Were they supportive?"

"Not really. My dad said I'd gotten myself into a big mess. And my mom— she was very hurt and angry."

"Yeah, your dad's reaction was a bit perplexing. I guess he was in shock," I replied, although I thought there was more to it than that. "And your mom was very upset."

And angry at me, though I'm not the one she should be angry at. I kept my thoughts to myself, not wanting to start another argument with Finn.

"Yeah, she told me she was distraught at finding out that another one of her children has bipolar disorder. She's worried people will find out and think it's a reflection on her," Finn confided.

I could understand her concern – mental illness often comes with a stigma attached. Still, Myra infuriated me with her fear of exposure. That was part of the problem with mental illness. Maybe if she had been less secretive and less ashamed, Finn would have found a way to get help when he was in high school or college.

I had hoped that his parents, especially his mother, would have been more concerned about helping their son get the help he needed rather than worrying about what people would think. But I had to admit that I was worried about what people would think, too.

When we returned home, the message light on the answering machine was blinking. There were several messages.

Finn pushed the play button tentatively but was relieved to hear Jack's voice.

"Hi Finn and Kassidy, it's Jack. I'm checking to see how things went with telling Mom and Dad. Madeline, Joy, and Hayden also called me to see how you were doing. They were all shocked, but I think everyone will be supportive. I'm going to give Mom and Dad a call and check on them. But give me a call when you get a chance."

The rest of the messages were from Hayden.

"Hi, Finn, it's Hayden. I just heard what happened. Call me as soon as you get this. I can't wait to talk to you."

"Hi, it's Hayden again. Give me a call back, Finn. We have so much to talk about!"

"Hi, Finn, it's Hayden! Call me back. I'm really anxious to talk to you about bipolar disorder."

"It's me again, Finn, I really want to talk to you. Call me back!"

"Finn, where are you? Call me!"

We'd just listened to the last message when the phone rang again.

"It's Hayden," Finn said, as he read the caller id and picked up the phone. "I hope he's not manic!"

I suspected after listening to the messages that he was.

"Hi, Hayden. We just got back from walking the dogs," Finn told his brother as he answered the phone.

I could hear Hayden's anxious voice but could not understand what he was saying. But I got the gist from Finn's responses.

"Yeah, it's true. I have bipolar disorder, too," Finn replied to Hayden.

Finn paused as he listened to Hayden.

"Yeah, I guess you're not alone anymore. I guess I'm not either," Finn said softly, as a tear slid down his cheek.

I hadn't considered what a relief it would be for Hayden to know that someone in the family would finally understand some of what he had been through. And I was glad Finn had Hayden to talk to about bipolar disorder, too.

I could only hear Finn's part of the conversation. Hayden must have asked him about the arrest.

"I met an 11-year-old girl online and went to meet her, except by that point I had been chatting online with her mother and then a female detective. So when I went to meet her, it was not the girl and I got arrested," I heard Finn say.

He's finally being honest! As painful as it is to hear, I'm relieved that he feels comfortable telling Hayden the truth. Hayden might be the only person that can help Finn start owning up to his actions.

"I'm going to counseling," Finn responded to another of Hayden's questions.

And then he said, "I do have a prescription for meds. But I don't like taking them."

Maybe Hayden can convince him to take his meds, I thought. Although I didn't have faith that Hayden took his regularly. But maybe now that they were both diagnosed, they could help each other.

They talked for a long time, and then Finn said, "I'm exhausted, Hayden, but we can talk again soon."

Finn paused and then said, "Yeah, Kassidy is right here."

"Hi, Hayden, how are you?" I asked when Finn handed me the phone.

"Hey, Kassidy, I'm doing great." he told me. "I'm sorry about what's happening with Finn. I wish you had told me sooner."

I understood what it meant to him not to feel so alone. I had felt alone for the last three months while we kept Finn's secret. I knew that not being the only one in the family with a diagnosed mental illness relieved him of some of the strain.

"I know, Hayden! I wanted Finn to tell everyone sooner. But he wasn't ready. It was a lot for us both to deal with," I replied. "But I'm so glad you and Finn are discussing it now. Please keep talking with Finn and Jack. Maybe together you can help the rest of the family understand."

"Thank you, Kassidy. I'm sorry that you and Finn are getting divorced," Hayden replied.

"Thank you, Hayden! Take care!" I responded, before hanging up the phone.

Then I turned to Finn.

"Do you want to call Jack back now?" I asked.

"No. I'm too drained to talk to anyone else tonight. I'll talk to him tomorrow," he replied, wearily.

"Yeah, I'm exhausted, too." I responded.

Finn went up to his room, and I let the dogs out one last time before heading upstairs to mine. I realized that neither of us had eaten dinner, our exhaustion overtaking our hunger.

But there was such great relief at having shared the secret. Sharing had lifted a huge weight. Although I knew there was still a lot to deal with, I was beginning to see the light at the end of the tunnel.

CHAPTER 20

RESCUE MISSION

The next day, I woke up feeling lighter. When I realized today was the day I told my family, that soon changed.

I went downstairs, passing the closed door of Finn's room. The house was still, and I knew he was sleeping. Then I continued into the kitchen to start a pot of coffee.

The sun was just beginning to rise, washing the room in a pale, uncertain light. I let the dogs out and bent to pick up the Sunday paper from the front step. The sight of it made my stomach tighten. Ever since the article exposing Finn, I had avoided newspapers altogether, as if headlines themselves could wound.

But he would need it now—to search for an apartment, a job, some next step that no longer included me. I carried it inside and set it on the table, leaving it there for him.

I needed some time to collect my thoughts before calling my parents. I always called them at eight, and I didn't want Finn within earshot—didn't want his interruptions, his presence shaping what I could or couldn't say. If I could persuade him to take the dogs on their morning walk, I would have the privacy I needed.

At 7:30 I rose for a second cup. As I poured it, I heard his footsteps coming down the stairs. My chest tightened. I grabbed another mug out of the cabinet.

"How are you doing?" I asked as I handed Finn a cup of coffee.

"I'm doing alright. A lot of mixed emotions after talking to everyone yesterday," he responded.

"Yeah," I agreed, "I feel that way, too. But I feel like we have more support now. And I think Jack can help you work through some of your feelings and help everyone else in the family now that they know."

He nodded but didn't say anything. I wasn't sure he wanted to talk to Jack again yet.

"Are you going to call your parents today?" he asked.

"Yes," I said. I paused before continuing, "I thought maybe you'd like to take the dogs for a walk so that you wouldn't have to be here when I talk to them."

I wasn't sure if he would take that as a sign that I didn't want him here or if he would take it as an act of kindness to spare him from having to go through it again. Honestly, for me, it was a little of both.

"That's a good idea," he replied, "I don't want to hear what you say to them or their reaction. Yesterday was more than enough for now."

I was relieved I'd be able to speak to my parents privately. A small part of me wondered if he'd wanted the same when he called his.

But I didn't trust him enough to give him that space. Even with me sitting right there, he hadn't told them the whole truth.

Who knows what story he would have crafted if I hadn't been listening?

As soon as Finn left with the dogs, I sat with the phone, a cup of coffee, and a glass of water. I wished then that I had Lizzie with me. I would have felt less alone with her there. But I knew what I had to do.

When my mom answered the phone, her cheerful "Hi, Honey!" nearly undid me.

I asked her to get my dad on the line. My voice was steady at first, but the moment I said, "It's about Finn," something in me began to shake.

I told them. Not every detail—just enough. The arrest. The minor. The chat rooms. The affairs. The counseling. The divorce. Each sentence felt like dragging something heavy across gravel. I could hear my mother's sharp intake of breath. My father went quiet in that way he did when he was trying to stay calm.

They asked questions—when, how, why hadn't I told them sooner? I explained that there had been so much to untangle. That I'd needed Finn to tell his family first. That I had a plan. That we were meeting with a lawyer. That he would be getting his own place.

Admitting we were in debt was almost as painful as admitting the rest. I waited for disappointment. Instead, I heard concern.

"Are you safe?" my father asked more than once.

"Yes," I told him. And I believed it.

They urged me to get away from him immediately. I reassured them I was handling it. For the first time since all of this began, I felt calm when I said I was divorcing him. Certain. Counseling had helped me find that steadiness. This was my decision—not fear, not pressure. Mine.

We ended the call with them repeating how much they loved me and how proud they were that I was taking steps to protect myself.

A few minutes later, the phone rang again.

They were coming.

They had already decided. They would drive from Ohio to Texas and be there the next evening. There was no arguing with them. My mother was packing; my father was mapping the route.

After I hung up, the house felt different. Less hollow. I had been carrying everything alone for months. Now, help was on the way.

I made them a hotel reservation nearby and called back with the details. When we said goodbye, I realized something had shifted inside me. I could stand on my own—but I didn't have to.

For the first time in a long time, I felt cared for.

I had just hung up the phone with my mom when Finn returned with the dogs.

"Did you talk to your parents?"

"Yes, I did. They are on their way to Austin."

"What? They are coming here?"

"They are going to stay in a hotel, but yes, they are coming to Texas to make sure I'm okay," I told him.

"Wow! That's a long drive just to make sure you're okay," he replied. "I'm surprised they would do that!"

He still doesn't see that this is happening to me, too. That his choices harmed me. That I was hurt and needed support, too.

When I arrived at work on Monday, I told my boss what was happening. He didn't hesitate to give me the time I needed. I planned to work through the morning and leave early, even though I didn't expect my parents to arrive until evening. I wanted to be home when they called.

It was lunchtime when the kitchen phone rang. The caller ID showed the La Quinta Inn. I assumed it was the front desk with a question about my parents' reservation.

Instead, I heard my mother's voice.

"Hi, Honey. We're here. We just checked in."

"Already?" I laughed in disbelief. "Didn't you stop overnight?"

"We did," she said, hesitating. "But neither of us could sleep. So we got up early and finished the drive."

"I'm on my way."

When I reached their room, I barely had time to lift my hand to knock before the door swung open. My mother wrapped me in her arms, and I held on tighter than I meant to, fighting back tears.

"I'm so happy to see you," I whispered.

"Oh, Honey… are you okay?" she asked, her voice breaking. "We're so sorry you're going through this."

"I'm okay, Mom." And for the first time, I felt steady saying it.

She stepped aside so I could hug my dad. He didn't say anything at first—just held me close, his embrace firm and protective.

"You must be exhausted," I said once we were seated in the small hotel room.

"We didn't even think about that," my mom replied. "We just needed to get here."

"I don't even remember most of the drive," my dad admitted. "We were on autopilot."

"Like a daze," my mom added.

I sighed heavily. "I'm just grateful you made it safely. Are you hungry?"

I had left my own lunch unfinished in my rush to see them.

"We should probably eat," my mom said, "though we haven't had much appetite since your call. Maybe after we talk."

"We could grab something and talk," I offered.

She shook her head gently. "It's better here. More private."

My dad leaned forward. "How are you really doing?"

I took a breath. "I'm okay. I know this is a shock to you. But I've had three months to process it… to make decisions."

"But are you sure you aren't in danger with Finn in the house? What if he does something drastic?" my mom asked.

"I don't feel that I'm in any danger. Really, there is nothing to worry about," I assured them.

"But what about Finn's bipolar disorder? Didn't you tell us that Hayden acted erratically when he visited you? How has Finn been behaving?"

"Hayden's behavior was erratic because he stopped taking his medication. And Finn's behavior, well, he seems depressed more than anything," I replied.

"And you're not worried he might hurt you?" my mom asked.

"No, when a bipolar person is depressed, they're more likely to hurt themselves. When they are manic, like Finn probably was when he was interacting with the girl, they are more likely to hurt themselves or others," I replied.

"Even so," my dad said carefully, "we think you should come home with us."

My mom nodded beside him.

For a moment, I couldn't speak. They had driven twenty-two hours to take me back to Ohio.

"I love you for that," I said finally. "But I'm not coming home."

They exchanged a look.

"I've talked with a lawyer. Finn will be getting his own place soon. The divorce should be straightforward." I paused. "I have a plan."

"You don't have to do this alone," my mom said softly. "You could stay with us while everything settles."

"I know I could," I replied. "But this is my life. My job is here. My friends are here. If I leave now, I'm running away from something I've already faced."

My dad leaned forward. "What if he doesn't move out? What if he makes this harder?"

"Then I'll handle it," I said. And I meant it.

Silence settled between us—not tense, but searching.

"I've been in counseling," I added. "It's helped me think clearly. I didn't make this decision out of anger or fear. I waited until I was sure."

My mom looked down at her hands. "We just wish you'd told us sooner."

"I know," I said gently. "But I needed to come to this on my own. If I had left because someone told me to, I might always have wondered if I'd given up too soon."

My dad studied me for a long moment. "And you're certain now?"

"Yes." My voice didn't waver. "I didn't take my vows lightly. But trust is gone. And without trust, there's nothing left to stand on."

He exhaled slowly.

"We raised you to be strong," he said.

"You did," I replied. "And that's why I can stay."

Something shifted then. They had come prepared to rescue their daughter. Instead, they were meeting a confident woman.

My mom pulled me into another hug. "We're proud of you," she whispered.

And for the first time since all of this began, I felt it—not just their protection, but their respect.

"Oh! We were supposed to call your sister when we got here!" my mother suddenly exclaimed.

She quickly dialed the touchtone phone next to the bed.

"Hi, Sela! We made it!" she said, when my sister answered. They chatted for a few moments, then she handed me the phone. "Sela wants to talk to you."

"Are you okay? This is insane! I can't believe this is happening," Sela burst out. "What the hell was he thinking?"

"Clearly, he wasn't," I replied, calmer than she expected.

"How are you this calm?"

I almost laughed. I'd had months to absorb what was still crashing into everyone else. They were just arriving at the beginning; I was already at the end. I reminded myself to be patient.

"I'm okay," I said. "Really."

"I heard Mom and Dad got there already. Of course they did," she muttered. "You know they'd pack you up and haul you back to Ohio if they could."

Her voice dropped into a dramatic whisper, even though no one could hear her. I smiled. It felt good—having her quietly on my side.

"They won't," I assured her. "I'm staying."

"Good," she said firmly. "We'll talk more later when you're alone. I just needed to know you're okay—and that they're not kidnapping you."

I laughed. "No kidnapping. I promise. How are Grant and the kids?"

"They're fine. The puppy is currently ruling the house. Grant's still in shock about Finn, but we're good."

We said goodbye, and when I hung up, I felt lighter. Between my parents' steady love and Sela's fierce loyalty, I wasn't alone in this anymore.

"What did your sister say?" my mom asked.

"Just that she can't believe this is happening, and not to let you drag me back home!" I laughed.

"We're not trying to drag you back home against your will!" my mother said, slightly annoyed.

"I know, I was just teasing. And really, I'm fine. I think the worst part is over, and I'm ready to move forward," I reassured them. "And moving home would not be moving forward. But it's nice to know that you are there if I ever need to come home for more than just a visit."

I could tell that they were still uncertain, but they seemed to accept my decision.

"How long are you staying?" I asked, realizing we had never even discussed that.

My parents looked at each other and laughed.

"We didn't talk about that! We thought we'd be helping you pack up your things," my dad said, still laughing. "We just knew we needed to get here as fast as possible."

I hugged them again and then suggested that we get something to eat. I was getting hungry by then and thought they must be, too.

"I guess I can eat now," my dad said. My dad could always eat, so it was a big deal that he had been too upset to eat.

"Yes, I'm feeling better now," my mother agreed.

"Oh, thank goodness! It's three o'clock already and I'm starving!" I admitted, laughing.

Breakfast was always my dad's favorite meal to eat out, so we went to Kerbey Lane, a café that served breakfast, lunch, and dinner all day.

We laughed when, without planning it, we all ended up ordering bacon and eggs. It was such a small, ordinary thing—but it felt like proof that something in my world was still normal.

I could see my parents beginning to relax, their shoulders lowering, their voices softening. And I felt it too. The heaviness of the past few months loosened its grip, if only for an hour.

I needed that break. Sitting there, laughing over coffee and toast with the two people who had known me my entire life, felt like stepping into sunlight after a long storm.

After our meal, we went back to the hotel.

"You can stay here with us tonight," my mom suggested.

"We're still worried that you might not be safe with Finn," my dad added.

"Thank you, but no, I'll be fine. Besides, you need to get some rest," I replied.

"Yeah, we're exhausted!" my mom admitted, my dad nodding in agreement.

I hugged them goodbye, then even though it was just early evening, I left them to rest.

I planned to take the next day off. Since we didn't need to pack up my stuff as they had expected, I suggested a trip to the Lady Bird Johnson Wildflower Center after breakfast. That was always a favorite place to go when they visited. I headed home, sure the dogs were ready for their walk.

CHAPTER 21

CALMING THE STORM

When I walked in the door, Finn was in the kitchen, chopping vegetables for his dinner.

"Where were you?" he asked, without saying hello when I walked through the door.

I stopped to say hello to the dogs, who were happy to see me, before answering him.

"My parents are here," I replied without looking at him, "I went to see them, and we went to get something to eat."

He stopped chopping and looked at me.

"They're here already?" he asked, surprised. "And you went to eat without me?"

I was surprised by his second question. "Yeah," I said, "they got here in record time. And yeah, we went to eat without you. They don't want to see you. They don't feel comfortable with everything that has happened."

Finn huffed and muttered, "They never really liked me, anyway!"

That made me angry.

"That's not true!" I shouted. "But after everything you did, they have a different opinion of you now."

I stomped upstairs to change out of my work clothes. When I came back down, he was still in the kitchen. I didn't say anything to him, put the leashes on the dogs, and took them for a walk.

The fresh air helped to clear my head. I kept reminding myself that it was almost over. We were meeting with the lawyer the day after next. That would put the divorce in motion. I would give him no more than two weeks to move out. I was anxious to move on from this disaster.

I didn't know if Finn had made any progress toward finding an apartment or a job, but that was up to him. After months of living under the black cloud of his actions, I could finally see glimpses of myself again and was ready to be completely free.

I returned to the house, and as soon as I walked in Finn said, "I'm sorry about that." He wiped his hands on a kitchen towel and continued, "I'm just not used to being left out of family stuff. And it hurts that they don't even want to see me."

I paused before answering, not wanting to lash out since he was trying to apologize.

"I understand," I replied calmly. "But you have to understand that because you hurt me, they are hurting, too. These are consequences to your actions. I can't do anything to change that."

Finn's eyes welled with tears. "Can I?" he asked, sadly.

"I don't know," I said, shaking my head, "I honestly don't know."

And although it wasn't even dark outside yet, I went upstairs to bed, the dogs dutifully following me. I was exhausted, too, from the day and from the months of holding his secret and living in this house with a man who was now like a stranger to me. *Just hang in there a little longer*, I told myself. And for the second night in a row, I slept deeply.

The next morning, I picked my parents up and, at my dad's request, we went back to Kerbey Lane for breakfast. I didn't mind one bit. The fact that he wanted to return felt like a small victory, proof that he'd actually enjoyed himself the day before.

Afterward, we headed to the Wildflower Center. While driving, I asked them if they had decided how long they wanted to stay. I was happy to have them there, but thought we should have a plan.

"You're going to see the lawyer tomorrow, right?" my dad asked. "We would like to come with you."

That was not what I was expecting to hear.

All kinds of thoughts raced through my head. *This is a very bad idea. What if they confront Finn?*

Distracted by my thoughts, I almost missed the turn at the light. *What if they voice their opinion about how to split things? What if Finn feels outnumbered and gets defensive?*

A woman walking a dog that looked like Sam caught my eye.

He might not be as agreeable to how and when to separate. I can't have this separation delayed. I need this meeting with Jordan and Finn to go smoothly.

"That is very nice of you, but I don't think it's a good idea. I need to do this myself," I responded, hoping they would understand.

"Are you sure?" my mom asked.

"Yes, I'm prepared. I have gone over all our finances. I know what I will demand and what I'm willing to negotiate and give up. I don't think he will fight much; he has no leg to stand on," I declared confidently.

My parents sat quietly for a minute before my dad spoke again.

"If you're sure," he said.

"Yes, I'm sure," I replied confidently and smiling.

"We're so proud of you, honey!" my mom said, fighting back tears. "And frankly, I'm a bit relieved. I didn't want to see Finn, anyway!"

I got choked up then but tried to stay composed. "Thanks," was all I could manage to say.

We spent the day wandering around the grounds of the Wildflower Center. Although it was still late winter, a few spring flowers were already blooming in the warm Texas sunshine. The air felt soft, almost forgiving.

We talked as we walked, avoiding the subjects of the lawyer, the divorce, and all that had happened. My body relaxed as we wandered around. For a few hours, I was happy just to be together.

On the drive back to the hotel, dad said they wouldn't return to Ohio until after Finn and I visited the lawyer. They were still concerned that Finn might react badly and somehow take it out on me. And although I tried to convince them otherwise, I was glad they were staying. I would need their love and support to face whatever might happen at Jordan's office.

CHAPTER 22

INITIATING THE DIVORCE

Jordan Jensen offered us a discount, so I saw no need to find another lawyer. I hoped it was the right decision since he also represented Finn in his legal case. But if it was a conflict of interest, it was more for Finn to worry about than me.

"Before we begin, I want to let you know that I will charge you a flat fee of $200 for handling the divorce. It's just to cover my time here today and to file the paperwork. Do you agree to that fee?" Jordan asked.

I breathed a sigh of relief. Compared to everything else, that was a modest sum.

"Yes, we agree," I responded for both of us.

Finn looked at me but didn't say anything.

Jordan cleared his throat and continued.

"The divorce will be very simple. Texas is a no-fault state, so neither party will need to show fault. The court will not consider either spouse's misconduct when granting the divorce or awarding property or support."

"All you need to do is agree on splitting your assets. Are you mutually agreeing to this divorce?" Jordan asked.

I said yes, but Finn hesitated.

"I don't have a choice," he muttered.

"Oh, you had choices!" I shot back.

Jordan leaned forward in his chair and addressed us.

"I know this is difficult for both of you. I want to make this as easy and painless as possible for you. But we need to work together. Okay?"

We both nodded our agreement, and he continued.

"Have you talked about how you want to split your assets?" he asked.

"No," we answered in unison.

Before he could continue, I interjected. "But I would first like to discuss splitting our liabilities."

Jordan looked surprised.

"Okay," he replied, drawing out the word as he said it, "But may I ask why?"

"Because we have more of those," I stated firmly, my arms crossed defensively across my chest. "And I want to ensure our debts are managed properly."

Finn squirmed in his seat. Jordan had another question for me.

"Do you have something in mind?" he asked, nervously tapping his pen on his notepad.

I sat back in my chair, uncrossed my arms, and breathed deeply. "I've thought about this very carefully. I will take on all the debts in both our names. That way, I can guarantee they get paid. I don't trust Finn to pay them."

Finn sighed and fidgeted again. But he said nothing.

"And as for the debts that are in his name only, and I honestly don't know how many there are since he has been hiding them from me, I want those to be his responsibility, and I want it in writing that I'm not legally responsible in any way," I declared sharply.

I handed Jordan the list of the outstanding debts in both our names, as well as the stack of our statements for all of them. He let out a long whistle as he reviewed the extensive list, which totaled over $40,000.

"Are you sure about this?" he asked, looking directly at me and ignoring Finn for the moment.

"Absolutely."

I was not going to risk debts in my name not being paid. I had no idea how soon I could pay them off, but I was determined. No matter how long it took.

The lawyer asked Finn, "Are you okay with this?"

I couldn't help but smile at that. I had no idea how much debt Finn had racked up on his own, but I was certain that being relieved of this burden would make him very happy.

But he surprised us both by angrily replying, "It's not like I'm a deadbeat who can't pay my way!"

"Are you agreeing or not?" Jordan sighed.

Finn looked at me and spit out a single word, "Fine!"

I hadn't expected him to thank me, but his anger was unexpected.

The lawyer looked at me and moved on. "I will write it up as you have requested."

"Thank you, Jordan," I replied.

"Ok," he continued, "Now let's go over the assets."

Again, Finn said nothing. I took a deep breath before responding.

"Our largest asset is our townhouse. As the primary income earner, I intend to keep it without a buyout. My retirement accounts will remain mine, and I plan to keep the joint money market account as well. He can keep his Acura, and I'll keep my Honda.

We have furniture, much of which came from his family, and some we purchased. We can discuss how to split that."

I paused before continuing.

"And we have two dogs—I get sole custody."

I kept my voice even, determined not to let emotion creep in. Finn sat rigidly beside me, arms crossed, jaw tight. He hadn't said a word—until then.

"No!" he shouted, "There are two dogs. I get Sam, and you get Lizzie!"

Jordan waited to see what agreement we could come to on our own.

I took another deep breath to calm myself and said firmly, "The dogs stay with me. They are bonded, and we can't split them up. And what happens to Sam if you go to jail? This is not negotiable, the dogs stay with me."

Finn's eyes welled with tears.

"You really hate me, don't you!" he screamed at me.

"No, I don't hate you. I just want what is best for Sam and Lizzie. And that is that they stay with me," I said wearily.

"Are you even going to let me see them?" he asked.

I sighed and said, "Yes, we can work something out so you can see them."

Of course, I would never let him see them without me being there. I was worried he would take Sam, and I could not let that happen.

The lawyer went through other potential assets, and the only other thing that we had was life insurance. I would be changing the beneficiary on mine immediately. And if he wanted to keep his, he would need to pay for it himself going forward. And then there was the checking account.

"Jordan, what do we do about the checking account and debit card?" I asked.

"Is that account also in both your names?" Jordan asked.

"Yes," we answered in unison.

"It would be considered joint property. You'll have to each set up your own accounts, then close the joint account once the divorce is final," Jordan said.

"So Finn will still have access to the joint account until after the divorce?" I asked.

"Yes, legally. You can't drain the joint account completely until after the divorce is final. But you don't have to wait to set up your own accounts. I recommend you start putting your income into your own accounts and start using those for your own expenses," Jordan explained.

I wasn't happy that Finn would continue to have access to our joint account. But at least I could prevent him from accessing my income going forward.

Jordan went over it all again to ensure he was clear on everything and that we were in agreement. He told us he would draw up the paperwork and submit it to the court. He didn't think it would take long to process it since no one was contesting anything. He said he would let us know when the paperwork was ready for us to sign. He suggested we come back to his office to sign rather than having it sent out to us, and we agreed.

"There's one more thing I need from you, Finn. Please give me all the credit cards that are in both of your names," Jordan said.

We were both a little shocked at that, and Finn protested.

"Why do I need to do that?" he asked angrily.

"Because Kassidy is also my client, and I need to protect her interests as much as yours. I don't want you to run up the credit cards she is taking responsibility for before the divorce is final," he said as gently as he could.

"I'm not going to do that!" Finn shouted.

"Then you should have no trouble giving them to me now," Jordan said, smiling politely.

Finn took out his wallet and angrily threw a stack of credit cards on the desk. He had a few more in his wallet.

"Is that all of them?" the lawyer asked me.

I picked them up and looked through them. One of the gas cards was missing, and I said so. Finn reluctantly pulled the missing card from his wallet and threw it on the desk.

"How am I supposed to put gas in my car?" he demanded.

I just shrugged. Jordan picked up the cards and a pair of scissors.

"Kassidy, may I have your permission to cut these up?" Jordan asked.

I nodded my approval. Finn slumped in his chair. I smiled slightly and sat back comfortably in mine.

"Kassidy, there's just one more thing we need to discuss. Are you planning on changing your name? If so, I can include that in the divorce. Or you can petition the court to change it later," Jordan explained.

"Oh, I hadn't even thought about that!" I replied, surprised. "Yes, let's go ahead and change it as part of the divorce."

"Yeah, just go ahead and erase me from your life, Kass!" Finn said, bitterly.

"Finn, you're divorcing, and this is a normal part of that process. Kassidy has every right to change her name." Jordan said evenly.

Finn sank back into his chair, shoulders folding inward, a dark look settling over his face.

Then, Jordan turned to me and said calmly, "I'll get that done for you, Kassidy. You'll still need to go to the Social Security office to make it official, and change it on all your accounts, and such. But you'll have the paperwork you need to do all that once the divorce is final."

When it was all done, we thanked Jordan and left his office.

We drove home in uneasy silence, both of us feeling depleted.

When we got home, the dogs greeted us, unaware of what was happening. I went upstairs to change into something more appropriate for walking the dogs. When I came back downstairs, Finn was getting ready to leave.

"I'm going to look at an apartment. Do you want to come with me?" he asked somewhat cheerfully.

"No," I responded, "this is something you must do alone."

He nodded, the slight smile leaving his face. I waited until he had gotten in his car and driven off. Then I picked up the phone and called my parents, who were still waiting at the hotel.

"Hi Kassidy! How did the meeting with Finn and the lawyer go?" my mom asked.

"Everything went well. But I'll tell you and dad more over dinner. What time would you like me to pick you up?" I replied.

"How about 4:30? I hope that's not too early, but our stomachs are still on eastern time," my mom responded.

"No, that's fine, I just need to walk the dogs, and then I'll come get you."

As I walked, I started making a mental checklist of things I needed to do—update beneficiaries on my life insurance and retirement accounts, take him off the car and house insurance, and change the locks as soon as he moved out. Jordan was helping us get the title for the townhouse put in my name only, and getting each of the cars titled to each of us individually. I wasn't prepared to deal with all my emotions, so it was a relief to make plans and organize my thoughts.

My marriage was ending, and I would soon be divorced. That was not something that I had ever thought would happen to me. Yet here I was. My marriage may not have been officially over yet, as decreed by a court, but it was certainly over for me.

When I returned to the townhouse with the dogs, Finn pulled his car into his spot next to mine. I unlocked the door and let the dogs in, waiting for Finn to get out of the car.

"Hi! How did it go?" I said, perhaps too brightly, as he approached the door.

"It's kind of small, but it's nice and clean. And it's all I can afford, so I put a deposit on it," he responded without looking at me.

It surprised me to hear he had put down a deposit. I was about to ask him how he did it when I remembered he still had access to our joint bank account. I started to get angry, but stopped myself. If this was required to get him out of the house, then so be it. It was a small price to pay in the bigger scheme of things.

"How soon will they let you move in?" I asked instead.

He shrugged, "They will let me know as soon as they do a background check."

My heart sank into my stomach. A background check! I hadn't thought of that. He had just been arrested for a felony, and our credit was maxed out, even though our credit score was good because I paid the bills. Either of those could have been a red flag for a landlord, and he had both! But regardless of whether this apartment worked out for him, I was determined to stick to the timeline I had given him. He needed to move out, and where he went was none of my concern. I just hoped they would return the deposit if he were rejected.

"Have you opened up a checking account for yourself?" I asked.

"No, not yet. I haven't had time," he said bitterly.

"That needs to be on the top of your to-do list. And how is the job search going?" I continued. I was not holding back anymore. I wanted him to have his own account so I could remove him from our joint account.

"I have an interview with a chip manufacturer for their clean lab on Friday," he sighed.

I was surprised and relieved to hear that. And that sounded like a good fit since he had worked in a clean lab at the university. I was hopeful that things were heading in the right direction.

"I also get my check from Ed on Friday. I will open my checking account then," he said less bitterly.

"Great," I replied.

He went to the living room and turned on the television. I headed upstairs to change into something more suitable for dinner with my parents. When I returned down the stairs, he was still on the couch watching television.

"I'm off to go have dinner with my parents," I reported as I grabbed my purse and said goodbye to the dogs.

Finn grunted something unintelligible as I walked out and shut the door.

CHAPTER 23

FINN MOVES OUT

When I got to the hotel, my parents quickly opened the door and hugged me. I felt wrapped in warmth and safety, a sharp contrast to the tension and anger I felt when dealing with Finn.

My parents wanted to hear everything—what the lawyer had said, how Finn had reacted, whether there had been tension in the room.

They didn't know I had agreed to take on all the debt. When I told them, I softened the numbers, minimizing the total. It didn't seem necessary to burden them with the full weight of it.

They were proud of me for taking responsibility, even though they insisted it wasn't fair that I would shoulder it alone. And they were especially relieved that I had secured it in writing—that I would not be liable for any future debts Finn might incur.

We had a quiet, pleasant dinner afterward, the kind where conversation drifted to safer topics. Later, I drove them back to the hotel.

"Are you sure everything's okay?" my mom asked again.

"Yes, everything is fine. Finn has a job interview on Friday and may have found an apartment. It's almost over!" I said to reassure her and my dad.

Whether or not they believed me, they decided to drive back to Ohio in the morning. We hugged and said our goodbyes, and they stood in the doorway of their hotel room, watching me drive away. I was sad they were leaving, but there was nothing they could do except offer emotional support. And that support easily reached from Ohio to Texas.

I was grateful for my parents and comforted to know I could always go home. Finn's parents had been much less supportive of him in that regard, and I felt bad for him. They did not come to see him, and they didn't offer any financial support. Finn's mother also didn't want to talk about it any further. She felt that his actions reflected on her and that people would judge her. Finn would have to find his way going forward, and he still had the criminal issues to deal with. I was relieved I would not have to worry about that soon.

When I got back to the house, Finn was still watching television, and take-out leftovers were lying on the kitchen counter.

A fresh wave of anger rose in me. After everything—after the lawyer, after the debt—he was still spending money as if nothing had changed. Part of me suspected it was deliberate, a small act of retaliation for not being invited to dinner with my parents.

He still carried himself like the injured party.

I hated that he still had access to the joint account, but legally, there was nothing I could do for now. I knew that things would be uncomfortable in the house until Finn moved out.

A part of me still cared about what happened to him, but only to a point. I didn't want to be in the courtroom to hear any of the testimony because I did not want to learn any more about the horrible things he had done. I did not want to pay for legal bills. I certainly did not want to be a character witness for him. I just wanted it all to be behind me.

The next several days were tense while Finn waited to hear about the apartment. On Friday, he went to his interview for the clean lab job. The interview went well, but they would also run a background check and have him do a drug test. The drug test was not the issue.

Finn came home from work with his car loaded with boxes. He had to move regardless of whether he got the apartment or the job. He started by packing up his bedroom, which had also served as his office. When I passed by on the way to my room, I saw him bent over a box of textbooks, running a finger along the spine of one of his favorites. I noticed a tear running down his cheek, a miserable homage to the promising career he had destroyed.

The phone rang, pulling us both from our thoughts. It was the apartment complex calling to tell him he'd gotten the apartment. I was so relieved that he had been approved. Whether they didn't care about Finn's felony charge or it didn't come up in the background check made no difference to me.

"When is the apartment available?" I asked optimistically.

"Tomorrow, but I need to work. I can pick up the keys on my way home, then I'll start moving things tomorrow evening," he replied.

Most of our furniture was too big for his apartment, so he didn't take much of it. He could move his things in several loads in his car and did it himself without my help. I was happy that he did not try to involve me.

By Sunday night, he was living in the apartment. There were still some odds and ends that he needed to move, but he could do that later.

When he packed the last load on Sunday evening, he paused and asked if I wanted to get dinner with him.

I declined, explaining that I thought it would be best if we didn't.

He knelt to hug the dogs goodbye, his voice catching as he whispered to them. I stood back, watching, unsure what I felt—pity, maybe, or simply distance.

Then he turned to me. The hug we shared was brief and awkward, our bodies remembering something our hearts no longer did. He was not the man I had loved and married. Still, the gesture felt like a necessary punctuation mark at the end of a long, painful sentence.

And then he grabbed the last box and walked out to his car.

I closed the door behind him.

He got in his car, and I watched from the window as he drove away. I had a mix of emotions - sadness, joy, relief - as I saw his car turn the corner, and then he was out of sight.

My chest was heavy, but my shoulders relaxed as my body reacted to my jumbled emotions. I was sad that my marriage was over. But I was also happy and relieved to be moving on.

The next day, while I was at work, Finn returned to get the last odds and ends he had left at the house. He came late in the day to be there when I got home. Although I didn't want to see him, I was glad he hadn't left before I arrived. I was still worried that he might try to take Sam with him if he had the opportunity.

I had stopped by the hardware store over the weekend and picked up new door locks. I left them in my trunk, where he wouldn't see them, but I planned to install them that night after he left. Once he was out, I did not want him to be able to come back in. We had said our goodbyes the night before, so we kept the conversation to a minimum.

"Did you get everything?" I asked.

"Yeah," he responded sullenly.

"Then I guess the only thing left is the key," I said, holding out my hand.

"What if I want to come and see the dogs?" he queried, raising his voice.

"If you want to see the dogs, you'll have to call me first, and we'll set a time," I stated firmly.

"Don't you trust me?" he asked incredulously.

"No," I replied softly, "if I did, we wouldn't be getting divorced."

He took the key from his ring and slammed it on the table. And then he stormed out the door without saying a word. I locked the door behind him and checked that the front door was locked as well.

I waited about twenty minutes after he had driven away before I unlocked the back door and got the new locks out of the trunk. I quickly went to work, changing them. I did not trust that he had given me all his keys. I would not allow him to come back for Sam. One of my neighbors, a nice single guy who lived two doors down, walked by on his way back from the mailboxes, and he saw what I was doing.

"Do you need a hand?" he offered cheerfully.

"No, thank you," I smiled, "I've got this!"

He smiled back and continued into his townhouse.

When I finished with the locks, and the dogs and I were safely locked inside our townhouse, I grabbed a beer from the refrigerator, popped Alanis Morrisette's "Jagged Little Pill" into my CD player, cranked up the volume, and danced around the living room in my bare feet, claiming the space as my own.

A few days later, as the dogs and I approached the townhouse on our way home from a walk, I saw Finn's car parked beside mine. He was at the back door, trying to open it with a key.

"What are you doing here?" I asked as I neared the door, stopping before I got too close.

"Did you change the locks?" he asked angrily in reply.

"Of course!" I retorted, "And I can see it was the right decision since you kept a key!"

Finn walked a few steps toward me, and I backed away.

"What are you doing here?" I asked again, more forcefully.

We were outside in the open, and I knew I could call out to my neighbors if I needed help.

Finn stopped walking toward me and said, "I forgot a few things. I just came to get them. I knocked, and you didn't answer."

"You should have called first," I replied angrily. "And why do you still have a key?"

"This is still my house, too!" he shouted at me. "I have every right to have this key! Why did you change the locks?"

"Because this isn't your house anymore, and you don't have the right to come into my home without my approval!" I shouted back. "I haven't found anything that was yours. What is it that you forgot to take with you?"

He didn't respond, so I asked again. "What did you forget?"

He looked down at the ground as he responded. "I didn't forget anything. I just wanted to come back and see you and the dogs."

I sighed heavily. "You should have called first," I repeated, frustrated.

"So, can I come in?" he asked, annoyed.

"No. You can't come in. You can say hi to the dogs, but then you must leave. And you need to call next time."

I was not about to relent. If I did, I knew he would just keep coming back.

As he approached the dogs, Sam greeted him eagerly, but Lizzie was more reserved, perking up when he pulled a couple of treats from his pocket. I gave him a few minutes with the dogs, then told him it was time to go. He gave them each a last pat and walked to his car.

"I'm sorry," he said. "Next time, I'll call first. But my mom told me that you talked to Madeline last week. So, I thought it would be alright."

"That has nothing to do with you coming over here!"

"Fine," he sighed, "I'll call next time."

I stood in the parking lot with the dogs while he drove away. I wanted to ensure he was gone before I entered the house. I was a little shaken at his showing up unannounced. And I was not surprised that he had kept a copy of the key. His deceit was pathological.

A few days later, he showed up at the house again. I had just gotten home from work and had changed clothes to walk the dogs when the doorbell rang. The dogs barked and ran ahead of me to the door. I looked out the window and saw Finn holding a pizza. I made sure the chain was latched before I cracked the door.

"Hi!" Finn said enthusiastically before I could say anything. "I brought a pizza and thought we could have dinner and watch television together. I know your favorite show is on tonight."

The dogs were jumping around excitedly; I wasn't sure whether it was for Finn or the pizza.

"You can't just show up on my doorstep without calling." I reminded him.

"But I brought pizza!" he exclaimed. "And the dogs love pizza bones."

When they heard that, they started barking again.

"Alright," I relented against my better judgment, since the dogs were in a frenzy, already anticipating the pizza crusts. "You can come in, but after we eat you need to go. You're not staying to watch television with me."

I shut the door, removed the chain latch, and let him in. The dogs danced around him, sniffing the pizza he set on the table. As I got out plates, forks, and napkins, he asked for a beer, so I got one for both of us from the fridge. We sat down opposite each other, and each helped ourselves to a slice of pizza. He had gotten my favorite – sausage, peppers, and onions. Obviously, he was trying to get into my good graces, but I was still skeptical about why he was there.

"How's the new apartment?" I asked him in between bites.

"It's small and lonely, but it's nice enough," he replied. "The futon is uncomfortable, but I can't afford a bed until after I start my job."

"And when will that be? Did you get the job at the clean lab?" I asked, hoping that they had hired him.

"Yeah, I start next week," he said, smiling. "I have to go through training, and I will be on a ninety-day probationary period before I will be eligible for benefits. But I think it is going to work out."

Relieved, I congratulated him.

"Mom said you talked to Joy this week. I'm glad you're keeping in touch with my sisters."

It dawned on me then that he had shown up at my door the first time after I had talked to Madeline, and now, he was here again after I spoke to Joy.

Did he think that because I was keeping in touch with his sisters, I also wanted to stay in touch with him? Is that why he showed up unannounced?

I needed to make that clear.

"Just because I'm in contact with your sisters does not mean you can come here without calling first. My relationship with them has nothing to do with you," I stated firmly.

"They still think of you as family," he responded, smiling.

"And I still think of them as family. But that still does not give you the right to show up here. Next time, call first. I don't want to have dinner with you and watch a movie. We are no longer a couple. I agreed to let you see the dogs occasionally, but that is it."

By the end, my voice had risen despite my intention to stay calm.

"Fine!" he shouted back at me. "I try to do something nice for you, and you just get mad at me!"

"You're not trying to do something nice for me! You are trying to manipulate me into doing what you want! You are doing it because you want to spend time with me, the dogs, or both. But we are not a couple anymore. You have to stop doing this!" My voice showed my frustration, but he took it as anger.

"Fine! I'll leave!" he shouted, grabbing the leftover pizza and heading for the door. "I tried to be nice, but you keep holding a grudge. I don't need this!" And with that, he stormed out.

I locked the door behind him and thought, *Now that he's paying his own way, he takes the leftovers home.*

I returned to the table and handed each dog a pizza bone from my plate. They gobbled them down greedily. I took the plates to the sink and dropped the beer bottles into the recycling bin.

Finn hadn't left any crusts for the dogs. He hadn't even thought to give them one before he left.

He's even selfish with the dogs!

I had not yet walked the dogs and had time to do so before my favorite show, "ER," started. I looked out the front and back of the house before stepping outside, ensuring Finn was gone. His car was nowhere in sight, and I breathed a sigh of relief as Sam, Lizzie, and I cautiously crossed the parking lot.

I was extra vigilant for the next few days, especially with the dogs. I did not know if Finn would show up unannounced; mercifully, he had not. A week passed, and it was the night of my favorite show. I was feeling anxious, expecting him to show up unannounced again. I had no contact with anyone else in his family that week, either. I didn't want to provoke a visit from him. I finally started relaxing after the show ended, and he did not appear on my doorstep. Maybe he finally understood that he could no longer get what he wanted from me.

CHAPTER 24

FREEDOM

A couple weeks later, Jordan Jensen called us back to his office to sign the papers. I arrived at Jordan's office a few minutes early. He was finishing up a telephone call and waved me in to have a seat. Finn had not yet arrived when Jordan hung up the phone.

"How are you doing, Kassidy?" Jordan asked, smiling.

"I'm doing fine. Just anxious to get this over with," I replied, smiling back.

We made small talk until the door to the small office opened, and Finn hurried in.

"Sorry I'm late!" he said, without offering any explanation for his tardiness.

I had not seen or heard from him since he showed up unexpectedly with the pizza two weeks ago. He looked a bit disheveled in his wrinkled shirt, and his stubble looked as if he hadn't shaved in a couple of days.

"How are you doing, Finn?" Jordan asked.

"I'm doing alright. I'm settling into my new place. I've never had my own apartment before," Finn replied.

"Have you found a job yet?" Jordan queried.

"Yes, I started working at my new job last week. It's in a clean lab, and I'm enjoying it. It makes me feel like I still have a connection to science," Finn said, smiling slightly.

"Congratulations, Finn! That's good to hear. Now, let's get down to the matter at hand," Jordan replied.

He handed each of us a copy of the divorce decree. Then he went through it with us, page by page, ensuring we both understood the terms we had decided on when we met previously.

Then he asked, "Do you both agree to these terms?"

I agreed and then held my breath, waiting for Finn to respond.

"Yeah, I agree, too," he said, no edge in his voice.

I was relieved that it went smoothly and that Finn didn't make any angry remarks. And then it was time for us to sign the official copy to be filed with the court. Jordan explained that the divorce would not be final until a judge approved and signed the divorce decree. He went on to tell us that we would each be sent a final copy of the signed decree and that we could keep the copies he had given us to review in the meeting.

After he had gone over everything, he walked across the hallway to another law office and asked a young lady to come over and join us. She was carrying an ink stamp and a large black book resembling a ledger.

"This is our notary," he said. "She'll witness your signatures."

Then Jordan handed me the official copy to sign, smiling and saying, "Ladies first."

When I had signed and added my initials in all the appropriate places, he handed the document to Finn and asked him to do the same. I was worried that Finn would protest, but he didn't.

I breathed a sigh of relief. It was almost over!

The notary stepped forward, pressing her stamp firmly onto the paper before adding her signature. We watched as she recorded the details in her ledger, the scratch of her pen sounding louder than it should have. When she finished, we thanked her, and she slipped quietly back across the hall.

I straightened in my chair, my shoulders relaxed. The tight band that had lived at the base of my neck for months finally began to loosen.

As part of the divorce services, Jordan then offered to draw up wills for us. I accepted the offer and set up an appointment with him. Now that Finn would no longer be my husband, I would be leaving everything to my family, including the dogs, should anything happen to me. I wanted to take care of that right away.

"Thanks, but I don't have enough assets to even put in a will," Finn proclaimed.

We stood up to leave, and Jordan shook my hand and said goodbye to me. He asked Finn to stay for a few minutes to discuss something that had come up in Finn's case.

I don't know if Jordan had detained Finn on purpose, but I was grateful I could go to my car without having to deal with Finn on the way to the parking lot.

The papers were signed! Even though the divorce wasn't final, I felt free. I felt like the world's weight had been lifted from my shoulders. And I was happier than I had been in months. I was relieved that Finn had signed the papers and didn't cause any trouble.

On the drive home, I cranked up the radio and sang along.

When I arrived at Jordan's office for my will appointment the following week, he welcomed me with a big smile.

"I have some great news!" he exclaimed.

And then, he handed me my copy of the final divorce decree.

"Congratulations! You are officially divorced!" Jordan beamed.

I could not believe that I was holding the divorce decree. I was overcome with joy and relief. Tears of joy rolled down my cheeks, and I couldn't stop smiling. I felt giddy!

"How did you get this so soon?" I asked, remembering that he had said it would be mailed out to each of us.

"I was at the courthouse yesterday on another divorce case with the same judge. She said she had just signed off on yours. Since I was going to see you today, I asked if I could deliver it. The mail might have taken another week, and I knew you were anxious for this to be over."

"Yes, thank you! Thank you! So that's it – it's official?" I asked, not really believing it could be true.

"Yes, it is official." He was smiling as broadly as I was. "I know that divorce is never easy and that this whole situation has been difficult for you. But I hope this can give you some peace going forward."

"Yes. I want to put this all behind me now. It has been the worst thing I've ever been through."

I was sad about the end of my marriage, and I was still hurt about all that had happened. But I suddenly felt empowered to move forward now that the divorce was final. And that made me smile.

But there was just one thing I had to confirm.

"I want to see in writing where I'm not responsible for Finn's debts," I stated as I started flipping through the pages of the decree.

Jordan gently took the papers from my hand and flipped to the page before handing them back to me.

"Here it is. You have nothing to worry about with regard to Finn's debt that he incurred on his own and any debt he takes on going forward," he said warmly. "And here's the new deed showing you are the sole owner of the house."

"Thank you so much," I said, biting back more tears of joy.

I had it in writing: I was free from paying Finn's debts. And the townhouse was mine.

"Okay," Jordan continued enthusiastically, "let's get your will done."

Jordan entered everything on the computer and then printed out copies for me and his files. He stepped across the hallway to the other law office and asked the notary to come in. It didn't take me long to sign the will.

"So I guess that's everything," I said as I started to stand to leave.

"Not quite," Jordan replied, "if you don't mind, there are a few things I'd like to discuss with you regarding Finn's case."

That stopped me in my tracks. I was not expecting to have anything more to do with Finn's legal troubles. I sat back down a little carelessly and almost knocked the chair over.

"Finn's case?" I asked with trepidation as I gripped the chair.

"Sorry," Jordan offered, "I didn't mean to startle you. I just wanted you to know that the investigation is going forward. You will likely get a call or a summons from a federal investigator. Even though you didn't know anything about Finn's activities before his arrest, they will still want to question you. You have nothing to worry about. I just wanted you to be prepared."

I sat there stunned for a moment before speaking again.

"I appreciate the heads up. What kinds of questions do you think they will ask me?"

"Just basic stuff – did you know what Finn was doing, where were you when he was on the computer chatting with the girl – that sort of thing. Since you were married when this happened, they just want to know if there is any evidence you may have or…" His voice trailed off.

"Or what?" I asked, already surmising what he hadn't wanted to say.

"Or if you were involved in any way," he said flatly. "I know you weren't involved, and I'm sure that they don't believe that you were, or they wouldn't have waited until the divorce was final to question you. They just have to be thorough in their investigation. I just didn't want you to be blindsided."

"How do they know the divorce is final?" I asked.

"They are tracking everything related to Finn very carefully," Jordan responded, his tone more serious.

I did not want to talk to the investigators, not because I was worried or had anything to hide. I was just ready to put this all behind me. But it was necessary - just one more unpleasant piece to wrap up before I was truly free of the mess Finn had created. I decided to focus on that rather than simply dreading it.

"I'm not going to worry about it," I replied as lightly as I could manage. "I really am glad you told me. It's better to know what's coming next."

I rose from my seat and thanked him again. We shook hands, and we said goodbye. Since I already had a copy of my signed and notarized will, it was likely the last time I would see Jordan. I was not planning on going to Finn's trial if it came to that.

Before leaving the building, I turned for one last look at the grand staircase. The terrified, hurt woman who first climbed those stairs was not the triumphant, independent woman who walked down them today.

CHAPTER 25

FREEDOM INTERRUPTED

When I got to my car, I pulled out my new cell phone. It was easy to find in my purse, since it was heavy and sank to the bottom. It was nearly the size of my home phone with an antenna that could be extended for better reception. I pushed the rubber buttons and dialed my best friend, Stephanie.

"Hi, Stephanie! I saw the lawyer today about my will, and he had my final divorce decree. It's done!" I shouted into the phone exuberantly.

"Oh my God, that's great news!" she replied with equal excitement. "We need to celebrate!"

"I agree! Why don't you come over for dinner tonight?" I asked, a spark of excitement returning to my voice. Stephanie had been my biggest supporter through this ordeal, and it only seemed right to celebrate this moment with her. "We can grab some take-out and watch ER."

Stephanie loved that show just as much as I did.

"Perfect," Stephanie declared, "I'll pick up a sausage and onion pie from Frank & Angie's Pizzeria on the way over. I'll be there at 6:30."

"Great, I'll get some red wine. Can't wait! See ya soon."

When I pulled into the driveway, the dogs were already waiting at the door, their tails thumping against the wood. They knew the routine. Walk time.

I changed quickly into shorts, a t-shirt, and sneakers, the dogs trotting after me as if they might miss something. Back downstairs, they sat expectantly as I clipped their leashes on. Then we stepped out into the late-March afternoon.

The air was warm but not yet heavy, the kind of gentle warmth that hints at what's coming. Sunlight brushed my face as we left the townhouse complex and turned into the neighborhood.

As we passed the straw house, I noticed it was nearly finished. Fresh paint gleamed in the light, and a realtor's sign planted in the yard announced Coming Soon.

I slowed for a moment.

That house had risen board by board while my marriage had quietly come apart. Now it stood complete—ready for someone new to walk through its doors.

And I was, in my own way, standing at a threshold too.

As we finished our walk, I stopped by the mailboxes to pick up the mail. A couple of pieces of mail were addressed to Finn. Even though he had assured me that he had changed his address with the post office, I still received his mail. I hoped that would soon stop. I made a mental note to pick up a large envelope to mail to him.

Inside, I gave the dogs some water and then grabbed a glass for myself. The paperwork from the lawyer was sitting on the counter where I had left it when I came home. I picked up the divorce decree, smiling to myself. I had made it through. And even though the lawyer had given me the heads up about the interview, I knew I had already survived the worst.

I got plates, utensils, napkins, and wine glasses to prepare for dinner with Stephanie. The dogs soon alerted me to her arrival with barking and tail wags. I looked out the window and saw that she had parked next to my car in the parking lot. I opened the door and yelled out to her.

"Hi, Stephanie! Do you need a hand?" I asked as she got out of the car.

"No, I've got it, thanks!" she replied as she shut the car door and headed toward me with a large pizza box. "I hope you got wine! I think we need wine!"

"Of course," I responded, laughing. "We're celebrating!"

She came inside, set the pizza on the counter, and hugged me.

"Finally!" she cried, "Your nightmare is finally over!"

"Well, not completely," I said with a sigh. "The lawyer told me that the federal investigator wants to interview me for the investigation. They purposely waited until after the divorce was final to talk to me."

"Why?" Stephanie asked, surprised, "You didn't know anything about it!"

"I know, but they need to make sure I don't have any evidence against Finn and that I wasn't involved in any way. The lawyer said it's just part of the process and nothing to worry about," I shrugged. "But after that, I think it will finally be over."

"But why is a federal investigator involved?" Stephanie asked.

"Because Finn used the internet to contact the girl," I replied.

I poured the wine while Stephanie loaded our plates with slices of pizza. The dogs circled excitedly, anticipating the pizza bones they were sure they would be getting. We made our way to the couch and turned on the television. Our show was just about to start.

Suddenly, there was a pounding on the front door. We all jumped, including the dogs, who had been so preoccupied with the possibility of treats that they had not heard anyone approach. The pounding was so fierce it worried us both. As I went to the door, Stephanie ran to the kitchen and grabbed the phone, ready to dial 9-1-1 if needed. I looked out the peephole and saw Finn, red-faced, leaning on the door and holding a pizza. I quickly secured the door chain.

I yelled out to Stephanie, "It's Finn!"

Finn must have heard me and shouted, "Open the door! I know you're in there, and I know you have someone with you! Our divorce isn't even final, and I can't believe you're already dating!"

He was furious. With the chain secured, I carefully opened the door just a crack.

"What are you doing here? You're not supposed to come over without calling first!"

He tried to push the door open, but the chain prevented him.

"I came to bring you dinner and watch television with you. But I got here and saw a car already in my parking space!" he responded sharply.

"First of all, it's not your parking space anymore, it's mine. We are divorced, and I own this house. I got the final decree today!" I shouted back. "And it's none of your business if I'm dating. But, just to be clear, it's Stephanie who's here, she came to help me celebrate."

Finn tried to push the door open again. But on hearing her name, Stephanie came forward far enough so Finn could see her.

That seemed to calm him a bit until something I said dawned on him.

"What do you mean you got the final divorce decree? I didn't get anything! You're lying!" he bellowed.

"I'll show it to you," I offered, "and I also have some mail for you. So step back so I can close the door while I go get it."

"No!" he shouted furiously, "you need to let me in!"

"Stephanie, call 9-1-1!" I shouted.

Finn backed away from the door when he heard me say that. He had seen the telephone receiver in Stephanie's hand and knew I was serious and that Stephanie would make that call.

"Okay, okay!" he relented, "I'm stepping back!"

As soon as he was away from the door, I shut it and locked it. The dogs had stayed by my side but now guarded the door as I walked into the kitchen to get the divorce decree and Finn's mail.

"Are you okay?" I asked Stephanie. "I'm so sorry, I had no idea he would show up like this and then think I was on a date!"

"Yes, I'm okay. Are you?"

"Yes, but stay ready to dial 9-1-1 just in case and run out the back if needed. I will only open the door a crack to give him his mail and show him the divorce decree. I will not let him touch it."

"Alright," Stephanie nodded, "I'm ready."

I walked back to the door and opened it just a crack. Again, he tried to push it open further, but the chain caught it. I held his mail with two fingers and let the ends of the pieces pass through the opening enough so he could grab them without grabbing my arm. He took them with one hand and reached for me with the other. I slammed the door on his arm.

"Aaagh!" he exclaimed. "Open the door! You're crushing my arm!"

"That's what you get for trying to grab me!"

I released some pressure from the door so that he could pull his arm back. Once he stepped back, I held up the divorce decree so he could see it without being able to reach it. His eyes filled with tears as his new reality sank in.

"I got it from Jordan today," I said gently, "when I was there to prepare my will."

I waited for him to say something, but he just stood there, staring through the crack in the doorway at the piece of paper I was holding.

"You need to go now," I declared firmly. "And don't come back, or I will call 9-1-1!"

With that, I shut and locked the door. Stephanie ensured the back door was locked as well. I picked up our wine glasses from the living room and met Stephanie in the kitchen. She had already uncorked the wine bottle, and I set them on the counter and watched her pour.

"Well, that was interesting!" Stephanie proclaimed sarcastically, grabbing her glass.

My hand was shaking from the surge of adrenaline through my body. I took a big sip of my wine before responding. After setting down my glass, I grabbed the counter's edge to steady myself.

"Unbelievable!" I said, "What was he thinking, just coming over here and banging on the door like that, assuming I was on a date!"

"Would you like to stay at my house tonight in case Finn comes back?" Stephanie asked.

"No, I'll be alright. How are you doing? The show is half over, do you want to watch the rest?" I asked, hoping Stephanie wasn't ready to leave yet. I was okay, but having her there was still comforting.

"Yeah, of course! We will not let him ruin our pizza, TV, and wine night!" she said with relish. "Who does he think he is?"

That made both of us laugh.

We brought the wine bottle back to the living room. Surprisingly, the pizza we left on our plates was still there. Evidently, the dogs were as distracted by the mayhem of Finn's visit as we were.

"Are you sure you don't want to come and stay at my house tonight?" Stephanie offered again after the show.

"No, I'll be fine. But thank you for offering! I don't think he'll be back!" I reassured her.

"Okay, but call me if he does or if you change your mind. The dogs are welcome to come, too," Stephanie replied.

I watched from the door as Stephanie got into her car, and then she made sure I had closed and locked it before she drove away. I was grateful that Stephanie was there and watching out for me. But there was no sign of Finn, and I doubted he would return.

The next morning, I went to work and ran into Stephanie in the parking lot. As we walked into the office, she inquired about the rest of my night.

"Did Finn come back?" she queried.

"No, he didn't. I think he got the message when we threatened to call the police," I replied. "I went to bed after you left and read for a while before falling asleep."

Just then, my cell phone rang. I did not recognize the number, and the caller ID did not give me any indication of who the caller might be. But my intuition told me to answer it anyway.

"Hello?" I said, more of a question than a greeting.

"This is Federal Agent Mark Barnes," the voice on the other end of the line announced. "Am I speaking with Kassidy Haggerty?"

My heart leaped into my throat, and I croaked my response.

"Yes, this is Kassidy," I answered hoarsely.

"I'm investigating the actions of your ex-husband, Finn, with regard to his felony case. I have a few questions and would like you to come to my office. Does Monday at three o'clock work for you?" Federal Agent Mark Barnes asked.

"Yes. Okay. Yes. I can make that work," I stammered nervously. "And how did you get this number? I just got this cell phone."

Agent Barnes chuckled. "I'm a Federal Agent, ma'am."

"Right."

Stephanie was watching me and mouthing, "What is it?" I shrugged and focused back on my conversation with the agent.

"So, Monday at three o'clock," I repeated.

"Yes. Let me give you the address. Do you have a pen and paper handy?" Agent Barnes continued.

I fumbled in my purse and quickly found a pen and an old envelope.

"Yes, I have something to write with. Go ahead," I replied. I wrote down the address and repeated it back to him.

"See you Monday at three o'clock," he said, then hung up the phone.

When I was certain we were disconnected, I turned back to Stephanie, who was anxiously waiting to hear what the call was about.

"That was the federal agent investigating Finn's case. He wants to interview me on Monday." I tried to sound nonchalant about it, but that was not how I felt. I was feeling anxious, and Stephanie saw through my act.

"Well, you knew this was coming. It'll be fine, Kass, don't worry!" Stephanie said.

"I know," I said, sighing. "But what should I wear to be interviewed by a federal agent?"

"Something very prim and proper?" Stephanie offered with a smile.

"Maybe the dark blue dress that I wear for job interviews?" I suggested. "It's not the same kind of interview, but I guess it would work."

CHAPTER 26

THE AGENT INTERVIEW

I arrived fifteen minutes early. Finding the building was easy—too easy, given the weight of what I was walking into. I stepped into the elevator and hit the button for the fourth floor, just as Agent Barnes had instructed. Alone in the mirrored capsule, I caught my reflection in the polished chrome doors. The blue dress with the jacket - the quintessential interview outfit that Stephanie and I had laughed over—back when nerves hadn't replaced laughter. Matching pumps. Conservative, yes. Safe. I hoped it struck the right tone for whatever version of an "interview" this was going to be.

When the elevator doors slid open, I stepped into a stark reception area. A large desk commanded the space like a sentry post. Behind it, a young woman in a crisp dark suit and white blouse barely looked up, her expression practiced and unreadable.

"How may I help you?" she asked as I approached the desk.

"My name is Kassidy Haggerty. I'm here to see Agent Barnes," I told her.

"Please have a seat, and I'll let Agent Barnes know you're here," she said as she motioned to the uncomfortable-looking waiting room chairs.

A few minutes later, a tall man in a tight tan suit came out of a door on the opposite side of the room. He looked at the young woman at the desk, and she nodded in my direction. The man approached where I was sitting and offered me his hand.

"Hello, Kassidy. I'm Agent Mark Barnes. Thank you for coming in today. Please follow me," he said, getting right down to business.

He held the door for me and then led me down a hallway to a small conference room. The room was decorated in government drab – everything was a shade of beige, from the walls to the carpet. Agent Barnes was a match in his suit. The blinds may have been white once, but had yellowed in the Texas sun. Agent Barnes took a seat facing the door and motioned for me to sit in the worn tan chair across from him.

Another young woman in a black suit and white blouse came in, carrying a tray of coffee and water, and set it on the table between us. She came and went without saying a word, and Agent Barnes said nothing to her.

"Would you like something to drink?" he offered me, waving a hand to the tray with the coffee and water.

"Yes, thank you. I'd like some water, please," I replied.

He poured a glass of water from the pitcher and handed it to me.

"Thank you," I said as I accepted the glass.

He poured himself a cup of coffee then opened the file folder on the table before him and sat back in his chair.

"Thank you for coming here today, Kassidy," he said again. "I'm going to ask you some questions about your ex-husband. I just want you to answer honestly. We're investigating him, not you. I want to make sure you understand that."

"Yes, of course," I replied.

He began with a simple question to which I was sure he already knew the answer.

"How long were you and Finn married?" he asked.

"We had just celebrated our tenth anniversary in July," I replied.

"Ten years. That's a long time. And did you know each other long before you married?" he continued.

"We dated for two years before we got married, and we knew each other through school for a couple of years before that. We took geology classes together in college. That is how we met."

"And you lived together at 1742 South Elm Street, Unit 5, Austin, Texas, is that correct?" he asked.

"Yes, that is correct."

"And when did you become aware of his online contact with the young girl?" he asked.

"Not until after he had been arrested, and I picked him up when he was released from jail. He told me the story on the drive home."

"And what was your reaction?" he asked.

"My reaction? I was shocked! I couldn't believe what I was hearing!" I felt hot tears in my eyes.

A box of tissues was on the table, and Agent Barnes reached out and pushed the box closer to me. I took a tissue and dabbed my eyes. I didn't want to cry. I had already cried enough over this mess.

Agent Barnes gave me a minute to compose myself and then continued. "Did you know he had been participating in online chat rooms before his arrest?"

"Chat *rooms*? You mean there were more than one? No. I didn't even know there was one before his arrest."

Was that a form of denial and self-protection? I'd have to ask Dianne during my next session with her.

Agent Barnes interrupted my thoughts with another question. "What did your husband tell you?" he queried.

"Ex-husband!" I corrected, surprising myself as I said it.

"I'm sorry. What did your ex-husband tell you?" Agent Barnes asked again.

"Finn told me that he had been in an online chat room. That he had met women there. Then he started talking to the girl, but he originally thought she was eighteen. But that was a lie; I found out when I read the newspaper article about his arrest. He said he went to meet her, and he was arrested because, at some point, her mother found out. And after she engaged online with him as her daughter, she then turned it over to the police. The police were the ones who continued interacting with him as the little girl, and then they were there when he went to meet her."

"Did he say anything about his interaction with her online?" he asked, eyeing me closely.

"No. He didn't share any details. He said that at some point in the conversations with the girl, things turned to a sexual nature. I asked him who took it there, and he admitted he had." I stopped to dab my eyes again. I noticed that Agent Barnes was scratching some notes on his pad.

"Did he mention sending her any pictures?" he asked as he shuffled through some of the papers in the folder before him.

"No, he didn't mention any pictures. That was another detail I learned from the newspaper article," I replied.

Agent Barnes paused before continuing and looked at me intently. I met his gaze for a few uncomfortable seconds, not understanding where this was headed. He finally sighed deeply and pulled a few copies of photos from the folder.

"Have you ever seen these photos before?" Agent Barnes asked.

I took a quick glance at the photo on top of the stack and turned away. On the table in front of me were pictures of a man's genitals. I had not seen the photos before, but I instinctively knew they must have been the photos Finn had sent.

My head was spinning, and I felt sick to my stomach. I could not look at the photos. And now I was full-on sobbing, no longer able to keep my emotions in check.

How could Finn do this? How could he send such graphic photos to a little girl? Yes, I knew he had sent the pictures to the girl, but seeing the photos was completely different. Again, I felt a wave of anger for not knowing and not being able to stop him.

"I'm sorry. But I had to show you the photos to gauge your reaction. We did not think you were involved, but we had to be sure," Agent Barnes offered apologetically. "I know how hard this must all be for you. If it is any consolation, he sent these when the mother had taken over the girl's chat account. The little girl did not see them."

"I guess that is somewhat comforting," I admitted to Agent Barnes.

"I just have a few more questions," Agent Barnes continued again, "Do you know Tom Mullen or Jeffrey Sunderson?"

"No, I've never heard those names. Who are they?" I asked.

"I can't disclose that, sorry. Your ex-husband never mentioned them?" he asked.

"No, I've never heard of them!" I declared emphatically.

My brain was racing with unpleasant possibilities. *Were these guys he had met in the chat rooms? Were they child pornographers?* Agent Barnes noticed my distress.

"It's nothing for you to worry about, ma'am. It's just something we're trying to sort out on our end," he said to comfort me.

It wasn't comforting, and it just raised more questions for me. But clearly, I was not going to get any answers from Agent Barnes. I waited for his next question, hoping it would be less disturbing.

"Can you confirm that you and Finn are now divorced?" he asked.

"Yes, we are divorced," I confirmed flatly.

"And can you confirm that you no longer share the house with your ex-husband?" he queried.

"Yes, he no longer lives with me," I said wearily.

"And can you tell me whether or not you are still in contact with your ex-husband?" he asked, looking up from his notes.

"I'm not intentionally still in contact with him. He has come by my townhouse unannounced to see my dogs and me. We had agreed that he would call before coming over if he wanted to see the dogs, but he has not respected or adhered to that," I said sharply.

"Has he ever threatened you?" Agent Barnes asked, suddenly concerned.

"Yes. Twice. The first was when I told him I was divorcing him. He grabbed my arm very roughly. And then he got very angry the last time he stopped by unannounced because I had a friend over, and he thought I was on a date. He pounded on the front door, but I didn't let him in. I had the chain on the door, but he tried to grab my arm. Luckily, I was able to avoid his grasp. My friend was ready to dial 9-1-1 if needed and was ready to run out the back door. But it didn't come to that. He left. I haven't heard from or seen him since," I stated.

"When was that, and is there any pattern to when he shows up?" Agent Barnes asked.

"It was last Thursday night. And yes, he usually shows up on a Thursday night, sometimes with dinner. He knows that I like to watch a show that night. He seems to think that is a way to return to my good graces. But it's not."

Agent Barnes made a note on his pad.

"Alright," he said, closing the folder abruptly and tapping it on the table to straighten the papers inside. "I think that is all I need to ask you now. I'll contact you again if anything else arises in our investigation that we have questions about. Thank you for coming in today. I appreciate your time. And it was a pleasure meeting you, Kassidy."

"Thank you," I replied as I stood up to leave. We shook hands, and then he led me back to the elevators and pushed the down button for me. After a quick wave he returned to his office.

I wasn't alone in the elevator. As the doors closed, I became aware of a few sideways glances. That's when it hit me—I probably had mascara streaked down my face from the tears I'd shed when Agent Barnes showed me the photos.

When the elevator reached the ground floor, I stepped out quickly and headed straight for the nearest restroom. One look in the mirror confirmed it. I was a mess.

I hadn't brought any makeup with me. Using damp paper towels, I wiped beneath my eyes and did what I could to make myself presentable before walking back out into the world.

As I drove home, I could not get the image out of my head of the one photo that I had glanced at. I felt disgusted and was shocked again at what Finn had done. I hadn't known what he was capable of. And who were the men that Agent Barnes had mentioned? Had Finn been involved in something more? I shuddered. *It's probably best not to know.*

In my next session with Dianne three days later, she asked how I was doing.

"Not so well right now," I responded.

"Tell me what's going on," she replied gently.

"I was interviewed on Monday by the Federal agent investigating Finn's case," I told her.

"That must have been difficult," Dianne soothed.

"Well, most of it went well. But he showed me the photos Finn sent to the girl. They were very disturbing," I replied, closing my eyes and wrinkling my nose in disgust.

"I'm sorry you had to see those. How did that make you feel?" Dianne asked.

"It made me sick," I said, my voice trembling. "I felt guilty for not knowing. For not stopping him. I didn't think he was capable of this. I didn't know my husband at all."

My tears were flowing now, and Dianne, as usual, handed me the box of tissues.

"You are not responsible for his actions. There was no way that you could have known what he was doing because he took great care to hide it from you. And there is no way you could have stopped it," Dianne repeated.

"My brain knows that, but my heart doesn't," I cried. "I'm just so glad the mother received those photos, not the little girl."

"Yes," Dianne agreed, "you can take some comfort in that. No one could have stopped Finn except Finn. And the mother was there to protect her child, which was her responsibility. You are not responsible for any of it. You must let it go."

I nodded, still crying and having difficulty finding the words to respond. I knew Dianne was right, but it was hard to let go and not feel some responsibility.

"Was there anything else that came as a surprise from the interview?" Dianne asked.

"Yes, something strange came up. The agent read off the names of two men and asked if I knew who they were. I had never heard of them. I don't know how they were connected to the investigation. But it has had my mind racing about the possibilities ever since. And the investigator mentioned that Finn had been in different chat rooms. I just thought he had been in one. It never dawned on me that there would be more than one. Why did I think there was only one?"

Dianne thought for a minute before responding.

"What did Finn tell you? I recall you saying he said he had been in a chat room, not plural. It was probably enough of a shock to hear that, so you didn't think beyond that. He didn't share all the details; you took them at face value at the time because that was enough to process. That's a natural response," Dianne offered.

"Yeah, I guess so. But now I'm wondering what other details I missed. I know Finn never mentioned the two other men. I just wonder who they are."

"You might never find out," Dianne replied. "And you're going to have to accept that."

I knew she was right, but it was hard not to wonder. Part of me also had no desire to know all the details. I knew things already that I wished I had never known.

"Is there anything else you'd like to discuss today?" Dianne asked.

"Yes. Finn has been coming over unannounced with dinner, hoping we can watch television together. Like we used to when we were married," I told her. "And it's usually after I've talked to one of his sisters."

"How does he know you've talked to his sisters?" Dianne queried.

"His mother tells him. And then he seems to interpret that as an invitation to come over," I replied angrily.

"What are those interactions like?" Dianne asked.

I described what had happened the evening Stephanie was over—the accusation, the tension, the way I'd had to calm him down. Just thinking about it made my muscles tense and my heart race.

"That sounds terrifying!" Dianne responded. "I will make sure that I mention this to Robert so he can address this with Finn. That is not acceptable at all!"

"What do I do if he comes back again?" I asked. "Tonight is usually the night it happens – my favorite show is on, and he knows that."

"Do not answer the door. Ignore him. And if he doesn't go away, call the police," Dianne said firmly. "And consider cutting off contact with his family."

"That will be hard. But if that's what I have to do to get rid of Finn, then that is what I'll do. I don't want him to come back," I sighed.

I left Dianne's office and headed home, thinking about what we had talked about. I hated the thought of ending my contact with Finn's family. But he was escalating, and I was worried for my safety. I also took to heart what she said about ignoring Finn and calling the police if he showed up again.

When I got home, I entered through the back door, as I always did. The dogs greeted me enthusiastically. Before letting them out, I went to the front window and scanned the street—a new habit since the last incident with Finn. Seeing nothing unusual, I opened the door and let them into the yard.

After changing clothes, I took them for a walk around the neighborhood.

When we returned, I noticed a police car parked in the guest spaces a few doors down, positioned with a clear view of my townhouse. The officer inside gave a slight nod as I passed, and I lifted my hand in acknowledgment.

At the mailboxes, I spotted a second cruiser on the opposite side, angled toward the back of the building, toward my door.

Had Agent Barnes arranged this?

If Finn showed up tonight, he wouldn't find me alone.

I don't know whether he came by. The evening passed quietly, and by morning the police cars were gone.

I hoped that if he had driven past, the sight of them was enough.

CHAPTER 27

MOVING ON

It had been about four months since my divorce was final. I no longer went to counseling weekly and only saw Dianne every few weeks. Once we were settled in her office, I told her the latest news.

"I got a call from Finn's lawyer," I began. "Finn has been sentenced to three years in prison."

"I heard. Robert got a similar call from Jordan," she replied. "And how are you feeling about that?"

"Well, I can't help but feel bad for him despite everything. Finn completely destroyed his life, and now he's in prison. But I'm also relieved that I don't have to worry about where he is. At least for the next three years."

"It's normal to have mixed feelings about something like this," Dianne said.

"Also, his mother called me. I wasn't home when she called, and she left a message," I told her.

"What did she say?" Dianne asked.

"She told me that Finn was going to jail. She asked me to visit him, because I was his only family here. But I'm no longer his family and will not visit him," I declared.

Dianne smiled.

"That is an unusual expectation," she said. "But you can understand she is just looking out for her son."

"I do," I said. "But protecting him has always meant protecting the secret. And the secret is what kept him from getting help."

Dianne tilted her head. "Tell me more."

"In that family, everything was managed quietly. Covered. Explained away. If his struggles had been named instead of hidden, maybe he would've faced them sooner. Maybe he wouldn't have had to pretend. Maybe he wouldn't have spiraled."

Dianne was quiet for a moment. "Fear and stigma around mental illness run deep. Sometimes families think they're protecting someone when they're actually protecting themselves from shame."

That landed.

"You don't have to carry anger for her," she added gently. "Understanding the pattern doesn't mean excusing it. But holding onto resentment will only tether you to it."

I exhaled. "Yeah, I know. I don't want to stay angry forever, but it may take some time," I replied.

"How are you feeling otherwise?" Dianne asked, "How are things going in general?"

"Things are going well! I got a job promotion, which came with a small pay increase. And I'm so glad Stephanie talked me into joining the cycling group! I've met some great people. I had forgotten how much I like riding my bike! I've recently started dating a guy from the cycling group. It's been nice!"

"You've started dating! That's wonderful!" Dianne said. "How are you feeling about that?"

"Honestly, I was very apprehensive at first. But we've just been taking things slowly and keeping it light," I replied.

"Taking it slow is good! What made you apprehensive?" Dianne asked.

"After what I've been through with Finn, I'm not sure I can trust myself to see red flags. I missed so many signs with Finn."

"That is understandable. But you are more aware now. And you know to listen to your intuition when something feels off," Dianne replied.

"I also wasn't sure how much to share about what happened with Finn."

"Just share what you are comfortable with. No more, no less," Dianne replied.

"That's what I have done so far. I told him I was divorced and that my ex-husband had bipolar disorder. I wasn't comfortable sharing that my ex-husband is a convicted felon or what he did," I told her. "It's been fun going out and getting to know someone new. It's fresh and exciting. I don't know if I'm ready for a serious relationship yet. But I'm having fun figuring it all out."

"It's good that you're having fun and not worried about getting too serious. You have been through a lot, and there is no rush. You just take all the time you need and enjoy the experience," Dianne suggested.

"Hey! This is my first time in your office without needing a giant wad of tissues!" I laughed.

Dianne laughed, too.

"You've come such a long way since you first came to see me, Kassidy. I'm so glad you have such a great support system because I know how much that helps. Honestly, you would have gotten through this without me. I only helped you do it a little faster. And I don't think that you need my help anymore. What do you think?" Dianne asked.

I was shocked to hear that, but I was also pleased. I had come to enjoy my time with Dianne, but I felt I was back on solid ground again. I believed I could continue without her counseling.

"Yeah, I think you're right. I am ready," I agreed.

"That's wonderful!" Dianne said, "And just know I'm always here if needed. But I think you are ready. Counseling is not meant to go on forever in a situation like yours. It's just to help you through the crisis, and you are through the crisis."

"Thank you for everything, Dianne! I don't think I would have gotten through it without you. But we can agree to disagree on that point," I laughed.

Dianne quickly called Robert and walked me to the reception area, where he met us. They both hugged me goodbye and wished me all the best. I thanked them both again and left the building for the last time. It felt good, but also strange, knowing I wouldn't return there again. But Dianne was right. I was ready to stand on my own again, and I had her, my family, and my friends to thank for that.

I returned to the office, eager to tell Stephanie my good news. But Stephanie was waiting anxiously and also had news for me.

"Mine first!" I told Stephanie excitedly. "I just had my last session with Dianne!"

"Really?" Stephanie asked, surprised. "How did that happen?"

"Dianne thinks I'm ready to move forward without her. And you know what? I think so, too," I beamed.

"And I totally agree!" Stephanie said.

"I could not have done it without you, Steph! Truly, thank you for all your support over the last eight months. You are the best!" I exclaimed as I hugged her. "Now, what's your news?"

"We just heard that there's a management position opening in Denver. They said it's open to everyone, but they've already picked their top candidates. They've picked a couple of people - one here in Austin and one in Houston - to interview for the position," Stephanie explained.

"Do you think Max will be one of the candidates?" I asked.

"Apparently, they don't want to move someone who is already a manager. They have a few up-and-comers in mind. People who have been ready to promote, but there wasn't a position available until now," Stephanie shared.

We speculated about which of our co-workers in the office had been eager for a promotion. We eliminated a few who we knew would not want to leave Austin. Then, we narrowed it down to two of the guys we worked with. Gavin had family in Denver and was itching to get back there, and Adrian was interested in climbing the ladder, even if it meant moving his family.

The next morning, Max called me into his office. I shrugged at Stephanie, indicating I didn't know why Max wanted to see me.

When I reached his office doorway, I asked, "Hi Max! You wanted to see me?"

"Come on in and shut the door, Kassidy. Have a seat," Max said to me.

Max only had closed-door meetings for reviews or when he had to deliver bad news. It wasn't review time, and I was suddenly a little worried. Things had been going well, but maybe I had made an unknown mistake.

"Have you heard about the open position in Denver?" Max asked.

"Yes. Stephanie mentioned it yesterday when she was filling me in on what was discussed at the staff meeting that I missed," I replied.

"The Director would like you to interview for the position if you are interested. And I think you would be a good fit for the job," Max declared.

I sat there for a minute before responding. I couldn't believe they offered me the opportunity to interview for the position. I made the short list of candidates!

"That's great! And yes, I'm interested, I'm honored to be considered!" I replied.

The opportunity was exciting, but the chance of moving to Denver intrigued me. As much as I loved my life and friends in Austin, I was also ready for something new and to put my past behind me.

"Dominic in Houston has also been asked to interview for the position," Max continued.

Dominic and I were friends. He had more experience and had been a team leader longer than I had. I wasn't surprised he had been selected.

"Dominic will probably be your biggest competition. The other candidates so far are from the Denver office. If they had been happy with those candidates, they would have just promoted one of them," Max shared.

Max was not one to mince words or hold back his opinions.

"I'm not surprised that Dominic is in the running. He's a great choice," I replied.

"And so are you. You have just as much chance of getting the job as he does. I think it will come down to who they think will fit best with the team," Max said.

"Thank you, Max," I replied.

It was nice to get a compliment from Max. He did not give them very often.

"I'll let Sean, the hiring manager in the Denver office, know that you are interested," Max replied.

At my desk, Stephanie was eagerly waiting to hear what Max said. As soon as I sat down, my chat app alerted me to a message.

Stephanie: What was that all about?

Kassidy: He just told me I'm one of the candidates they want to interview for the Denver job!

Stephanie: That's awesome! I'm sad you'll have to move to Denver, but I'm happy for you.

Kassidy: Thanks, Steph, but I don't have the job yet. :)

Stephanie: Did he tell you who they picked from Houston?

Kassidy: Yes, it's Dominic. But don't say anything to anyone. I'm not sure I was supposed to share any of that.

Stephanie: Dominic, yeah, that doesn't surprise me. But don't worry, you deserve the promotion as much as he does.

Kassidy: Thanks, but if he gets the job, I'll know they picked him because he is more qualified.

A little while later, I received an email from Sean, the manager in Denver, inviting me to an interview and telling me that the office administrator there would contact me to make arrangements. They wanted me to fly to Denver on Monday and interview on Tuesday. Dominic's interview was also on Tuesday. They wanted to make a quick decision.

It didn't give me much time to plan, but I agreed to the interview schedule. I immediately called my dog sitter to arrange care for Sam and Lizzie.

The trip to Denver the following week was a whirlwind. On Tuesday, Dominic and I interviewed with various teams throughout the office, followed by separate final meetings with Sean. The schedule was staggered so we were never in the same room at the same time. We passed each other briefly in the hallway between conference rooms, exchanging quick smiles and quiet good-luck wishes. Even lunch was arranged separately.

By late afternoon, we were back on a plane home.

We didn't have to wait too long for the answer regarding the position. I got Sean's call when I returned to the Austin office the next day.

"Hi, Kassidy, this is Sean," he began, "Do you have a few minutes to talk?"

"Hi, Sean, yes, I do," I answered, feeling nervous and excited. "Have you made a decision already?"

"I have. After careful consideration and discussion with the team, I'm offering you the QA Manager position in Denver," Sean said enthusiastically.

"Thank you, Sean, I'm honored and excited!" I gushed.

Sean outlined the salary, and I felt a quiet surge of relief when I realized it meant another raise. He explained that formal paperwork would follow and that, once I officially accepted, they would begin arranging the transfer and my move to Denver.

"I spoke with Max," Sean continued. "He'd like you to stay through the end of your current release. I was hoping to bring you on sooner, but I understand. That's about a month from now. Does that timeline work for you, Kassidy?"

A month! I will be moving to Denver in a month! I thought, suddenly feeling a little panicked.

"Yes, that sounds great," I said. My heart raced at the thought of all that needed to be done quickly.

"Terrific, I will send you the paperwork, and we'll get things started. I'll call Dominic next to let him know we've decided. You are certain you are accepting the offer, correct?" Sean asked.

"Oh yes, I'm accepting the offer. Thank you so much, Sean," I replied eagerly. "I'm looking forward to working with you and the team."

"I look forward to working with you, too, Kassidy."

I went to Max's office to tell him my news, and before I could even speak, he greeted me with a hearty "Congratulations!"

I suggested we use the next month to transition my replacement and recommended Stephanie for the role. Max smiled.

"I've already made my decision," he said. "And I think you'll be pleased."

An hour later, Stephanie and I were sitting in his office. Max began by talking about the upcoming release, drawing it out just long enough to make her nervous.

Finally, he got to the point.

"Kassidy has accepted a management position in Denver. We'd like you to step into her role."

Stephanie's confusion dissolved into pure excitement.

"You got it?" she exclaimed, turning to me.

"I did," I laughed. "And you're going to be amazing."

The team responded with easy congratulations, already shifting into transition mode. I was thrilled—but also aware that a month was not much time to untangle a life and prepare for a move.

Back at my desk, reality settled in. An email from Dominic congratulated me. Sean confirmed my acceptance. Human Resources outlined the transfer process—movers, a realtor, and help finding housing in Denver. It was all happening quickly.

Driving home that evening, I thought about how far I had come. The ordeal with Finn had nearly undone me. There were moments I wasn't sure I would make it through.

But I had.

Now I was stepping into something new—something I had earned.

For the first time in a long time, I was facing forward. And the view felt wide open.

CHAPTER 28

A NEW LIFE

When I got home, I called my parents right away. They were thrilled about the promotion, though still uneasy about my moving to a new city alone. I assured them the company was handling the details—realtor, movers, housing support—and that helped ease their fears.

Things moved quickly after that. The transfer company assigned a realtor and scheduled a house-hunting trip to Denver. Once Max and I found a window in the release schedule that wouldn't cause too much disruption, I called Sean to confirm my visit. Sean arranged for me to spend an afternoon in the office while I was there and join the team for happy hour so we could get to know one another. The house-hunting portion of the trip was a success; I found a beautiful brick ranch with hardwood floors and a nice backyard for the dogs.

The release ran longer than expected, but my timeline didn't change. Stephanie had grown into the role faster than any of us anticipated. Max was confident she could handle it, and I knew I'd still be a phone call away if needed.

On my last day, the team took me to lunch. It was simple and warm—less of a goodbye and more of a sendoff.

On our last morning in Austin, I took the dogs on one final walk through the neighborhood. I didn't rush them and let them stop to sniff every last bush and tree. It also gave me time to take in the sights of the neighborhood for the last time. I had really enjoyed living in Austin, except for the time between Finn's arrest and the divorce. But most of my memories here were good ones. I was going to miss this neighborhood, and I was going to miss this town. I was going to miss my friends the most. But I knew that I would be back to visit. And the excitement of moving to Denver overshadowed my sadness about leaving.

When everything was packed in the car, I allowed myself one last walk through the townhouse. With the dogs following behind, I went into each room. I started in my bedroom and thought about how excited Finn and I had been when we moved in. The bedroom was spacious, and we had ample room for both of us to have a dresser. It was much bigger than the bedrooms in our previous apartments. I tried to focus only on good memories with Finn, not on the ones from after his arrest.

I stared at the spare bedroom door. I didn't want to go inside. That room was the most painful for me, and I hadn't been in there much since Finn's arrest.

I walked through the living room and put my hand on the mantel that had held our stockings every Christmas. First, it was just Finn's and mine. Then we added Lizzie's when we got her, and then next came Sam's. My new home in Denver had a beautiful stone fireplace in the family room. I was looking forward to hanging three stockings there this Christmas.

Finally, I walked through the dining room and kitchen. Finn had not taken the dining room furniture from his aunt because he had no room for it in his small apartment. It had never been to my taste, and I didn't want to take it to Denver with me. I found a buyer for it - a friend of Stephanie's who needed furniture for her new home. She and her boyfriend came to pick it up a few days earlier. It was another tie to Finn that I was leaving behind. I would get something new in Denver. I smiled at the thought.

At ten o'clock, I met the buyer of my townhouse at the title company and signed the final papers. Just like that, it was no longer mine.

I picked up the dogs and headed north, determined to be gone before the new owner's moving truck arrived. The drive to Denver would take two days—nearly one full day just to cross Texas. I had booked a pet-friendly hotel in Amarillo for the night.

The dogs bounced in the back seat, convinced we were headed somewhere fun. They had no idea we were beginning a sixteen-hour journey toward a new life. I did—and despite the miles ahead, I felt lighter than I had in years.

Everything happened very quickly, but the transfer company made it all go smoothly. The buyer's offer on my townhouse was double what I had paid for it six years earlier, thanks to a big upswing in the Austin market. That allowed me to buy the house in Denver. Because of my windfall from the townhouse sale, I could put a nice down payment on my Denver house and pay off the debt that I had taken on in the divorce. It was my last big tie to Finn. I felt even freer now than when Jordan had given me the final divorce decree.

Even though the dogs hated being cooped up for so long, the 16-hour drive to Denver was uneventful. I often stopped for breaks to let them out and stretch my legs. I was not going to close on my house in Denver for two weeks, so when I got there, I drove to the corporate housing the transfer company had set up for me. It was a nice apartment complex, and the dogs were happy to find the grounds inundated with rabbits. They watched them from the window and tried to chase them on our walks, an instant source of fascination.

I had just two days to settle in before starting work. The welcome from my new team was warm and genuine. In the evenings, I walked the dogs as I always had, keeping our routine steady while everything else shifted.

Two weeks later, I closed on my new house.

I drove straight from the title office to the property with cleaning supplies in the trunk and a change of clothes in the back seat. The movers arrived that afternoon, unloading my furniture into rooms that were finally mine. By the time they left, the garage was stacked with boxes, but I didn't mind. It was the good kind of mess, the kind that comes with beginnings.

That evening, I loaded the dogs into the car one more time and brought them to see our new home.

Having lived in a townhouse, the dogs had never had a yard to themselves. It was like having their own park! They surveyed the perimeter first, with Lizzie following Sam, who stopped to taste every single plant. Lizzie was content to let Sam take all the risk. They were still slightly confused by moving again, and they would check on me often to ensure I was still there. But they liked their new surroundings. And with our furniture in place, it felt more like home than the apartment had.

That evening, they snuggled on the couch and fell asleep easily. We were home.

I loved living in Colorado. I walked the dogs every morning around my new neighborhood before heading for work and again when I got home in the evening. And on the weekends, I took the dogs hiking and exploring the trails near us.

I painted and decorated several rooms in my new house. I gave my doily, the one Finn and his mother tossed out, a place of honor in my new home office. And I found a photo of a starfish that a local artist had taken in a shop one of my co-workers had recommended. It was the perfect piece to hang on the wall of my dining room.

Since my new house was bigger than the townhouse in Austin, I bought some new furniture to fill the space. My new bedroom set was a crowning jewel. I hadn't had a headboard since I left my parents' home, and it made my room feel more complete and adult.

I liked my new job. It was challenging, but the people I worked with helped me settle in. We went to happy hour every Friday night, and I got to know my co-workers on a more personal level. And of course, on Thursday nights, I ordered pizza and watched *ER* from my couch with Sam and Lizzie sleeping on either side of me.

Stephanie and I talked often, sometimes about work, sometimes about *ER*, but mostly just about what was going on in our lives. I missed seeing her every day, but it was good to talk to her regularly.

Since I knew no one in Denver except the people I worked with, I found cycling, running, and hiking groups. I made new friends and started dating again.

Dating was fun, but I found that I had some residual trust issues from my relationship with Finn. Most of my relationships did not last long because my dates would feel that I was holding back.

And I was.

I was hesitant to share anything about Finn's misdeeds and how my relationship with Finn ended. It was hard for me to let go and fully trust them or myself. So, I just took things slowly and tried to enjoy the experiences without getting too serious.

One sunny Spring day, about two years after I had moved to Denver and about three years after Finn's incarceration, I received a letter in the mail. I recognized the handwriting immediately. The way the letter was addressed was also a dead giveaway, as it was addressed to "Mrs. Finn Haggerty."

It was from my former mother-in-law, Myra.

My heart raced, and my face flushed hot with anger. How she had found me in Colorado, I didn't know. I had not had any contact with any of Finn's family since before his trial.

I stared at the letter for several minutes, reluctant to open it. I had put my past behind me and didn't want to revisit that chapter of my life.

I dropped it into the trash.

Then curiosity got the better of me, and I fished it out and opened it.

Our Dearest Kassidy,

I hope this letter finds you well. We had difficulty tracking you down since you did not tell us you had moved to Colorado.

I wanted to let you know that Finn will be released from jail in Texas soon. He has served his time, which was more than he deserved. We miss you very much and hope you and Finn can put your differences behind you and reconcile. I still don't understand why you divorced him in the first place. He loves you very much. As we all do. And he will need all our support when he is released from jail. It has been a very difficult time for him.

I look forward to hearing from you. Please give me a call so that we can talk.

With love,

Myra

I was speechless, staring at her letter for several minutes.

I realized I had no regrets. I may have stayed in my marriage to Finn longer than I should have after his arrest, but I did what I needed to do to take care of myself. I had moved so far past my life with Finn that it almost seemed like it had happened to someone else.

I was in a good place now. I was healthy and happy.

I marched back to the kitchen, threw the letter in the trash, then washed my hands at the sink.

I returned to the living room and sat on the couch. Lizzie and Sam assumed their positions on either side of me, as usual. I gave them each a hug, then petted their heads.

"This is why I have two hands," I told them, smiling.

EPILOGUE

It's been nearly 30 years since Finn's arrest. I rarely think about that part of my life now. And when I do, it feels unreal like it had happened to someone else. As if I'd read it in a novel or watched it unfold on a screen, rather than lived it.

I was only twenty-three and had been out of college for one year when we got married. I never thought Finn's arrest and all that came with it were anything that would happen to me. I had not yet experienced much of the world and knew nothing about mental illness or bipolar disorder. People hardly ever talked about mental illness back then. And it was largely with a lack of understanding or compassion when they did.

Mental illness awareness has come a long way since that time. But there is often still a stigma associated with it. And this prevents people from getting the help that they need.

Finn knew something wasn't right. I believe that. But fear, denial, and shame can be powerful barriers. Whether he continued counseling after our divorce, I don't know. I hope he eventually took his diagnosis seriously and chose the support available to him.

One thing that I learned in all of it is that you cannot help someone who is not ready or willing to help themselves. You can support them and be compassionate, but they need to take action to care for themselves. You can offer love. You can offer compassion. You can stand beside them. But you cannot walk the path for them.

At some point, responsibility becomes theirs.

And learning that truth set me free.

And sometimes, you must walk away to protect yourself. Walking away from Finn was one of the hardest things that I have ever done. But it was necessary for my own well-being.

Two of my steadiest supporters after Finn's arrest were my two dogs, Lizzie and Sam. I needed their support emotionally, and I cannot fully express the therapeutic effect that they had on me. When I was upset, they would calm me. When they thought I was in danger, they would protect me. They were my constant companions, so I was never alone. And they ensured I got fresh air and exercise daily through our walks and runs. They helped me maintain a sense of normalcy and improved my health. They were there for me through it all. I was grateful to have them with me, and I will always have a dog (or dogs) in my life.

I'm also grateful that I had Dianne's counseling to help get me through the crisis after Finn's arrest. She helped me get back on solid ground. And I gained the confidence I needed to end my broken marriage and do it without regrets.

I also learned that I was not responsible for Finn's actions or anyone else's actions, only my own. I took care of myself and made my own mental health a priority. Counseling was not something I ever saw myself needing, but I strongly recommend it. We all go through things in our lives that are bigger than we are – divorce, grief, illness, and more. There is no shame in seeking help; it can make a huge difference to your mental well-being.

During the counseling, Dianne and I focused on what I needed to get through the immediate crisis. But we never really touched on any lingering effects that my situation with Finn might have on my future relationships. Although I have had some good relationships over the years, there was one area where I continued to feel the aftershocks of my relationship with Finn for a long time.

Trust.

I had a hard time trusting others, and just as importantly, I had a hard time trusting *myself*. I still had a lot of doubts about having missed the red flags with Finn and worried that I would make the same mistake. Even though Dianne had reiterated to me many times that Finn had purposefully hidden his feelings and actions from me, it was hard for me to get over that and trust my own instincts again.

My experience with Finn made me overly suspicious, so I also worried that I would see red flags where they didn't exist or ignore those that did in my relationships. That caused me to stay in relationships that didn't work for much longer than I should have. I would tell myself *He's not Finn! Focus on his good qualities,* and I would try to make it work. That was never a successful strategy.

Eventually, I became aware of these patterns. I journaled about my experience with Finn and the other failed relationships, using this information to identify and avoid the patterns in the future. I also journaled a lot about what I really wanted and what kind of man I wanted to be in a relationship with. This helped me prepare for a happy, healthy relationship with a kind, generous, smart, fun man, which is exactly what I found. I met and married Drew a few years ago, and he is one of the best humans I know.

Journaling also helped me forgive Finn. He was dealing with something he did not know how to handle, and he was afraid to let anyone else know about it. What Finn did was reprehensible. Forgiving him was not condoning his actions or letting him off the hook. I understood that he was hurting, and hurting people hurt others.

I have also forgiven Myra for the same reasons. I recognize that she did the best she could. Forgiving Finn and Myra allowed me to release the pain and anger that I had. I had to let go of the suffering Finn had caused. Carrying it any longer would harm me. Forgiving Finn was essential for my own well-being.

And I have forgiven myself for not knowing that Finn intended to harm a child and for not being able to stop him. That has been the hardest to forgive and let go of. But I couldn't have fully healed without doing so.

If you ever find yourself in a situation with a loved one who has an issue, such as mental illness or addiction, and they are not seeking help, you can feel empowered to walk away or just take a step back, if needed. You cannot help anyone else if you're not taking care of yourself first. Your safety and well-being are just as important as theirs. It's okay to make that your priority.

ABOUT THE AUTHOR

Karen Krueger is a former geologist and software tester who is now pursuing her lifelong dream of writing fiction. Her debut novel, *Arrested Love*, draws on personal experiences and explores the complicated terrain of relationships, resilience, and self-discovery.

Karen lives in Colorado with her husband, Dean, and their dog, Nutmeg. When she's not writing, proofreading, or copywriting, she enjoys reading, hiking mountain trails, tending her garden, and running. An avid traveler, Karen has explored destinations across Europe, Asia, and the Americas—experiences that continue to inspire her curiosity about people, cultures, and the stories that shape our lives.

Karen can be reached at Karen@KarenKruegerWriter.com.

www.ingramcontent.com/pod-product-compliance
Lightning Source LLC
Chambersburg PA
CBHW050023040726
47599CB00015B/1514